Shifted

Siren Prophecy 1

by
Tricia Barr, Joanna Reeder, Angel Leya, Jesse
Booth & Alessandra Jay

Shifter Academy

Myreen

Rule #1: Never go out after dark.
Rule #2: Never go into large bodies of water.
Rule #3: Stay off of social media.

"So, how strict is that rule?" Kenzie asked, tossing a French fry in her mouth.

The two girls were sitting at a picnic table outside the school cafeteria, making the most of their half hour lunch break.

Myreen's previously comfortable posture stiffened at the question, and she put down the burger she'd been about to bite into. "Rule number one? Pretty unbreakable." She sighed. "Why?"

These were the rules Myreen had lived by her entire life, rules put in place by her eccentric mother. If a friend ever threw a birthday party after five in the afternoon, Myreen wasn't allowed to go. When all her friends were enjoying dips in the lake for summertime fun, Myreen wasn't allowed to go. And when everyone started getting smart phones and chatting on Facebook or Twitter, Myreen couldn't join them. Myreen was allowed a phone, but only one that could make and receive calls and text messages.

These rules made it difficult for Myreen to make friends. Not that it mattered much, as she was hardly ever in one place long enough to get to know anyone. Her mother moved them every few months, leaving one small town to start a new life in another one. Myreen hated it growing up. She would finally make one good friend, and then her mom would spring a move on her and she'd have to abandon them to start over somewhere else. And with the no-social-media rule, keeping in touch was damn near impossible. Myreen would send letters, but nobody participated in snail mail anymore. Myreen was stuck in the Stone Age while the rest of the world passed her by.

For the last three months, they'd been living in Short Grove, a tiny town in Illinois. The town was so small, it had one school, no mall of any sort, and was pretty much invisible on any map of the state. Luckily, it was only an hour's drive from Chicago, so Myreen was able to experience city life when she could manage to get away on weekends— with a strict curfew, of course.

Myreen had the sneaking suspicion that another move was, though. She had made one good friend: Kenzie.

Kenzie was great. She had approached Myreen on her first day at the new school, and the two had become fast friends. They did everything together: homework, weekend trips to the city, gossiping on Myreen's couch all hours of the night. Kenzie was aware of the no-going-out-after-dark rule, and rather than prying, she was content to stay at Myreen's house to hang out once the sun set.

Or, at least, she was before today.

Kenzie flipped her wavy brown hair over her shoulder. "There's a party tonight. I think we should go." Her fingers tapped an excited beat, betraying her casual tone.

2

"Someone in this town is actually throwing a party?" Myreen asked, raising her brows in surprise.

Kenzie leaned forward, a fire burning in her hazel eyes. "And it's at Michael Guido's house." She raised a brow, but when Myreen didn't spark with recognition, she added, "He's a football player. Family's got big money, at least for this small town. So you *know* it's going to be epic."

Myreen dropped her shoulders and shook her head. "Kenzie, as much as I would love to go, you know I can't."

"I was afraid you'd say that." Kenzie's nose crinkled, and she jammed a fry into her plate. "Nothing fun ever happens in *Shallow Grave*," Kenzie said, using her nickname for their sleepy town. She leveled her gaze at Myreen, an unspoken challenge there. "Until now. You're a teenager, Myreen. When was the last time you ever did something you weren't supposed to?"

Myreen snorted. "Um, never."

"Exactly." Kenzie pointed her mashed fry at Myreen's chest. "A little rebellion is healthy—no, *necessary*. I refuse to let you skip this important rite of teenage-hood."

Myreen imagined it, telling her mom that she wanted to go to the party and then the deathly stern look and lecture she'd receive in return. She'd heard that lecture so many times, she had the dang thing memorized by now.

She opened her mouth to object, but Kenzie cut her off. "Robby Fletcher'll be there." Kenzie raised her brow and smirked. She was using Myreen's pseudo crush as a bribe, and it was kinda working.

"Robby doesn't know I exist," Myreen said, rolling her eyes.

"So you get to be Cinderella. Wiggle that perfect little body of yours into an even smaller dress. Before you know it, you'll be sweeping him off his feet."

"Aren't guys supposed to do the sweeping?" Myreen asked with a smirk.

"This is the twenty-first century," Kenzie said. "Where's your sense of empowerment?"

"Stuck in the twentieth century, with my *dumb* phone," Myreen said, holding up her flip phone.

"Your mom's weird," Kenzie said. "No offense," she added quickly.

"None taken," Myreen said with a shrug. "You don't even know the half of it."

"I guess I can kinda understand the no-social-media thing," Kenzie said, dipping another fry into her mound of ketchup with one hand as she tapped the screen of her phone with the other. "Kids our age really shouldn't be on social media."

"You're literally on it right now."

"That's my point," Kenzie said, stuffing her phone into her pocket. "It's addictive and it horrible for your social skills. Why do you think *I'm* so unpopular?" She leaned back in her chair, throwing her half-eaten fry onto her plate.

"You're not unpopular," Myreen said in Kenzie's defense. "You're just...very honest, and not everyone appreciates your brand of honesty."

In appearance, there was no reason Kenzie shouldn't be popular. Though she was a tad on the thicker side, she had a curvy figure with nice, wide hips. Her hair had a natural rock star wave that required little maintenance, and her face was pretty enough on its own that she never needed makeup, which was more than half the girls of the cheerleading squad could say. If popularity was just a beauty contest, Kenzie would definitely be in the running.

But this was a small town, and everyone in their school had known each other their whole lives. Kenzie spoke her mind, and unlike most teenage girls, stood up for herself and didn't take crap from anyone.

Because of that, the "popular" kids didn't like her very much. She wasn't some lemming they could push around, or some bee looking to follow a queen.

"Whatever," Kenzie said with a shrug. "But we're talking about you and your rules right now. I might even get the after-dark rule. Maybe your mom's afraid you'll get abducted or something. Or," she said, dragging out the word, "your mom's a spy. No, a superhero. That's it. All her enemies are out to get her and she's afraid they'll snatch you for ransom or something. You said you guys move every few months, right?"

"I've considered every scenario you can think of," Myreen said. "But my mom is too clumsy to be a spy, and not nearly strong enough to be a superhero. I have entertained the notion that she might be in the Witness Protection Program, but why she would keep that from me, I don't know."

"So you have no idea why you guys move around so much?" Kenzie pried, and Myreen thought she saw her eyes flash for a moment. A trick of the sunlight, or something.

"Nope," Myreen sighed. "I stopped asking years ago because she would never give me a straight answer. For all I know, it's something stupid, like she owes someone money. She does have loads of it, even though she never works."

"Really?" Kenzie's hazel eyes sparkled, a faint smile on her lips.

Myreen had never told a friend this much about her personal life, and she felt a sort of guilt for betraying her mom's trust in such a way. But there was something about Kenzie that made Myreen trust her. And it was refreshingly uplifting to be able to confide these sordid details of her life to someone she considered a true friend.

As if sensing Myreen's discomfort on the topic, Kenzie changed the subject. "She could be something else. Like a werewolf. Or a vampire."

5

Myreen laughed. "Seriously?"

"Right. You all don't go out after night. Werewolf it is."

"Yep, that must be it." Myreen shook her head.

"So, tonight. You're going."

Myreen frowned. It wasn't at all that she didn't want to go. She'd never been to a party, not since she was in elementary school and everyone had their birthday parties at lunch time. A real high school party sounded like the event of a lifetime! Her chest burned with the yearning to go. But her mom would never, ever, in a million years, let her leave the house after dark.

"I really do want to," Myreen prefaced with a sigh.

"I know there's a 'but' coming, so save it," Kenzie said. "If your mom won't let you go, then I say you should sneak out."

"Sneak out?" Myreen parroted, as if the words were a foreign language to her.

"Yeah, you know, climb out your window while your mom is busy making dinner or something. If you tell her you're sick, she never even has to know. Besides, you deserve a reward for being a perfect daughter. Until now." Kenzie smirked.

"So my reward for good behavior is deviance?" Myreen asked.

"Teenage rebellion. Remember?" Kenzie flipped her hair over her shoulder again, turning sideways so she could drape her arm over the table.

The more she thought about it, the more Myreen wanted to make this party happen. But how? She didn't like the idea of sneaking out. Maybe she could reason with her mom. Myreen wasn't a child anymore. She was sixteen. In two years, she would be considered an adult. She had felt for some time now that she deserved a little taste of freedom, and if there was any real reason for the crazy rules, she was old enough to hear it. A little bit of truth was long overdue.

"Okay," Myreen decided. "I'll find a way to go. Meet me at my house at seven."

"Make it eight," Kenzie said. "Only losers go to a party on time. Or so I've heard."

"Eight it is." A bubble of excitement bounced in Myreen's belly, followed by a stab of doubt threatening to pop it.

***

"Dinner's ready," her mom called from the kitchen.

Myreen had been pacing in her room, putting together just the right words to make her case to her mom. It had been years since Myreen had pushed for any kind of lenience on the rules, accepting them as just a way of life. For the most part, she had never really minded. She was content to stay in with her mom every night and watch movies or play cards and board games. She was content not to be addicted to a device as most teens were these days. She was even okay with the fact that she had never really been swimming before.

But this party was a chance to have some real fun, to be normal for a change. Until Kenzie had brought it up, Myreen hadn't admitted to herself how desperately she wanted to be a normal kid. Moving around all the time was exhausting. Her mom owed her this one small exception to the rules.

Myreen took one deep breath in front of her mirror, fixing her hair just right, as if preparing for a speech in front of a large audience. Her shiny, thick black hair flowed down past her shoulders in wayward waves, currents of dark blue peeking out here and there—thanks to a bottle of dye and Kenzie's goading. Her sky blue eyes stared back at her with uncertainty, shadowed by thick black eyelashes that never needed mascara.

You can do this, she told herself, then turned away from her reflection and headed for the kitchen.

Her mother was setting the table and turned to smile at her when she entered. Her long pale blond hair always seemed to waft around her, as if unbound by the laws of gravity, forever floating in a sea of its own imagination. Myreen had no idea where she'd gotten her black-as-midnight hair, but she undoubtedly got her eyes from her mom, whose were bright with happiness this evening. Myreen felt an extra twinge of guilt knowing that she was about to snuff out their light.

"I made your favorite," her mom said, placing a full plate on the table. "Pesto grilled salmon and fettuccine alfredo."

"Thanks, Mom," Myreen said, ignoring the lump in her throat. She sat at the table and looked down at her plate, the delicious smell taunting her.

"How was school today?" her mom asked, sitting across from her and poking a fork into her food.

"It was alright." Myreen wondered: when was the best time to bring up this overdue conversation?

She looked out the window. The last bit of daylight was clinging lazily to the horizon, slowly dragging its glow across the late autumn sky.

"Just alright?" her mom asked before popping a bite of herb-covered fish into her mouth.

The clock would be striking seven soon. *Now is as good a time as any.*

"Actually, something kinda cool did happen today," Myreen began, poking at her food. "One of the football players is throwing a party tonight, and I was hoping I could go."

Her mother's jaw froze mid-chew, and the light immediately vanished from her eyes.

"Kenzie will be there," Myreen added quickly. "We won't stay long, just one hour would be enough. And I promise not to drink any—"

"Not tonight," her mom cut her off.

Myreen had expected this answer. "Mom, I never get to go to any social functions. I'm not asking for something outrageous here. Just *one* party. At which I promise to be on my best behavior."

"There will be other parties," her mom said, a casual tone masking a dark and heavy secret.

"Parties that you still won't let me go to," Myreen said, unable to keep a bit of sass out of her voice. "I don't get it. Every girl my age gets to go out after school. Everyone gets to hang out with friends and do things at night."

"But those girls aren't my daughters."

"I never ask for anything," Myreen said, her big speech rushing out, skipping over words she had prepared. "I never complain when we have to pack all our things and rush out all of a sudden. I never ask for fancy clothes or gadgets or anything like that. I get almost all A's in school and have never gotten in trouble. In case you haven't noticed, I'm a really good kid. All I'm asking for, just this once, is one tiny hour of freedom, to have some fun with kids my own age."

Her mom looked down at her food, stoic. "I'm sorry, honey. The answer is no."

Anger bubbled up from under the surface, an anger Myreen was so used to bottling up. Her mother was her best friend, and she was a very secretive person. Myreen didn't like to pry, but she deserved an explanation.

"Why is the answer no?" Myreen tried to sound like an adult deserving of the respect she was asking for, and not like the indignant teenager she felt bristling on the inside. "Why don't you ever let me even go into the backyard after sunset? What's so scary about the dark?"

"We're not having this conversation right now," her mom said flatly, continuing to eat her food as if their talk was over.

"Then when?" Myreen asked. "I'm sixteen years old. I'm not just some child you can cart around with you anymore. I'm almost an adult, and I need to know why. Why do you hop around from place to place? Why can't we do anything online? And what's the deal with water? What are you so afraid of?"

"That's enough, Myreen!" her mom snapped.

The silence that ensued made Myreen realize how loud her voice had been, which made her feel very young and naïve now. She hated feeling so small, so helpless to control anything in her life. She wasn't willing to just go with the flow anymore.

"Unless you can give me an explanation for your rules, I will no longer abide by them," Myreen declared in a low but strong voice.

A spark of panic lit her mom's blue eyes, and Myreen saw a fear behind them that part of her believed had always been there, hiding.

"Did it ever occur to you that those rules exist to protect you?" A note of desperation raised the pitch of her mom's voice.

"Protect me from what?" Myreen asked, hiding her own desperation. She had always suspected her mom was running. That something bad had happened to her that related to night and water.

Her mom stayed silent, looking at her with pleading eyes.

"If you have something to tell me, now would be the time," Myreen said. "Whatever it is, I'm ready to listen."

Her mom's eyes fell to the floor, darting back and forth in deliberation. Anticipation sizzled in Myreen's belly like pop rocks in soda. Was she actually going to get to hear about her mother's mysterious past? Myreen knew nothing about her mom's history. Nothing about grandparents or extended family. Myreen didn't even know who her father was. Every time she'd asked, her mother always changed the subject. But it seemed she might finally get some clue, some missing piece of this almost empty puzzle.

Then her mom's eyes stopped their pacing. They returned to meet Myreen's gaze, and she knew. Her mom had decided to continue the secrecy.

Myreen pushed away from the table and stood. "Then I'm going."

"No, you can't." Her mom jumped out of her chair.

"I'll be back before midnight," Myreen said firmly, pushing her chair into the table and heading for the door.

"Myreen Lee Fairchild, you are not leaving this house!" her mom yelled in her well-practiced maternal tone.

Some young, skittish side of Myreen wanted to do as her mother said, to please her and avoid repercussion. But her determination to make a stand was behind the wheel, and she had no intention of turning around. Maybe this one act of mutiny would finally get her mother to confess something, anything.

She strode for the door, but her mom ran ahead of her and gripped the knob.

"Let me out," Myreen insisted with narrowed eyes.

"I can't do that."

"Let me out!" Myreen yelled. Her voice sounded strangely musical, not her own.

Her mother gasped and dropped her hand. Myreen was startled by her own shout, ashamed that she had talked back so brazenly, enough to make her mom jump. But she had gone too far to give up now. Her mom had released the door knob. Myreen had to take her chance before the opportunity closed.

She rushed out, slamming the door behind her and running down the street. Her pulse was racing, her hands shaking as she pulled out her phone to dial Kenzie's number and put the phone to her ear.

"Hey, Kenz, things didn't go so well, can I come over before the party?" Myreen asked into her phone.

"Of course, come on over," Kenzie's worried voice replied. "Is everything okay?"

"I don't know," Myreen said honestly. "I'll see you in a few minutes." She hung up the phone and stuck her hands in her pockets as

11

she strode to Kenzie's house down the street.

She hated what happened back there. But it needed to happen, one way or another, and had needed to for some time. She'd had enough of secrets and changed subjects, enough of blindly complying to ridiculous requests. Things were never going to be the same after tonight, and that both excited and terrified her.

Myreen

"I'm sure everything will be okay," Kenzie reassured Myreen as the two walked back from the party. "I can't even tell you how many times I've argued with my mom and Gram, and it always turns out alright."

Myreen had tried to enjoy the party, but she spent the whole time wrangling a giant knot of stress in her gut. Her mom hadn't even called or texted her, which was incredibly uncharacteristic of her. Even when Myreen was at school, her mom would text her at least once to check in. Had she broken her mother's heart? Sent her into a nervous breakdown? Myreen was dreading going home, and she was grateful that Kenzie had offered to accompany her. She really needed that support right now.

"I hope so," Myreen said. "My mom and I have never fought like this. I've never even talked back to her before. I know it's a silly thing for a teenager, but she's kinda my best friend—besides you, of course."

"I don't think that's silly at all," Kenzie said. "I think it's kinda sweet, actually. I wish I could say that about my mom. I mean, I love her, but I wouldn't call us 'friends'." They continued walking in silence for a moment, and then Kenzie added, "I'll stick around as long as you want me to. Or, I can leave right away to give you guys time to talk. Whatever you want."

"Thanks, Kenz," Myreen said, managing a half-smile.

Myreen's house was in sight, and the stress knot constricted even tighter. She had no idea what to expect, and part of her hoped that they could just go back to the way things were. She'd rather have a happy relationship with her mom, even if it was shrouded in secrecy.

As they got closer, Myreen saw there was something amiss. The front door was wide open. Her mom never left the door open after nightfall; as soon as the sun went down, she would turn the deadbolt. The stress knot flared with a wave of panic, and Myreen picked up the pace, her brisk walk quickly turning into a run.

"What's wrong?" Kenzie asked, running behind her.

"I hope nothing," Myreen said as they made it to the door.

Nothing in the house was out of place, everything was just as it had been when she left.

"Mom?" Myreen called out.

No answer.

Myreen made her way across the small living room to the last place she had seen her mom—the kitchen.

"Mom?" she called out again, receiving the same empty silence in reply.

"Myreen, something about this doesn't feel right," Kenzie said, hovering in the doorway and looking around. "We should go."

Myreen didn't have time to wonder at the curious caution of her usually reckless friend. "I have to find my mom," Myreen said, as if the idea of leaving her house was ridiculous.

She stamped into the kitchen, then froze.

Lying on the floor, pale blue eyes open wide and beautiful face fixed in anguish, was her mother.

Myreen dropped to the floor, her hands fumbling, finding their way to her mother's face.

"Mom? Mom!" she yelled, trying to shake her mother awake.

Her mom's body was cold and unresponsive. Remembering from movies she'd seen, Myreen pressed her index and middle fingers to her mom's neck under her jaw, feeling around for a pulse. But there was none.

"Oh no!" Kenzie gasped as she came into the room behind her.

"Call 9-1-1!" Myreen shrieked, then turned her mother's head the other way to search for a pulse on the other side of her neck. But as she did, her fingers ran into an angry red bite mark. A *dry* bite mark. No blood. With a bite this deep, there should be blood everywhere, shouldn't there?

Panic spiked in her chest as she tried to comprehend what was happening. Something had bit her mom! But what? How could a bite hurt her this badly? Badly enough to… No, she couldn't be dead. She just couldn't!

Myreen's head was a din of white noise as she fought the heavy sob that threatened to constrict her chest. But she couldn't cry. Crying would mean admitting defeat, facing the reality that her mother was…

She was vaguely aware of the sound of Kenzie dialing on her phone as she paced nervously around the kitchen, and of the sound of heavy feet coming in through the front door.

A large hand landed on Myreen's shoulder, and she sucked in a breath and spun her head around.

"You have to come with me right now," said a man she had never seen before. His build was threatening enough. He could have easily attacked her mom.

She jerked her shoulder away from his hand. "Who are you? Did you hurt my mom?" she accused with a tremulous voice, her mind a clashing storm of sorrow, anger and paranoia.

"No, but if we don't leave now, the ones who did will get you, too," he said.

"I'm not going anywhere with you," she protested, lips twitching between a sneer and a pout. *Don't cry, don't cry!*

"If you don't, you will die," he said. "Please, we don't have much time." He held out a strong hand. "If I wanted to kill you, don't you think I would have already done so? I am not your enemy."

Myreen looked up at Kenzie, who was staring at the stranger with intense eyes, holding her phone to a deaf ear.

"Please," the man urged once more, and Myreen heard sincerity and desperation in his voice.

Her mother was dead. Someone or something had killed her. And Myreen believed this man when he said she was in danger of being next. She didn't have a lot of options. Stay here and wait for the cops to arrive—and risk whatever fate awaited her if the murderer returned—or take a leap of faith and trust this man, who seemed to genuinely want to help her.

Without a word, she reluctantly accepted the man's hand. He pulled her to her feet, and together she and Kenzie followed him briskly out of the house, Myreen's legs jumping ahead of her body as if whatever had attacked her mom was going to jump out at her at any second.

He charged toward a sleek black Camaro parked along the curb and opened the back door. Trepidation rooted her to the sidewalk at the thought of getting in this stranger's car, but she couldn't find her voice.

"You never said anything about getting into a car," Kenzie said, voicing Myreen's thoughts for her.

"We have to get off the streets," he said, holding the door open. "We're too exposed here."

"Then we can go to my house," Kenzie said. "It's just down the street." She pointed in that direction.

"It's too close." The man shook his head. "They will follow Myreen's scent there."

"Follow her scent?" Kenzie said. "Are you talking about what I think you're talking about?"

He cut a narrowed gaze at Kenzie. "I'll explain everything, but we have to get to a safe place first." His broad shoulders bristled with urgency. "Please, they may already be on to us."

Myreen passed a hesitant look to Kenzie.

"I'm not leaving your side," Kenzie promised, taking her hand and squeezing it firmly.

They nodded to each other and got in the car. The man closed the door and rushed into the driver's seat, wasting no time in starting the engine and speeding down the road.

Now that she had a chance, Myreen took a good look at the man sitting in front of her. He looked to be in his late thirties, with short brown hair and handsome dark stubble framing his rugged face. He had the look of a gladiator, rough and strong, with scars marring the bulges on his arms.

"Who are you and what do you want with me?" Myreen hiccupped, now wishing she had just stayed with her mom and waited for the police.

He looked at her in the rearview mirror. "My name is Oberon. I came to personally invite you to a school for… special people like you. I had no idea you were in any kind of danger. We didn't realize you were a target."

"A target for who?" she asked, trying to remain calm. "Who did that to my mom?" Tears welled in her eyes, but she knew if she let them break, they would render her useless.

"Vampires," Oberon replied, dead serious.

"Vampires?" Myreen asked, not bothering to hide her skepticism.

17

"Do you think I'm an idiot?"

"This isn't a joke, Myreen," he said, radiating authority. "You don't live in the world you think you do. Do you even know what you are?"

She narrowed her eyes. What was he talking about?

"What *is* she?" Kenzie asked beside her. Myreen turned to Kenzie, who looked like she completely believed every word this Oberon guy was saying.

"Myreen, have you ever experienced anything strange? Anything you couldn't explain?" Oberon kept his gaze on Myreen in the mirror, ignoring Kenzie's question.

Myreen's mind flipped through screenshots of her life. There was nothing normal about the way she grew up, but nothing to indicate she was something otherworldly, as this man was suggesting.

"No," she answered honestly.

"What about your mother?" he asked.

Myreen shook her head, not yet ready to say anything relating to her mom.

"You've never... been to the beach? Or had anything weird happen to you while swimming?"

She met his steely gaze in the mirror. Why was he asking her about swimming? Was there really something to the stupid "no water" rule?

"I've never been allowed to swim." She leaned on the edge of her seat in anticipation of some explanation at last.

Oberon's brows raised in an understanding that was completely lost to her. What did he know that she didn't?

"So your mom knew, and she tried to keep you from it," he said with a nod.

"From what?" Myreen asked at the same time as Kenzie.

Oberon sighed, flicking another look at Kenzie through the rearview mirror. "Myreen, you are a mermaid."

The balloon of excitement that had been growing inside her

popped, the sound like a whoopee cushion in her head. She didn't know what she was hoping he would tell her, but that certainly wasn't it.

"A mermaid?" she said flatly. "Okay, that's it. Just let me out of the car."

"It's true," he said.

"First you say vampires attacked my house, and now you expect me to believe that I'm a mermaid?" she summarized in a mocking tone. "I don't know if you're crazy or just toying with me, but my mom just died! This is sick!"

"Think about it, Myreen," he said. "I know you saw that bite mark on your mom's neck. What do you think that could have been from?"

"Not vampires," she said, throwing up her hands in exasperation. "They don't exist."

"Actually, that's not true," Kenzie said, her voice low. She couldn't even meet Myreen's gaze.

Myreen rolled her eyes. She knew Kenzie was into weird stuff, but now wasn't the time for her to defend this psycho. Myreen was not going to buy into this nonsense. Her mother's dead body back at home was real, and she needed to do something about it.

"Please let me out of the car," she said.

"I can prove it to you," Oberon growled, clearly getting frustrated.

"And how exactly are you going to prove to me that I'm a mermaid?" she asked, all sass.

"Mermaids aren't the only shape-shifters in the world," he said, harshly turning the steering wheel. "There are more species than you can imagine. For centuries, we've been hunted down by vampires and certain humans, but we finally have a place where we can be safe from them."

He reached back over his seat to hand her an envelope. She narrowed her eyes at it for a moment, then took it, afraid to leave him driving one-handed for too long. On the flat side of the envelope was a label that read THE DOME with a strange insignia beneath it, a crest divided into four sections, each with a different symbol inside: talons, a wing, a spiral and claw marks.

"Like I said earlier, I came here tonight to personally invite you to the school," he continued as she inspected the envelope. "We don't often get stray mermaids, so I knew it would be best to have this discussion in person. To explain to you who we are and why you should come to the school." He looked back over his shoulder. "Open it."

Myreen looked at Kenzie, who was watching with large eyes full of anticipation. Kenzie nodded in encouragement, so Myreen figured why not.

She ripped the envelope open and unfolded the letter inside. The same insignia was in the top right corner in full color. At the top were the words "The Dome" and under that "Academy for the Gifted". But as she read it, impossibly the "G" turned into an "Sh" to read "Academy for the Shifted." She blinked hard several times, but the letters kept changing back and forth. If this was a prank, it was a very well thought-out one.

Shrugging off that weirdness, she continued to read the letter.

Myreen Fairchild,

We are excited to invite you to study at our most prestigious school for gifted individuals. You are receiving this letter because you have been found to be one of us, and we would be honored to guide you through your journey of self-discovery and make you a valued member of our community. The choice is yours, but we must warn you that failure to accept this invitation may put your family and others at risk. A representative will be in touch shortly to give you further instructions. We look forward to studying with you.

Sincerely,

Oberon Rex, Director

"Normally, initiates either grew up in families that are already affiliated with the school, or have begun to exhibit abilities that would make them aware of their status, so the form letter usually suffices. We rarely have to meet in person," Oberon said. "But like I said, you are a rare case."

"You keep saying 'we,'" Kenzie said. "Does that mean you're a shape-shifter too?"

Myreen shot her a look that said, "Don't be ridiculous," but Kenzie was focused on Oberon.

"I am," he said with pride.

"Kenzie, you can't really believe all this," Myreen said.

"Actually, I do," Kenzie said.

"Well, I don't," Myreen said. "And I want no part of this sick game he's playing with us. Please take me home so I can call the cops and find out what really happened to my mom."

"I said I can prove it to you." He pulled the car over onto the side of the road. Then he got out of the car and yanked open her door. He waved out his hand in an invitation for her to get out.

Myreen didn't hesitate. She didn't know what he was planning to do, but now was her chance to make a run for it. She got out of the car and realized they were on a long stretch of road that led to the city. There was nothing but green field around them for miles. It would be a long run back, if she even made it that far.

Kenzie hopped out after her, and it was clear that she had no interest in running; her eyes were trained unblinkingly on Oberon. Myreen stayed close to Kenzie so that she could grab her arm and drag her away if she had to.

Oberon stepped away a few feet into the grass and began unbuttoning his black shirt.

"What the!? Why are you stripping?" Myreen shrieked.

"Just wait," Oberon said with a hint of irritation in his voice.

He threw off his shirt and pulled down his pants, and Myreen was now truly terrified of what he was planning to do. She grabbed Kenzie's arm and squeezed, trying to tell her telepathically to escape with her now that his pants were around his ankles. Kenzie didn't get the message, and Myreen's sudden tug on Kenzie's unmoving arm caused her to trip to the ground.

She pushed herself up with her hands in time to see something that just wasn't possible.

Oberon had turned from a large, muscular man into an even bigger, mythical beast. All over, his skin sprouted small brown feathers. His rugged face transformed, his nose and mouth growing and twisting into a huge black beak with a dagger-sharp tip. His hands and feet enlarged to smooth black talons that dug into the grass as he landed on all fours. And out of his broad back emerged the most magnificent pair of brown wings, furling and expanding, making the air crack with their power.

Standing before her was a gryphon. A beast of legend. This creature didn't exist, and yet here it was, not three feet from her, looking at her with Oberon's golden-brown eyes.

Kenzie

Kenzie watched with a slack jaw as the man before her turned into a spectacular gryphon. Myreen's panic barely registered, and she couldn't seem to bring herself to move to help her friend, who had fallen flat on her face.

Every nerve Kenzie's her body sizzled.

She'd known about the shifter world, had even heard stories from Gram, but she'd never been this close to it. Oh sure, there were the occasional whispered conversations or clandestine meetings that she was never allowed to watch. Not that she hadn't tried to snag a peek, but the wards Gram knew could keep even the most curious cat away.

And now she was in the middle of the shifter world. She could almost taste the excitement—a wild citrus flavor, if she had to guess. She wanted in that school, more than she'd ever wanted anything in her life. And that was saying a lot, considering all she'd ever dreamed of was learning more about the magic her family possessed.

Of course, with no grimoire to guide her, the chances of *that* ever happening were about a million to one.

But Myreen. Kenzie looked down at her raven-haired friend at last, who was just managing to pick herself up off the ground. A mermaid. That's what Oberon had said. It didn't entirely surprise Kenzie. She'd known something was special about Myreen from the first time they'd met. Something about those sky blue eyes had demanded the impromptu blue streaks now running through her friend's hair—and the immediate friendship that sparked between them. Besides, Myreen was a little too pretty to be human. Seriously. Most people had to be photoshopped to look that good.

Kenzie cleared her throat, a bubble of nerves fluttering in her stomach. "I wanna go to the school, too."

Oberon looked at her, his feathered brow raised. He turned and shifted back to human, pulling his clothes off the ground. Kenzie wasn't normally into older guys, but dang, he was hot. He didn't even need to put on his pants, with those fancy tighty-whiteys he was wearing. She was surprised those hadn't shredded when he turned into the gryphon.

"Are you a shifter?" Oberon asked, before pulling his shirt over his head. *Dang it.* "I'm assuming no, since we likely would've found you before now." His eyes shifted to where Myreen stood, one arm wrapped around her waist.

Kenzie's heart dropped a touch. It seemed selfish, trying to get into a shifter school when her best friend had just lost her mom. She put a hand on Myreen's shoulder, giving her an encouraging smile.

"I'm a selkie. Shifter enough for you?" Kenzie raised a brow at Oberon, who was frowning. Myreen gasped, pulling away from Kenzie's touch.

"We need to keep moving." Oberon waved them toward the car, looking around the area as if he expected to be attacked at any moment. It might've seemed absurd if it wasn't the middle of the night and Myreen's mom hadn't just been killed by a vampire. Yeah, they needed to get moving.

Kenzie grabbed Myreen's hand and tugged her toward the car.

"No," Myreen said, pulling back. "This is insane."

Kenzie sighed, her shoulders slumping. "I know it's a lot to process, but it's all true. I swear."

Myreen's eyes narrowed. "What do you mean, selkie?"

"I can turn into a seal." *And use magic.* Well, sort of.

Myreen crinkled her nose, a look that was altogether too cute for someone who was obviously in so much distress.

"Only if you have an enchanted seal skin," Oberon cut in. "And we need to leave. Now!" Seeing Myreen's hesitation, he added, "Unless you would prefer to become a vampire's snack?"

Myreen shook her head, but followed Kenzie into the back seat. Her normally pale features looked even whiter—if that were possible—with just a hint of green around the edges. She was practically bioluminescent in the shadows.

Once they were all settled and Oberon was clipping down the road once more, he leaned back into his seat. "We only allow shifters at the school."

Kenzie scoffed. "But I said—"

"I heard you. You're not a shifter, you're a magic user. There's a difference."

Magic user? Myreen mouthed, her brows arching toward her hairline. Kenzie patted Myreen's hand, trying to convey with just one look that she'd explain everything.

"Difference?" Kenzie snorted. "I don't see how."

"Shifters don't exactly have a choice. You do. We need a safe place to practice and perfect our powers. You don't."

"I don't think it's that simple."

"The answer is no," Oberon ground out.

"But Myreen'll need me." She felt almost dirty for using her

25

friend's trauma as a bargaining chip. Surely Oberon would see the girls' bond and realize it was for the best. And Kenzie really did want to be there for her friend. She hadn't felt so close to anyone since kindergarten, when she'd accidentally set fire to her best-friend-at-the-time's skirt in an attempt to show off. Yeah, that got her labelled "freak" faster than a die-hard Cavalier fan at a Bulls game. Ugh.

"The answer is still no."

"What kind of monster are you?" Myreen asked Oberon, the green to her skin replaced by a flaming red. "My mom just died, and you want to separate me from my only friend in the world." Her fists clenched, and Kenzie could see her eyes starting to brim with tears.

She had to bail. Oberon wasn't likely to bend, and Kenzie didn't want her friend hurting any more than she already was.

"There are plenty of her kind at the school," Oberon said, directing his comment at Kenzie. Addressing Myreen, he added, "You will be well taken care of, I promise you."

Myreen growled, but Kenzie caught her eye and shook her head. "Let's just call this a draw." *For now.* This wasn't over, not by a long shot. But she couldn't put her friend through anything else. "We'll text or write or something. Our friendship isn't going to end. You can count on that. Maybe you can finally get that social media account you've been drooling over." Kenzie gave Myreen a half-hearted smile, desperately hoping to lighten the mood.

Myreen let out a short and bitter burst of a laugh, then hiccupped. "Right."

"Myreen, we'll talk about your options when we get to the school." Oberon pulled into a parking lot after paying the toll for entrance. "For now, Kenzie, you'll have to catch a cab home." He reached into his pocket, pulling out a wad of bills. Peeling some twenties off the outside, he handed them to Kenzie. "Here's some money for the fare. I'm sorry I can't take you back myself, but it's not safe."

"What if the vampires come looking for *me*?" Kenzie asked, jutting out her chin. She slipped the money into the back pocket of her skin-tight jeans.

"They won't. It's not you they're after." Oberon ran a hand through his hair, then got out of the car.

The girls slid out of the back seat, Kenzie watching her friend to see what she would do. But Myreen was back to hugging herself, her gaze dark as the night sky. Kenzie thought she detected a hint of a shiver from Myreen's suddenly frail looking body.

She threw her arms around Myreen's neck, squeezing her tight. "It's gonna be okay," Kenzie whispered. Myreen's head nodded against her shoulder. "I'll always be here for you. No matter what. Okay?" Myreen nodded again, sniffling.

Kenzie slowly peeled herself away. She shot a glare at Oberon, who was still wearing that hunted look, his foot tapping an impatient tune. *I mean seriously, does this guy ever smile?*

"Your mom's a selkie too, right?" Oberon asked Kenzie.

"Uh, yeah," Kenzie said, sarcasm lacing her words. "Why?"

"You should be fine, but you'll want to tell her what happened. She should be able to make sure they don't follow Myreen's scent to your house."

"Ah." Of course. She didn't bother asking why Oberon assumed she couldn't do it. That was a sore enough point without arguing it over with Mr. Hottie McMoody. "Well, thanks. I guess."

Oberon nodded, then put a hand behind Myreen's back and steered her toward the subway entrance—one of the few below-ground ones in the city. Myreen cast a backward glance, and Kenzie waved her hand and tried to smile. She wasn't all that close with her mom, due to their differing opinions on magic, but she couldn't imagine losing her and then being forced to go to some school—albeit a rather cool school—all in one day. And the rules... Kenzie always knew those rules

27

were weird, even for Myreen's helicopter mom, but why would she keep her own daughter from the shifter world? What was she hiding from?

Kenzie watched Myreen and Oberon until they disappeared. After looking around the parking lot to see if anyone was watching her, she ducked her head and jogged to where the pair had disappeared. If she could just see which line they were taking, she might be able to figure out where the school was. If she could get inside the building, maybe she could gather some respect. Or support. Sparking a little rebellion might help give her an in. Besides, she wasn't letting even a fabled gryphon take her friend somewhere without knowing where. Roughly, anyway.

Kenzie crept down the stairs, crouching to see past the ceiling. She didn't need Oberon knowing she was spying on them. Oberon nodded at the attendant and handed a ticket to Myreen. She took it, and they slid through the turnstiles, Oberon flashing his own pass. Kenzie frowned. The man had a car, so why was he taking the subway to the school? And it must be he did that a lot, considering he had a pass. She waited, frozen on her step, until they had disappeared from view once more.

Rushing down the stairs, she looked for Oberon and Myreen, but they were likely down the next set of stairs, well out of view. Kenzie slowed her walk to something a bit more casual, trying to look as harmless as possible. A couple of people were approaching the turnstiles. Kenzie tried to position herself between them and the guard as she swung over the contraption.

"Hey!" came the indignant response from a woman behind her.

Kenzie turned a little, lifting her hand. "Not riding. My friend needs her phone." And she took off, to the alarmed protests of fellow passengers and the angry glare of the guard on duty. Kenzie wasn't sure when the next train would pull through, but she had to get a sight on her friend before she boarded.

The guard caught her arm just as she reached the platform.

Kenzie held up her free hand in surrender. "Not looking for any trouble. Just wanted to get this phone to my friend before she boarded." Kenzie looked around, spotting Myreen's tell-tale blue-black locks, Oberon's impressive form beside her. Kenzie's gaze flicked to the sign hanging overhead, the unmistakable green strip beckoning to riders seeking to take the green line south.

"Likely story," the woman said, looking Kenzie over. Her brow arched. "You don't look like one of our regular jumpers. You're not a runaway, are you?"

Kenzie shook her head. "No, ma'am. And I wasn't trying to ride. Look, see?" Kenzie pulled out her own phone, showing it to the woman. "My friend accidentally left this. She's going to be devastated."

The woman snorted. "Kids. Hey, what's your name?" She had a badge on that said Officer L. Ward.

"Kenzie. Kenzie MacLugh," she volunteered, hoping to inspire some good will. "Please, Ms. Ward. I won't do it again."

Officer Ward grimaced, but led Kenzie to the turnstile, opening a side gate to let her through. "I better not catch you doing anything like that again."

Kenzie nodded eagerly.

"You have what you need to get you home?"

"Yes ma'am."

"Good. Now get." Officer Ward shooed Kenzie away, putting her hands on her belt.

Kenzie gave a final nod and a smile, her heart beating about a hundred miles a minute. She'd rather not have an offence on her record, and she *really* didn't want her mom to know. Things were complicated enough without a court date hanging over her head.

Kenzie forced a deep breath as she headed back up the stairs. There had to be some way to track Myreen's phone, but at least she knew they were headed south on the green line. It wasn't a location, but it was a start. She pulled out her phone, checking out all the stops on the green line, wondering where her friend would get off.

Too bad she didn't have magic for this kind of situation. Lighting a candle, basic object moving, sure. Most of the magic she knew was the garden variety, but what she really wanted was the opportunity to find out what her magic was really capable of. Without a grimoire to guide her, she'd need someplace safe to test and study—or maybe another selkie to help her find new incantations and potions, though that was more unlikely than getting into the school. *Stupid selkies and their secrecy.*

Besides, her friend needed her. Of that, she was certain.

Myreen

The subway tunnel was a blur as their train sped through it. Myreen felt detached from the world around her. She was still struggling to keep reality from crashing down on her. She wasn't ready to face what happened at her house, not yet, not in the presence of this stranger. She couldn't afford to fall apart, not when she still knew so little about what was actually going on.

She cleared the lump from her throat and looked at the man who was her seemingly reluctant escort. He was all puffed up like a lion, watching the passengers of the train like they were predatory hyenas in his savanna.

"Where is this school you're taking me to?" she asked.

He regarded her with those steely eyes, and his features softened slightly. "I'll explain soon. Our stop is coming, and then we can speak more freely."

Myreen nodded, understanding that he still considered them

unsafe. She looked around the uncaring, distracted commuters around her. They looked harmless, ordinary. Could one of them be out for her?

She tried not to think about that, either. Grief and fear were playing tug-of-war with her heart, and she didn't want either one to win.

Stop by stop, all the passengers disembarked, until she and Oberon were the only two left on the train. She looked at the digital map on the wall. The next stop was the end of the line. Where were they going?

The train slowed for its final destination.

"Come on, this is where we get off," Oberon said, rising from the bench.

Allowing a sense of curiosity to fill her fretful mind, she followed him to the door, and they exited as soon as it opened. The platform was dim and completely empty. The stairs to the right led to an industrial part of Chicago that she had never been to before, but she couldn't imagine a school for supernatural beings dwelling in this neighborhood.

She headed for the stairs, but when Oberon didn't take the lead, she stopped short and looked back. He was walking toward a janitorial closet in the darkest corner of the platform. She cocked her head and walked up behind him, watching as he pulled the same subway pass out of his pocket and swiped it through the reader on the closet door. A little green light came on and a click sounded. Oberon pulled the door open and nodded for her to precede him inside.

Myreen crossed the threshold and found herself on another subway platform. A secret platform. Oberon followed her in and closed the door behind him.

"There, now we can talk freely," he said. "This subway will take us to the Dome. Here, this is your pass now. It's the only thing that will unlock that door and allow you to ride this private subway." He offered it to her.

With a mild sense of privilege, she accepted it. "You're trusting me with this?"

"All students get one," he said with a nod. "None of our students are prisoners of the school. They can come and go whenever they want, with a chaperone, of course, if they're minors."

That was comforting. She trusted Oberon, even though she had no solid reason to yet, but knowing that she wasn't expected to be confined to the school he was taking her to made her feel so much better about her situation. Not like she had anywhere else to go.

"Let's get on," he said. "The train will be leaving soon."

With his hand on her back, he gently guided her toward the waiting train.

"But where is the school?" she asked.

"You'll see," he said, a hint of a smirk on his face. "I don't want to ruin the surprise. There's nothing like the first time you see it."

She raised a curious eyebrow, but stepped onto the car anyway. They both took a seat on opposite benches facing each other, and the train began to move forward.

"Look, for what it's worth," Oberon began with an awkward expression. "I'm truly sorry about your mother. About all of this. It wasn't supposed to be this way. I was supposed to come to your house and talk to you and your mother about the school, and ideally you both would have come back with me. If we had any idea the vampires were targeting you, I would have come much sooner."

"How did you know about me?" she asked, choosing to avoid the subject of the night's previous events. "If I really am what you say I am."

"We have a seer," he said. "She helps us locate and welcome shifters from all over the world. Yesterday when she was doing a routine search, she saw you."

"A seer?" Myreen asked, trying not to sound as skeptical as she felt. She had to remind herself that this stuff wasn't as crazy as it seemed—after all, she did just see him transform into a gryphon.

"Yes. Her name is Delphine," he replied, braiding his fingers and putting his hands on his lap. "She's actually the head instructor of the mermaids at the school. You'll meet her tonight."

"Is she a mermaid, too?" she asked.

Oberon nodded. "A rare talent among mermaids is the ability to see the future. She is the most talented seer I've ever met, and she's been using that skill to find lost shifters like yourself since the school started over twenty years ago."

Myreen nodded, trying to wrap her head around all this. They thought she was a mermaid. But how could that be? She'd never experienced anything to suggest she was something other than human, and she'd certainly never sprouted a tail with a flashy flipper.

But, then again, she'd never really been in open water before, either. Her mom hadn't even allowed her to take baths when she was growing up; it'd been nothing but showers since before she could remember. Could her mom have known?

"How does someone become a mermaid?" she asked. "Is it random?"

Oberon shook his head. "Mermaids are born mermaids. It's hereditary."

"So that would mean that my mom was a mermaid?"

"One of your parents would have to be, yes," he answered. "Do you know anything about your father?"

Myreen frowned and shook her head. "I guess my mom was hiding more than I thought."

She leaned back and looked out the window, watching the darkness outside zoom by. She knew she should be taking this time to ask more questions, but she didn't have it in her.

How could her mother keep this from her? The no-swimming rule made so much sense now. Her mom knew she was a mermaid and had intentionally kept it from her. But why? And did that mean she had been a mermaid, too? Or was it Myreen's mysterious father, whom her mom would never talk about? Myreen didn't even know his name.

Despite all that she was learning, she couldn't cast any blame on her mom. How could she? All she could think about was how she'd never get to talk about any of this with her. She'd never see that secretive expression again. Never hear her voice, her laugh. Her mom was gone.

Tears brimmed again and Myreen blinked them away. Her entire being was begging to cry, to shed the weight of all this anguish and regret, but now was the not the time or place to give her body the release it needed. According to Oberon, they would soon be at the school, and she didn't want to be a wailing, soggy mess in front of so many strangers. She had to keep it together, for just a little while longer.

Out of the corner of her eye, she saw Oberon move. He came to sit beside her.

"I know what you must be feeling," he said in a low voice. "Twenty years ago, my parents and my wife were killed by vampires."

Myreen looked at his face, which was tight with tension. She could now see the sorrow behind his stoic eyes. Was this loss the reason for his roughness?

She had no words of comfort to give, as she was just as broken by the loss as he was. Instead, she asked, "Why do vampires come after shifters?"

He sighed and leaned forward, his elbows resting on his knees. "They believe they are the truly superior race on this planet, and they want to rule over humans. Shifters believe that all races of humans are equal and should stand together. We've been fighting their advances for centuries. Venoms and bites from certain shifter species are fatal to vampires, so we are the only thing standing in the way of their dark dreams."

A sudden hatred sparked inside Myreen, focused toward the

demons that took her mom from her.

"Is there a way to beat them?" she asked.

"I hope so," he said, giving her a strange look, as if he expected her to explode at any minute; it was a look of anticipation.

Feeling uncomfortable under his intense gaze, she turned to look out the window again. As she did, the darkness outside suddenly broke and gave way to a beautiful blue. The lights within the train slowly dimmed, allowing the blue around them to brighten and cast an almost magical glow on the benches and walls.

"Whoa," Myreen said, turning her whole body around to take a better look. The train was now passing through a glass tunnel that was completely underwater. Fish of all sizes and colors swam beyond the glass. Where were they?

"You haven't seen anything yet," Oberon said with a smile in his voice. "Look out the other side."

She turned around to do as he suggested, and she couldn't believe what she saw.

In the distance a few miles away, an enormous glass dome winked at her through the surprisingly clear water. She couldn't tell just how big it was from here, but it looked as though it spanned at least a mile. Magnificent metallic buildings filled its womb, twinkling like a modern city of Atlantis. Myreen had never seen anything so wondrous in her whole life.

"Myreen Fairchild, welcome to the Dome," Oberon said.

"This is incredible!" she gasped. "Where are we?"

"At the bottom of Lake Michigan," he answered. "It's our greatest and most important secret."

"How long has this place been here?" she asked, unable to take her eyes off the glass structure.

"Twenty years. After our previous school was destroyed, we needed to find a new location that the vampires would never find. So far, our plan has worked."

Myreen had no other words. She was mesmerized by the sight beyond the windows. It made her forget for a moment the tragedy of this night. She stared at it until it was out of view as the train curved away, anticipation building to see what the inside looked like.

Finally, the train came to a stop, and Myreen rushed out the doors with a newfound eagerness. Landing on the platform, she went to the glass that framed this tunnel, placing a tentative hand on it as if she could reach right through it to the dense water on the other side. She looked up directly above her, amazed by the fact that she couldn't see the surface. She knew they had to be deep under the lake, but seeing all the water on top of her was no less miraculous.

Having never been anywhere near open water before, she realized she should feel at least a little claustrophobic, being stuck under so much of it. After all, she didn't know how to swim. If the glass should break, she'd most certainly die. And yet, she felt absolutely no fear, only extreme wonder and a sense of well-being.

Oberon came onto the platform and stood beside her. "Are you ready to see the inside?"

Myreen could only nod fervently.

Oberon led her to a large vault-style metal door at the end of the tunnel. He opened a little metal box that was roughly head level, leaned close so that his face was within inches, and pressed a button. A tiny green laser flashed and moved over his right eye. Then large bolts clanked loudly within the door, and it opened.

"Retina scan," Oberon said. "Shifters have unique retina structures. That way even if a vampire did make it to this point, they wouldn't be able to get in."

Oberon pulled the door open the rest of the way and invited her to follow him through. They crossed the threshold into a large entrance hall whose floors, walls and ceilings were made completely out of some dark matte metal. Directly in front of them was an archway, framed by metal columns around which long Japanese-style dragons were coiled, shining like silver on the lackluster metal. At the zenith of the arch, the same crest from her invitation letter perched proudly, welcoming her. A large desk sat to their right, and behind the desk sat a large man with a fiery orange beard, his hair buzzed nearly bald. He smiled and nodded at Oberon and Myreen as they passed.

Through the archway, she could see only a fraction of a long and massive corridor, like something found only in palaces of old. Breathless, she emerged from the entrance hall, staring with wide eyes at the towering grand hall in which she now stood. The ceiling was at least three stories up, and shining metallic creatures of ancient lore crawled and slithered up and down the unpolished gray walls. Dragons snaked up the vaulted ceiling, meeting to hiss at each other at the upper-most point. Mermaids stood in the doorframes of every adjoining corridor, as if holding them up. Werewolves howled here and there at an unseen moon, and magnificent gryphons stood like gargoyles on the ledges of each story that overlooked this grand hall.

Myreen could never have imagined architecture like this in her wildest dreams, and all crafted and molded out of metal, either polished to a glorious shine or left flat and unrefined. There wasn't a single brick or wooden beam or even a dab of plaster in the entire place, and yet the darkness of it all was nothing short of beautiful.

She reached out to touch one of the wolves that seemed frozen in his climb up the wall, amazed at how meticulously each spike of ruffled fur was molded to look so lifelike.

"Is this whole place made out of metal?" she asked, staring straight up.

"Yes. It's a silver-steel alloy. The student population is mostly made up of weres, who are vulnerable to silver. This helps them better control their shifting ability and be less governed by the phases of the moon."

"Weres?" she asked, lowering her head to give him a quizzical look.

He gave a gruff chuckle. "There is much you have to learn about our world. Weres include hounds, which you probably know as werewolves, maos, which are werecats, and ursas, the werebears."

"How many different shifters are there?" she asked, her head already spinning.

"In the most common varieties, ten," Oberon replied. "But every now and then, something new or something thought to have been extinct will pop up. I'm sure this all seems like a lot right now, and you don't have to learn it all tonight. There will be plenty of time for that later."

A group of teenagers came out of one of the many corridors. They were chatting happily, but when they saw Oberon and Myreen, they stopped and fell silent. They looked at Myreen with question marks on their faces, making her feel like some freak on display at a circus.

"It's late, and you've had a very long and difficult night," Oberon said, guiding her away from the onlookers and toward a staircase with a firm hand on her back. "Let me show you to your room so you can get some much-needed rest."

At his suggestion, she suddenly felt very tired, and nothing sounded better than curling up in a bed with a blanket over her head and crying until the pain went away; even though she knew that no amount of spilled tears could ease this pain.

She nodded and allowed him to lead her up the stairs. As they walked, more and more students crossed their path, and stopped to watch. Whispers followed them all through the building. Myreen didn't care to try to catch any of their words. She just wanted to get away from it all.

They came to a large pair of doors that were molded to look like water with elegant mermaids swimming through it. Just as he was raising his knuckles to knock, the doors parted inward, and a tall, beautiful redhead greeted them.

"My dear girl," the woman said. "I have been so looking forward to your arrival, and I'm so terribly sorry it had to be under these circumstances."

How does she know? Oberon didn't call anyone.

The woman passed a knowing glance at Oberon for a second, and he nodded.

"This is where I leave you," he said to Myreen. "Delphine is the head of the Mermaid Prime, and she will take it from here. I'll be by again in a few days to check on how you're doing."

"Uh, thank you," she said, not knowing what else to say.

He bowed his head, then turned around and vanished down the hall.

"Come, Myreen," Delphine said, beckoning her with an open hand that was creamy white and delicate. "Let's get you settled in."

Myreen nodded and followed the woman through the double doors.

They came into a lounge room of sorts, where a few teens were sitting on couches, talking or reading or staring at illuminated laptop screens. Once again, students turned their heads toward her.

Myreen chose to ignore this unwanted attention, eager to get to a private space.

"How did you know?" she asked, casting sheepish eyes on Delphine.

Delphine nodded, her powerful green eyes glinting in understanding. "Some mermaids have the ability to see the future. I was the one who had the vision of you that brought you to us. But visions don't always come in a timely manner. I only saw the death of your mother as it happened. I am so sorry." Her pretty brow furrowed in genuine sympathy.

Myreen had forgotten about Delphine's ability. There had simply been too much information in the last hour to process it all. She sighed, resigned to the fact that she knew less about this world than any other person in this school.

They went up another short flight of steps and stopped at one of the many doors along the hallway. Delphine pulled a key card out of the pocket of her black dress pants and unlocked the door, then handed the card to Myreen.

"This will be your room for as long as you're a student here," she said. "There is a campus map and a class schedule on your desk."

Myreen walked into the modest bedroom and looked around. There was a comfortable-looking twin bed—complete with blue sheets and comforter—a dresser, a desk with a chair, and a closet. No window.

"Your teachers are expecting you in classes tomorrow morning, but I understand completely if you need a few days to mourn," Delphine said softly.

Myreen turned around. "No, it's fine," she said, resolute. "I'm already behind. I'd like to start classes tomorrow if that's okay."

Delphine gave a long nod. "As you wish. In that case, I'll see you tomorrow in Transformation." The woman backed out through the doorway and began to close the door, then stopped. "My door is on the main floor of the common room, under the stairs. If you need anything, please feel free to come and talk to me."

The smile she offered was so warm and motherly, it reminded Myreen of her own mom's smile. Queue the lump to constrict her throat.

Myreen coughed unevenly and said, "Thank you."

Delphine mercifully closed the door, leaving Myreen to herself at last.

Myreen stood in the middle of her new room for a few minutes, the weight of her sorrow crashing down on her like the first wave of a tsunami. Drowning in it, she no longer had the strength to make it to her bed.

She crumbled to the floor and sobbed.

Myreen

What's more intimidating than a first day at a new school? A first day at a school for shape-shifters as the only one who knows nothing about the shifter world.

Myreen had hardly slept that night, so she was up when she heard shuffling and chatter in the hall outside her door. Delphine had said the other students in this section were all mermaids—like her, supposedly. Yet she was terrified to go out there. How would she possibly fit in? The only thought that finally compelled her to get out of bed was that maybe her fellow "mermaids" could help her learn about what she was, and maybe she could make a friend.

She sluggishly slid off the bed and picked up the tablet that that sat on her desk. A quick tap revealed the class schedule.

Monday-Wednesday-Friday:
8:00 Mastery
9:00 Algebra

10:00 Chemistry

11:00 English

2:00 Defense

Tuesday-Thursday:

8:00 Shifter Biology

9:00 Shifter History

10:00 Transformation

11:00 Music

2:00 Defense

There was a note at the bottom to skip Defense class for the first day, which she was okay with because it sounded far too intimidating.

The day was Thursday, which meant she had Shifter Biology first. She looked at the digital clock sitting next to the closed laptop on the desk. 6:45 AM. Which meant she had about fifteen minutes to get herself dressed before venturing to find some breakfast.

Myreen had no idea what she would wear. She hadn't had the chance to grab clothes before rushing out of her house. She was still in the same slimming jeans and t-shirt from the party last night, and while they didn't smell like they'd gone through a rough night, she didn't think them appropriate for a first day.

Hoping against hope, she slid her closet door open. To her surprise, the closet was full of black uniforms, each with slacks and a button-up dress shirt with a little blue swirl on the left breast. Apparently, this school had a uniform policy, which she was surprised to find she was grateful for. She usually hated schools like that, as she liked to express herself through her appearance—hence the blue streaks in her hair—but wearing the same outfit as everyone else would help her stand out less.

She quickly changed into one of the sets, brushed her hair and teeth, and tied her shoes. She grabbed tablet, loaded with the schedule and the school map, and readied herself to start her day, when she realized she had no school supplies whatsoever. No pen, pencil, paper, nothing. Myreen couldn't just show up to classes empty-handed, regardless of the haphazard way she arrived here. She looked around the room, hoping to once again find a surprise resource. But there was nothing in the desk drawers or anywhere else in this modest space. Just a detached keyboard that had apparently been hidden beneath the tablet.

Sighing, she looked at the keyboard. Maybe she could type notes. What else was she supposed to do? Leaning against the desk on the floor was a stylish laptop bag with the school's crest embroidered in shiny colorful thread. She stuck the keyboard and tablet in the bag and slung it over her shoulder, then took a deep breath before opening her bedroom door.

The common room was a buzz of activity, with students moving all about. And just as last night, when they saw her enter their space, they all quieted to look at her.

"There she is, the *new* mermaid," she heard one of them whisper, followed by barely stifled giggles.

Not knowing what else to do, she smiled and nodded at those who didn't look away from her gaze. Whatever courage she was depending on finding her was nowhere in sight.

Myreen rushed out of the common room and into the massive grand hall, her nerves sizzling with the sense of inadequacy. If she couldn't woman-up to ask someone for directions, then she'd have to find the cafeteria on her own. She grabbed her tablet and pulled up the school map and took a good look at it for the first time. She found the mermaid dorms, and the grand hall at the center, from which several hallways branched out. Her eyes scanned the screen until they caught sight of the words DINING HALL, which was on the ground floor to the left of the grand hall.

There, that wasn't so bad. She wasn't some helpless damsel in distress; she had to remind herself of that. She could certainly find her own way around, or at least she hoped so.

She put the tablet back away and smoothed the front of her shirt, then made her way to the stairs that would take her back down to the grand hall. Unlike in the mermaid common room, when she passed other students, they didn't stare and whisper. The uniform was doing its job after all. She did get the occasional up-down look from some of the male students, which on a day like this was a welcome confidence booster.

Many of them were filing into the archways to the left of the grand hall, so she followed the masses, hoping they would lead her to the right place. Once she passed under the arch, she realized there wasn't much farther to look. The entire span of the left side of this building *was* the dining hall. Tables packed with people filled the open space, and all the way to the back of the room was a huge buffet station. The smell of bacon and eggs assaulted her nostrils, and she realized how hungry she really was, having hardly eaten the night before.

After waiting in line for a few minutes, she left the buffet station with a tray full of delicious-smelling food. Now she just had to find a place to sit and devour it. Myreen looked around the large hall, scouring for an empty seat.

There was a round table not too far away with two empty seats, and upon closer inspection, Myreen saw that all the girls at that table were wearing the same symbol on their shirts as her own. Mermaids.

She put on a friendly face and approached the table.

"Hi girls," she announced herself with a chipper voice. "Mind if I sit with you?"

The three girls stopped their conversation and shot her a look down their noses. The strawberry blond in the middle had a polished beauty, the kind one sees in magazines. She was flanked by a girl with hair so dirty blond it appeared to have a greenish tint to it, and another with long black hair that resembled Myreen's. The strawberry blond was clearly the queen bee, and Myreen wished she had noted that fact before coming up to them.

"This table is full," said the strawberry blond in an unashamedly catty tone.

"Ohh-kaay," Myreen said, pursing her lips. She turned away from the table without direction.

For creatures that mythologically spend a lot of time in water, they sure know how to burn, she thought.

She tried not to read too much into that encounter. Maybe there really were two other people occupying those chairs and they had just gotten up for more food. Myreen inwardly shook her head; she knew better.

Luckily, she found an empty seat at the end of a long rectangular table, and she wasted no time digging into her food. The group of boys to the right of her were in a loud debate about something, and she was happy that none of them noticed her.

As she ate, she saw that all the students had varying symbols on their shirts—one of the four symbols that made up the school crest. The boys arguing next to her all had the three red slashes on their shirts. She knew that the blue swirl was for mermaids, and she couldn't help but wonder what the other four symbols meant. Oberon had said there were nearly a dozen different shifters in the world, so did this school only accept four of them?

When her tray was empty and her belly pleasantly full, she hastened out of the dining hall and went in search of her first class. According to the map, it was out the double doors at the far end of the grand hall and across the campus in a big pie-slice-shaped building.

She followed a flock of students out of the end of the hall and

47

found herself looking at something she had not expected—but then, nothing about the school was within the realm of her expectations. The campus appeared like a regular school campus, complete with the most vibrant green grass filling the space between every connecting sidewalk. Grass was the last thing she thought she would see under a dome at the bottom of the lake. There were even fruit-bearing trees standing here and there, offering shade from the surprisingly bright turquoise light that filtered from the surface through the depths of water above the Dome.

Myreen realized she had stopped to stare—right in the middle of the pedestrian traffic on the wide sidewalk—and continued her trek toward the pie-slice building, which in actuality was much bigger than the digital map could convey.

"Jesse, calm down, man."

Myreen looked up and saw a group of boys on the grass that appeared to be in a fight—or on the brink of one. She would have ignored them completely if the sound of growling hadn't caught her attention.

A boy in the center of the quarrel had his hands firmly on the chest of the one who was growling, trying to calm him down. But the growling boy heard none of it. His breathing came louder and more forceful, and his eyes began to glow a bright red. Myreen thought she was seeing things and blinked hard.

"Jesse, no!" the mediator yelled, and before the last word was out of his mouth, the growling boy's body ripped out of his uniform, sprouted a thick coat of ashy brown fur and mutated into a giant snarling wolf.

Myreen gasped and jumped away from the scene, clutching her bag to her frantically beating heart.

No one else around reacted in such a way. Many either rolled their eyes and shook their heads, or laughed in derision, making fun of the boy who was now a huge hairy dog.

"Jesse Barnes, what do you think you're doing?" a woman yelled as she made her way across the yard.

"Oh, he's in for it now," another student snickered before fleeing the scene like everyone else. All too eager to get away, Myreen did the same and rushed even quicker to her first class. She didn't know if she would ever get used to seeing people turn into oversized beasts, but it didn't look like she would have a choice.

***

Once she entered the building, finding her classroom was easy. All the doors were labeled by subject, and Shifter Biology was the eighth door down, between Chemistry and General Biology.

Myreen was the first student to arrive, and she was happy that she wouldn't have to awkwardly struggle to find her seat in front of a full class.

A woman—who she assumed was the teacher, dressed in the same style of formal clothing as Delphine had been last night—looked up from her laptop when she saw Myreen enter.

"Ah, you must be Myreen," she said, rising from her desk and walking over to Myreen. "I'm Mrs. Coltar. I'm very pleased to have you in my class." The woman offered her a warm smile.

"Uh, thanks," Myreen said, smiling back. "Are the seats assigned?"

"Yes. Your seat is in the second row, third column." Mrs. Coltar held out an open hand toward the seat in question. "I know you're a bit new to all of this, but we get new shifters in class at least once a month, so we often go back over the basics. If you have any questions during the lecture, feel free to speak up."

Mrs. Coltar's demeanor was so sweet, almost motherly. Myreen already felt calmer for being in her presence, and the reassurance that a refresher course was in order was also a big relief.

Myreen nodded and took her seat. As more students began to fill the seats around her, she studied all the educational posters and diagrams on the walls. There were diagrams of about a dozen different creatures, complete with skeleton, musculature, organ structure and vein maps. There was a dragon to the right of the dry erase board, a griffon next to that, some kind of large furry creature with nine tails—and again, Myreen wondered just how many different shifters there were. The mermaid diagram was especially interesting, and Myreen stared at it until class started, attempting to commit the skeletal structure to memory, and imagining just how a human's bones could mutate and combine in such a way.

"Good morning, class," Mrs. Coltar announced. "As we've had a couple new students recently, I think it best to go over the basics."

There was a collective sigh from the class, and Myreen sunk into her chair, hoping to avoid blame for the repetition.

She saw all the students pulling tablets out of their cases, some with keyboards attached and others just putting them on, and setting them on their desks. *So I don't need a pen and paper after all,* she thought, and was glad that she had the sense to take the tablet with her. She pulled it out and started it up on her desk, finding the keyboard pretty much attached itself with some sort of magnetic clasp, then set her sights back on the teacher, eager to type down everything she said.

Mrs. Coltar flipped a switch to dim the lights, and a machine projected an image onto the whiteboard. The image was of ten different creatures, separated into groups.

"All shifter species are classified into the four major primes," Mrs. Coltar lectured. "Who can tell me the four primes?"

A girl somewhere behind Myreen must have raised her hand.

"Joanna," Mrs. Coltar said.

"The four primes are archaic, avian, were, and the best of all, oceanid," the girl said with a haughty tone.

Mrs. Coltar frowned at the girl, but continued to say, "That's correct. There are three major shifter species under the archaic prime, which are gryphons, kitsunes, and nagas. Avian houses dragons, phoenixes, and harpies. Currently, mermaids are the only species classified under oceanid, simply because they have just recently come out of the water, so to speak, and we don't have enough knowledge of what other species may reside in the depths. And as for weres, the three major types are hounds, maos, and ursas."

Myreen studied the projected image harder, learning what each of the creatures were. Of course, she already knew about gryphons, which was the first one on the left. Next to that was the furry creature with nine tails, which said kitsune under it, and beside that was what appeared to be a giant humanoid lizard with a snake head. The idea that a creature like that actually existed was a bit terrifying.

The dragon, phoenix and harpy were pretty obvious, as those were popular mythological creatures, as was the mermaid. And upon studying the were images, she remembered Oberon's summary from the other night—hounds were werewolves, maos were werecats, and ursas were werebears. So, the boy that had turned into a giant dog not five minutes ago in the yard was a hound. As she had gathered from the teacher's reaction outside, students weren't allowed to just shift whenever they wanted, for which Myreen was deeply grateful, because if she thought she had to see even one more person transform into a monster today, she was going to freak the heck out.

"Now, who can tell me which is the only species that is forced to shift under a full moon?" Mrs. Coltar asked the class.

The boy in front of Myreen raised his hand. "Trick question," he said with a smug chuckle. "There are three: hounds, maos, and ursas."

"Correct. And what is special about their creation that is different from all other shifters?"

"Weres become weres because they are either bitten or scratched by another were, while all other shifters are born as what they are," the boy answered.

"Very good. Can someone else tell me what makes mermaids different from other species in terms of birth?"

The class was silent in response. Myreen looked around the room at the other students, and saw that a few rows behind her, one girl was raising her hand.

"Come on, guys, we just went over this last week," Mrs. Coltar prodded. She gave them all a moment to remember. "All right, take it away, Joanna."

"Mermaids are the only shifters that are born in their shifter form," Joanna answered with pride, making Myreen's brows jump. "We are the one true shifter species."

Mermaids are born mermaids? So there was no way her mom couldn't know she was one.

Mrs. Coltar sighed, and Myreen now understood why she was reluctant to call on her to answer the question; Joanna must be a mermaid.

"Thank you, Joanna, but in the future, please keep your opinions to yourself."

The rest of the lecture was on the puberty trigger, which basically was a hormonal stage of development that caused most of the shifter species—excluding weres and mermaids—to have the ability to shift. This usually happened anywhere between twelve and sixteen. This was when most students were invited to study at the school, mostly so that they could learn to control their abilities in a safe place, away from the human population.

When the lecture was over, Myreen felt infinitely better about being here, like she could at least comprehend most of what was going on. She now knew which prime each of the symbols referred to—the blue swirl was mermaid, of course, the red slash for weres, the wing for avians, and the talon-looking symbol for archaic. As she walked to her next class, she could tell roughly what type of shifter a student was by which symbol they wore on their shirt.

Next on her schedule was Shifter History, and she was pleasantly surprised to see that Oberon was sitting behind the desk at the front of the room. She knew that he was the school director, but not that he taught classes as well.

This room was structured like a lecture hall with theatre style seats of red upholstery. Myreen assumed that these seats were not assigned, and sat in a seat at the front of the class. She opened her tablet on her lap, excited to take more notes.

A shadow fell over her, and she looked up from her screen to see the three girls from the dining hall standing in front of her, all of them giving her a dirty look. It was only then that she recognized that the arrogant mermaid who'd been making all the comments in Shifter Bio—the one named Joanna—was the greenish-blond one. The arrogant strawberry blond leader hmphed at her, then turned her head in a demeaning gesture and led her trio up the stairs to sit at the back of the class.

Myreen's lips trembled, and she tried to stifle a pout. Now she *knew* that their rejection this morning was exactly that. What had she done to make them dislike her? Her asking to sit with those girls were the first words she'd spoken to any student since she'd gotten here.

It wasn't like Myreen had never been dissed by other girls before. Under any other circumstances, such a thing wouldn't have fazed her. But she was already vulnerable, like cracked glass, ready to fall apart at the slightest ding.

She wanted to cry, not just for their hazing, but for everything that had happened in the last twenty-four hours. But she was in the middle of a class full of at least fifty other students. Now was not the time nor the place, so she bit her lip and sucked in a breath.

Oberon started class just then, giving her the perfect distraction.

"Today, we're going to talk about the Mer Allocation. Do any of you what this refers to?"

There were some giggles in the class behind Myreen, some she knew came from Trish and her trio, but it was a guy who raised his hand. Oberon pointed his index finger at the guy.

"This was when the mer migrated from living in the ocean to living on land."

Oberon nodded. "Yes. I'm sure you're all too young to remember, but it was a big shock to many of us to learn that mers even existed. They had always been a subject of legend, a fairytale even to us shifters. They trickled in at first, testing the waters, so to speak, then assimilated into human society, assuming human identities to live on land full-time. Due to global warming, over-fishing and pollution, along with upgraded hunting technology by human hunters, the mermaids no longer felt safe in the depths, and believed their only way to escape the dangers of humans was to join them. Does anyone know when this happened?"

Another hand went up. "1985?" a girl in the back answered.

"Correct. The movement began in the early eighties, and by 1985, the entire mermaid civilizations of the Caribbean and Pacific Ocean had merged with humans."

Oberon pointed to a student Myreen had not seen raise their hand. "Is it true that Delphine was one of the pioneers that led the mer to land?"

"Very good, Jenna. Yes, in fact, were it not for Delphine's brilliance with financial gains, the mer might never have made the switch. And were it not for Delphine, none of us would be here in this room. When the Dome's predecessor school was destroyed by vampires, Delphine came forth with the vast funding she and other mermaids had amassed using their fortune-telling skills. She offered to help create a new school for shifters of all origins. Delphine made the Dome possible, and it has proven to be the greatest shifter shelter of all time."

Myreen found all this fascinating! She was blown away by the history of a people she never knew she belonged to—and still questioned that relationship. After all, she had yet to see proof that she was actually a mermaid. What if Delphine and Oberon had gotten it wrong? What if that was why those other girls dogged her, because they could tell she wasn't one of them? After learning about mermaids, she would be so honored to be a part of that community, to be welcomed into their culture and learn all she could.

"Are there any questions on the lecture?" Oberon posed to the class.

"I have a question," a gratingly familiar voice said from the back of the room.

"Yes, Trish," Oberon said. Myreen turned around to see who had raised their hand. Sure enough, it was the strawberry-blond diva.

"Why have all the teachers been searching for a stray mermaid all these years?" Trish asked, shooting a venomous, mascara-lined look at Myreen.

A stray mermaid? The teachers have been searching for someone like me? Why? Myreen turned her quizzical gaze on Oberon, as did the rest of the class.

Oberon faltered momentarily. "I'm sorry?" he asked, obviously feigning ignorance.

"What's so special about this new mermaid you brought in last night?" Trish rephrased, this time directly targeting Myreen. "I think we all want to know."

"Ooo, I smell blood in the water," some boy yelled in the background, and some snickers followed.

Myreen stared at Oberon with anticipation, barely breathing. If there was something special about her—something other than being a mermaid, which was already incredible if it was true—then she wanted to know about it. Maybe it could shed some light on the vampire attack on her house, on her mom...

"I think you should leave the gossip in the dorm rooms, Trish," Oberon said, dismissing the issue entirely. "Now, does anyone have any questions *about the lecture?*"

The class was quiet for a moment, but then one student raised their hand to ask something trivial.

Myreen didn't hear it.

Her brain was abuzz with speculation. What did those mermaid girls know that she didn't? It seemed that everyone knew more than she did, and not just about the shifter world, but about her.

Now that she really thought about it, it did seem strange for a school director to come to a prospective student's home in the middle of the night to invite her to a school, shifter or not. Not that she didn't appreciate him swooping in to save her, but what was so urgent about her placement at the school that it couldn't wait until an appropriate hour during the day?

But if they did expect something special from her, what if she disappointed them? Her next class was Transformation, and she had no idea how to transform, or if she even could. What if she failed, and proved herself to be nothing but human? They would kick her out for sure. She had already seen too much of their world. Would they kill her to protect their secret?

The period bell rang, announcing the end of class. Myreen left the lecture hall and made her way to the gymnasium where Transformation was held, with a similar dread as if she were walking to the gallows.

Myreen

Finding the Mermaid Transformation class was easy; all Myreen had to do was follow the stench of arrogance and privilege. It wasn't just the sea witch trio that gave her that impression of mermaids. Every student that carried themselves with a sense of self-importance had the mermaid symbol on their shirt.

The training room was on the far side of the second largest building on campus that appeared to be used for physical activities. According to the map, there was a gymnasium on the top floor with all manner of sports and exercise equipment, and a pool.

She walked through the door, the pounding of her heart against her eardrum beating in time with her footsteps like a death march cadence. The space inside was almost completely monopolized by an enormous swimming pool, with diving boards of various heights at one end, and several metal hoops hanging from the ceiling here and there. There were already several students in the pool, all of them wearing the same fitted swim top of black elastic.

The realization that she would be expected to swim shot white hot panic into her chest. She had never been in any amount of water, and she was almost certain to drown if she tried to swim, or at the very least to make a fool of herself flapping around gracelessly.

As she stood paralyzed with anxiety over the matter, someone jumped out of the water like a dolphin, heading toward one of the hanging hoops. The woman's speed was remarkable, but Myreen did manage to catch sight of something breathtaking before she landed in the water—a long, shimmering green tail where her legs should be, delicate gossamer fins decorating her hips and the bottom of the tail like glorious streamers celebrating its majesty.

Myreen was aware that her jaw had fallen open, but she couldn't connect her brain to her body to close it. All this talk of mermaids today, but she still hadn't fully accepted them as *real* until that moment. Unlike the two other shifters she had witnessed, this mermaid wasn't monstrous in any way. On the contrary, it was probably the most beautiful living thing she'd ever seen.

The jumper's head resurfaced a few feet away from where she landed. She pushed her hands up over her face and down the back of her hair, and Myreen saw that it was Delphine.

"Myreen," Delphine greeted with a beaming smile. "I'm so excited to give you your first lesson! Go into the locker room and you'll find a swim top in your locker. Just look for the locker with your name on it, third one on the back row."

Rendered too dumb to speak, Myreen simply nodded and made her way to the back of the room where there was a pair of doors, each with the appropriate gender stick figure on it. The only difference was that these figures had tails instead of legs. *How cute*, Myreen noted.

As she walked, she noticed more beautiful mermaid tails splashing through the water. Even as she knew everyone was giving her derisive looks, she couldn't help but stare at all of them. One of the most interesting things she noticed was that not all of their tails were the same color. In fact, no two tails looked the same. The majority were varying shades of blue and green, but every now and then there was a splash of red or yellow.

She playfully imagined what color her tail would turn out to be…if she was what they said she was. Her heart fell at the question.

Myreen pushed open the door to the ladies' locker room and ignored the stares and whispers as she made her way to the last row to look for her locker. Third one in, she saw her name on a digital readout. At the bottom of the screen there was a flashing oval, PRESS FINGER HERE displayed above it.

She pressed her index finger to the circle, and after a moment there was a beep and her locker popped open. The screen now said CALIBRATED. GOOD MORNING, MYREEN. She couldn't help but be impressed. They sure liked their gadgets here.

Just as Delphine had said, a long black swim top hung inside the locker. Myreen took it out and inspected it. Something was missing. It had to be. There were no bottoms included. She scanned every corner of the inside of the locker, but it was completely empty. Did they actually expect her to go out with no bottoms, or was this some kind of hazing prank?

Myreen looked around, half expecting to see Trish and her cronies giggling in a corner, but they were nowhere in sight. A few lockers down, another girl was pulling on her swim top. It went down past her buttocks to just above her knees, looking almost like a dress. Then the girl discreetly slipped out of her panties and placed all her clothes in her locker.

So, we really are expected to go commando.

Myreen's cheeks instantly burned at that realization. After a moment of thought, the reason behind it came to her: any bottoms they might be wearing would get in the way of two legs becoming one fin. Though she understood the logic, she felt uncomfortable with the idea of leaving her nether parts completely bare—in a class with boys, no less.

She would just have to be extra careful. No bending over, that was for darn certain!

Accepting her wardrobe fate, she disrobed her uniform and pulled on the swim top. The fabric clung to her like a second skin, and she happily found that no part of it hiked up when she made different movements. In fact, the more she moved, the more she realized how difficult it would be to show anything she shouldn't, even if she tried. *This must be some kind of smart fabric.*

As ready as she would ever be, Myreen put her clothes and laptop bag in her locker, the door automatically locking when she closed it, and went back into the training room.

Delphine stood outside the locker room, waiting for her. It was almost a shock to see her walking around on two creamy legs after that spectacle in the pool.

"Wonderful! Are you ready?" Delphine's green eyes were bright as she gazed at Myreen. Even soaking wet, her long red hair looked amazing.

"Um, actually, I'm not so sure about this," Myreen said with a timid shrug. She lowered her voice to say, "I've never done this before. I don't even know if I can shift. And I definitely can't swim."

Rather than becoming upset or disappointed, Delphine gave an indulgent laugh and put her hand on Myreen's back to guide her toward the pool. "Don't worry about any of that. The water in the pool is salt water; mermaids automatically transform in salt water."

"Really?" Myreen asked in a hushed tone.

Delphine gave an encouraging nod. "You won't even have to try. Just let your body do what it was meant to do. Don't fight it—that lesson comes later." She winked at Myreen.

"Okay," Myreen said, doubt weighing down her tone.

She looked at the crystal clear water as they came closer and closer. There were no stairs to step easily in as she'd seen in movies. From the looks of it, every part of this pool was just as deep as the rest, and it seemed to be at least two meters deep, deep enough to go over her head and then some.

"Just ease in at whatever pace you feel comfortable with," Delphine said as they stood at the edge of the pool. "And don't be alarmed when your skin starts to react."

"What will happen?" Myreen asked, unable to take her eyes off the water in front of her.

"Dip a toe in and see," Delphine encouraged.

Her fear overridden by curiosity, Myreen stretched out a leg and allowed her toes to submerge into the pleasantly warm water. Instantly, a prickling sensation devoured every inch of her wet skin, and she instinctively retracted her foot. Looking down at her toes, she saw that the flesh that had been previously smooth and unblemished had begun to peel, revealing shimmery scales beneath.

Myreen gasped, in awe of the reaction a tiny amount of salt water could produce.

"Oh, just dive in already," Trish's unmistakable voice said behind her, and suddenly swift hands thrust into her back, knocking her off balance and forcing her to belly-flop into the pool.

Myreen tried to scream, but water rushed into her open mouth and filled her lungs. She threw out her arms to find something to hold onto, splashing fruitlessly and grabbing nothing but water.

And then the whole-body circus of sensations took hold of her consciousness, and she could see, hear, feel nothing else. That same prickling covered the surface of her entire body, an itch that no amount of scratching could satisfy. Before she could even process that, the bones in her hips, legs and feet began to shift, unsetting and resetting, breaking and healing, so quickly that the pain began and ended in the blink of an eye. Half blinded by the sting of the water in her eyes, she hunched over to look at her legs. She could just make out that they had connected into one piece.

Another piercing pain rippled through her chest and neck, and she felt the skin on her throat splitting. She cried out again involuntarily, releasing bubbles into the water around her like an over-shook soda, and clutched at her neck as it seemed to tear apart.

All at once, the experience was over, and the world, both inside and outside of her body, was silent and calm. She opened her eyes, surprised to find that the water no longer stung, and that she could see perfectly. She gasped, only to realize that she could breathe. Water filled the inside of her mouth, throat and lungs, yet somehow she could still inhale and exhale without struggle. She took in a deep breath, and tiny bubbles appeared at the corners of her eyes. With her hands still clutching her throat, she could feel that those bubbles were releasing from three long slits on either side of her neck.

Holy crap, I have gills!

Burning with the thrill of her new reality, she looked down at her legs, and found a long and magnificent tail in their place. It was the most beautiful shade of pearlescent pink. Tissue-thin fins formed a make-shift skirt around her waist and blossomed from the end of her tail, long and flowing, like silk swaying in the wind.

It was true. It was all true! She really was a mermaid!

Her heart leaped with a newfound freedom and joy. She twirled in the water, the liquid submitting easily to her will. Myreen flexed her legs, marveling at the revelation of having only one limb instead of two. Rather than having only the knee and ankle joints, it was as if her new tail had hundreds of joints, and they obeyed her every internal command, bending backwards and forwards like a snake's spine. She flicked the end of her tail and watched as the water rippled in its wake. For a girl who had never set foot—or any other body part—in water, she felt like an Olympic swimmer.

The sound of arguing echoed through the water from the surface, and Myreen remembered that she had been pushed into the pool. Though it caused her no harm, Trish certainly hadn't been helping.

Myreen spun around and swam to the surface.

In her current form, the dry world felt painfully loud and overbearing, assaulting all her senses. She blinked through the brightness of the fluorescent lights to see Delphine sternly chiding Trish, whose expression looked bored.

"Look, she's totally fine," Trish said, pointing at Myreen. "I did her a favor. It would have taken her all period to get in there at the rate she was going."

"That's no concern of yours, and your little act of charity has earned you a week's detention," Delphine scolded.

"What?" Trish snapped, stomping her foot in protest.

"Want to make it two?" Delphine threatened.

Trish hmphed and scowled at Myreen, then stormed off to the girl's locker room.

Turning her attention back to Myreen, Delphine knelt at the edge of the pool. "I'm so sorry, she had no right to do that. How are you feeling?"

"Actually, I feel incredible," Myreen confessed. "I can't believe I went my whole life without knowing this part of myself."

"Well, I won't pretend to know anything about your home life, but I'm sure your mother had a good reason." Delphine's emerald eyes were sincere yet cryptic as they looked down on Myreen.

Myreen looked away, unable to comment. The mention of her mother caused the joy of transforming to evaporate, the buzz in her chest turning into a sour taste in her mouth.

Delphine thought her mom had a reason for hiding this. Myreen only wished she knew what that reason was.

Juliet

Head down, don't make eye contact, headphones on high, try to keep cool. Literally.

Juliet repeated this mantra to herself whenever she left the comfort of her room, which today had only been for music class and the one-on-one training she was forced to do with her dad. This day, especially, the chant echoed through her head.

Today marked one month since the *incident* occurred; a month since she found her father after not seeing him for years; a month since she was told that she could transform into a phoenix. And yet, she was still processing everything at a slow and steady pace. But that was good, in her case.

So far, the pressure of attempting to discover the phoenix within had caused her to set fire to two classrooms. She was lucky that the first fire was in her phoenix mastery class, which her father, Malachai Quinn, taught.

"Juliet, just to be clear, I'm only requesting a verbal answer. Do you feel the

heat of your fire lingering anywhere in your body?" She felt the spotlight on her, as her father asked her so nonchalantly in front of the entire class. The question alone brought back the memory of the incident, *because the warm feeling in her stomach was how it started.*

Her emotions got the best of her and she knew it was too late. Juliet felt her palms sweat with heat that rose into flames and escaped her fingertips. The sound of a mocking snicker got her to retract the fire.

"Brett, be useful and get the other extinguisher from the closet," her dad said.

Brett had a smug smirk on his face, and it made Juliet want to recoil even more. Who knew how many other students would tease her for that?

Thankfully, there wasn't too much damage, due to the smart extinguishers that Mr. Suzuki, head of Tinkering and Technology, stocked in the room.

That hadn't been the case a week ago, when she set fire to the second classroom. That one was much worse, and much more humiliating.

While her mantra had saved her many times, the mean girl mermaids just poked her too deep that day.

It didn't help that she was awkward in every way. She kept her head down and her music on blast to avoid socializing with anyone. Only, she tripped over and ran into everything. It wasn't like she had long legs to trip over, either. She was average in height and weight. Being half-Indian and half-Irish, her appearance stood out enough to catch everyone's attention—as if she wasn't doing that enough with her clumsiness.

But being the hot-headed school jinx, quite literally, was nothing compared to the fact that she was the daughter of the most intense professor at the school. As if any of the students needed more reasons to stay away from her.

Not that she wanted to make friends in the first place.

It surprised Juliet that the three mermaids had decided to pick on her, considering who her father was. But they just didn't care.

Juliet had wanted to react like she had in the past—with her fists. It was easy for her to solve her problems physically, because that was the one thing she distinctly remembered from her father before he left. Even at such a young age, he made sure she knew that standing up for herself would always be in her best interest.

If she had met the mermaid trio before she had fire in her blood, she would have pummeled them without hesitation. But now, she couldn't even let herself get to that point of anger, or something or someone would most certainly catch fire.

And that day, flames sparked out of every cell of her body, incinerating the clothes that she wore and leaving her completely nude and even more vulnerable. She was supposed to be wearing her smart clothes, but she hated the way it felt. Besides, that stuff was for shifters, and she still had yet to find her phoenix form. It took a week for her to leave her room after that.

To avoid a third catastrophe, Oberon suggested that she uncover the facts at her own pace. Every professor quickly agreed. Juliet's father only settled on the decision after adding a mandatory one-on-one session with him. She was more than happy to be given that choice. Well, mostly.

Growing up, she'd lived in the same three-story house in St. Louis. She went to the same school, studying with the same kids that never wanted to give her a chance. Her brown sugar skin and bright orange hair—which cascaded in long soft waves down her back, framing her heart-shaped face and round, almost yellow eyes—made her stand out. And her temper only made for her reputation worse.

But everything changed the day her dad came back. Now, even though a month had gone by, the relationship with her dad was still fragile and complex. Even if she now better understood the importance of the school's protection, that it was his priority to the shifter world that made him leave. Still, his presence made her uneasy, and trying to control the phoenix inside when he was around was nearly impossible.

So she fell into a routine, spending her days reading about the shifter world on her own—in her room, by herself. Where she wouldn't hear the whispers of the other students, and where she didn't have to embarrass herself with another fiery explosion.

And Juliet once again turned to her music and herself for comfort.

Music class was the only class that Juliet felt at peace. She felt connected to the beautiful, soothing sounds. It was the only way she could tune out the background noise of the world around her. She made sure to attend the class every chance she got. If it weren't for the mean girl mermaids, that class would be perfect.

Juliet waited outside of the Music Class doors with her headphones on as loud as they could go. But even the relaxing melody couldn't drown out the noise of the students gossiping about a new student. A new mermaid student. *Great, another stuck up mermaid.*

She rolled her eyes and picked up her phone to switch to the next song, but it was too late. Trish and her posers rounded the corner, beelining right to her. Taking a deep breath, Juliet abandoned her mantra and slid the headphones off her head, giving them the attention that they craved.

"Well, well, well, if it isn't the school's very own walking hazard. Who let you out of your cage, bird?" As Trish began.

Juliet laughed sarcastically. "Very clever, Trish. Word is there's a new mermaid in town. Hear she's prettier than all three of you put together. How does that make you feel?"

Joanna lunged forward, but Alessandra held her back.

"Ooh, did I hit a nerve?" Juliet taunted.

Trish gave her a snarl of a smile. "You aren't even on the same scale as one of us, little bird. This school was safe before you and your floppy flames stumbled in. And as for the new mermaid, she's just as pathetic as you are. You're a failure, a forgotten baby chick, and an absolute disaster, which is why *we* will always be better than *you*. In each and every way."

Juliet could feel the burning embarrassment growing inside of her. And just when she was going to give up on the class for the day, a new face stepped in front of the heartless brute.

"Don't you have three have anything better to do?" the new girl asked, standing beside Juliet as if they were good friends. "Your lives must be really boring if your only source of enjoyment is making others feel bad."

Trish snickered along with the rest of the staring mermaids. "Whatever you say, Myreen."

Grabbing Juliet's hand, Myreen led them inside of the now open classroom. Juliet retracted her hand from Myreen's grip and sheepishly found her seat in the far corner of the room.

Myreen followed quietly behind and took the seat next to her, placing her bag by her feet. "I know this won't mean much coming from me, but I'm sorry for what she said back there."

Noticing how nice this mermaid was, Juliet allowed her curiosity to pique. "Thanks. For helping me, too. But I wouldn't be seen talking to me if I were you. You'll be sure to get labeled on the low scale beside me, the school jinx."

Sadness grew in Myreen's eyes. It brought back all the looks Juliet would get from adults who knew her mother. She despised receiving pity for her life, or being anyone's charity case, but Myreen seemed to relate.

"Well, who's to say that isn't total crap? Or that I even want to be on it. I just got here, but I can't find one mermaid that isn't stuck up."

That comment caused Juliet to crack a smile. "That's 'cause they all think they're convinced they're the royalty of this school."

Myreen rolled her eyes. "No wonder Trish and her posse are such

68

monsters."

Again, Juliet chuckled. "I've only been here a month and, for a mermaid, you're pretty cool."

As Myreen turned in her seat to face Juliet, she sent her a comforting and honest smile. "Your sarcasm reminds me of a friend back home." Myreen extended her hand. "I'm Myreen by the way. Oberon picked me up yesterday." Myreen's voice cracked and she grimaced.

Juliet returned the smile. "I'm Juliet, beginner phoenix. My dad picked me up a month ago."

"Wow. Another newbie shifter. It's really nice to meet you. To meet anyone that isn't whispering about me behind my back." Myreen gave Juliet a knowing look.

Mrs. Smith, the music instructor, entered the classroom, her long red hair coiled in a bun on top of her head.

"Same here. Thanks again. You saved me and possibly this entire classroom from another fire. I haven't exactly gotten the hang of the whole shifting into a fiery bird thing yet." Juliet said the last sentence quietly because the teacher had begun speaking.

Myreen laughed softly as she turned to give her attention to the teacher.

For the first time in her entire life Juliet felt a real friendship forming with someone who got her. If she thought music class was her favorite before, having Myreen in it with her had made it even better.

Kol

"Nik," Brett Claud said, lightly smacking his friend in the arm in his lazy, surfer-type way—even though he wasn't a skater or a surfer. "I *dare you* to ask Beth Ann out." He directed his boisterous laugh down the hallway—flicking his blond hair as if it were still long—so it was sure to echo along the silver-steel walls to where Beth Ann and her friends walked ahead.

Nikolai Candida aimed a raised eyebrow at Malkolm Dracul or *Kol*, who rolled his eyes in response. Kol's friends were idiots sometimes. Or most of the time. And really, it was mostly Brett who was the idiot.

"Why don't *you* ask her out, Brett?" Kol asked in a lower tone. The way Beth Ann snapped her sky-blue hair over her shoulder suggested that she'd heard Brett loud and clear. Kol wasn't going to give her the same satisfaction. "She's more your type."

Brett threw his hands in the air. "Well... *duh*!" He talked through his teeth, suddenly *not* wanting the girls to hear. "She's a phoenix. But what would be the fun in that? Not exactly a dare."

"Not a dare huh?" Nik folded his arms across his chest. "Then do it! Show us how *not a dare* it would be!"

Kol cringed. He wanted to spout something about Nik needing some serious grammar lessons, but refrained. His friends hated it when he went all *English Harpy* on them in the exact *opposite* way Mrs. Coltar— who was definitely not a harpy and was actually one of the few humans at Shifter Academy—did.

"Honestly, I'd rather eat lead," Brett said, drawing out the words with a lazy expression and walking backward so he could face them as he spoke. "She's a little bit too high maintenance for my blood." He snapped his fingers. "No! Ask out *Juliet Quinn*!"

"Also a phoenix," Nik said.

"And one who would probably be hazardous to your health," Kol interjected. "That girl is going to burn down the school one of these days."

"But we're underwater," Brett argued.

"Again, *hazardous* to his health," Kol said. "And ours. Why are you *daring* Nik to ask Juliet out anyway?"

He resisted the powerful urge to flick Brett on the head the way his father always did when he said or did something stupid. Towering over both of them physically brought out the dominance in him. And when they acted so idiotic, it was all he could do to not turn into his least favorite parent. It didn't help that the entire school seemed to bow at his feet, either. Mostly the Avians, of course, but he'd caught more than one nod from a were or kitsune.

Brett shrugged and fell back into line with Kol and Nik. "Because she'd say yes, and *then* you'd have to tell your parents that you kissed a girl who wasn't a dragon." He cracked his knuckles loudly in triumph.

"Who said anything about kissing her?" Nik's expression was pure horror as he rubbed his fingers over the carved swirls of stubble on the sides of his head.

"C'mon!" Brett nearly shouted. "School scandal! We need some excitement around here. And it's not like I dared you to go proposing to a selkie or that…" he paused and looked around to make sure they didn't have an audience anywhere near. "Or that new chick who showed up in the middle of the night and somehow went her whole life not knowing she was a mermaid." His whisper sounded more like a Naga hiss.

"That's impossible," Nik said. "Brett, you're an idiot. There's no way a mermaid would *not* know she was a mermaid."

"It's true," Kol said sobering them both with his tone. "I overheard that her mother was totally clueless, or something. And maybe she was afraid of water? Anyway, the girl had no idea until Oberon told her."

"How do you know—?"

"Malkolm."

The baritone voice Kol would know anywhere cut off Nik's sentence. Nik and Brett knew the voice, too, and said a quick and respectful hello before skittering off toward the cafeteria. *Cowards.*

Kol straightened his back, filling the full six-foot, six-inches of his height. He was grateful he'd filled out more from the beanpole stages and felt sturdier in his skin. Yet, he still felt ten years old in his father's presence, and so felt like he had to show that he wasn't.

"Hello, Father," Kol said, bowing slightly. It irked him that he hadn't noticed his father standing right in the path he walked. "What brings you to the Dome?" he asked and was proud that there was no hint of a quaver in his voice. It boosted his courage. So he clasped his hands behind his back, in the same way his father did when talking with someone he considered his equal.

His father did not mirror him, though. "Oberon offered his office—"

"Lord Eduard," Miss Dinu, the dragon mastery teacher interrupted with a pinched smile. She was a relative of the Draculs. "I was not

72

aware you were visiting the Dome today." She pushed aside her brown hair and touched the frames of her glasses, which were a fiery red color that day.

"Hannah!" Eduard's smile was uninhibited and clearly not forced. A stark contrast to the look he'd given his own son. But Kol didn't care.

He relaxed his stance slightly, since his father's attention was elsewhere. And then he caught sight of his mother rounding the corner to meet them. Her long, thick auburn hair hung around her shoulders. And Kol noticed she wore the light blue pant suit he'd bought her for her last birthday.

"Hey, Mom." He met her halfway and leaned over to wrap both arms around her shoulders. She was tall for a woman, but barely reached his shoulder. He towered over everyone.

"Hello, Malkolm," she said in the soft tone he liked to think was reserved only for him, but was certain his sister, Tatiana, got an equal dosage of it.

"I didn't know you were coming to visit," Kol said, pulling back from her.

"Your father wanted to discuss something with you," she said, and they both looked at Eduard and Miss Dinu who were fully engaged in their conversation.

Kol tried to avoid looking directly at his mother's face as she watched them, but failed, and he felt the stab of pain that always accompanied it.

Victoria was beautiful. She was his mother, but Kol couldn't argue that fact. He'd heard more than one of his friends comment on her beauty, despite her age, and he'd seen the looks other men gave her, though she never noticed. She looked twenty years younger than her age, with her thick auburn locks, near-flawless porcelain skin, and amber eyes. Kol's black hair, thick eyebrows and strong features were straight from Eduard, but Kol's amber eyes came from his mother.

And Victoria always looked a hundred times more ethereal whenever she watched Eduard. The reason she never noticed the gazes from others—the admiration or envy of her beauty—was because of the pure and irrevocable love that drew her eyes to the face of Eduard, and *only* Eduard. She could gaze unabashedly if his attention and her thoughts were distracted. But the second his eyes met hers, the spell was broken.

Though her expression only changed a fraction, small enough that an acquaintance or even a close friend might miss it, Kol had the expression laced with pain burned in his memory. He didn't see it now, but knew it would come the second Eduard finished his conversation with Miss Dinu, so he stared at the polished floor.

"I've accepted it, Malkolm," she said softly, tilting her head to force him to meet her eyes.

"He doesn't deserve you," Kol said bitterly. It wasn't the first time he'd said it to her, either. "Do you still feed Adam and Alex and... *her* every other Sunday night?" He accused. "Does Tatiana put up with it? Or has she started making excuses to miss out? She said she would," he grumbled the last part under his breath.

Victoria tilted her head down, so she could look at Kol through her eyebrows. It was her way of showing him authority, ever since he grew an inch taller than her when he was eleven. It was still effective. "It's not your father's fault," she said.

"Bullsh—"

"Malkolm Torq Dracul," she cut him off in her firm tone. The one that demanded the attention of every creature around her. "You will *not* curse at me." Since she directed it at Kol and no one other than Eduard and Miss Dinu were nearby, he got the full force of it. His father and Dragon Mastery teacher didn't even glance over at them.

Kol straightened, but lowered his head and laced his fingers in front of him. "It's not fair," he said so quietly she shouldn't have heard him.

But she was his mother. "I know it's not fair," she said in her soft tone and he felt a hand reach out to loosen the grip his fingers had on each other.

He looked at her only to see another expression of pain on her face. "Are you...?" She couldn't even finish the sentence. "Have you...?"

At first, he wasn't sure what she was trying to say, but it only took a second. "Have I fallen in love?"

She nodded, her brows pinching together.

Kol looked down at his hands, but made sure his words rang with truth to put his mother at ease. "No, Mom. I haven't fallen in love." He almost added that he vowed to *never* fall in love, but wasn't certain if he had any control over it. He didn't know the exact words of the curse on the Dracul line, but was pretty sure *falling in love* was just as certain as that love being *unrequited*. It was the reason Victoria looked at Eduard the way she did, but never got a look in return. It was the reason Kol had half-brothers. Eduard loved Adam and Alex's mother, and the reason why she'd left him when Alex was a baby. It was the reason Tatiana would have an arranged marriage. Kol probably would, too. He just didn't know which was worse: loving his future wife as she yearned for another, or turning into his father. There was no way around it, no matter what a Dracul did or didn't do. He was pretty sure a relative tried to escape it by becoming a hermit, but ended up falling for the poor Hunter girl who got lost and fell into—and then out of—his arms.

Victoria blew a sigh of relief.

"Don't worry, Mom," Kol said, lightening his tone. "I'm only seventeen. Who falls in love at seventeen, anyway?"

She smiled at him, but he didn't meet her eyes. They both knew there was nothing she could do to protect her son from the inevitable.

"Hello, Victoria," Miss Dinu said formally as she passed, adjusting her glasses.

"Nice to see you, Hannah," Victoria said in her genuine way.

"I'll see you in the morning, Kol," Miss Dinu said over her shoulder before disappearing around the corner.

"Malkolm." Eduard also approached. "I have some business to discuss with you." He seemed to be in a better mood after talking with Miss Dinu.

Kol internally groaned; he'd hoped to ask his mother what the reason for their visit was, to prepare for whatever his father's *business* was. But he'd gotten so caught up in being angry at Eduard, he'd completely forgotten.

But… what could he do?

"Oberon's office, you said?" Kol asked.

His father led the way.

***

"Malkolm, I'm impressed with the progress you have made at the Dome."

Kol was speechless. He was expecting a lecture, not praise from his father. And the fact that Eduard came unannounced made him think that he'd majorly screwed up without knowing it. Kol bowed his head slightly in gratitude.

"What do you know of this *Myreen* girl?" Eduard was never one to beat around the bush.

"Who?" Kol didn't know if he was more baffled that his father had come all the way to ask about the new girl in school, or that Eduard actually knew the *name* of that new girl.

"Yes, the mermaid Oberon recently found."

"Only the gossip that has been circling around the school," Kol said with his chin held high.

"And what gossip is that?" Eduard's thick eyebrow arched toward the ceiling.

"Just that she somehow never knew she was a mermaid until Oberon contacted her. And that her mother died in some shifter or vampire attack?"

The muscles in Eduard's face relaxed slightly.

"Why? What should I know about her?" He knew he was inching toward the line where his father would snap and put him in his place, but Kol couldn't help it. He was curious. And he'd been out of the presence of his father for so long that his manners slipped.

But Eduard didn't snap or even silently disapprove. Instead, his features softened as they often did when he was deep in thought, then he placed both hands behind his back.

Kol resisted the urge to let his jaw land on the floor. He didn't he expect that reaction.

"Intelligence tells us that she could be the siren from the prophecy."

Eduard wasn't the type to joke or tease. Kol was pretty sure he'd never even heard of sarcasm. So although he was in disbelief, Kol knew his father would never talk lightly about something as serious as the prophecy.

"You think she's *the siren?*" Kol had to make sure his ears were currently working.

Eduard nodded once.

"But she's a teenager! And she thought she was human only hours ago! How could she possibly—?"

"Malkolm," Eduard interrupted sternly, but not condescending, like Kol was used to. Still, it silenced him. "It is imperative that we find out if she's the siren from the prophecy before anyone else."

Kol didn't dare ask what would happen if someone else found out first.

"This is your chance to prove yourself, Malkolm." Had Eduard actually smiled?

"You want me to find out?" Kol asked. "But how? If she didn't even know she was a mermaid, how do you expect her to know she's not only a siren, but *the* siren? And it's not like the prophecy is common knowledge, anyway."

"Befriend her Malkolm, gain her trust."

"Befriend her?" He knew that wasn't the word his father meant. "You mean seduce her?" Kol hid the thick feeling of disgust from his expression.

Eduard shrugged uncharacteristically. "If that's what it takes to get close to her, then yes, seduce her."

"I'm not charming some poor girl into thinking I'm interested in her." Kol folded his arms over his chest and stood up straighter, so he towered just a bit more over his father.

"I'm not asking you to fall in love with the girl," Eduard said, laughing once. "We all know where that gets a Dracul. Just get close to her and find out if she's the girl we've been waiting for."

Kol wanted to punch his father in the face for speaking so casually about the very pain he saw on his mother's face every day—or at the very least, flick him on the top of the head. But he refrained. And here he was, asking Kol to do the exact thing to Myreen that Eduard had done to his mother for decades.

Eduard might not have said the words, but seducing Myreen was exactly what he intended Kol to do. Kol had no intention of obeying orders, or having anything to do with Myreen, for that matter.

"I won't do it," Kol said, turning his back and reaching for the door. He was willing to do almost anything for his father—mostly out of fear rather than love—but this was the one thing he could never agree to.

"You will *not* storm out on me, boy!"

Kol froze in his tracks and suddenly felt ten years old again.

"You will face me when I'm speaking to you!"

Kol turned slowly and set his jaw. Bracing for the lashing.

"Malkolm, you are a *disgrace* to the royal Dracul line," Eduard's voice was low and cruel. "I would have done *anything,* and I would have sacrificed *anything* to protect our people."

Eduard threw the door open and stomped out before slamming it inches from Kol's nose.

Oberon

The final steps of the departing students left the classroom quiet and peaceful after a long day of teaching. Oberon rubbed at his temples as he glanced down at the screen built into his desk. Another set of assignments had been graded. Reaching down, he tapped the *Submit* button, sending off the newly posted grades to their respective students.

Running a hand through his brown hair, he let loose a heavy sigh.

"What has your feathers ruffled?"

Oberon jumped at the voice that disrupted his peaceful silence.

"Ren!" Oberon called in annoyance. "Why do you find it so hard to knock?"

"The door was open. Why would I knock?"

"A tapping on the door is a lot less jarring than your enthusiastic voice."

Ren Suzuki, the math teacher, entered and made his way toward Oberon. He was wearing a button-down tan shirt, the top button undone and a cardinal tie pulled a little loose around his collar. He was

Japanese-American, and Oberon's oldest friend. They'd been around each other so long, he could almost see Ren's fox-form features, even in human form, except for the nine tails the kitsune sported when shifted.

"I think the door was ajar-ring, but that's just me," Ren replied casually.

Oberon rolled his eyes.

"Besides, I could have just phased through the closed door anyway," Ren said. "On a more serious note, I just wanted to swing by and talk to you about some new tech we're developing. It's just about ready for field testing with the shifter military."

"I've got a lot on my mind, my friend," Oberon replied, looking back down at his screen. "Now isn't a very good time."

Ren tilted his head. "A vampire tracking system. The latest and greatest."

Oberon's eyes made their way back up to Ren. "Better than the ones your team has come up with in the past, I hope."

Ren moved forward, taking Oberon's words as an invitation to explain things.

"We have been trying to track vampires using ineffective methods. Our current gear picks up patterns of attacks by searching reported attacks on news and social media databases to locate large groups of them. But the problem is, we're tracking attacks, not vampires."

Oberon's heart rate increased as he realized what this could mean. "And your new tech could locate any vampire, anywhere, anytime?"

Inhaling deeply, Ren's features crinkled. "Not exactly. But we're getting closer to that ultimate goal."

Waiting expectantly, Oberon raised his eyebrows.

Ren cleared his throat. "The new tracking system has been fine-tuned to detect the chemical that vampires expel when they are in need of drinking. You know, when their animal instincts are kicking into gear, so to speak."

Oberon nodded slowly. "That's getting us a bit closer to what we really want to be able to do." He saw Delphine quietly standing at the door, unbeknownst to Ren. Oberon had sent her a message between classes, asking if she could stop by at the end of the day to talk with him about Myreen.

"It's progress," Ren said. "I sent the schematics for the system directly to your tablet, so when you get a chance, could you take a look at them? And if you like what you see, maybe use your impeccable gryphon charm to persuade Delphine to approve the finances?"

Oberon stared at the kitsune, waiting for the punchline.

Ren's serious face grimaced, then cracked into a huge grin as he laughed. "Impeccable—get it, Oberon? Im-peck-able? Because of your beak?"

Oberon just shook his head.

Delphine spoke form the doorway. "Just like you, Ren, your jokes don't improve with age."

Ren jumped in surprised, whirling about to face the doorway. There, Delphine was leaning against the frame with folded arms.

"We call that karma, Ren," Oberon said. "You scared me, then you got it worse."

"Delphine!" Ren said sweetly. He'd always been taken with her, ever since they'd first met her at Framboise Island. "Er, how much of the conversation did you hear?"

She didn't move from her position. "That really isn't the question, is it? The question is: how much money is this tinkering project going to cost?"

Ren pointed a finger in the air. "You can't put a price tag on kitsune-made inventions, my dear. That's like trying to figure out how much the sun is worth."

"Actually, that analogy makes no sense," Delphine replied, her hands dropping to her sides and striding forward. "But I'll work with

Oberon to see if your foxy little project is worth it."

"Wonderful," Ren said, slightly bowing his head. "That's all I ask."

"I have some important matters to discuss with Oberon now, Ren," Delphine said. "I'm sure you have your hands full of tinkering projects."

Ren nodded. "I'll be on my way. Thank you both for considering this new project. Once it is approved, we will get right to work."

Oberon's thin friend slipped past Delphine and out the door.

"He's a good man," Oberon said getting to his feet. "Please, Delphine, take a seat. And thank you for coming to speak with me."

A few loose strands jumped out from the smooth bun of Delphine's otherwise perfectly kept red hair. In the twenty years he'd known her, she'd hardly aged a day.

She eased into one of the chairs that sat before his desk, and he sat back down as well.

"Your message sounded urgent," Delphine said, starting the conversation. "Is everything okay?"

Oberon shrugged. "I wouldn't say it's urgent, exactly. I just need somebody to talk to about some things that have been weighing on my mind."

Delphine half-smiled. "I'm assuming Ren wasn't cutting it?"

"Like I said, Ren is a good man, but he's hardly one I can talk to about serious matters."

"Understood," she replied. Oberon knew that while Delphine and Ren got along, she didn't care much for the kitsune's company. "What's been on your mind, Oberon?"

Looking past Delphine, he saw that the door to his classroom was still open. He navigated to the room controls on his desk tablet and sent the command for the door to shut.

"Today in one of my morning classes, a student had the nerve to ask me why we've been searching for a stray mermaid. Myreen happened to be in that class, and all eyes went straight to her."

Delphine nodded expectantly. "Our students are sharp. Where did the conversation go after that?"

"I was able to shift the conversation back to our class topic pretty quickly," Oberon replied. "But Myreen now knows, at the very least, that we were looking for somebody out of the ordinary. She can't know about the prophecy, not yet."

The prophecy. Oberon had been present when Delphine had received it sixteen years before, and he now heard her voice replay that moment in his head.

A siren will emerge as a stray mermaid and bring destruction to Draven, leader of the vampires, summoning ultimate peace between shifters and vampires once and for all.

Ever since then, he'd been searching for *the one*—this stray mermaid. And he was convinced it was Myreen.

"We've been over this before, Oberon," Delphine said cautiously. "While Myreen does fit within the parameters of the prophecy, I can't be completely sure she is the mermaid we've been looking for."

"Why else did it take you so long to find her?" Oberon asked. "She's sixteen years old—"

"And before today, she'd never shifted," Delphine interrupted. She was one of only a handful of people that could do this without setting Oberon off. "Even for a shifter that we find after their puberty trigger, sixteen is a late age to be found. But Myreen is a mermaid—the puberty trigger doesn't apply to her."

"Yes," Oberon agreed, a little annoyed with the proud reminder. "All mermaids are lucky enough to be born with the ability to shift."

Delphine bit her upper lip. "Although I hate to admit it, my clairvoyance isn't all-inclusive. There are billions of people in the world, and while a small percentage of them have shifting abilities, there are many we don't know about who would benefit from what we have here at the Dome. And the mermaid from the prophecy? She could still be out there."

Deep inside, Oberon felt that Myreen was the one. He couldn't prove it, but in the moments he'd been around the girl, his instincts screamed that she was the prophesied mermaid.

"And we'll keep looking," he replied.

"That being said," Delphine continued, "I have hope that Myreen is the siren. But only time will tell if she truly is."

"Time and training," Oberon added.

"Speaking of which, thank you for assigning her to music class. Having her in close proximity will help me keep a better eye on her outside of my other interaction with her and the other mer people."

"Music is a powerful form of art that has a magical quality to it," Oberon said. "And as we both know, music can bring forth incredible things."

"With Myreen, that is the hope," Delphine said with a smile.

Oberon nodded. "Yes, it is."

A quietness fell around them as they let that last statement settle in. It *felt* right. They'd work with Myreen and help her the best they could. Draven had to be stopped. No. Not just stopped. The vampire leader had to die.

His thoughts pulled him into painful memories of the school, shaped like a plus sign, on Framboise Island in South Dakota. His wife's helpless scream pulling him from the sky, the image of her bloodied, lifeless form on the ground of their quarters. The bruised, broken bodies of his parents in gryphon form lying nearby, stripped of their wings, their barren eyes staring at him. And Draven's pale, taunting face catching in the moonlight as he crouched in the window.

Say one last goodbye to your family.

Explosions erupting from the school, burying his family—his parents, wife, and unborn child...

"Do you wish to discuss anything else, Oberon?"

Delphine's question stole the terrible memory away, as if it were caught in a breeze, blowing away from him.

He blinked a few times, processing her words. "I don't believe so. We'll just want to keep our ears out for any more of these rumors about our *stray* mermaid. The less people know, the better we can protect Myreen. She's dealing with enough already, what with the death of her mother and being whisked away to a new world with foreign abilities."

"Agreed," Delphine said with a nod as she got to her feet. "I will keep you posted on the training Myreen goes through, as well as her progress."

"Any and all information is helpful," Oberon said. "Thank you, Delphine, for all that you have done and are doing for our cause. We couldn't do this without you."

She chuckled. "I agree with that statement, too."

Her pride used to bother Oberon, but he'd grown to see past it. The head mermaid really did care for all shifters, despite the front she put on.

A few gestures on his desk tablet opened the classroom door, and Delphine made for it.

"One more thing," Oberon said quickly, stopping her before she made it to the door. "Could you please send Myreen here? I'd like to see how her first day of classes went."

"I'll gladly have her sent your way," she said, then stepped out of the classroom.

Oberon watched her leave.

A notification from his tablet chimed, and he looked down. It was Ren's schematics for the revolutionary vampire tracking system. This only brought back the image of Draven's sneering face.

Oberon gritted his teeth, finding his eyes stinging with the formation of tears. He pounded his fist on the desk in an attempt to let his emotions flood a different way. It wouldn't do for Myreen to see him sobbing like an infant.

He tapped on his tablet, opening Ren's schematics, trying to distract his mind from the intruding, painful memories. Upon reading the description of the project, he found he couldn't concentrate on the technical terminology.

I could use a flight right about now, he thought.

And then Myreen entered the room, hands in her uniform pockets, looking tired and a little out of place.

He smiled, shoving his other feelings aside for the moment.

"Myreen, come in," he said, getting to his feet and gesturing for her to come forward.

"You wanted to see me?" she asked, moving closer to the desk.

"Just for a moment," Oberon replied. "I know after a full day of being stuck inside classrooms, the last place you'd want to be right now is back here."

She shrugged. "This place is incredible—even the classrooms. I've been to a lot of schools, and this one? It's amazing."

Oberon chuckled. "Yes, it is quite an amazing school, and it will only get more amazing for you. But tell me, how has your day been?"

She breathed in heavily, then let it out in one big gust. She paused for a moment, looking above him for a few moments, then made eye contact again. "Overwhelming?"

"I can imagine so. This school, although amazing, is quite different from any other school you've ever been to. And while there are good differences, there are likely probably some that aren't so good."

"It's actually the similarities that make it hard," she said quickly, her lips instantly becoming a line, as if she felt she'd overstepped some boundary with her words.

Oberon cocked his head. "What do you mean?"

Myreen shrugged. "You know… cliques. I've already run into

some."

"I suppose you'll find cliques just about anywhere you go," he replied.

"That's just how it goes." Her tired eyes suddenly widened as a wave of excitement lit up her face. "I shifted into mermaid form for the first time today!"

Smiling, Oberon said, "That's wonderful. You'll find that shifting into your mermaid form will be an excellent outlet for you, something you'll be able to turn to whenever you want to. At least, with enough practice."

"Hopefully it won't take me too long," she replied.

"The best advice I can give you is to have patience," Oberon replied. "Have patience and keep trying. A mix of those two things will get you there."

She looked down at her hands and nodded.

"One more thing before you can head back to your afternoon," Oberon continued, taking on a more serious tone. "It's not something that is easy for me to discuss. But I know what you are going through, and that a lot is hitting you at once. Most of all, I know what it's like to lose family members."

She continued to look down, and Oberon saw a forced swallow in her neck.

"If you *ever* need someone to talk to, and you don't feel like there's anybody else, you can come to me, okay?"

Myreen nodded quickly, sniffling.

"Thank you," she said with a brisk voice. "Can I go now?"

Oberon studied her for a few seconds. "Of course."

She stood up and hurried out the door.

Oberon leaned back in his chair, exhaling deeply as he pondered the girl and the prophecy, contemplating how the future would unveil itself.

Kenzie

It was a full day before Kenzie could get back to the subway where she'd last seen her friend disappear. She'd heard nothing from Myreen. Not that she'd expected to, really. She was in a super-secret school for shifters, after all.

The stalker-tracker app worked, but the results left Kenzie a little confused. The dot disappeared somewhere over Lake Michigan. Or more likely, under. That was part of the reason it had taken her so long. She'd needled her mom and grandmother for any kind of magic or spells until they started asking questions.

And when the questions became too heated, she'd retreated to the anger she kept bottled up. The anger born of magic unspent, of a lifetime of knowing that what she was capable of was well out of reach. The magic she'd possessed since the day she'd sparked with life could never be accessed, not to its full potential. Not without being taught—which her mother and grandmother were loath to do—and not without the grimoire her family had lost.

And so they'd fought. They fought about the lost magic. They fought about her desire to start a new grimoire. And she'd blamed them, like always, for refusing to tell her about how the grimoire was lost in the first place, or how they were involved in the shifter world today, or how they performed the more skilled spells.

It was an awful fight. They always got just a bit ugly. Guilt still gnawed at her insides for starting the thing. But they'd stopped asking questions, and for now, her interest in the school was safe. Because telling her mom and grandma was out of the question. They'd just tell her no, like all the other times before. Why they were so bent on keeping her from the shifter world, she had no idea. She just knew she belonged there, and she wasn't going to let them stop her.

Kenzie glanced around the street to see if anyone was looking, then partially lifted the flap on her bag and peered inside. Her seal skin was there and safe. She lowered the flap, but let her fingers slip below it to linger over the soft fur. Her mom would kill her if she knew Kenzie had taken out their only skin. They'd lost the magic necessary to create new skins, and this one was the only one her family owned. Not like you could hit up a department store for a new one. But she needed to prove to the shifters that she was one of them. Finger crossed, she hoped this would do the trick.

Kenzie took a deep breath and headed down the stairway that led to the subway. She had her money ready—in her pocket, not her bag so she wouldn't accidentally flash the precious material—and a quick glance around told her she didn't have to worry about the scrutiny of that one guard who'd caught her jumping the turnstile. Just as well. She wasn't looking to do anything stupid this time.

At least, not until she got to the school.

Ticket in hand, she made it through to the green train, waiting at the same terminal that Myreen had disappeared through. The overhead display said it would be a few minutes before the next train arrived. She looked around at the other passengers milling about the platform, shuffling on and off cars. Kenzie wondered if any of the others were shifters. If Oberon had brought Myreen this way, it served to reason that other students would take this route. Right?

But she didn't feel anything. Not like she had with Myreen. Now that girl had some serious shifter juju going on. Kenzie was surprised she hadn't realized it before. But then again, she didn't have enough experience with shifters or her magic to realize when she was getting a nudge.

The train came to a quick stop, the doors hissing open. A flood of travelers got off, and when they thinned, she swam upstream with the passengers looking to get on. The doors hissed closed again, and Kenzie looked around, finally deciding on a handrail for stability as the train sped away.

Kenzie turned on her phone and watched her GPS move over the map. She wasn't even close to where she'd last seen Myreen's phone disappear. She sighed and patted her bag again, looking to the seats. Might as well get comfortable.

Kenzie's toe tapped as she held onto the handrail. She scanned the faces around her for anything useful. Would she get a feeling that she was looking at a shifter? She'd thought that was the reason she'd been attracted to Myreen, not realizing her own magic was speaking to her, but now she wasn't so sure. And it wasn't like her Spidey-senses were tingling at the moment.

The next stop thinned out the crowd around her, and she grabbed a vacant seat. She couldn't help but notice the guy barreling toward her car, barely squeezing through the doors as the muffled voice announced their departure.

He sighed as he looked around, then plopped into the seat next to her. He huffed and puffed, then leaned over.

Kenzie smirked. "Just made it, eh?"

The guy smiled. "Yeah. Didn't want to wait the fifteen minutes for the next one, you know?"

Kenzie nodded.

"Name's Wes," he said, holding out his hand.

Kenzie accepted and gave a firm shake. He wasn't exactly stacked, but he had a nice cut to his physique. She wondered if that was the result of diligence or pure male hormones. "Kenzie."

"Nice," Wes said, nodding. He leaned back in his seat, his legs extending into the aisle. "You take the L often?"

"Not really. Why? You the 'L police'?" Kenzie asked, lowering her voice to a mocking tone, complete with air quotes.

Wes laughed. "Nah. I'm just on and off these things all day, and I'm pretty good with faces. I would've remembered yours."

Kenzie blushed, pursing her lips. "Think so?"

It was Wes's turn to blush. Kenzie smiled as she watched him stammer. She'd spent so much time in Shallow Grave that she'd forgotten that not *all* guys were idiots. Wes seemed pretty cool. Okay, and yes, he was kinda cute. In a granola sort of way. Dang, she had to get out more.

"Don't hurt yourself," Kenzie said, flicking her hair over her shoulder. "So why exactly are you on and off the subs all day?"

"Uh, would you believe I'm a courier?"

Kenzie shrugged. "Sure."

"Yeah, well I run errands for people, deliver messages and stuff."

Kenzie lifted her brows. "We are still in the twenty-first century, right? Cell phones and email and all that?"

Wes laughed, running a hand over his short brown hair. "Yeah. But believe it or not, some things still require a personal touch."

"No kidding?"

The overhead speaker buzzed with information and the train slowed.

Wes stood and stretched, then looked back at Kenzie. "End of the line for me. And you're not standing. Does this mean your stop is next?"

"Could be."

"It's the last one on the green line."

Kenzie folded her arms, a stubborn smirk on her face.

"Ah, it's gonna be like that, huh? Well, maybe I'll see you around."

"Assuming you can remember my face."

Wes grinned. "Oh, trust me. That won't be a problem."

"Goodbye Wes." Kenzie's eyes darted to where the doors were hissing closed behind him.

Wes snaked through the narrowing opening just in time. He rapped on the window and waved as the train took off for its next destination. Kenzie waved, feeling the tiniest bit of regret. She wasn't stupid enough to give him the stalker-411, but she almost wished she had. Yeah, she *really* needed to get out more.

Kenzie patted her bag again, still plump with the fur, and waited for her final destination. It didn't take long. Her phone still told her she wasn't far enough—not nearly in, under, or over lake Michigan. Kenzie took one last look at the few remaining passengers as they unloaded. None of them looked like shifters. *And still no tingling feeling.* She hesitated, then darted off the train before it lurched to life once more. There had to be something else. A ferry, perhaps?

Kenzie passed by a closet door before stopping and turning back. Something about the lock had caught her attention. Kenzie peered at it, then snapped her fingers. It was an electronic lock. Way too high-tech for janitorial supplies. She wasn't sure those things even *had* a regular lock, but they certainly didn't need this.

Kenzie looked around the emptied platform. There would be more people stopping here in a bit, and others might be looking to get on as the train headed in the other direction. She had to work quickly.

Kenzie wiped her sweaty palms on her jeans and took a deep

breath. Unlocking spells were simple enough, but she had no idea if they worked on electronic locks. They definitely didn't work on computer passwords. She'd tried that once, in a failed attempt to learn more about the world her mom and grandma were a part of.

Kenzie flexed her fingers.

"Díghlisál." The glow of magic moved through her, a warmth and tingling in the tips of her fingers. Kenzie smiled. There wasn't a better feeling in the world than tapping into that well of power—almost as good as tucking into your favorite sweater on a comfy couch with a tub of ice cream, your best friend, and a good movie.

But the door stood unmoved.

"Fudgsicles," Kenzie said under her breath. So that unlocking spell didn't work. Kenzie wiped her hands on her pants again and then shook them out, her hips swaying back and forth as she geared up for another try. She only knew three spells that could work: unlock, like with a key—which had already failed—undo, like a button or clasp, and open, to allow passage. She decided on the third for her next try. The roar of the next train approached, and Kenzie rushed to cast her next spell.

"Oskílte," she breathed, her heart hammering in her throat. There was a faint click, and she gently pulled the door knob. It opened.

Kenzie took one last glance around to make sure she wasn't seen, then slipped inside. She was surprised to find herself on another platform, although this one seemed a little cleaner and brighter. She looked back at the door she'd just come through, wondering if there was some enchantment to it, but this was the other side, no lock to keep her from exiting. Instead, there was a small camera, so viewers could determine if it was safe to come out. Smart. Very smart.

And kinda creepy. Were there other cameras around? Was someone watching her right now? A chill spread goosebumps along her arms, her eyes darting around as she soaked up as much information about where she was as quickly as possible. She didn't *see* any cameras, so she decided to move on.

The rail was empty, and Kenzie wondered when the next train would come by. *And will it be full of shifters?* On one hand, that could work in her favor. But then again, maybe that wasn't the best idea. She had no idea if the shifters on the other side would be friend or foe. In an ideal world, they'd be friends. *Most shifters don't take kindly to selkies.* The warning popped into her head, one of the few tight-lipped and short-lived conversations she'd had with her mother on the subject. Apparently, the shifter world wasn't fond of those who used magic to shift, rather than being born or given the innate ability. And Oberon's reaction had confirmed that. It wasn't fair. They didn't even know her. But if she could just get a few shifters on her side...

She wanted to go to this school so bad. To learn more about who she was, to have a safe place to practice and unlock her magic. Away from her mom and grandmother, and away from humans. If she had to be honest, that last part was probably a big reason she'd just let Wes go. She wasn't so sure she could keep that kind of secret from a guy she was into. Even in her friendship with Myreen, it hadn't been easy. She'd opened her mouth to tell Myreen a thousand times, only to shut it again or bark out something lame, as if that had been her intention all along.

Now, she just wanted to be herself. She could have that with Myreen. And maybe others.

If she could get into the school.

Kenzie glanced down the track to see a car coming. She stepped behind a column and waited. The train stopped, and the doors slid open, but no other sounds came. She peeked around her beam, and when no one was there, she bolted for the car. The doors glided closed behind her, and the train took off, headed back the way it had come.

Kenzie took another breath, hoping to calm her nerves. She had to laugh. Secret platform. What was this, Hollywood?

The dark tunnels passed by for several minutes. Most of the transit system in the city was above-ground, and she marveled at how much of her journey had been below ground.

And then the view opened up, the tunnel she traveled through covered in glass. She was on the bottom of Lake Michigan, and a gleaming dome was her destination. Her eyes widened, and her breath stilled. Then the laughter came, turning almost maniacal. "This. Is. Incredible," she murmured, pressing her hand to the window. More than ever, this was where she wanted to be.

She stayed like that, even when the track curved and the Dome disappeared from sight. She barely even noticed when the train came to a stop, her mind swirling with possibilities. What did it look like on the inside? What was the history? The technology? The Dome looked like some alien world, and her mind wanted to create an interior to match.

Another train car hissed as it headed back the way she'd just come. *Two of those things. Smart.*

She stepped off and found herself at another impasse. This lock was way more high tech than the one on the platform, and the camera above the door said she was being watched. Kenzie squared her shoulders and marched toward the door with all the confidence she could muster. She had to look the part of a student here. Heck, she was the part, whether they wanted to believe that or not.

"First time here?" came a voice over the speaker, deep and authoritative.

Kenzie nodded, then decided he might be looking for a verbal response. "Yes."

"We'll just need a retina scan."

Kenzie stepped up and let out a breath as she positioned her face for the scan. Her lids fluttered as she thought and pleaded to whatever unseen forces that the scan would work on her. She didn't know what they were looking for, but she hoped whatever it was, she had it.

"Oscailte," Kenzie whispered, a last-ditch attempt to ensure she made it in. The door buzzed, and she grabbed the handle and pulled it open.

Her heart pounded in her throat.

"Welcome to Shifter Academy," the speaker voice continued. "Step inside and they'll get you settled."

"Thanks." Kenzie strode in. The door banged shut behind her, and she jumped. She shouldered her bag, hugging it tight. She wasn't sure when she'd have to pull out the seal skin, but she wanted to be ready, regardless.

Kenzie's mouth fell open as she took in the dark metals and intricate figures. Japanese-style dragons coiled around the archway, climbing toward the same symbol she'd seen on Myreen's letter. The hall beyond looked even more detailed, and Kenzie took a step toward it.

"Welcome," a woman's voice called out, drawing Kenzie back to herself. The woman—no, a goddess, for sure—sat behind a large desk, her bright red hair and green eyes arresting.

Kenzie felt about an inch tall, and she clasped her hands behind her back. "Um, I'm here to attend the school."

"Yes, of course. I'm Delphine, head of the school Acceptance Department, but you can call me Ms. Smith. Which kind of were are you, and who sent you?"

Kenzie's mouth hung open, her brows hanging low. *A were?* Why did Ms. Smith assume she was a were?

"Well?" Ms. Smith asked after Kenzie stood there staring dumbly for several long moments. Those green eyes bored into Kenzie, Ms. Smith's foot tapping beneath the desk.

"Not a were." Kenzie pulled her skin out of the bag and threw it over her shoulders. "Aon," she said, and the skin swallowed her whole. She shrunk as flippers and fins replaced her feet, but for each inch she decreased in height, she seemed to put in back on in pounds. Whiskers tested the air as they sprouted from either side of her wet nose. *See? I am a shifter,* she wanted to say. She looked up at Ms. Smith, hopeful, expectant.

Ms. Smith threw her head back and laughed.

Not the reaction Kenzie was going for. She released the magic and grew into her own skin once more. She bit her lip as she waited for Ms. Smith's verdict.

"You're no shifter, *selkie.*" The label rolled off her tongue like vomit, and Kenzie cringed. "I don't know how you got in, but you can be sure it won't happen again."

Kenzie swallowed and squared her shoulders, which knocked the seal skin to the floor. She bent and fumbled with the fabric, stuffing it back into her bag. "I'm as much shifter as you are," she mumbled before straightening up again.

"You don't belong here. You don't need this place. You will leave and never come back. Do we understand each other?"

"Why?" Kenzie cried out, every fight she'd had with her mom blowing the top off any cool she might have been able to conjure. "Why can't I be here? What do you people have against selkies?"

Ms. Smith's lip twitched in what looked like a failed attempt to snarl. "Everyone here shifts because they have to. Because it's what their bodies do when they *get bit* or *hit water* or *get angry.* You? You have to kill a creature to take its place. That's not shifting. That's murder."

Kenzie took a step back, her hands balling of their own accord. "I did *not* murder anything, and I can guarantee whoever took this seal skin didn't do so lightly. I'm a MacLugh and—"

"I *knew* there was something familiar about you," Ms. Smith said, standing up.

"Does that mean—?"

Ms. Smith pointed to the door. "Out."

Kenzie's heart stalled. "But—"

"OUT!"

Kenzie staggered back from the venom of that one word. Somewhere deep down she knew this would be the outcome, but still, she'd hoped against hope. Stupid. All this way for nothing. And she'd wasted her only chance at a good first impression.

Ms. Smith tapped a button on the phone at her desk and spoke into the device. "We'll need to escort this one back out."

"Yes, ma'am," replied the voice from the door speaker.

Ms. Smith turned her attention back to her desk, as if Kenzie didn't exist.

Kenzie sulked as she headed toward the exit, taking one last glance at the school she so desperately wanted to be a part of. Just beyond the entry way she could see a glimpse of the architecture, filled with mythical creatures, sleek and inviting. She did a double take as she glimpsed the blue-black hair and shocked face of— "Myreen!"

Myreen's eyes widened and her face split into a grin. She ran to Kenzie, and they embraced, Kenzie squeezing her friend tight.

All of Kenzie's anger and disappointment dissolved as she focused on Myreen. "How are you? Settling in?"

Myreen's smile faltered. "I'm... okay."

Kenzie raised a brow.

"So?" Myreen asked, hope sparking in her eyes. "Are you coming to school here?"

"Not while Ursula, over here, reigns," Kenzie quietly grumped, raising her brows in the direction of the desk.

Myreen's brows scrunched and she glanced that way. Kenzie nodded once. At Myreen's insistent stare, Kenzie stole a glance over her shoulder and saw Ms. Smith standing again, this time leaning on the front of her desk with arms and ankles crossed. Kenzie's face reddened. *Crap*.

"If you're all done, I believe it's time for you to go," Ms. Smith said, in that calm, infuriating manner of a woman who knows she's in control.

Myreen pulled Kenzie into another hug. "We'll get you in," she whispered. Her voice resumed a normal volume as she added, "We'll just have to figure some things out, first."

Kenzie pulled away when Ms. Smith cleared her throat. "Can you ever forgive me for not telling you about who I was?"

Myreen nodded. "It's probably better that you didn't. I can barely process it all now, and I'm a mermaid."

Kenzie chuckled. "If you need anything, anytime—"

"I know. Thanks." Myreen turned to Ms. Smith. "Do you mind if I ride with her, just to the other platform?"

Ms. Smith sniffed, but visibly softened as she looked into Myreen's eyes. "I wouldn't advise it, but you're free to come and go as you please."

Myreen nodded, then smiled at Kenzie.

A figure darkened the opening, more mountain than man. "Thanks, Malachai. I'd do it myself, but I've got some matters to attend to." Ms. Smith sat back down at her desk.

The girls took a step toward the exit, but Ms. Smith's voice stopped them. "Just so you know, Myreen, selkies are no friends of mermaids. You'd be wise to remember that."

Myreen dipped her head, and the girls hurried to the train, followed by Malachai, aka *Mountain Man*. Kenzie guessed this was speaker dude, and she was glad she'd met him by voice first. *If his bulging muscles and incredible height don't scare the pants off you, then the orange beard and crew-cut would,* Kenzie thought. She wondered what kind of shifter he was.

"So what's it like?" Kenzie asked as they settled into the train.

"Incredible. You've never seen anything like it." Myreen shook her head, her voice filled with awe. "Do you have any idea how many types of shifters there are?" Mountain Man cleared his throat and Myreen quieted for a few moments. "I took my first swim today."

"And?" Kenzie coaxed, desperate for details.

"I didn't drown."

"Duh." Kenzie smiled and gave Myreen a good-natured nudge.

"It kinda felt like I was slipping into my own skin for the first time." Myreen's eyes twinkled as she said, "My tail's pink."

Kenzie chuckled. "Figures. I always thought you looked like a Barbie."

Myreen laughed, but grew quiet again, looking at her hands as they rested in her lap.

"But?" Kenzie prodded.

Myreen let out a long breath. She glanced at Mountain Man, then back at her hands. "Let's just say, being a mermaid isn't all it's cracked up to be."

Kenzie grabbed Myreen's hand and squeezed it, trying to give her an encouraging smile. She didn't know what Myreen was going through, but they couldn't exactly speak freely with the big guy watching them.

Kenzie managed a wry smile. "Made any friends yet?" She asked, though she kinda hated to hear the answer. A "no" meant that Myreen still needed her, and there was nothing Kenzie could do to fix that, but a "yes" meant that she might lose her friend to a world she could never really be a part of.

"One friend. Juliet. She's nice. But Kenz, it's not the same."

"Heh. Did you really think you could top this?" Kenzie asked, letting go of Myreen's hand to gesture along the length of her body.

Myreen laughed and she shook her head. "No, Kenz, I don't think anything could top you."

That comment alone warmed Kenzie to her core.

The girls continued to chat amiably as the train carried Kenzie away from her dreams, the Dome shrinking and fading until it disappeared entirely. This wasn't over. Not by a long shot.

Still, all of it hurt more than Kenzie cared to let on. But she knew Myreen was hurting more. Her friend was strong, and Kenzie had a feeling she wouldn't give in to her grief until she absolutely had to.

She just hoped Myreen would be surrounded by friends, if—or when—she finally broke.

Myreen

How is it possible that after the incredibly long day I had and how exhausted I now feel that I can't sleep?

So many thoughts and questions were whirling through Myreen's head. Why did Oberon take such an interest in her? Why did all the other mermaids hate her so much? It seemed like new students arrived at the school all the time, and yet she was the topic of discussion on everyone's lips. Was there something special about her?

And then there was the topic of Kenzie. How on earth was she going to get Kenzie accepted at the school? Having her there would mean having a true friend. She liked Juliet and hoped that their friendship would grow, but it wouldn't be the same bond that she and Kenzie shared. Kenzie had been there with her through all the stuff with her mom, and she knew Myreen as something other than *that new mermaid girl.*

Transforming into a mermaid had been the most profound and magical experience of her life, and yet it was tainted by the fact that her mother had kept it from her all this time.

Oberon said that mermaid DNA was hereditary, so either her mom was a mermaid, or her dad was, and her mom had known about it. Myreen couldn't figure out why her mom tried so hard to keep Myreen from that part of herself. Being in the water, twisting and twirling in her natural form, Myreen had felt more herself than ever before. How could her mom keep that from her?

And Myreen couldn't even be angry at her mom for it, because her mom was dead. She could never be angry at her mom for anything again. She could only mourn her, miss seeing that bright smile, miss even hearing her recite the rules for the billionth time. If her mother came back to her right here, right now, Myreen wouldn't ask her about any of this shifter stuff, she would just hug her as tight as she could and never let go. She would give up all this knowledge about herself and where she fit in the world and go back to life as an ignorant, sheltered teen if it meant having her mom back.

A sigh escaped her lips as she opened her eyes for the umpteenth time. She looked at the digital clock on her desk. It was past midnight. Her stomach started to rumble, and she remembered that she had skipped out on dinner. Well, maybe a full belly would ease her body enough to push her over that sleep threshold.

Myreen got out of bed, slipped on her shoes and crept out of her room. The mermaid common room was empty, for which she was grateful. The last thing she needed right now was to run into another mermaid who disliked her for absolutely no reason.

The grand hall was so empty and silent that her steps echoed as she made her way down the stairs and toward the dining hall. It was strange to see the usually buzzing dining hall vacant and dark. Almost haunting, really.

She knew that the buffet station would be empty, but she hoped that she could at least find a vending machine. But the walls of the dining hall were bare. *Hmm, there has to be food in here somewhere.*

Behind the buffet station, Myreen saw a door she assumed led to the kitchen. She went around the counters and tried the knob. *Yes!*

The kitchen was about a third of the size of the dining hall, the biggest she'd ever been in. She imagined this was what a five-star restaurant kitchen would look like, with a dozen or so counters, three double door steel refrigerators, and a massive brick oven at the back, flanked by a tower of smaller ovens on either side. *Jackpot!*

Shaking with the hunger that now possessed her senses, she rushed to the nearest fridge, eager to pick out anything that looked appetizing. She placed an armload of goodies on the counter and began to dig in.

A sound from the entrance of the kitchen made her almost choke on the roast chicken she had just popped in her mouth, seized by the sudden fear of being caught. She didn't know if students were allowed to be in here after hours, and she really didn't want to get in trouble on her first day. Should she hide? Run?

When she looked at the door, however, another student was standing there, looking just as surprised to see her as she was to see him. The boy was freakishly tall, definitely over six feet, but with a proportionate build, making him quite intimidating. But his facial features were just the opposite—handsome, sultry, with a look that drew her in. His thick crown of black hair complimented his amber eyes and tanned skin nicely, making everything about him give off a pleasant warmth.

The boy stood there for a moment, looking uncertain as to whether he should complete the task he came there for or turn around and go. *Am I really that repellant?*

Finally, he made his decision. He cast his eyes away from her and went to one of the tall cabinets to rummage for his own midnight snack.

"You couldn't sleep either?" Myreen asked, hoping to ease the strange tension in the room.

The boy paused for a moment, the only acknowledgement he gave her before continuing his search.

Great, another person who doesn't like me, she thought, taking another slow, sad bite of her chicken.

She heard him open and close the fridge behind her, and resigned herself to just ignore him as he was ignoring her and finish her meal in silence.

To her shock, the boy placed a plate of smoked salmon in front of her. "As a mermaid, you really should have more fish in your diet," he said matter-of-factly before sitting down at the other end of the counter to focus on his plate.

"Oh. Uh, thank you," she said, not sure how to respond to his detached helpfulness. The salmon really did smell good, better than the chicken. If mermaids really lived underwater for thousands of years, it would make sense that sea-based foods would be better for her. That would explain why her mom had made fish so often.

She took a good look at her standoffish dinner mate. He wore the wing symbol on his chest. An avian. But was he a dragon, a phoenix, or a harpy?

"I'm Myreen," she ventured, hoping to get him to open up.

"I know," he said without looking at her. "The whole school knows who you are."

Okay? "You know who *I* am. Who are you?" she asked, unwilling to be brushed off that easily.

He sighed, as if accepting that they were going to have to talk. "Kol," he answered curtly.

Myreen took that as a win and smiled to herself. "What type of shifter are you?"

He rolled his eyes before reluctantly aiming them on her. "Why is that important?"

"Look, I'm just making small talk," Myreen said defensively. "I'm new here and I'm just trying to make some friends."

"And why do *we* have to be friends?" he snapped at her.

The pure disdain in his voice hit her harder than she expected, and all the pain of being so hated since she got here coalesced and imploded within her.

"Because I have no friends," she said, hearing her voice break as the words came out. "Because I have no one and nothing left in this whole world. I'm completely alone." Before she could stop herself, she was openly weeping over the salmon he'd given her. She put her head in her hands, wishing she could just disappear.

Kol gave another long sigh, and when she heard his chair scrape against the floor, she thought he was going to leave her to cry by herself. It was just as well, she didn't want anyone to see her like this. Not that anyone really cared.

"Please, don't cry," his voice said from beside her, catching her off guard. "I'm not usually this rude. I just had an unpleasant talk with my father. I shouldn't have taken it out on you."

Myreen lifted her face and looked at his through a layer of tears. The rigidness his face had previously been etched in had smoothed, leaving behind an almost apologetic expression. Almost.

"At least you have a father," Myreen sniffed. "What I wouldn't give to hear my mom lecture me one more time."

Curiosity pursed Kol's smooth brow. "What happened to your mom?"

Myreen gave a defeated laugh. "What? You don't know? It's not broadcasted all over the school? My mom was killed by vampires last night, and yet everyone in this school treats me like some pariah they can't wait to get rid of." The pain of that truth stabbed at her belly, and a deep wail of despair clawed its way out of her throat.

"Wow, I had no idea," Kol said, sincerity in his voice for the first time. "I really am sorry. I don't know what I would do if my mom died. My father, well, he's another issue entirely." He laughed nervously, maybe an attempt to lighten the mood, but Myreen's mood was too heavy to be budged.

A long moment passed where the only sound in the kitchen was Myreen's pitiful sobbing and occasional sniffle. She expected Kol to leave. Even a normal guy would be uncomfortable around a strange girl's crying. But he stayed. He offered no more words of support, and made no gestures; he just stood by her side like a statue, but somehow his presence was comforting. Maybe he did care. What other reason would he have to stay?

When her tear wells had dried up and her body was too exhausted to cry anymore, she looked up, and Kol was ready with a napkin.

Myreen accepted it and wiped the sticky tears off her face and fingers. "Thank you," she hiccupped. "Thank you for staying with me. You could have left at any time, but you didn't."

Kol shrugged. "Yeah, well, no one should have to go through that kind of loss alone. And… if it means that much to you, I guess we can be friends." His tone sounded so robotic, so uninterested, but the corner of his mouth rose in a joking smile and he winked at her. "As for your earlier question, I'm a dragon, if you must know."

This guy was a mystery, but Myreen kind of liked that. He played it off like he was above emotion, but she could see that a kindhearted, empathetic individual was hiding underneath those thick scales.

"Glad to meet you, Dragon Kol," Myreen said in as light a tone as she could manage.

He nodded his head toward their still-full plates. "You should finish your food. As a mermaid, you really need more omega-threes than the rest of us. I think there's a box of seaweed chips in the cupboard. You should take those back to your room for snacking while you study." He went back around the counter to attend to his plate.

"For a dragon, you sure seem to know a lot about mermaids," she teased, relishing the opportunity to get away from her sorrow.

"I know a lot about everything," he said, stabbing his fork into a piece a pork. "I'm a well of useless knowledge. If we're going to hang out, you might as well get used to my encyclopedic recitations."

Myreen laughed, and the two of them finished their food in a much more pleasant manner than they'd started. It had been a long and tumultuous first day, but she was happy to have made two new friends. Things were looking up.

Kol

Kol shoveled in his last bite. He was grateful for the silence to finish his meal. Any other girl would've insisted on keeping the conversation going. Clearly Myreen had more going for her than a pretty face and those piercing blue eyes he'd been avoiding the last several minutes. But seriously, how did the girl not know something was different about her with those blue streaks in her hair? Did she seriously think that was a normal human trait?

"Is it true you were unaware of your nature until Oberon found you?" he asked, setting his fork down and pushing his plate away.

Myreen's eyebrows furrowed for a split second before she shrugged. "Mom had rules," she said. "I wasn't allowed out after dark, I couldn't go swimming, and social media was completely banned." She held up her fingers as she rattled them off. "I'm not sure how they're all connected, but I'm convinced there was no way I could've figured it out myself." She laughed once. It was a sad sort of laugh.

It surprised Kol that she didn't seem to have any animosity toward her mother for having such strict boundaries. Especially ones that prevented much of a social life. Myreen seemed like the type of girl who craved attending pool parties that lasted past sunset and posting on Instagram to document her life.

All the mermaids he knew were precisely that type. Even the few humans he knew would've rebelled against rules that strict.

He certainly wished he could rebel more against his father's rules, and he shuddered at the memories of the consequences that followed when he'd dared to try. He shook off the thought.

"Anyway," Myreen continued. "I thought mermaids were a myth until… well yesterday. And *dragon shifters?* Aren't those supposed to be the hot guys on the covers of paranormal romance novels?" She laughed. It was a real laugh. "The ones girls daydream about and stupid high school guys wish they were?"

She stared longer than Kol was comfortable with. And those eyes.

"I'm not familiar with that genre," he said clearing his and Myreen's plates and taking them to the sink.

"Oh?" she asked. "What genre do you prefer?" She made her way to him as he squirted some dish soap and began to scrub.

"I don't have much time for novels," he said, keeping his eyes on the washing.

For being so talkative, she was suddenly quiet again. Maybe she thought he needed to concentrate on something as simple as washing dishes. *Strange.*

"So what *do* you have time for?" She asked as he turned the faucet on to rinse the first plate. "I m- mean…" she stammered. "What do you like to read? You said so yourself that you're a walking encyclopedia. Tell me something."

He looked at her—at those blue eyes that dared him to look away.

He had the sudden urge to run his fingers through his hair so he'd have an excuse to duck his head and *not* look at her anymore. But his hands were wet, so he reached for a drying towel. It wasn't where the staff usually left it. *Where is that blasted thing?* he wondered and ripped his gaze away as Myreen slowly took the now-clean plate from him.

Like she'd scare him away if she moved too quickly.

She probably would.

Smart girl.

And of course, she was holding the towel.

Kol turned back to the sink to scrub the other plate while Myreen dried. The rote action helped clear his head. "What do you want to know?" he asked.

"Well…" she said, her tone was thoughtful. "My mom kept this entire world from me. So, you can pretty much tell me anything about shifters and I *guarantee* that I probably won't already know it. Like the fish thing." She pointed at the plate Kol washed—for longer than was probably needed. "I mean, yeah, of course it makes sense that a mermaid should eat fish. But also, yeah, I didn't know it."

He rinsed the plate and handed it to her, then quickly washed and rinsed the utensils before answering. "So, your hair didn't clue you in?" He turned off the faucet then took the towel from her when she'd finished drying to wipe his hands.

"My hair?"

"The blue streaks didn't clue you in that you weren't exactly human?"

She held up a lock of black and blue. "Dyed," she said. "It was the one thing my mom actually let me do that was semi parental-shocking. Well, some parents might call it shocking." She leaned against the sink, with both hands behind her. Something seemed to dawn on her suddenly. "Is that why that Joanna girl's hair is that dirty blondish-greenish color?" She made a face when she said it. "Because she's a mermaid?"

Kol laughed out loud at her expression then quickly composed himself again. "It actually has something to do with food preference, in Joanna's case."

"Oh?"

"I believe she enjoys kelp."

Myreen made the face again. Kol held back another laugh, but a smile slipped out.

"But some mermaids have hair color that would never be natural to a human or other shifter. As a kid, I knew a mermaid who liked to frequent the lake at my family's vacation property. Her hair was brilliant violet. She was good friends with my mom."

That sad look returned.

Strange. Kol studied her, trying to decipher the change of mood. But it didn't take him long. *Stupid Kol. Her mom just died.* "I'm sorry," he said quickly, terrified that the water works would start again. "I shouldn't—"

"No, it's fine," Myreen said, but Kol could see her welled tears. "It's just fresh is all."

"I don't know how losing your mom could ever be *less than fresh*," he said. "Unless your mom was like my father—" Kol gripped his hair for an excuse to look at the floor, but he couldn't do it long, and he made it look like he was running his fingers through it, so she wouldn't think he was some freak.

Yeah, she'd probably already come to that conclusion.

Still, he needed to stop saying things like that about Eduard. It always made its way back to his father. Why couldn't he be one of the illegitimate sons, like Adam or Alex, who could say and do what they wanted? It was a burden being the heir. So much was expected. So much was required. He hadn't had a moment of peace since the day he was born. He was grateful puberty came early for him and he'd been

113

accepted to the school at thirteen.

But he'd never really wish to *not* be the heir, because that would mean that Victoria wouldn't be his mother.

And he couldn't imagine…

"I'm really sorry for your loss," he said, and for once his voice sounded like he actually meant the words. He wasn't the greatest at conveying emotion, so it surprised him that he actually sounded like he could. It didn't mean that he never felt anything. He just wasn't great at it.

She smiled sadly once more, but fortunately didn't begin crying again.

One of the kitchen doors creaked open. For an upscale, modern facility, one would think that some WD40 would be in the budget.

Kol was grateful for the warning, though, because suddenly he realized his proximity to Myreen was closer than he wanted *anyone* to see.

Especially Ms. Dinu. The teacher's eyes smiled—though her mouth didn't—as soon as they locked eyes.

Semi-covertly, Kol took a step away—with his long legs, one was enough. It probably wasn't subtle enough. He couldn't care, though. He wouldn't allow himself to care.

"Students should be in their dorms at this hour," Ms. Dinu said sternly with a raised eyebrow. The smile in her eyes was gone. "You know that, Mr. Dracul."

"Of course. Sorry, Ms. Dinu," Kol muttered under his breath and exited as quickly as his legs could take him. Which was fast. He only heard the end of Myreen's apology about being a new student and not knowing the rules.

Out of her presence, his head cleared. But Kol kept his pace brisk through the hallway—he couldn't have Myreen thinking he wanted to continue their conversation by stalling. Still, it wasn't long before he heard the click of heels behind him. He slowed. They obviously weren't student steps.

"Mr. Dracul!" Ms. Dinu was out of breath.

"I know, I know," Kol said. "I'm heading straight back." He tried not to sound annoyed that she apparently felt the need to tell him twice. And while he was clearly following the rules, no less!

"No, it's not that," she said, holding a hand out to stop him. For someone so much smaller than him—like most people—she certainly made him feel about a foot shorter in certain circumstances. Like this one.

"Is it about what happened last week? Because Brett—"

"It's not about Brett," she interrupted and squeezed her eyes tight. She exhaled. And then smiled.

What?

"Your father spoke to me today."

Okay... he thought, but didn't voice it. Instead, he crossed his arms over his chest. He didn't like the tone in her voice.

"He informed me of the *task* he assigned you."

Kol resisted the urge to react with a string of cuss words. Eduard assigned a task master? Faking a friendship with Myreen was *that* important? But cursing at a teacher past midnight in the hallway probably wasn't the best idea.

"He told you," was all he said.

"Clearly your father was wrong," she hooked a thumb back toward the kitchen. "But he wanted me to convince you of the importance of... *fulfilling* your assignment."

Assignment? Really? Kol thought. *I'm not in the damn military!*

Well, not yet. But he didn't like to think about that. Kol didn't grace his distant relative and dragon mastery teacher with a response.

"But I can see that you haven't wasted any time," she said, pride shining behind her glasses. "Perhaps I'll shirk my responsibility in checking the kitchen the next time I'm on curfew duty." She winked.

Kol couldn't help the scowl that came out.

"Look," she said, putting a hand on Kol's still folded arm. "You don't have to fall for her. He didn't ask you to do that."

"I know what my father asked."

"Okay." She let go of his arm, nodded once, then clomped down the hallway in the opposite direction. Running off to send back a report to *Lord Dracul* about Kol's obedience, no doubt.

Kol raced up the stairs to the second floor and barreled into the Avian common room. He wanted to crash face-first onto his bed and sink into unconsciousness. He wanted to be alone.

"Why, don't *you* look bright-eyed this evening?" Brett teased, ruining any hope Kol had of sneaking into his room unnoticed. Brett was shooting zombies on the large flat screen. Sneaking off to bed usually didn't take any effort with the pseudo-apocalyptic distractions.

Nik was snoring in the chair next to Brett. His controller lay loosely in his hands.

"Did ya find the teacher's stash of espresso to go with your midnight snack?" Brett asked. "Or did you corner Trish in one of the greenhouses again?" He winked just like Ms. Dinu had. Kol wanted to punch him in the face.

"You're the only one banned from the espresso," Kol deadpanned. "And since when do you even notice my sneaking by your virtual bloodshed?" Kol asked, resisting the urge to use violence. "Seriously, Brett haven't you beat this game yet?"

"Three times, actually." He grinned wide.

"You're a *dragon*, Brett. How is that game at all entertaining? Slow humans shooting dead guys."

"You're changing the subject," Brett said, then uncharacteristically turned off his game. And the TV.

"No, I did not corner Trish," Kol said, rolling his eyes at his friend's idiocy and moved to head to his room.

"Nope. Not done talking." Brett stood and stretched, but then sobered and looked Kol in the eye. "What did Lord Dracul want?"

"It doesn't matter," Kol said flatly, pointedly keeping his thoughts miles away from a pair of bright eyes.

Brett raised an eyebrow. For speaking as slowly as he sometimes did, and fronting the persona of a washed up surfer, Brett was smart, if not very observant.

"He needed me to do something," Kol said. "An assignment, sort of."

"Assignment?"

"Lame, I know."

"What is it?" His eyebrows rose.

"Top secret."

"Liar."

Kol shrugged. "I'm not telling you." *I haven't even decided if I'm actually going to do it*, he thought.

"Well… you're gonna do it, right?" Brett asked, suddenly looking concerned and weirdly reading Kol's mind. *Was he bitten by a Mao or something?* "Because whatever the General is asking you to do must be important, right?"

"Right." Kol narrowed his eyes, like it would help him read Brett's mind. He shook his head. "I'm going to bed," he said. "I've got an essay to write in the morning."

He had a responsibility to his family. Of course he'd do it.

Myreen

Myreen woke up feeling much better. The cry she'd had with Kol last night had really shed the weight of mourning she'd been carrying, and everything about the current morning felt lighter, brighter. Her arms were less shaky, her legs felt springy, and the pain that had been gnawing at her guts was now replaced by a gentle buzz energizing her.

She hopped out of bed and tapped on her tablet to look at her schedule. Surprisingly, today's classes looked like a typical day at school: Math, Chemistry, English. Everything, aside from her first class, which was Mastery—whatever that was—and her last class, Defense. She was actually looking forward to attending her basic classes. They might make her feel normal again. The idea of Defense did not give her that same comfort. PE had always been her least favorite subject, and Defense sounded like PE, tenfold. Although she understood the need for it, especially after what happened to her mom, she had no physical prowess, whatsoever. She realized that was the point of the class—to improve her physical abilities—but still, it did not appeal to her at all.

After getting dressed and grabbing her laptop bag, Myreen made her way down to the dining hall, happy to know that she would have someone to sit with while she ate. She filled her tray and easily spotted Kol sitting at a table with two other boys—he was hard to miss, even sitting, as he was at least a foot taller than everyone else in the dining hall.

Myreen claimed the empty seat next to him. His eyes almost bugged out of his head, and she thought she noticed his face turn a shade of pink.

"Good morning," she greeted him and his friends, whose mouths fell open as they looked at her. "I know, I know, new mermaid and all, big shocker." Myreen decided to break the ice by diving into it.

"Uh, sorry, do we know you?" one of Kol's friends asked, shaking his blond head as if he had long hair.

"Brett," the other friend hissed under his breath.

Kol gave a sidelong glance at the boy—who must be Brett—but didn't say anything. Myreen still hadn't quite figured him out, but she chose to interpret his silence as acceptance.

"Kol and I know each other," she answered Brett's question, pretending not to notice its rude intent. "We ran into each other last night and had a good talk. I thought it might be fun to get to know his friends." She offered a friendly smile.

Brett and the other boy slowly turned their heads in Kol's direction simultaneously, and Myreen got the idea that Kol hadn't mentioned her. *Is he ashamed for his friends to know that we talked? Maybe this was a mistake. Maybe he was just nice to me last night because we were alone and I was crying. Maybe he wants nothing to do with me, like the rest of the school.*

Kol looked at her for a moment, chewing on his bottom lip as if internally debating something, then said, "Uh, yeah, I ran into her here last night after the meeting with my father. She's alright."

119

Brett looked back at her and smiled wide. "Is it true that you had no idea you were a mermaid until you came here?" He was leaning forward, beaming at her like she was some kind of tabloid celebrity.

She shrugged, surprised by his about-face reaction. "Yep. I'm a shifter newbie in every way."

"Whoa, that's so weird," Brett said. "I've never met a mermaid who wasn't… well, an elitist snob from birth. Have you tried transforming yet? What was it like?"

"Brett, give the girl a break," the other friend chastised. Then he looked at Myreen. "Sorry, Brett has no filter. I'm Nik."

Myreen laughed. "It's okay, I don't mind. I've heard that my fellow mermaids can be quite… delightful. I can promise you guys that I'm nothing like them."

"Glad to hear it," Nik said. "Kol found a keeper." He winked at Kol, who just rolled his eyes and turned away.

"Hi, Myreen," Juliet's voice sounded from behind her. When Myreen turned around to look at her, Juliet was hovering there awkwardly, as if stuck in place by indecision.

"Oh, this is too perfect," Brett said with a clap of his hands. "The fish out of water and the accidental fire-starter."

"Dude!" Kol and Nik scolded Brett in stereo.

Nik half smiled at Juliet, his gaze bouncing from her face to the table. "You can sit with us, too, if you want."

Juliet's eyes had hardly left Nik's face since she appeared beside the table, and at his invitation to sit, those eyes lit up. Did Juliet have a crush on Nik? *I'll have to remember to ask her about it later.*

The breakfast turned out not to be such a fiasco. Brett spent most of the time asking Myreen random personal questions about her pre-mermaid life, and Kol and Nik argued about mermaid politics, which was all very educational for Myreen—she guessed that much of her time spent with Kol would be.

He was like a handsome computer, always calculating, always spouting facts, and at least making it look as though he had no emotions. But there was something about him that she liked, despite all the warning signs—especially the giant "Not Interested" label on his forehead whenever he looked at her.

After breakfast, Myreen went to the mermaid training room for her first class, Mastery. As she walked, she tried to guess what the class would entail. She'd never heard of anything like it at any other school. If it was in the mermaid training room, she knew it had something to do specifically with being a mermaid.

When she entered the training room, students were just emerging from the locker rooms in their swim tops and getting ready to get in the pool. She followed their example and went to the locker room to get into her own top, then sheepishly returned to the training room to see what the next hour had in store for her.

Delphine was at the opposite corner of the room, talking to a small group of students, and Myreen figured she would just wait for instructions. She sat at the edge of the pool and, with a thrill in her belly, dipped her feet in the water. Just as last time, a prickling itch swallowed the surface of her skin on her legs, and she watched as the smooth flesh was gradually replaced by glistening pink scales. She had been too distraught yesterday to get a good view, but now she could clearly witness her ankles and shins webbing together and stretching out into a tail that still astounded and excited her.

Myreen could happily sit here all day and splash her tail in the water. Nothing was more comfortable than the feeling of water surrounding her. The coolness on her arms, washing over her tail, it was like discovering the underside of a pillow. She was tempted to dive in completely, but she wanted to be alert for when the class started—and skip the not-as-pleasant emergence of the gills on her neck. That had been her least favorite part. She knew she'd have to get used to it eventually, but for now, she was enjoying this leisure moment.

A good ten minutes passed, and Delphine had not officially started the class. Many of the students were just playing in the pool. Myreen had clearly missed something. She watched the other mermaids, swimming, flipping, or just floating in groups and gossiping. Then something caught the corner of her eye, and she looked to the far left edge of the pool. One of the male students was waving his hands above the water, and impossibly, a stream of water rose upward and made a somewhat sloppy arc before splashing back to the surface from whence it came.

Myreen's mouth dropped open, and she blinked hard. *Did I really just see that?*

"Quite a trick, huh?" a male voice said behind her.

She turned around to see a rather attractive guy standing behind her. For a moment, Myreen lost herself in appreciation for his boy-band good looks. He had sandy brown hair that looked as though it had taken him all morning to get it to feather out so perfectly, and beach blue eyes that seemed to harbor some hidden hunger within their depths. Thanks to the skin-tight swim top, Myreen could see each sculpted muscle of his defined chest and abs.

The boy gave her a crooked smile, then dove head-first into the pool, his form flawless. Myreen watched his legs morph into a handsome dark blue tail as his body cut like a knife through the water. He spun around, and his head surfaced a foot or so in front of her. He rested his bent elbow on the edge of the pool.

"So, you're the new mermaid nobody will shut up about," he said with a laugh. "I'm Kendall." He extended a wet hand.

Myreen nervously reached out and accepted it, hating that her cheeks were burning so much. "Yep, I guess that's me." She looked back to the student that had manipulated the water. "How did he do that?" She tipped her chin in that direction.

"I know you're new to all this, so I'll break it down for you," Kendall said. "All shifters have secondary abilities—powers, if you will—aside from just transforming. Mermaids can control water in whatever form they find it. That's the main purpose of this class, teaching young shifters like you and me how to master this power."

Myreen nodded in understanding. *So that's why it's called Mastery.*

"Buuut, most of us mermaids have been playing with water since before we could talk, so the majority of the students spend this class as a free period," he explained.

"Ah. So are you a water manipulation expert?" she asked, a weak attempt at flirting. This guy was seriously gorgeous, and so far, the only mermaid who would give her the time of day.

"I guess you could say that. And I have other things to study in this class, which is why you won't find me lounging about like the rest of them."

"Oh? What is there to master aside from fancy irrigation skills?" she asked.

He chuckled. "I'm a seer."

Myreen brows shot up. She knew that Delphine was a seer, and that the ability was rare even among mermaids. Now that she thought about it, Kendall had been one of the students Delphine had been talking to on the other side of the room.

"At the beginning of each class, Delphine gives the small handful of us who have the affinity for future sight a brief lesson, helping to guide us through fine-tuning our visions," Kendall said.

"So you can see the future like Delphine?" Myreen asked, then felt stupid for letting those words come out. "I mean, do you get visions of new shifters when they're turned or come of age?"

"Haha, no. I'm nowhere near as good as Delphine," he said, shaking his head. "Delphine can target her sight to just about anything or anyone she wants. That's how she made her fortune, playing the stock market. You know she's the one who financed the school, right?"

"Oh yeah. I think they mentioned that in history, yesterday," Myreen said. She imagined a psychic could use future-sight to make millions. Delphine was craftier than Myreen realized.

"Nah, the only things I can see are random events specific to me," Kendall said. "I can't target my visions. Not yet, anyway. And the frustrating thing is, I can't see the causes, only the outcomes, so I can't figure out how to prevent what I see."

A shadow fell over his face for a brief instant, and Myreen wondered if there was something unpleasant he had foreseen that he wished to stop. If only Myreen had that affinity. She might have been able to see the vampire attack coming. She might have been able to save her mom.

"Good morning, Myreen." Delphine's voice jolted Myreen out of her thoughts. She turned to see that the mer teacher was walking toward them. "I apologize for not tending to you sooner, but my upperclassmen needed some briefing. I see you've met Kendall. He's one of the school's finest apprentice seers." Delphine didn't hide her favoritism toward him. "He might even have my job one day." She winked at him, and his brows furrowed with a flicker of nervousness.

"I'd better get back to practicing," Kendall said. "It was nice to meet you, Myreen." And then he dove into the water and swam away.

It was very nice to meet you, too, Myreen thought as his tail whipped in her direction and he zipped through the water. A gorgeous mer-guy who was nice, could there be anything better?

"I know this is all very new to you, so let me explain what we study in this class," Delphine said.

"Oh, Kendall told me a little bit," Myreen said. "Mermaids have the power to control water, and..." She gulped as she realized she was going to have to figure out how to do that. *Oh, crap.*

Delphine nodded at Myreen's unspoken dilemma. "It's all right, no one expects you to shape water into a sea dragon on your first try. There's no pressure here. We'll just take it slow and awaken your awareness of your connection to the water. Once you find it, everything else will follow."

"Okay," Myreen said with uncertainty, hoping that it would be as simple as Delphine led on.

Delphine claimed that there were no expectations of her, but Myreen could sense that just about everyone was expecting something from her, Oberon most of all. She didn't know what they were expecting, but she didn't want to let any of them down.

***

"So, uh, what do you know about *Kendall?*" Myreen whispered.

"You mean *Ken Doll?*" Juliet asked with a snicker. "He's your typical popular guy. If this school had jocks, he'd probably be the quarterback of the football team. I mean, I guess I could see why you'd be asking, as a mermaid. He is pretty."

"I know mermaids don't have the best reputation for being, well, human, but is he nice?" He had been nice to her, but she wanted to get the scoop on him, if there was one.

Juliet shrugged. "I'll put it this way—he's not the worst of them. But he did date the worst of them."

"What?" Myreen asked.

"Yeah, he and Alessandra have this on-again-off-again thing going on," Juliet replied.

The butterflies in Myreen's stomach fell dead to the floor. If Kendall could date a girl like that, maybe he wasn't the guy she hoped he was.

"Well, that sucks." Myreen sighed.

"But you're way prettier than she is," Juliet said. "Better in just about every way, in fact."

Myreen gave a doubtful snort. "It's not a big deal, really. He's just the first mermaid to even talk to me, so I got a little ahead of myself, I guess."

"He's definitely the cutest of the mer-guys," Juliet said, and Myreen smiled inwardly at the terminology confirmation. "Seeing as inter-shifter dating is kind of a no-no, he's your best bet."

"Wait, w- what?" Myreen stammered. "There are rules about dating?"

"Well, not technically," Juliet said, tilting her head to the side. "I mean, it's not written anywhere that two different shifters *can't* get together, but it's just an unspoken rule."

"Why?"

"I think because of the speciesism in the shifter world. Everyone is so obsessed with purity in bloodlines—well, aside from weres, obviously. But dragons, phoenixes and mermaids especially have a cultural heritage that dominates who they are. Parents want to be able to know what species of shifter their child will be, and with two different types, you just never known which side of the coin you're gonna get. You could even end up with a freak who's a mix of both, if you get pregnant at all."

Myreen frowned. So much for any leaning she might have had toward Kol. Maybe that was why he was so cold toward her. Because even if they did have a certain chemistry, nothing could ever happen between them.

The students in the dining hall began to shuffle. "Ready to head off to Defense class?" Juliet asked.

"Not really," Myreen admitted with a laugh. "What exactly is that class about?"

"It's mostly wrestling and sparring techniques, but every now and then Oberon pairs us up to fight each other and even has a few students give us a show in the Simulation Room."

"Simulation Room?" Myreen asked, intrigued.

Juliet gave a wicked smile. "You're in for a treat the first time you see it. Well, as long as you're not the one who has to test in it."

Myreen gulped. She hoped she never had to test in that room.

Myreen

"I— hate— this!"

Myreen panted as she threw a tired fist at the punching bag in front of her for what felt like the billionth time.

"You haven't— seen anything— yet," Juliet huffed beside her, kicking at her own punching bag like it stole her diary.

Defense class was every bit as horrible as Myreen had imagined it would be. The training room was enormous, divided into sections with different equipment. One section had ellipticals and treadmills, one had full body punching bags and gloves, one had weights, and then half of the ginormous gymnasium had nothing but a foam mat that covered the entire floor; Myreen assumed that was where the sparring happened.

Myreen took a moment to catch her breath and looked around. There were hundreds of students in here. The whole school must be in the gym. Many of them were training just as *enthusiastically* as Myreen was, but some of them, like Juliet, were really giving it their all.

"Sorry if this is a stupid question, but why are you pushing yourself so hard?" Myreen asked after her lungs had stopped screaming at her.

Juliet didn't stop her attack on the bag when she answered. "Students can test out of Defense— and seeing as my father is one of the highest— ranked— lieutenants— in the shifter forces— I kinda have to." She gave the bag one big punch and it rocked so hard that Myreen thought it was going to fly clean off the chains that held it.

"Wow, a lieutenant?" Myreen said on an exhale. "Tough shoes to fill."

"You have no idea," Juliet said, giving the bag a death stare.

The idea of testing out of this class was tempting, but Myreen had very little faith that her body would ever excel at this type of thing. She could barely go up a flight of stairs without getting winded.

"How do you test out?" Myreen asked, expecting a harrowing answer.

"You have to win the simulation," Juliet replied, a hint of a smile tugging at the corner of her mouth.

Myreen remembered Juliet talking about that at lunch. It would be interesting to watch, but Myreen had no intention whatsoever of going into a simulation, if she had a choice.

"Alright, class, that's time." Oberon's voice filled the gym. "Time to pair up for forty minutes of sparring."

"Oh no." Myreen sighed, her exhausted shoulders slumping as low as they could go.

The class gathered around the foam mat, and Oberon and his assistants paired everyone off. Myreen dreaded him coming to her, dreaded who she might get paired with. If it was Trish or one of those mer-witches, she was done for. Heck, if it was Juliet, she was done for.

"Myreen, you'll be paired with Kendall," Oberon said.

An exclamation point floated over her head at that designation. Myreen was both thrilled and dismayed. *Why did it have to be Kendall?* She was covered in a thick layer of sweat, and she was sure her hair looked like it had gone through a garbage disposal. Now she had to get up close and personal with the only cute guy at this school who was openly nice to her?

Kendall made his way over to her with an expression that said he was pleased with the match. And his shirt was off. And his chest was glistening like that of a Greek god. How the heck was she supposed to focus when he looked like *that*?

"Go easy on me?" she asked as coyly as she could.

"Of course," he chuckled.

So quickly Myreen didn't know what was happening, Kendall spun around, and kicked her feet out from under her. She was certain she was going to land painfully on her butt. She squeezed her eyes shut to brace for the fall, but strong arms caught under her back and knees. When she timidly opened her eyes, Kendall was cradling her against his firm, slick chest, his handsome face wearing a devilish smile.

Oh, this guy is good!

"You fight dirty," she panted.

He winked. "I just wanted to sweep you off your feet."

Swoon!!!

"I'm sorry, but that was really corny," she giggled.

"I know, but I couldn't help myself," he laughed back. "Okay, let's get to the actual training. I'll try to teach you some evasive maneuvers you can use against these other guys, because I don't think anyone else you might get paired with will go easy on you."

"Thanks," she said.

"Besides, you're small and thin enough that you could easily slip out of many hold positions. You just have to learn how to use your body."

Kendall was offering to teach her how to use her body. Was she dreaming? Now she was hot and flushed for another reason.

"Let's start with escaping a choke hold," he said, stepping behind her. "I'm gonna put my arms around your neck, and I want you to try to get out."

Myreen stood in place, feeling the heat coming off his body as he stood centimeters away from her back. He seemed to be waiting for her permission.

"Okay." She nodded. "Let's do it."

One large, muscular arm came over her shoulder and bent under her chin, his hand catching in the bend of his other arm that jackknifed on her opposite shoulder. The embrace was tight, but not horribly uncomfortable, and she could still breathe easily.

"Alright, now try to get out," he instructed.

All Myreen could think about was the fact that his warm body was wrapped around hers, and her head was a frenzy of hormonal fog. She wrapped her hands around his thick forearm and pulled. Despite his seemingly loose hold on her neck, she couldn't budge his arm, no matter how much she struggled. She squirmed and wriggled, trying to twist herself around or slip out. It ended with her looking undoubtedly foolish and somewhat crooked.

Kendall laughed, and she could feel the vibrations of his chest rumbling against her back. "Well, that was a good attempt, but let me show you the right way." He dropped his hands and moved so that he was in front with his back to her. "Put your arms around my neck."

She did as he said, putting her arms in the same formation that his had been on her. Just as he had, she made sure not to hold him too tightly, so she wouldn't hurt him. Not like she could.

"No matter how hard you pull on the choking arm, you're never going to break it free," he said, tugging on her right forearm as she gripped the bend in her elbow. "You have to go for the parts that can be moved, which in this case is the interlocking arm."

He grabbed the wrist of her other arm, the one that was bent and next her face, and pulled it down with ease. *Wow, I am weak!*

"Once you have that arm down, the lock is broken, and you can push the choking arm out of the way," he said. "But you have to also roll your shoulder into the disabled arm as you push away the choking arm so that you can escape."

She felt his shoulder blade gently push into the left side of her chest, which completely distracted her from the hand that pushed at her arm around his neck, and he slipped out of her hold.

Kendall turned around and smiled at her. "Now you try."

She nodded and happily let him put his arms around her again. Not a bad place to be, honestly. Once he had his arms in place, she reached up for his left wrist and pulled as hard as she could. The arm came down, no problem, and she rolled into his chest at the same time as she pushed his choking arm away, hopping out of his hold like a bunny.

Free and floating on air, she spun around with an ear-to-ear smile. "That was amazing! I actually did it!"

"That was perfect! See? You're a natural."

"It helps that you're such a great teacher," she said in a flirtatious tone. "Maybe you could help me with Mastery, too?"

"Sure, I wouldn't mind tutoring you. I think it really sucks that you missed out on growing up like a mermaid. Is it true that you were never in the water until yesterday?"

There it was, the small reminder that she was different from everyone else. Yet, Kendall wasn't saying it with judgment. The look in his beach eyes was honest, with a glint of sympathy.

"Yes," she replied. "They're calling me a fish out of water."

Kendall frowned. "I'm sorry. I can't imagine going my whole life without swimming. That really sucks."

Myreen nodded. "You have no idea. I feel like I've been robbed, and I never even knew it." Her smile faltered as instant guilt stunned her for making that claim. The person who supposedly robbed her was her mom, and saying such a thing was an insult to her mom's memory. After all, she knew that whatever her mom's reasons were, they weren't malicious.

"That's alright," Kendall said with a warm smile. "We'll try to get you caught up on everything you missed. I'll personally take you under my fin. I'm sure there are lots of things I can teach you."

Myreen didn't miss the innuendo there.

When he lunged for her this time, she saw it coming, but saw no reason to resist physical contact with him in this circumstance. He wrapped an arm around her waist and took her to the mat. "Now, let's work on your ground game."

Maybe Defense class wouldn't be so torturous after all.

Kol

"Malkolm Dracul."

Oberon Rex's booming voice snapped Kol from his thoughts. He'd beat his partner, a volatile hound named Jesse, several minutes before in his spar—Kol seriously needed another go at the simulation so he could finally test out of defense class. He hadn't lost to another student in almost a year, and it was seriously getting boring. Thanks to that, he practically had a front row seat to see Myreen's spar with *Ken Doll.*

Which didn't really look like a spar...

Sparring doesn't require that much... contact. At least not that long. Kol shook his head slightly to knock out the distracting images and turned his attention to the school director.

Oberon seemed to be hiding a smile as he held a hand toward Kol. "Show everyone how it's done."

Kol nodded and switched to autopilot while walking to the center of the large mat. The rest of the students gathered behind the *safe zone.*

He noticed Myreen and Kendall still stood close to each other, a little bit separated from the rest of the crowd. Crossing his arms over his chest, Kol snatched his gaze away and calculated whose turn it might be to face him and how much effort he'd need to put into the exercise.

It probably wasn't a day for fire manipulation, unless he was pitted against Nik again, but they'd been paired last week so he doubted it. Although he might make an exception for Kendall...

But the entire school rumbled in a collective chuckle, snapping Kol from his thoughts. He looked at Oberon.

Was he hiding a smile?

Uncrossing his arms, Kol looked back at the crowd of his classmates with a questioning look. *Why wasn't he calling another student?* He found Nik and Brett near the front. Brett pointed at Oberon with a wide grin.

Kol's thick hair lifted in a breeze and he instantly sparked his fingertips. Gryphons used wind. He snapped his head to Oberon.

"There he is," Oberon said quietly, causing anyone within hearing distance to laugh out loud. How did Kol miss the purple glow of Oberon's eyes?

"You mean, spar with *you? Sir?*"

A gust of wind pushed against the back of Kol's knees, forcing him into a kneeling position and his fingers splayed on the mat to keep him from face planting.

Kol silently cursed as his classmates rumbled with laughter again. Oberon hated being called by any sort of title. And Kol had to be corrected more than most, thanks to his upbringing.

Oberon remained stoic as the laughter died down. "That's what I meant when I said: *Let's show them how it's done.*"

Wordlessly, Kol pushed himself off the floor and took his stance.

Fire power it is.

How the gryphon managed to create a whirlwind that forced Kol to bend his knees and brace himself—yet didn't lift a single strand of hair from the kitsunes and nagas in the front row—always amazed him. But he couldn't think about it. He clapped his hands to conjure two yellow-orange fireballs, even as his eyes watered from the gusts.

With a flick of his wrists, Kol urged the fire orbs to grow four times in size within a matter of seconds, or else be extinguished by the increasing winds.

His foot slipped and with the same motion he tossed the fireball from his right hand—not directly at Oberon—but into the path of the funnel heading toward the director. Most thought it was his dragon nature that helped Kol win his fights. Or that he was a Dracul. He let them assume both of those reasons, but he knew his analytical calculations were what actually gave him the upper hand.

Oberon quickly ducked, avoiding getting a face-full of fire, but Kol smiled at seeing the tiny red glow on the tips of his defense teacher's sandy brown hair before the sparks extinguished.

With a smile, he managed a quick glance at the crowd before hurling his other fireball at a different point in the funnel to knock into the back of Oberon's knees. He hoped for a similar result, and maybe even a face plant, as payback for Oberon's cheap shot moments ago. But he couldn't help his eyes being drawn to the location of Myreen and Kendall, whose hand was brushing a dark lock of hair from her face.

Thanks to the minor distraction, Kol didn't release his projectile in time. It hit the gust centimeters off, and was flung away from the orbit around Oberon and into the ceiling tiles, incinerating several of them.

And before he could recover, he was flat on his back with one of the treadmills inches from his nose before Oberon put it safely back in its place. His eyes shifted from their brilliant purple glow, darkening until they were back to their hazel color.

The mood in the room shifted and the room quieted. No one expected Kol to beat an experienced gryphon, not to mention the defense teacher and director of the School for the Shifted, but they still seemed surprised.

The crowd dispersed. Oberon helped Kol to his feet, but didn't say a word, allowing Kol to keep his dignity as he rejoined his friends, who waited near the exit.

"You almost had him!" Nik clapped a hand on Kol's shoulder—which was tricky since he had to slap upward to reach it—but Kol appreciated the gesture.

"Yeah, I don't know what your plan was with that second one," Brett said as they walked from the room. "But *man!* Using Oberon's wind against him was freaking brilliant! If he hadn't ducked, he would've needed a new face!"

Even Nik laughed at that and ran a hand over the shaved swirls on the side of his head. "What happened with that second one?"

Kol shrugged. He wasn't going to admit where his focus was. "I miscalculated. I was trying to hit the back of Oberon's knees."

"Ah!" Brett said. "Payback. Genius."

"That would've been pretty epic," Nik agreed.

"Next time," Kol said, ready for the subject to be dropped.

"Hey, there's a party this weekend," Nik said, granting Kol's wish. "It's at Jackson's house off campus."

"The Hound?"

"Yep," Brett said. "And we're going."

Kol didn't answer, but figured he wouldn't have much choice in the matter. He made an excuse about homework—which wasn't really an excuse, Brett just always thought it was—and made his way back to his room.

Partway through his Calculus homework, Kol's email chimed on his laptop.

It was from Eduard.

He was being reminded just him how *"imperative it is"* that he *"befriend the mermaid."*

Kol rolled his eyes before closing his computer. He wasn't finished with his homework, but he was finished with the email. Though Eduard had worded it like a request, a *favor* Kol would be doing by continuing with his task, he knew it wasn't a request.

His instinct told him to push back, to rebel and do the opposite of what his father wanted. But he cared for his family. He was proud to be a Dracul, despite the curse that came with it. *I've pretty much decided to do it anyway,* he thought.

And besides, with Myreen cozying up to *Ken Doll,* certainly there wasn't any harm in Kol being Myreen's *friend.* If she wanted to be interested in one of her own kind—as she should—Kol could more easily guard his heart. And he was practiced enough that it wouldn't be an issue, anyway.

It is imperative—Eduard used the word imperative to near annoyance—*that we find out if she's the siren from the prophecy before anyone else.* Those were Eduard's words that day in Oberon's office.

Step one: Befriend Myreen. *Check.*

Step Two: Find out if she's the siren.

He wasn't getting any more homework done anyway, so Kol pushed from his desk and left to find her. He walked with a bit more determination and purpose than he had in a while.

***

Dinner wasn't for another hour, but Kol checked the dining hall, hoping to catch Myreen before everyone else began trickling in. Sure enough, she sat at one of the tables alone, with her laptop open and some notes sprawled.

"Did they forget to put a desk in your room?" he asked.

Her cheeks colored. "A friend was helping me sort through this

Shifter Biology syllabus."

He nodded. Mrs. Coltar's syllabus was famously confusing. "A friend?" he pressed, sitting down across from her without invitation. She didn't protest.

"Yeah. Juliet Quinn," she said.

Kol made a noise and leaned back. "The accident waiting—" He stopped himself. But she must've had an inkling what he was about to say and stared at her fingernails.

He contemplated the best way to needle her for any clues that she might be the siren that didn't include the obvious one: getting a blood sample and comparing it to other mermaids. She broke the silence first.

"Oberon was pretty rough on you today," she said her voice rising slightly at the end, finally looking at him. Was that pity in her voice?

He didn't like the way the conversation was going.

"Is he always like that?" she continued. Or maybe it was fear.

"He won't call you up like that," he assured her, leaning forward and resting his elbows on the table with his fingers laced together. "He reserves his show-off moments for..." he trailed off seeing her small smile.

"For show-off's like *you?*" she teased.

"Who says I'm a show-off?" Did she see his quick spar in class? Sure, he'd barely given that hound a chance, but he assumed she was too preoccupied with her own "*spar.*" "I'm not the one who thinks wrapping my arms around a girl is the best way to teach her defense." He didn't mean to say that out loud, and he shut her still-open-laptop to distract from the heat rising up his neck.

She raised an eyebrow up into the black and blue hair that swept across her face. She didn't look mad at the way he'd invaded her space. "Kendall was showing me how to escape if someone grabbed me. Really, it was basic self-defense." She rolled her eyes. "Like, *human* stuff."

"Yeah, well for someone who just barely learned she's a shifter, you should probably be focusing on learning your *shifter* ways of defense."

"Honestly, it was kind of nice doing something I might've done in my old life."

"Well, learning how to get out of a hold like that won't save you from a vampire."

"You think I don't know that?" Her voice rose. "That's how my mom died!"

"And vampires aren't the only things," he said, realizing that he was horrible for even bringing it up, but she had to know the seriousness of the danger. "There are rogue shifters out there. Weres that weren't found and brought to the Dome in time, Nagas who disagreed with the way the shifter military ran things and defected because of their own stupid self-righteous beliefs. My family has…" He hesitated. Myreen didn't know about his family heritage or even the fact that they were considered royalty. It was refreshing that she was the one girl who didn't treat him like he was a prince to be won. "There are dragon enemies out there," he finished vaguely.

She nodded and narrowed her eyes like she was scrutinizing him. Like she was determining if he told the truth. The temperature in his blood rose and he clenched his fists to prevent any accidental fire orbs from forming.

"Not to mention the hunters!" he said. Her ignorance to the dangers was infuriating. "Sure, they're human, but you catch one mercury bullet and *poof!*" He made an explosion gesture with his hands.

"Are you trying to scare me?" she asked, her tone eerily calm.

"No, I—"

"I'm not going to pretend that what you said isn't real or doesn't matter," she interrupted. "I *know* it's real. My world was shattered by something I never thought existed until it happened. But it's a little overwhelming learning that I grow a tail when I touch salt water." She laughed. It sounded forced. "The first time I went under, I sprouted gills!" She blew out a breath of exasperation. "It's just overwhelming and Ken..." she stopped. "It's nice that *some* people are helping me ease into this. And adjust." Myreen began packing her notes and computer into her bag.

Damage control. "You know, the first time I conjured fire, I set my mother's favorite rug on fire," he said, making an effort to change his tone. He prayed it was enough to make her stay. He hadn't even found out anything that would suggest she was the siren yet.

She stood to leave.

"I'm just saying that I get it." He stood too. "Figuring out your powers and where you fit in the shifter world can be overwhelming."

"You don't understand," she said and walked from the table.

"I know I don't understand." He rounded the table and walked behind her. "I was born knowing what I was, and struggled. I can't imagine what you're going through. It terrified me the first time sparks flew through my fingers. My father had to disable the smoke alarm for about three months until I gained more control." He was hoping for at least a smile but got nothing.

But she did stop walking to look at him. "How did you finally get control?" she asked.

He should've known she'd ask, but he'd spilled so much more than he'd planned that it caught him off guard. "I learned to play the piano."

"The piano?" There was that skeptical look again.

"Yeah, I mean, the playing wasn't what taught me control," he said. "Practice did that. But learning the piano is what finally calmed me enough to deal with all of the fear that was causing my powers to be so out of control."

He got a small smile from her.

And he realized he'd unknowingly led the conversation to the perfect line of questioning. "Do you play?" he asked.

She shook her head.

"Do you... *sing?*" Kol tried to sound nonchalant about it, but heard the emphasis in his voice.

"No, my musical talent is limited to Spotify playlists," she said. "I'll see you later Kol."

He didn't want her to leave. He'd angered her, and she infuriated him, but Kol craved Myreen's company. She was his friend, after all. He scrambled to think of anything that would make her stay just a second longer. "There's a party this weekend," he blurted out.

That did it. She turned back to him with that eyebrow raised beneath that lock of hair that insisted on covering part of her forehead.

"It's at Jackson's house off campus. A were."

"I uh—"

"You should come with me." He hadn't intended to add the *with me* part. But it was too late now, so he braced himself for the rejection.

"Okay," Myreen said with a smile, pushing that piece of hair behind her ear. "I'd love to come."

Then she turned and walked away.

What did I get myself into?

Kenzie

Kenzie sat in her room—a crazy mashup of childhood fantasy and teenage angst—and fiddled with the pencil in her hand. She put the pencil down and began tapping her nearly-black-but-actually-purple nails on the blank notebook atop her Rainbow Bright bedcover. The textbook sat open but still unread, despite the multiple times she'd tried.

She couldn't get Myreen, or the school, or her untapped powers off her mind. Her own school had been distractingly dull since she'd lost her only friend to the coolest school she could imagine. And she'd been rejected in her attempt to join. Twice.

But wallowing wasn't going to fix anything—she'd already tried that, and it was a miserable pity party. No, she needed a plan.

Mom's head popped in her door. "Time to wrap up. Dinner's going to be ready in ten."

Kenzie nodded, her eyes still glazed over from thinking.

"Is everything okay?" Mom asked, her brow creased. She came all the way in and sat on the edge of the bed.

Kenzie sat up, rubbing her face. "I guess. It's just..." She stared at her mom a moment, trying to decide if she wanted to risk getting in trouble again. Life in the house was just getting back to normal after their last fight. "Do shifters hate us?" The words rushed out of her mouth before she could change her mind.

Mom's mouth hardened into a thin line. Kenzie winced as she braced for another lecture.

Instead, mom sighed. "Oh, Kenz, where would you get an idea like that."

Kenzie turned her face away, guilt seeping into her. She hated lying to her mom, but she hated being excluded even more. She wanted to take her place in the shifter world and find the magic that had been stolen from her family. To be so close but not part of it nearly killed her.

"I don't know. You and Gram keep me away from it all the time. I thought, you know, maybe shifters hated us or something." That was as close to the truth as she wanted to stray.

Mom's arms wrapped around Kenzie, and Kenzie snuggled in, letting out a contented sigh. As a little girl, she'd wondered if mom hugs were laced with magic.

"No, not hate, really. Distrust, certainly, but not hate."

Kenzie had definitely caught hate vibes from Delphine. She wondered what that woman had against selkies. Besides the killing seal thing, of course.

Kenzie pulled away from her mom's embrace to look her in the eyes. "Why, though? Why would anyone hate or dislike us?"

Mom looked at the ceiling. "Do you remember the stories of creation I used to tell you?"

Kenzie nodded. They were stories of war and hate. About how the vampires were created to dominate the other races, and then shifters to combat the vampires. She never understood why humans turned on the shifters afterward, but something had driven them into hiding. Of course, the Hunters might have something to do with that.

"What I've never told you was that selkies were the magic users that helped turn armies into the shifters and vampires we have today."

Kenzie's brows hit her hairline. That was some seriously powerful magic.

Mom nodded. "Many of our kind found sealskin magic in order to blend in with the shifters, but it's not quite the same." Mom ran a hand through her hair, suddenly looking weary beyond her forty-some years. "And without the grimoire..."

Kenzie leaned forward, stilling her breath. Would today be the day she finally opened up?

The faint sound of the oven timer chimed, piercing the moment more effectively than a scream.

Mom stood up. "Right. Dinner. Wrap this up and come on," she said, pointing to Kenzie's homework.

Kenzie slumped. "Right."

Mom stopped at the door. "You'd tell me if you met a shifter or a vampire, or if someone was harassing you, right?"

Kenzie pasted on a smile. "Yeah, mom. Sure."

Mom stood there, searching Kenzie's face. The oven timer wailed on. *It's done! It's done!* came the insistent cry.

Kenzie's phone started ringing, vibrating toward the edge of her nightstand. Kenzie grabbed it, her eyes lighting up as she scanned the screen. Myreen. "Gotta take this."

Mom pursed her lips, but nodded and closed the door.

"Ahhh, I've missed you!" Kenzie squealed into the phone when she picked up.

Myreen laughed. "Missed you more. That's actually why I'm calling. There's going to be a shifter party tomorrow night."

"At the Dome?" Kenzie wasn't sure she should try her luck again so soon.

"No, a were house. We're all headed topside for it. You should so come. We need to catch up."

Kenzie's grin started to fade as she remembered her mom and Oberon and Delphine. "Do you think...? I mean, would it be okay, me not being a student and everything?" *And I'm a selkie, which no one seems to like,* she wanted to say.

Myreen hesitated a moment. "I don't see why it wouldn't be okay. And it's not like we're all going to be walking around in shifter form. I think? Anyway, if anyone asks, just tell them you're new and haven't gotten the hang of shifting yet. The friend I told you about, Juliet, is a phoenix who can't shift, and she's been here a few months."

Kenzie's smile was back, full force. "Ooh, fire." An idea was forming. She jotted down the details as Myreen rattled them off. They said their goodbyes and hung up.

Kenzie checked her closet for something to wear. Jeans and t-shirts—quirky as they were—didn't feel quite right. But she didn't want to wear a dress. And not one thing felt fresh or exciting. What exactly *would* shifters wear? She laughed at herself. *Yeah, like there's some dress code for people who look like animals part-time.* She fingered through her all-too-familiar outfits, then gave up with a sigh. Maybe she'd have time to get a new outfit before the weekend hit. Then again, she didn't want to look like she was trying too hard.

"Kenzie, come on! Dinner!" came Mom's voice from down the hall.

Kenzie sighed. There was one other thing she needed to do before she could officially pose as a phoenix. Fire. The spell was simple enough—and one of the few she knew—but she couldn't remember the word. Something like... "Turn on," she mumbled, though she knew it wasn't right. Fire wasn't one of her usual tricks, not after that incident in first grade. She stuck to unlocking and moving stuff. Moving was especially useful for pranking people, so long as they couldn't see her eyes when she did it. Despite her mother's insistence that she not play with magic, her grandmother had demanded that Kenzie at least know a few spells to defend herself. Still, Kenzie wasn't much of a candle girl, so she didn't have much reason to burn anything.

Kenzie snapped her fingers repeatedly, trying to jar her memory. "Duty? No. Dotty? Unh, uh. Ummmm."

"Kenzie?" Mom called again.

"Just a minute!" Kenzie called back. She could always ask her mom, though she didn't want to raise any suspicions. "Oooh! Dóiche—Ow!" Kenzie shook her hands as the burning sensation dissipated from her fingertips. She was on the right track.

"Food's getting cold!"

Kenzie groaned, her shoulders slumping. "Coming, mom," she grumbled to herself. Maybe it was time for a refresher course.

Kenzie went down the hallway to the dining area, a small table and four chairs nearly filling the space. It was just off a cramped galley kitchen, and opened right into the living room, all decorated in a kitschy-country manner. Mom was sitting at the dining table, chatting away with Gram, who had come from her townhouse next door. They'd bought the pair of units soon after Dad died, so they could both raise Kenzie. And owning two separate places had certain perks—like keeping all shifter business away from Kenzie.

Kenzie plopped into the seat closest to her mom, inhaling the warm, comforting aroma of spaghetti. "Ah, mom, you outdid yourself."

Mom laughed and shook her head. "I make potpie and you don't bat an eye, but throw some noodles in some water?"

"And don't forget the frozen meatballs you cooked in the oven."

"And how's my favorite grandchild?" Gram chimed in. "Not getting into any more trouble, are you?"

"Not me." Kenzie shot her a mock-angelic smile, shoveling some spaghetti in her mouth, the sauce-covered noodles smacking against her chin.

Mom and Gram had been on alert since Myreen's mom died. Not because of the death, but because of the lie Kenzie had told them about thinking a vampire had been following her. It was the best lie Kenzie could come up with, not wanting them to know about Myreen being a shifter and all. And it's not like the police were broadcasting vampire theories in their search for the killer. Mom and Gram had warded up the house like there was an army of vampires after them. Kenzie still wasn't allowed to go out after dark.

Kenzie slurped up her noodles, then grabbed a napkin to wipe her face, while Mom gave her classic *mom face*. "Speaking of trouble..."

"Uh, oh," Mom said, setting down her fork.

"What's the spell for fire again?"

"Dóicheáhn," Gram said, and Kenzie's napkin lit on fire.

Kenzie yelped and threw it at her glass of water, and Mom shook her head. Gram laughed and muttered something else under her breath that extinguished the flame.

"Honestly," Mom said, giving a sidelong glance at Gram. "You could burn the place down."

"No. *She* could burn the place down," Gram said, pointing to Kenzie.

Kenzie shrugged. "Not my fault all you've taught me to do is cause trouble."

"It's all you *need* to know," Mom said, grimacing. "I just hope I raised you to be responsible enough not to abuse those powers."

Kenzie waggled her eyebrows. She spun her fork in the spaghetti, the amusement of the moment waning. She hated that they kept so much from her, hated that they hadn't even *tried* to rebuild what had been lost. But she couldn't say any of that. At least, not this time. She needed to be on her best behavior if she wanted permission to go to the party.

"How's Myreen?" Mom asked.

Kenzie swallowed her water down the wrong pipe and ended up coughing on it. "Good," she croaked out. One more cough did the job, and Kenzie cleared her throat. "Sorry. Yeah, she had to transfer schools, since her mom, you know... So I'm not able to see her as much."

Mom sat back. "Oh, no. Poor girl. I'm sorry, honey. I know you really liked her."

Kenzie half-smiled. "Yeah, but it's not like she's disappeared off the face of the planet. She's actually in Chicago. We'll keep in touch." Mostly true. "And actually, there's this party this weekend, and Myreen invited me."

Mom and Gram looked at each other.

"I don't know, honey. It's so soon." Mom was referring to the vampire thing. Kenzie knew that might be a tough work-around.

"I'll be extra careful. And maaaaybe, you could teach me a spell to protect against any otherworldly beings?" Kenzie batted her eyes.

Mom groaned, but Gram nodded.

"I think she can handle it, don't you?" Gram asked Mom.

Mom shook her head. "I suppose. It's just—"

"I know," Gram said. "The spell is higher level stuff. But it's just this one thing. We can practice tonight and all day tomorrow."

Mom sighed, looking at Kenzie. "Fine. You get the hang of that spell, and I'll let you go to the party." She held up a finger, and Kenzie bit her lip to keep from squealing. "*Only* if you promise me to be home by midnight."

"Aw, Mom. What am I, Cinderella?"

"Promise me."

Kenzie rolled her eyes. "Fine. I promise."

"Good," Gram said, a glint in her eye. "Finish up your dinner and we'll get started."

Juliet

Juliet walked over to the Avian training room that was just down the hall, her nerves building up little by little. And when she saw the door to the training room, instantly her stomach sank. She knew that on the other side of the door was her father, who waited to begin their mandatory one-on-one lesson. She knew he would stand there with the same apologetic look on his face that he'd had since the day he brought her to this school. It made her uncomfortable that she made him so uneasy.

She knew he was sorry for leaving her all those years ago, and she knew how badly he wanted to rekindle a relationship with her, but it just wasn't that easy. Every time she saw the sorrow in his eyes—thanks to learning about how horrendous her mother had been to her—she became angry all over again. And that anger led to the fiery pit that formed in her stomach, warning her that her emotions were about to cause another explosion.

Her perspective changed, though, as she thought of Myreen who had no one. At least Juliet had her father, who could help her through these new changes in her life. She placed her hand on the door and took a deep breath, pushing to reveal her frighteningly large father, who was standing with his back straight and arms crossed.

"Um, hi?" Juliet squeezed around his broad muscles to set her bag down.

"Oberon tells me you have a new friend?" He had a hint of annoyance in his voice as he cut straight to the chase. His pale skin turned a light shade of red. The bright orange color of his hair stood out, which caused Juliet to struggle to hide her smile.

"That's a disappointment? I didn't set anything on fire today, *yay*..." Sarcasm seeped out of her response.

"Do you really think it's smart to bring someone new into your life when you're so... fragile?"

"Fragile?" Juliet felt her temper rise, but reminded herself that she was still lucky to have him. Taking another deep breath, she stood and took her stance in the center of the training room. "Let's just get this over with, please."

Raising her hands and slightly bending her knees, she readied for the impact from her father. Thankfully, her eagerness to begin was enough for him to drop it. For now.

This was slightly more intense than defense class. But she couldn't help but love seeing the pride in his eyes whenever he saw her fight. They started out the lesson with sets of jabs, uppercuts, and hooks. In between were the sit ups, pushups, planks, and rope jumps. And they ended the lesson sparring off against each other.

It was their only common ground, and up until now, it usually began and finished in the same silent manner. He didn't broach the subject of her friendship with Myreen anymore until they were done and dripping with sweat. And even then, he knew not to push her... too much.

"So, you still disagree? A new friend, especially one like her, could be hazardous." He didn't even try to hold back how harsh and judgmental he sounded.

"I *am* the hazard! And what do you mean, *like her*?" If he just let them finish the session silently, her nerves wouldn't be getting so worked up so easily. She felt her hands go clammy and she knew she had to get out of there.

"Honey, you are not a hazard. You just need… practice. And what I mean is, you don't know anything about this girl and what life she had before coming here. Or who she chooses to be her friends outside of this school. I just need you to be more careful with who *you* decide to call your friend."

"Right, because there are so many people lining up for the job." She grabbed her bag and stomped to the exit. Her head spun as she squeezed her fist closed like a toddler about to have a tantrum.

"Juliet, you are not to be seen with her around the school, and that is final." Not once had her mother ever ordered her around this way— not that she even cared.

Seething fury sparked in her bones as she spun around to face him. Juliet felt the fire beginning to make its way out of her body, starting with a warm, sinking feeling in her stomach that flowed through her arms to her fingers. But she didn't care enough to try and stop it from happening.

"You don't get to tell me who I can and can't be friends with," Juliet said, which caused Malachai's nostrils to flare and his eyes to grow round.

He didn't even think to get one of the extinguishers. She could feel the intense heat spreading to every inch of her body. But her hands got the hottest before any other part of her. And with them squeezed into tight fists, she could sense that the heat needed to leave her body.

She opened her hands with a bitter force. The exhilarating heat left her fingertips, setting the pile of training mats ablaze first. The exercise equipment sparked as the fire crawled up its metallic surface. As if in slow motion, the flames turned to wildfire. Juliet stared in awe as she watched the heat dance along her skin, as if it belonged there.

If it weren't for the vile stench of the flaming vinyl from the mats, she would have stayed longer to feel that entrancing warmth. And before her dad could stop her, half of the room was already lit up. She ran out while he scrambled to extinguish the blaze.

With her head spinning, she stumbled through the halls. Her breathing was heavy, and she felt the sweat build up on her forehead. She knew she had to sit down to compose herself.

***

Thankfully, a blazing hot shower was exactly what she needed. Finally at ease, she almost jumped out of her skin when someone knocked on her door.

"Well, you look much more approachable," Myreen teased Juliet as she threw herself on the foot of her bed, playing with the edges of a fringe pillow that was by her hands.

"And you look rather delighted… like you have a secret."

"Oh, you're good. Kol invited me to this were party. It's tonight."

And there go her red cheeks. "Sounds like fun. Are you going?"

Juliet couldn't help but feel a slight pang of jealousy. She'd been at the school a little longer than Myreen, and not once had anyone ever invited her to anything, let alone a legendary were party. She always heard the stories of the epic party games, and there was a rumor that their houses were massive.

"I'd like to, but I'd like it even more if you came with me."

Juliet stared at her with unblinking eyes.

"So, is that a no?" Myreen's eyes fell to her hands, and Juliet felt her heart swell—whether with excitement or nervousness, she wasn't sure.

"I'll go."

Myreen's eyes lit up.

"Is Nik going too?" Juliet blurted out. Myreen's bright blue eyes practically bulged out of her head as she nodded enthusiastically.

Juliet ran over to her closet and began throwing different outfits on the bed. "What am I going to wear? What are *you* going to wear?"

Suddenly Myreen cursed under her breath. "I don't have anything. I didn't have time to pack any of my old things before coming here."

"I didn't either. My dad gave me his card for emergency situations, so I go out every now and then. There's a sale at this cool store I found. And this sounds like an emergency to me. Wanna go shopping? Or you could borrow something of mine."

"Well, you do have cute stuff. But… it's all black. It's not really my color." Myreen teased Juliet as she fussed with the messy pile of clothes.

"Shopping it is. We can grab some dinner before the party, so we don't have to come back here. Let's go before my dad sees us leaving."

Ironically, her dad was still busy cleaning up the fire mess that she left him with, so he wasn't at his usual post checking to see who entered or left the Dome. She felt a slight pang of guilt that made her stomach clench, but quickly remembered how upset he made her.

Although, she knew she was going to hear the wrath of the terrifying Malachai Quinn when they returned.

Juliet was excited to show Myreen the cute hole-in-the-wall store that she stumbled upon, but she wasn't sure what kind of style Myreen liked. She'd only seen her in her uniform. And at that place, all the clothes looked like they belonged in a hipster's closet. The skeptical look on Myreen's face said that wasn't quite up her alley.

There was an entire section dedicated to the color black, and while

Juliet spent most of her time there, Myreen floated around the brighter side of the store. After they tried on a few pieces—Myreen finding something she liked—Juliet paid for their new clothes and searched for a place to eat.

With hands full of shopping bags, they found a pizzeria close by. During dinner, Juliet couldn't hold back the question any longer.

"So... did Kol invite you there as his friend, or as his date?" She wiggled her eyebrows comically, causing Myreen to practically choke on her pizza.

"He asked if I would go with him. But I don't know how he meant it, J." Myreen played with the straw in her drink.

"Don't look at me. I don't speak 'guy'. But if you want my observations... both Kol and Kendall have the hots for you."

"I'm not even sure what I want him to mean. But Kenzie would know exactly what he meant. She's meeting us at the party—we'll have to ask her. I'm so excited for you two to meet."

"Another friend, awesome!" Juliet said with nervous excitement. Introductions always made her feel awkward and tense.

Juliet wondered if this was the friend her father mentioned before she blew up on him. Regardless, she wasn't in any position to turn down anyone who actually wanted to be her friend. She would give Kenzie the fair chance she deserved.

Finishing their dinner, they hurried to the bathroom to change into one of their new outfits. Once in her cute, short, and of course *black* overalls, Juliet waited outside of Myreen's stall.

"So, Nik, huh?"

It was a simple, yet loaded, question. Clearing her throat, Juliet felt her heart rate pick up.

"He's... nice." It was all she could say, but even Myreen chuckled at the obvious simplicity.

"And hot." They both laughed.

Myreen stepped out of her stall in an aquamarine, short-sleeved dress that made her eyes sparkle. Juliet whistled her approval as Myreen shyly did a twirl.

"Now *that* is definitely going to get you the attention you want from Kol. Or Kendall," she teased while applying a little make up to her eyes and lips. Only, Myreen took the gloss away from her and replaced it with a dark burgundy red that Juliet would never be brave enough to wear on her own.

"Put it on. Trust me. Nik won't be able to pull himself away from you."

Giddy, Juliet spread the lipstick on her lips. She was ready to go to her first ever school party. Her first ever *shifter* party.

The walk back to the subway entrance to meet Kol, Nik, and Brett was faster than her nerves could take.

And the guys looked even more handsome outside of the Dome walls. Each of their styles were different and their own.

But Nik was who had Juliet's attention.

There were fresh spirals shaved into the side of his head that were almost hypnotizing to look at. He wore a light blue, button-down shirt with the sleeves rolled up to his elbows. Her heart fluttered.

Myreen looked just as flustered. The girls awkwardly waved. Juliet was too aware of how Kol kept stealing side glances at Myreen to see if Nik noticed her. The cab van got there seconds later.

"Shotgun!" Brett called. Kol tapped the seat next to him for Myreen, leaving Juliet to apprehensively sit by Nik. Brett turned the music up so loud that they couldn't hear each other, so they sat silently, bopping along to the music.

Thankfully, the were's house was close by. She knew they had almost arrived when the houses began to grow in size. When they pulled up to the lakefront mansion, she could hear the music blaring from outside. The large all-white pillars were crowded with students she wasn't so thrilled to see. She vowed to herself that she would leave at the first sign of teasing.

Juliet didn't know which was more nerve-wracking—being in such close proximity with Nik or walking into this party known as the kleptomaniac who couldn't keep her emotions in check. With not much time to obsess over the embarrassing details, Juliet followed behind Myreen towards the side of the mansion. A girl their age that she'd never seen before waited alone by one of the enormous pillars. Juliet knew it was Kenzie just by the way Myreen ran to her.

Immediately, Myreen and Kenzie embraced each other with the tightest of hugs. The guys stood a foot away in their own conversation. When Kenzie pulled away to get a better look at her friend, she looked Myreen up and down. "Dang, girl. You must be a phoenix, because you're on fire!"

"Kenz this is Juliet. Juliet, Kenzie."

Juliet extended her hand, but Kenzie pulled her in for her own hug. Instantly, Juliet liked her. *Who cares what dad thought?*

"Thanks for being there for Myreen. It's nice to know she has a friend at the school." Kenzie's smile was so big that it was contagious.

"No problem. She's there for me, too. You should have seen her stand up to Trish on my behalf. The worst mer-bully of them all." Juliet gently shoved her elbow into Myreen's.

"That's my girl. Tough as nails." Kenzie put her hands in the back pockets of her jeans, rocking back on her heels. "So, anyone know what happens at a shifter party?"

And as they both shrugged their shoulders, Kenzie could only shake her head. Standing in between Myreen and Juliet, she hooked her arms with theirs and straightened her back.

"Three misfit-teers. What better way to make an entrance?" Kenzie led them inside with the confidence of an Emmy-winning actress, the boys trailing them inside. Juliet tried to absorb some of that swagger for herself and swore she wouldn't let anything happen to make her clumsy reputation worse.

Especially not a fire.

Myreen

"This is the best. Night. Ever!"

Kenzie was practically bouncing to the pumping music as the two of them went to the counter to grab their cups. But the smile on her face and the spring in her step had more to do with the good vibes she was getting from the crowd than the beat. Kenzie had spent the previous hour mingling, performing interesting fire tricks and telling jokes that had everyone roaring with laughter. She was the life of the party. Myreen's plan was working out perfectly so far.

Well, one of her plans at least.

She had no idea where Juliet had gotten off to, and she wondered if she should go find her.

But when Kol had invited her to this party, she hoped it would be a turning point in their hot-and-cold relationship. He had seemed almost desperate for her to come with him tonight. It had been really cute, actually. But now that they were here, he had been treating her like a cootie-covered kid sister he was forced to drag around with him. He was polite enough to keep her drink full, like a gentleman, but he rejected every opportunity for them to get close.

Myreen took a swig from her red plastic cup as Kenzie skipped back to her adoring public. Kol was standing against the wall, looking all dark and sulky in his perfectly fitting jeans and just-snug-enough black t-shirt. *Smoking hot.* After seeing his fight with Oberon yesterday, that was the phrase that would now always come to mind whenever she saw him. Why did he have to be so appealing and yet so distant?

Maybe she just wasn't being obvious enough. She needed to take a note from Kenzie's playbook and go for what she wanted, lest she end up like poor Juliet, pining silently over a guy who might never know how she felt about him.

Putting her concern for Juliet on the back-burner for a moment, she sauntered up to him, swaying her hips in time with the hip-hop beat, and took his hands. "Dance with me," she invited as enticingly as she knew how.

"Oh no, I don't dance," he objected, shaking his head and pulling his hands back.

"Sure you do," Myreen said, tugging him gently, playfully toward the dance floor. "Come on, I'll teach you."

"Seriously, Myreen, I'm not the dancing type," he said, removing his hands from her grasp.

His rejection burned. It was as if one of those fireballs had found its way right to her chest. *That's what I get for being interested in a dragon, I guess.*

"Not a very noble thing to do, Dracul," Kendall said as he appeared at her side. "Refusing a lady's invitation to dance. I, for one, would be honored if you would dance with me."

Kendall's handsome smile and unabashed attention was like cool water over her singed ego.

"Yeah, let's dance," she said, looking at Kol as she spoke. She let Kendall take her hand and guide her to the middle of the living room where people were dancing. They fell into step with those around them.

"What are you doing with the *Prince* anyway?" Kendall asked as he swerved around her.

"The Prince?" What was he talking about?

Kendall nodded his chin in Kol's direction, a look of disdain on his face. "All the girls at this school fawn over him because he's descended from dragon royalty. Never mind if he's a different species from them. I thought you were different."

Myreen frowned at that and jerked her head. "I had no idea Kol was royalty. And I wasn't fawning over him. He invited me to this party. We're… friends, I guess."

"Ha! No girl is *friends* with Kol Dracul," Kendall snorted. "I wouldn't say he's a player, exactly, but he's burned more than one girl at this school."

Her heart fell. Had she been all wrong about Kol? She didn't know what to feel or how to proceed.

"And what about you?" she asked, eager to take the subject off Kol, to forget about him for a moment. "I've heard that you and Alessandra have a thing."

"*Had* is the correct word," Kendall said. "Trust me, that whole nightmare is one-hundred percent over. I kinda have my eyes on someone new." He winked at her, and her crestfallen heart fluttered, like a butterfly getting back up after a harsh wind had knocked it to the ground.

She liked Kendall. She could picture herself ending up with him. He was funny and sweet, and he had abs that could cut diamonds. And yet, as she twirled and swiveled around him with every sexy trick in her dance book, she knew that she wasn't dancing for Kendall but for Kol, trying to make him jealous. She knew he was watching. She could feel his hot gaze on her, like the heat of an old light bulb, and it was getting more and more heated with every twist of her hips.

After a while, her body gave in to the dance, and the music took over. Now she was dancing just for the sheer joy of it. Music was always her escape, and tonight, it whisked her away from her conflicted feelings over Kol.

"Ready for a drink?" Kendall asked when one of the songs ended.

Myreen nodded, and they went to the kitchen to scrounge for something—preferably non-alcoholic. Now that she knew she was a mermaid, she was much more aware of the fact that she needed to drink three times as much water as a normal person, and it really showed when she exerted herself.

Kendall found some bottles of water in one of the many ice chests and tossed one to her. They both unscrewed the tops and chugged down the chilled liquid.

"So, I know you're having some trouble fitting in with the other mermaids," Kendall said as he tossed his empty bottle in the trash. "Most of that is from Trish just being nasty. But if they got to know you, they'd see that you really are one of us. You've just been missing."

His words sparked a desire in her that was as old as time—to fit in. In all honesty, she had never put in too much effort before. With every new school, she knew it would be just a matter of time before she had to leave again and forfeit any progress. But this was different. Her mom wasn't going to uproot her life and drag her somewhere else. This school was where she was going to stay for a long time, and she had no one. Fitting in was absolutely imperative, otherwise she didn't know how long she'd survive. Befriending dragons and phoenixes was nice, but why shouldn't she want to be liked and welcomed by her own kind, too?

"I would really love that," she said, screwing the cap back onto her bottle. "But I can't even get them to acknowledge I exist. How can I show them who I am?"

"Because I'm going to help you," he said with a smile. He held out his hand. "Let's go reintroduce you to some merpeople."

With a giddy bubble in her stomach, she took his hand and practically skipped after him toward a group of mermaids that were currently laughing at one of Kenzie's jokes.

"Lenore, Trevor, Helena," Kendall greeted the trio as they approached, and he and Trevor fist-bumped. "You might have seen her shyly gracing the halls of our common room, but I don't think any of you have formally met Myreen."

Their smiles slowly fell as they took her in, and looked down their noses at her.

"Come on, guys, she's a mermaid, just like the rest of us," he said.

The girl with the bob-cut dark brown hair shot him a narrowed glance. "She's an outsider," she whispered to him, not-so-quietly.

"Lenore, just because she didn't grow up in our tribe doesn't mean she doesn't belong in it," Kendall argued, putting his arm around Lenore's shoulders. "All our ancestors were once outsiders to each other, but they learned to come together for the sake of the species. Honor their memory by doing the same."

"But Trish said—" the curly-headed blond, who must be Helena, started to say.

"Screw Trish!" Kendall cut her off. "Why the heck would you believe a word Trish says, anyway? You remember that nasty rumor she spread about you two summers ago."

Helena looked down and shrunk with shame. Myreen wondered what the rumor had been, and more to the point, what rumors Trish was spreading about her.

"You brought Kenzie, didn't you?" Trevor asked, tipping his cup toward Kenzie who was doing something with fire.

Wait, what? But Myreen didn't take too long to see exactly what party tricks Kenzie was performing. She didn't want to snub these three in any way. So she nodded.

Trevor shrugged. "Well, mermaid or not, Kenzie's pretty cool, so anyone who's friends with her must be cool, too."

Myreen felt a smile spreading across her lips.

"And by the way, I never believed a word Trish said," he intimated with a smile.

"Alright," Lenore said. "I guess we can give this stray a chance."

"You can start by calling her by her real name," Kendall said.

"Oh, right," she said with a fake smile. "Myreen, right?"

Myreen nodded.

"Why did your parents give you a Mer name?" Helena asked.

"What?" Myreen was totally stumped.

"Your name. It's a Mer name. Mermaids don't use the old language much anymore, especially not for names. When we surfaced, we started using colloquial names. I just think it's weird that you have a Mer name." Helena looked slightly irritated as she explained, like Myreen was stupid for not knowing any of this.

She always knew that her name was weird, but even after coming to this school, she never imagined it was from another language, much less the language of her people. She didn't even know they *had* their own language, although it made sense that they would.

"Sorry, but what does it mean in… Mer?" she asked. She didn't want to seem as ignorant as they already thought she was, but she really wanted to know. She *needed* to know.

"Treasure," Helena answered, rolling her eyes, and Lenore giggled. "Honestly, with a pretentious name like that, can you blame any of us for hating you just a little bit?"

Myreen knew that this was Helena's attempt at a joke, but Myreen couldn't laugh with them. For all the ways her mom had kept the shifter world from her, she had blessed her with the most precious thing of all—a Mer name. And not just any Mer name, but one that really meant something.

Tears welled up in her eyes, but she refused to let the mermaid girls see her cry.

"Would you all excuse me for a minute?" she was able to say with a stable voice before turning around and rushing to the backyard.

Her vision was blurry as she stepped onto the back porch, but she could see that anyone who was outside was preoccupied—apparently this was the make out section of the party. At least none of them would witness her struggle not to fall apart. She didn't want to be known as the emo chick who cries at parties.

"Myreen?" Kendall's shadow fell over her from the open kitchen door. "Are you alright? Don't mind Lenore and Helena, they can be a bit catty sometimes."

"No, it's not that." She shook her head and rolled her eyes up in an attempt to pull the tears back in.

Kendall came around to face her, his brows pinched. "Then what is it?" His full focus was trained on her, like he genuinely cared.

"You wouldn't understand," she said, her breathing tripping over itself.

"Try me," he said, and he put a hand softly on her shoulder.

She inhaled deeply to try to stabilize her breathing.

"I knew nothing of mermaids before I came to this school a few days ago. My mom had hidden it from me my whole life. The night Oberon brought me here, he rescued me just after vampires killed my mom. So now I'm learning all these amazing and terrifying things about myself, and I can't even ask her about any of it. And to know that she named me a Mer word… I don't know anything about who she really was, and now she's gone, and I'll never get to hear her side…"

She tried so hard to keep the tears at bay, to lock her emotions deep inside, but they spilled over the mental dam she had built and forced their way out the only way they knew how. Miniature rivers poured down her face, and all she could feel in that moment was the crippling regret surrounding her mother.

Kendall's other hand landed on her other shoulder, his thumbs gently kneading into them. "I'm so sorry. I had no idea. You're right, I don't understand. I don't understand why a mermaid would keep their child from finding their tail. It seems almost cruel."

Myreen cried even harder, her shoulder rocking under Kendall's hands.

"Oh, I'm sorry! I didn't mean to imply... I just meant... I can't imagine what you're going through, but I'll do everything in my power to make this transition easier for you. I promise. I'll tutor you myself every day if that's what it takes."

She nodded, unable to actually say thanks just yet.

Suddenly, Kendall's hand was wrenched off her shoulder, and strong hands pushed Kendall backward.

"What did you do to her?" Kol barked, clenching his fists as he closed in on Kendall.

"What are you talking about?" Kendall rebuked, smoothing his hands down his shirt.

"She's crying!" Kol snapped. "What did he do to you?" he asked, turning on Myreen.

"Wh– uh," she stammered.

"I didn't do anything to her," Kendall said. "And what do you care, anyway? You brought her here and then practically pretended she didn't exist."

"That's no concern of yours." Kol's jaw stiffened as he turned glowing blue eyes back on Kendall.

Myreen had only seen shifters' eyes glow when they were about to use their powers, and that realization made her heart jump in her chest. As much as the teenage girl part of her was silently reveling in the fact that Kol at least believed he was coming to her rescue, she didn't want to see either of these boys hurt each other, especially not over her.

"Kol it's fine, really." She put her hands on his chest, keenly watching his eyes in hopes that the glow would fade away. "I was just having a moment about my mom and Kendall was talking me through it."

Looking frightening as he towered at least half a foot over her, he looked down at her, his calculating eyes scanning over her, she assumed for marks of abuse. When he found none, the tension slowly eased all over his body, and the glow dissipated, leaving only those warm amber eyes that were finally giving her their full focus. "So, he didn't... hurt you?"

She shook her head, very relieved.

"What right do you think you have accusing *me* of hurting a girl?" Kendall asked, stalking toward Kol.

Maybe she hadn't prevented the fight after all.

"I'm not the one who breaks their hearts," Kendall continued. "Who makes out with them behind the greenhouses then never calls them again. Trish is the hardest girl I know, and yet she cried for days after you used her."

Myreen gasped. *Kol made out with Trish?* Her stomach twisted with disgust, and she thought she was about to be sick.

"Shut up!" Kol yelled, his pride clearly wounded.

"Why don't you dragons just stay away from our mermaids," Kendall said, puffing up like a blowfish.

The two guys were practically chest-to-chest, and Myreen needed to find some way to stop this from escalating. She slipped between them and put a hand on both of their chests to push them away from each other. But as her vision passed through the open back door, she caught a glimpse of Trish and her squad circling Kenzie, whose hands were balled into fists, her chin jutting stubbornly forward.

"Oh no, this can't be good," Myreen whispered. She pushed past the two testosterone-filled guys and rushed to the aid of her friend.

"I knew there was something off about you as soon as I saw you walk in with that bottom-feeder," Myreen heard Trish saying as she came into the living room. "You're no phoenix. You're a *magic user.*" Trish said the pair of words like they left a bad taste in her mouth.

"Actually, I'm a selkie," Kenzie said, standing up tall.

Trish laughed. "That's even worse! You're a wannabe shifter. How pathetic!"

"What's your problem, Trish?" Myreen stomped into their circle to stand beside Kenzie. "Why do you have to try so hard to tear everyone else down? Do you really think it makes you look better?"

Trish narrowed her eyes on Myreen. "I *am* better. I'm Mer nobility, not that you would know anything about that."

"Big freakin' deal!" Myreen snapped. "You think the status of your blood gives you the right to treat others like crap? Well, you're wrong." Myreen climbed onto the couch and stood on it so that everyone at the party could see her. "Kenzie may not be a shifter by conventional means, but she has just as much right to study her craft as we do. I think she belongs at our school. Every single one of you enjoyed her company tonight. Clearly she fits into our world. If we rally together, I'm sure we can get her accepted into the Dome."

While a scattered few were nodding their heads, most of the partiers were averting their eyes—or rolling them. Kenzie was looking at them all, probably tallying the response, her jaw twitching, the hope draining out of her eyes.

Helena stepped forward. "Magic users can't be trusted, least of all selkies."

"You told us you were a phoenix," Lenore added, staring daggers at Kenzie. "You lied to everyone."

"I never said I was a phoenix," Kenzie said, crossing her arms.

"Someone assumed. I didn't correct them."

"But you let us believe it, and omission is the same as a lie," Helena said.

"Mark my words, seal-killer, you will *never* be a student at the Dome," Trish hissed, looking more naga than mermaid. Then she turned her venomous gaze on Myreen. "And you're a traitor for just being with her, but telling her about the Dome? Our kind's most protected secret? Some mermaid you are."

The mermaids all glared at Myreen.

"You will never be one of us," Lenore said, hammering the final nail in her outsider coffin.

The sting of rejection on such a large scale was almost more than she could bear, but her failure on Kenzie's part hurt even more. She stepped down off the couch and looked at Kenzie.

"Kenz…" Myreen began, unsure of what else to say.

"This was a mistake." Kenzie shook her head, her fingers running through her hair. "I shouldn't have come here tonight." Then she turned around and rushed to the front door.

Myreen ran after her, grabbing her arm as they came outside. "This isn't the end."

"No," Kenzie stopped her, looking down at the ground. "I don't belong here, and nobody in my world will teach me anything. Maybe I'm just not meant for this. Maybe I'm not meant for anything."

Myreen had never seen Kenzie so down. Kenzie had a never-say-die attitude, a fire inside of her that couldn't be put out. But tonight, that fire's light was barely visible. And Myreen knew she was at fault. How had this night gone so horribly wrong?

"Kenz, you can't believe that," Myreen said.

"Sorry. I'm going home," Kenzie said with finality. "I'll talk to you later." Then she pulled her arm out of Myreen's gentle hold and walked off into the night.

That's just great, Myreen. In one night, not only did she pit her only two guy friends against each other, but she humiliated her best friend and completely alienated herself from the mermaids. How was she possibly going to fix any of this?

Kol

"Why don't you dragons just stay away from our mermaids," Kendall said, jutting his chest out.

When Myreen suddenly disappeared into the house, Kol poked a finger into Kendall's ribs, which were still invading his space. "And who are *you* to tell *me* what to do?" Kol lowered his voice.

He saw the slightest flicker of fear in the mer's eyes, but it disappeared as quickly as it appeared, replaced by a smirk. "What? You think because you come from the *famous* Dracul line that you can do whatever you want?"

Kol bared his teeth and resisted the urge to flick this moron on the head.

"I've got news for you, bro," Kendall backed up with his hands in the air, as if addressing the people who were gawking at them, although his eyes remained on Kol. When did they get an audience? "I'm royalty, too."

Kol tossed his head at the group of onlookers in a way that made them jump and scatter in different directions.

"Not only that, but I'm a *Mer*," Kendall emphasized.

Kol didn't miss the way Kendall's misdirection of addressing the crowd covered his cowardly retreat. But he didn't mention it.

"Like Myreen," Kendall continued. "And our kind stick together. So if you think you have even the tiniest chance with that girl—"

"It's not like that," Kol interrupted. "But why *her*? Weren't you dating that... what's her name... *Alexandra* or whoever... who looks *just* like Myreen?"

"*Alessandra*," Kendall corrected. "But that doesn't matter. Alessandra and I mutually broke up, and yes, now I'm interested in Myreen."

"And how's she gonna feel when she finds out she looks the same as your old girlfriend?" Kol crossed his arms over his chest in triumph.

"I hope she's flattered. Since I upgraded and all."

There was something about that blue tail that made Kol want to punch him in the teeth.

"So, to make myself clear," Kendall said, approaching Kol again. "Dragon royalty may come with its perks. I suspect you can get *almost* any girl you want. Dragon. Phoenix. Probably even Naga or a Kitsune." Kendall waved a hand before getting back in Kol's face. "But Dragon royalty means nothing to a *Mer*. So. Back. Off."

***

Kol shrugged off the *Ken-Doll* incident. His knuckles barely connected with the fish's jaw. No big deal.

Or at least Kol tried to shrug it off. He'd made it a point to keep his distance from the mer-guy since he'd first laid eyes on the elitist—or *his majesty*—but the guy seemed to lean more to the extreme in his arrogance and entitlement than some of the other merfolk. And it wasn't like him to resort to violence, but Kendall asked for it.

Kol had barely registered the guy's existence until Myreen's appearance and Kendall's sudden interest in her. And it was annoying that his interest interfered with Kol's task of befriending her. Part of him wanted to find a way to end their connection.

But who was he to dictate who Myreen chose to spend her time with?

Even if he was a vamp-sized moron.

Kol located Nik and Brett in the living room and with a nod ushered them into the game room. It was clearly the *it* place to be, and though Kol usually avoided being the center of the party because everyone expected him to, he decided to take his place in the role for once.

At least Kendall wasn't there. Probably off licking his wounds.

Jackson, the were whose house they'd invaded, handed Kol a cue stick—without prompting—and reset the pool table, though it looked like they hadn't finished their game. Two other guys who'd been playing handed their cues to Nik and Brett, and though Nik waved a hand to decline, the ursa insisted that he was finished playing anyway, then leaned against the wall instead of leaving.

Kol hated when he, and his friends by default, were treated this way, but decided to ignore it and lined up the purple-chalked end of his stick to break.

The room was quiet at first, but when the observers settled in to the fact that *Kol Dracul* and his friends weren't playing the *royals and their friends only club*—which wasn't a thing, Kol just didn't like the attention or the effort it took to socialize with others outside of his little circle—the chatter picked up again, with side conversations and the occasional tip about the best way to get the ball in a pocket.

It was obvious by the way they weren't whispering or giving

sideways glances that none of them had heard about the incident out back.

"What happened out there?" Nik asked in a low voice when it was obvious that most of the observers were focused on their own conversations.

Kol shrugged, then smacked the cue ball, knocking the three into the side pocket.

"Yeah, didn't you ask the new girl to come with you?" Brett asked. His volume wasn't as subtle and a few of the girls in the corner stopped their conversation to eavesdrop.

"I was just trying to be nice," Kol said, realizing that maybe they didn't know about everything that went down. "And her name is Myreen."

"But she was dancing with that *Ken Barbie* kid," Brett said, right as Nik missed his shot.

Brett walked around to line up his stick, aiming to get the nine-ball into the corner pocket nearest Kol.

"His name is Kendall," Nik corrected. "And Kol didn't ask Myreen to come as a *date*. Like he said, he was just being nice."

Brett made his shot and leaned against the table.

"Thank you, Nik," Kol said, keeping the girls in the corner in his peripheral. One had her hand cupped to the other's ear and whispered something.

Time to end this conversation.

"Loser buys chili fries at Mack's before we head back to the Dome," Kol said after the four-ball practically cracked the wood of the table before dropping into the pocket.

Nik nodded. Defeated. "Fine."

"Deal," Brett said.

Kol felt bad for doing that to Nik—he wasn't as practiced in the game as the dragons were—but he had to change subjects.

"Hey," a familiar voice said from behind. Myreen's voice. He'd been so busy changing the subject away from the topic of *her*, he hadn't seen her approach. "Can I talk to you for a sec?"

Kol looked at Nik and Brett who lifted their shoulders in unison. But Kol didn't miss the wink from Brett before turning back to her.

"Me?" Kol stupidly asked.

Myreen raised an *are-you-serious?* eyebrow.

Nik let out an irritated sigh.

Brett cough-laughed, that sounded something like, *he's in trouble!* Or *she's trouble!* Kol wasn't exactly sure which.

He wasn't in the mood to get into whatever it was she wanted to talk about, so he waved a hand to indicate he was in the middle of something. He knew it was a jerk move, but did it anyway.

"I can wait," she said, leaning against the wall.

Nik and Brett suddenly became traitors and excused themselves before Kol could make some lame-ass excuse. Chili cheese fries apparently weren't enough.

"You're both buying!" he shouted at them as they melted back into the crowd in the living room.

And when did the rest of the room clear out? He thought at least the girls in the corner would stick around for some gossip fodder.

"Whatdoyawant?" Kol half-mumbled, leaning against the opposite wall with his arms crossed.

Now that his friends were gone, her annoyed wall fell. Slightly. Not completely. She still looked furious, her mouth pinched tight and the lines creasing her forehead. Gathering all her hair, she twisted it into a bun, then pushed away from the wall and, with her free hand, tossed the eight ball at the cluster of balls at the opposite end of the table.

Does she know? he wondered. Did the snitch go crying to her about the mean dragon who punched him in the face?

"I wanna know what that was about," she said, releasing her hair so it fell in waves of black and blue around her shoulders. She mimicked his stance with her arms crossed and looked him dead in the eye.

With those penetrating blue eyes.

Kol averted his gaze and pushed away from the wall, uncrossing his arms. "What are you talking about?"

She threw her hands in the air and let out an exasperated breath. "With Kendall!" she nearly shouted. "First you're angry at the way he helped me in defense… like it's any of your business."

Kol laughed once. This he could handle. He looked back at her. "Kendall just isn't the best person to be teaching a newbie defense." He laughed once.

She glared at him.

He shrugged it off and rolled his shoulders back.

"And then tonight," she said. "I can handle myself, Kol."

His discomfort grew again. Remembering the way she had cried on the back porch caused a sinking feeling to drop in his stomach like a rock. He was so certain that Kendall… He closed his eyes to banish the memory. He knew what sort of things happened on the back porch. This wasn't Jackson's first party.

He banished that memory, too.

"Look, whatever," he said holding his hands up in surrender. "I guess I was wrong to interfere." He wanted the conversation to end before the part about his fist messing up Kendall's orthodontic work was brought up, so he moved past her, through the living room and out the front door.

"Yeah, I know you invited me to come with you," she said, trailing behind.

"Why are you following me?" he asked. And that was a strange thing for her to say at that moment.

"Because I'm not done talking to you!" She jerked his arm, forcing him to stop and turn to look at her. Her face was lit by the nearby streetlight with an eerie yellowish glow. It made her sky blue eyes colorless, and the way the shadows played on her features, sharpened the edges. She was... *nope*. He wouldn't allow himself to even entertain the thought about how beautiful she was or how it was affecting him.

He kept his expression stoic as he looked over her shoulder at the shadows of the trees behind her. "Then talk," he said, his voice low.

"You may have invited me to come with you," she said, her tone matching his, cool and calm. "But you are not my boyfriend."

His eyes snapped to hers. "Did you think—?"

She held up a hand, stopping him. "You didn't seem to mind when Kendall asked me to dance." She said it with one of those *so there!* looks girls—specifically mermaids—seemed to have perfected. *Myreen's fitting right in.*

"You're right," he said, smirking, proving that he absolutely had no problem with it. "I didn't. You can dance with whomever you wish."

"Kendall was comforting me," she said. "You didn't need to come barging in. You're not my boyfriend."

Kol tried to think up another retort. Another comeback, but he was at a loss. *You're right*, he wanted to say but didn't. *I'm not your boyfriend.* Like she felt the need to say. Twice. It was something that could never happen. He wanted to convey that to her somehow, for both of their sakes.

But then he realized that she might not even think of him in that way, and he remained quiet.

With a triumphant look, Myreen then said, "Goodnight." She left him, heading back to the party.

What was I thinking? He lamented, stomping a few steps to kick the edge of a trash can. She was correct. He had no right intervening in that girl's business. He wasn't her boyfriend, nor would he ever be, thanks to the stupid Dracul curse. He'd already decided that long before all the stuff with *Ken-doll* happened. In fact, he'd decided that about every girl.

No girlfriends. It was just as well.

Even if suddenly, for the first time, he worried that he might actually want to.

But he couldn't. Not now. Not ever. Not as long as the Dracul curse was still in effect. He couldn't allow himself to fall for anyone or allow anyone to fall for him.

It was the reason he planned to join the military with his father as soon as he graduated, because he could never do to someone what his father did to his mother every single day.

Over a hundred years ago, a Dracul named Aline or Elana did something to piss off a vampire, or a group of selkies—the exact reason had been lost over the generations—but a selkie had cast a spell on her and the entire Dracul line and anyone connected to it by marriage, that they would be cursed with unrequited love.

Therefore, his mother loved his father deeply. But was unrequited.

But Eduard hadn't come out unscathed, either, because he clearly loved Adam and Alex's mother without the feelings returned. It was probably the reason she'd never asked Eduard to leave Victoria.

The Draculs were forced to have arranged marriages to keep the line from dying out. But anyone who agreed to the marriage knew the risk of the inevitable tragedy that would occur if one spouse fell for the other. And it almost always happened, since no Dracul had discovered a single clue about how to break it.

So… no girlfriends.

He hated to admit it, but Myreen dating that jerk of a mer-guy was exactly what was best. If she was dating someone else, it would be that much easier to keep his *friendship* strictly business. It would be easier to stay on task and get the information his father wanted without… complications.

But man, Myreen was certainly a tenacious one. He didn't expect her to come at him like that and put him in his place. Kendall hadn't done anything wrong. *Besides existing.* He hadn't done anything Kol had done himself—flirting with a girl.

Kol just hadn't expected it. Though he'd never tried, Kol was certain he could steal the attention of any girl away from the attention-seeking *pseudo* royal. But Myreen didn't fawn over Kol, all doe-eyed and star-struck, like he was some kind of untouchable celebrity, the way some of the other girls did, either.

Granted, she probably had no idea who he was in the shifter community. But he suspected when she did find out, she wouldn't act any differently.

He respected her for that.

And it terrified him.

Leif

Leif took the tip of his straw between his thumb and index finger and spun the cup of ice water until a tiny vortex formed in the middle. The cubes circled around and around, following the current of water he'd created. His eyes followed the rotation until the ice clinked together and came to a stop, then he started it again.

Running his other hand through his jet-black hair, he sighed heavily. Leif remembered a time when water quenched his thirst. That had been over a hundred years ago.

Since then, there was only one liquid that could satisfy his thirst. And there were several humans sitting in the restaurant with him that could provide him with that liquid.

Blood.

Leif hated that it was the only way to hold his animalistic urges back. Fortunately, before leaving his home, he'd drained several blood bags he'd stolen from a nearby hospital. Sure, he could sense the blood flowing in the veins of the humans around him, but the urge to drink at this particular moment was hardly noticeable.

The late afternoon sun streamed into the windows of the corner restaurant he was sitting in, and although Leif still preferred the darkness, he was the only known vampire who could survive in daylight.

A young waitress with braided auburn hair walked up to his table.

"Sir, you've been here for over a half hour now," she said sweetly, holding a pot of coffee with steam sizzling out of the spout. "Are you sure there's nothing else I can bring for you while you wait for your friend?"

Friend. Leif bounced the word around in his head. Was Oberon a friend? Sure, they were on friendly terms. But their relationship was strictly business. Leif had a lot of baggage when it came to shifters, and he knew for a fact that Oberon had major hang-ups with vampires.

He glanced at the waitress's name tag. "No thanks, Vicky. I'm actually not hungry at all."

Swishing the pot of coffee, she said, "Coffee?"

Her persistence bothered him, and he breathed deeply to keep his emotions in check. Feigning a smile, he said, "I'm fine, really. Hot drinks and I don't mix well." He actually preferred his blood bags to be refrigerated.

She threw a thumb behind her. "We've got cold drinks, too. Sodas, fresh-squeezed lemonade…"

"I'll stop you there, Vicky," he said, his tone becoming darker. "I just… really don't need anything right now, okay?"

The waitress stood there looking at him as if he'd slapped her across the face.

"Well, forgive my service," she said, her own emotions showing just how off-kilter he'd set her. "This is a restaurant, you know?"

Leif nodded. "A fine establishment, to be sure. Check back when my *friend* arrives. He might want something."

Vicky gave a quiet *hmph* as she moved on to another table a few feet away.

I just hate *public places,* he thought, putting a finger on top of the straw and creating a seal. Pulling it up and out of the water, he removed his finger and watched the stream fall out of the bottom and back into the water.

With the fingertips of his other hand, he tip-tapped the rhythm of Beethoven's *Andante Favori*, remembering the fingering with ease. For a century, Leif had gone from being an inept tinkerer to a master pianist.

The bell attached to the door's crash bar handle jingled, stopping the song Leif was imagining he was playing and drawing his attention to the newcomer.

"Finally," he mumbled, watching as Vicky approached Oberon. The man's brown hair was untidy, the remnants of a part just able to be seen.

During their short conversation, Vicky glanced Leif's way with annoyance, then pointed at him.

Leif heard Oberon say, "Thank you," then he left the waitress and headed for the table.

As the man sat down, he said, "I see you still have a personal touch with people, Leif."

Leif snorted. "I see you still have a way of being late to everything."

"It's not as if I could just fly right into downtown Chicago without being marked."

"True," Leif conceded, then dropped his voice to a whisper. "But it's not as if I could order human food and pretend to enjoy it. I've been bugged five times, Oberon. Five times by different waiters and waitresses."

"It was a long day at the school," replied Oberon. "It's been a series of long days, actually."

Vicky approached with her steaming pot of coffee. She glared momentarily at Leif. He pretended like she wasn't standing there.

"Here you go sir," she said. Oberon quickly slid over the mug that was preset on the table and she poured the dark-brown coffee in. "I brought cream and sugar. Use as much as you like."

Leif risked a sideways glance and found her looking at him. "As for you…"

"I'm good," Leif said quickly, rubbing a mark on his sweating glass of water.

Vicky looked back at Oberon. "I'll stop by in a few minutes to check on you, okay? It's dinner time, and we've got a daily special that will knock your socks off."

"Thank you very much, Vicky, you've been most attentive," Oberon replied. "The coffee is just fine right now."

"You're welcome very much," she said, glancing once more at Leif, then shoved her nose in the air and walked off to help a family that had just entered the restaurant.

"You see, Leif, it's not too difficult to show some kindness," said Oberon.

Leif set his jaw. "The world hasn't been too kind to me. It's extremely hard for me to be kind to the world."

Oberon studied him for a few seconds. At last, he said, "Fair enough," then began fixing his coffee to his liking.

"So tell me, why the emergency meeting?" Leif asked. He wiggled his phone. "Your message seemed quite urgent."

Oberon took a sip from his mug, then rested it back down on his coaster. His brown eyes bore a weary sincerity, and his face seemed to have more wrinkles than Leif remembered seeing the last time they'd met.

The school director sighed. "I need to ask another favor of you."

Leif blinked a few times. "Does this have to do with the way I've been monitoring vampire movement in the vicinity? Oberon, I swear the school is safe. Nothing out of the ordinary is happening here. Not even the beginnings of what happened in South Dakota twenty years ago."

Oberon shook his head. "You're doing a fine job on vampire surveillance. This would be… an added responsibility."

It was Leif's turn to study Oberon. "I don't like the sound of that. What do you mean?"

After taking another sip, Oberon dabbed at his mouth with his napkin. "In the past, we've talked about the prophecy. The siren."

Leif nodded. "You're referring to the mermaid prophecy. The one who is supposedly going to take down Draven and end the shifter-vampire war."

"Yes, that's the one," Oberon confirmed.

Leif tilted his head. "You know I don't hold much credence in such a prophecy, right? I've never known *any* mermaid who would be able to kill Draven. If you don't mind me pointing out, you were unsuccessful with that very task."

A fire lit in Oberon's eyes that made his cup of steaming coffee look lukewarm.

"How dare you bring that up," the gryphon said dangerously.

Leif raised his hands defensively. "I didn't mean it as a personal attack. You're talking to a guy who couldn't stand up to Draven, let alone fight him. I'm just saying that it's hard for me to see a mermaid take on the big bad Draven when somebody like you—who I respect as a capable fighter—had difficulties doing just that."

The fire in Oberon's eyes simmered down to low embers, a warning to Leif that the gryphon was still agitated.

"You believe what you must," Oberon said. "But I believe we have found the siren."

Leif hadn't been expecting that. "What?"

"Several nights ago I went to her door, only to find her mother dead," Oberon continued. "The mermaid had luckily been away from the house at the time. Otherwise, she would have suffered the same fate as her mother."

"And this mermaid's mother was killed by vampires?" Leif asked.

Oberon nodded.

"Where did it happen?"

"In Short Grove," Oberon said.

Leif nodded. "Yes, there has been vampire activity in Short Grove, but nothing out of the ordinary."

"This particular attack has me extremely concerned. Is there any possibility in your mind that Draven knows about the prophecy?"

Leif shrugged. "How in the world would Draven know about the siren?"

Oberon sighed. "I need to know if you have told him anything."

His own heart surged with a burning anger—not for the gryphon, of course, but for the vampire leader. "Oberon, I swear to you that I haven't seen Draven since I outcasted myself from the other vampires."

Nodding slowly, Oberon said, "Thank you for that reaffirmation."

"More coffee?" Vicky said, appearing from seemingly nowhere.

"Sure, sure," Oberon replied quickly. "Top it off, please."

"Anything else I can bring you?" she asked sweetly. She was simply pretending like Leif didn't exist at this point. He was grateful for it.

"No thank you, my dear," Oberon replied. "We'll be out of your hair in a bit."

"You're such a sweetheart," Vicky said. "Your coffee's on the house."

"Are you sure?" Oberon asked, reaching into his pockets.

"Of course," she replied. She turned and gave Leif a look that said *I should charge you for breathing our air and* not *drinking our water,* then moved away.

"I just love this place," Oberon said.

"Clearly," Leif said, not impressed. "Back to what we were talking about... If what you're assuming is true and Draven is aware of this mermaid and the prophecy, then there are only two options that would explain him finding out such a thing."

"Enlighten me," Oberon said, mixing up his fresh cup of coffee.

He guessed that Oberon likely knew what the options were, but he humored the gryphon anyway. "First, somehow vampire spies have infiltrated the shifters in such a way that they were able to hear the prophecy."

Oberon nodded. "And secondly?"

"Secondly," Leif said, flicking water with his fingers from the exterior of his sweating cup, "you've got someone on the inside working for Draven."

At this, Oberon shook his head adamantly. "Nope. That's impossible."

Leif half-smiled. This was classic shifter ignorance. "Why would you say that?"

"Because the school hasn't had any vampire attacks," Oberon said. "If there was an informant within the confines of the school, the vampires would get to us somehow. Draven is that conniving."

Leif's smile broadened. "I'm supposing you don't know how informants work, do you?"

"Once again, enlighten me."

Leif shrugged. "They never share everything. Information has a cost. Whatever the informant decides to share is only worth how much they are being rewarded for it."

Oberon shook his head. "I can't start down that path of thinking, Leif. I'll never be able to trust anybody with that kind of thinking."

"Now you know how I live," Leif said. "Life is a lot easier when the only person you trust is yourself. That way, you never get burned."

Oberon hesitated for a moment, then spoke up. "Do you trust

me?"

Chuckling softly, Leif pointed a finger upwards and said, "I want to trust you."

"I *need* you to trust me."

"For whatever this favor is you're asking me to do?"

Oberon nodded.

"Which is?"

Oberon inhaled deeply, then let out his breath. Looking into his coffee mug as if there were a mermaid swimming within, he said, "I need you to rejoin Draven and the vampires."

Leif couldn't help but laugh out loud. He was probably drawing the attention of the other diners, but he couldn't help it. "You need me to what?"

Clearing his throat, Oberon softly said, "I need you to find out if Draven is searching for the siren. I don't think he'll let you just walk in unannounced and reveal that kind of information."

Leif placed both hands on the table and leaned forward. A bazillion red flags hoisted in his mind at the mere thought of rejoining the vampires. "Let me make this very clear, Oberon. I will *never* rejoin that monster for *any* reason."

"Even if it meant the prophecy was true?" Oberon offered. "Even if it meant the beginning of Draven's downfall?"

"Listen, I like you shifters. You're much better than the vampires—and that's saying a lot, because I *am* a vampire. But what you're asking me to do? I might as well shoot myself with a copper bullet. It would be a much better way of dying than what Draven would do to me."

Oberon looked him straight in the eyes and set his coffee cup back down. "If you do this for me, I will aid you in your quest to bring back the love of your life."

Gemma.

Leif remembered her breathtaking features so vividly, even though he hadn't seen her for a century. She had wide emerald eyes that were as pretty as the orchards he used to care for, and a smile that could scare away any worry or anger in an instant. Her perfect face was framed by red hair that was reminiscent of the reflective sunsets by the Columbia River.

How he missed her.

The love of his life, taken away too soon. She was the one who'd used her abilities to allow him to be protected against the sun.

Leif found himself dropping his hand down to the outside of his jeans pocket where her brooch was secured. He'd lost her over a hundred years ago when a shifter had killed her. Back when they were living at the Frost Boarding House. The very possibility that the magic to bring Gemma back to life was somewhere in the world kept Leif going. But he hadn't yet found anybody who could resurrect the dead.

Leif swallowed. It was his whole purpose for being alive. And he really did want to trust Oberon.

"If I do this, you must swear that my goal to bring Gemma back will become yours as well."

Oberon matched his stare. "I promise that your goal will become my goal once Draven is taken out."

It wasn't even an option anymore. Oberon's network of shifters was the widest in the world, and it was only getting bigger. If anybody could find a shifter skilled enough to bring Gemma back to life, it was him.

Leif would endure whatever Draven decided to do to him if it meant he'd be reunited with Gemma again.

"I agree to these conditions," Leif said at last, extending a hand to Oberon. The gryphon took his hand and clasped it firmly. "If you go back on this promise, you will have made an enemy of me."

Oberon nodded. "I understand. And I never break a promise."

Leif released their handhold, then looked around. "It's getting late. I should get going, and so should you."

"Agreed," Oberon replied. "Thanks for meeting with me. And keep me informed as you progress with Draven. His knowledge of the siren might not be important to you, but it is crucial to us. The sooner you get us the information we need, the sooner we can help the siren prepare."

Leif stood up, his chair screeching along the faux wood flooring.

"It might take me some time, but I'll get you the information you seek. It would make me extremely happy if you started looking for a shifter who could help me out. I know it won't be easy, but it will be easier than trying to live with Draven and the other vampires."

"I will begin my search," Oberon said. "I'm sure we will find somebody to help you."

Leif nodded, then headed for the door, not acknowledging Vicky as he passed by her.

The bells attached to the door chimed as he walked out into the busy Chicago streets.

Walking down the sidewalk, he decided to take the long way home.

Turning the corner, he stepped past a man walking his dog. The fuzzy mutt took a sniff at Leif as he moved by, forcing Leif to step off the curb and into the gutter.

"Sorry, sir," the old gentleman said. "He's a friendly pooch. Wouldn't harm a flee, even if it was biting him."

Leif pressed on. He hated dogs. Having been in too many fights with shifters back when he'd been on Draven's side, he couldn't look at any kind of canine and not think of the weres he'd fought—the weres he'd killed.

Walking a few more blocks, he took caution around the busy intersections. He wanted to use his super-speed to get home faster and think, but moving that fast would mark him in a hurry.

Pausing at the next intersection, he looked across the street. Leif's heart completely stopped as he saw a young woman. There was a familiar air about her, and he instantly recognized it.

"Gemma!" he cried out, not caring who was around to hear him. He was almost certain it was her. Leif had only gotten a glimpse of her from the side. He hurried down the street opposite of her.

Finally getting to the point he could keep pace with the girl, Leif could tell that she wasn't Gemma. She had brown hair and seemed to be a few inches shorter. Her face bore a striking resemblance, but what was most familiar to him was the air about the girl. He could sense her magic like he could sense human blood. And it felt almost identical to Gemma's magic. Could this girl be related to her in some fashion? Could she also be a selkie?

His thoughts of Oberon and Draven and the prophecy melted away. Leif *had* to find out more about this girl.

Kenzie

Kenzie trudged down the road to the subway entrance, cursing her luck. Of all the stupid things to do, she had to go and get herself caught. She was surrounded by beautiful people, shifter people, people she felt a deep kinship with, and in her rush to impress them, she'd botched it all.

That's the moment everything blew up in her face. Literally.

"I should've closed my eyes. I should've closed my eyes. Why didn't I close my eyes?" she mumbled. She stopped and closed them now, wishing she could go back and change what happened. The fire had felt so close, so hot. She scared herself, and she'd opened her eyes to make sure she was okay. She should've just released the spell. But as she opened her eyes, the faces around her went from gleeful to horrified.

Because I'm not one of them.

The warm Chicago night was just beginning, glowing lights popping up everywhere. The smell of hot asphalt and greasy food hit her, and Kenzie's stomach rumbled against the meager fare she'd eaten at the party. Okay, and yeah, she'd had a glass of spiked punch. Just to calm her nerves, though in hindsight, maybe it'd done more harm than good.

Kenzie moved herself forward again, wishing she had somewhere else to go besides home. This sucked. She didn't want the night to end this way. Pivoting on her heel, she turned back the way she'd come. *I could go back. Maybe convince them that... maybe... Wait. What's that?*

She stopped and looked at the sidewalk, her brows furrowed. Why did it look so strange? Seriously, it was just one glass. There was no way she was drunk, right?

Several people passed by, a few murmuring that she shouldn't be standing in the middle of a sidewalk. And finally Kenzie realized why it looked wrong.

There were no shadows.

In the dying light it was kinda hard to tell, but she was right next to a lamppost. That, at least, should've been casting a shadow.

Her mind raced with possible causes, but only one would explain the phenomenon: a vampire was near.

She actually knew more about vampires than she did about shifters, thanks to mom and Gram's paranoia on the subject. The surest sign of a vampire attack was the lack of shadow. It only worked for older vampires, who used the extra shadows to cloak themselves. *But if you ever see shadows disappear, you get out,* Gram had told her.

The hair on the back of her neck stood up, and she resisted the urge to scan her surroundings. *Crap! Crap, crap, crap.* Of all the luck, of course she'd be hunted, tonight of all nights. *It just keeps getting better.*

She stopped herself, slowing her breathing, balling her hands into fists. She was on the street, and it was relatively busy. No self-respecting, self-preserving vamp would attack her right here, right now. Right? She had to be smart about this. Shaking her head, she took a deep breath, hoping to clear away the last of the cobwebs.

Of course, there was always the off chance that she wasn't the target. Not that she was going to risk it, especially after what happened to Myreen's mom. *Myreen.* Kenzie sniffed her shoulder, wondering if she somehow smelled like Myreen. Not that she'd be able to tell, not being a vampire and all. Kenzie rolled her eyes. She was being ridiculous.

She turned around again, trying to be casual as she walked down the street. She kept looking side to side, peering in stores and around bends, but she avoided looking over her shoulder. She hoped she wasn't being too obvious. Staying cool was usually her thing, but she'd never been tailed by a vampire before. Could he smell her fear? Hear her heart beating?

She began to twirl her right hand at the wrist, as if she were stretching it. The spell Gram had taught her was the most complicated she'd ever learned. Not only was the incantation longer than one word or a simple phrase, there were hand motions that had to go with it. If she missed one step in the process, did anything wrong or out of order, she might as well be muttering the dictionary for all the good it would do her.

Kenzie looked down at the pavement, her shadow still eerily absent. *Yep, I'm being followed.* She continued to roll her wrist as she drew out the words under her breath, in no particular rush to finish the spell just yet. "Fiáscha na olch."

Spotting an empty alleyway, she ducked into it. She pushed her shoulders back and held her head high. No vampire would see her cower. She hated the isolation of the alleyway, which made her heart rate kick into high gear, but she had to make sure she was far enough away. People didn't need to see her do magic, didn't need to see her eyes glow white with the effort, and didn't need to see the blood-sucking parasite she was about to take care of. Sort of.

"Tóg go bog é na fola."

She slipped behind a trash bin, leaning up against the brick wall. There was a door here, the back of some establishment, no doubt locked. The trash smelled like old fish, and Kenzie scrunched her nose as she finished her charm, this time at full volume. "Diúltódha darshada."

She pushed her hands out in front of her, toward the part of the wall that steeped deeper in shadows than the rest. Wind pushed her hair back, a flash of light momentarily blinding her before the night returned.

But in place of the darkness was a vampire.

Kenzie's heart raced. He didn't look nearly as evil as she'd envisioned. Sure, he was pale. Kinda cute, in an old-fashioned sort of way. Or maybe a hipster kind of way, with that hair. Dang these stupid non-human types and their ridiculously good looks. He looked about as surprised as she felt.

They stared at each other for a long moment, sizing each other up. The spell was three parts—dispelling the darkness he used to cover himself, slowing his blood to weaken him, and binding him to where he stood. The darkness part obviously worked—*thanks, Gram*—but the other two she wasn't as sure of. Though, as intricate as the spell was, chances are the whole thing held or none at all. She hoped.

What do you ask a bound vampire? Kenzie hadn't thought that far ahead, concerned only with completing the spell correctly. But now that she had him, she couldn't help her curiosity. Maybe it was some sort of morbid death wish, after the rejection she'd just endured at the hands of shifters, but she wasn't ready to walk away just yet.

"Well, at least you're not sparkling," she began, frowning. "Why are you following me?" It seemed as good a place as any to start. She wanted to make sure Myreen was safe.

"You're a selkie, aren't you?" It was more a statement than a question, and Kenzie took a step back.

"Please, don't go."

Kenzie crossed her arms, trying to look tough. "Why? Afraid your next meal's gonna get away?"

The vampire flinched. "I don't drink fresh blood. Not if I can help it."

Kenzie raised a brow.

"And if I wanted to kill you, you'd already be dead. Not a smart move, luring a vampire into an alley."

"And yet you're the one stuck to a wall."

"I'm sorry. I've been told my manners are lacking. My name is Leif." He gave a small nod, or maybe a bow.

For a vampire who couldn't move, he seemed to be moving quite a bit. Lips, head, and did she see a finger twitch?

"Ooo-kay." She wasn't about to give him her name, no matter how charming he tried to be.

"It's just, you don't see a lot of magic users around these days. Especially not as powerful as you. You kind of remind me of someone I used to know..." His gaze momentarily darted away from her face, the first time since she'd uncovered the guy. "...a long time ago."

Kenzie narrowed her eyes. The haunted look in his eyes as he studied her, as if she were a ghost, made her almost believe him. Almost.

"Are you friends with shifters?" Leif continued. "Maybe you go to that school?"

Kenzie sucked her lips in, trying not to respond. She didn't trust this vampire. If it weren't for the binding spell, she'd probably be dinner. Maybe. And even if the shifters hated her, there was no way she'd give a vampire any information about them or their school.

But she must have shaken her head.

"Would you like to go to the school?"

Kenzie sighed. "Look, Leif. I appreciate the small talk and all, but I should be getting home." She looked back and forth, even glancing upward. "You're not stalling so your vampire friends can come rescue you, are you? Because I've got a whole lot more magic where that came from."

"No. I'm... alone. For now, anyway. And I believe you. Your magic, I can sense it."

That caught Kenzie's attention. He could sense her magic? Did he have any idea how powerful she was? She didn't even know the answer to that question.

Leif licked his lips, his voice taking on a more desperate tone. "This... *friend* of mine, she died. Many years ago. I've been searching for a way to... bring her back."

"From the dead?" Kenzie couldn't believe what she was hearing. She scoffed. "What was her name? Bella?"

"Gemma."

Kenzie closed her mouth, looking at the vampire a little closer. He didn't appear to be making this stuff up. "I couldn't raise the dead if I wanted to."

"I might have a way."

"Are you punking me right now? Is this some sort of twisted joke?"

"No. I have a grimoire—"

"How does a vampire get a grimoire?"

"—and it's very old. It may have a spell in there to help. My friend, she used it to help me once."

Kenzie's mind raced. A magic user had helped a vampire. "You didn't kill her, did you? This isn't some guilt trip or revenge or something?"

"No! I didn't... I'd never hurt her. And I didn't kill her. It's a long story. But if I give you the grimoire, do you think you might—?"

"No." Kenzie shook her head, unable to believe she was even

hearing this. "You're a vampire. These are all lies." She had to go. She didn't know how long the spell would last. At least he wasn't asking about Myreen. Maybe he didn't have anything to do with that.

"Dóicheáhn," Leif said, but there was no spark behind his words. "I can't do magic, not like a selkie, but I've seen some of the grimoire."

Kenzie took another step backward. "Only some?"

"The book itself is spelled, making much of its contents unreadable to anyone... to those without magic."

That sounded about right. Selkies were known for their distrust of others, so it made sense they'd lock the magic, especially the higher-level spells, to ensure it didn't fall into the hands of others.

"I can get you into the school," Leif continued, his look lighting with something—maybe desperation? "I know the director."

Kenzie spit out a laugh. "I've met him. Real charmer."

"Oberon can be blunt. And stubborn. But he owes me."

Kenzie shifted her weight to one foot, putting her hands in the back pockets of her jeans. The fact that she was even entertaining this vampire was beyond her. She should be gone by now, texting Myreen to be careful and singing the song Gram had taught her to mask her scent from vampires. She shook her head, turning to leave. "No. I'm sorry, I can't trust you."

A ping on the pavement caught Kenzie's attention, and she whirled back. She expected any number of things—a gun, a knife, maybe some brass knuckles. Instead, a piece of jewelry glinted in the dim light from the street. Some sort of pin or decoration or something. Maybe a leaf?

Leif's fingers were outstretched, as if a magnet pulled them toward the pin. "It's the only thing I have left of her. Please. You have to believe me."

Kenzie stared at Leif, long and hard. Maybe he'd gotten out of the spell. Maybe he was trying to lure her in for a bite. She wanted to believe him, wanted desperately to have someone—anyone—on her side. But she couldn't take that leap of faith. Not tonight. And certainly not with a vampire.

"Keep it," she said, backing away.

"Please."

The look in his eyes was so desperate, so clawing, her own heart wanted to break for him. She swallowed. "I can't. You've got the wrong girl."

"If you change your mind—"

"I'll slit a wrist or something. I'm sure you'll come running."

Leif paled—if that were even possible. "No. Don't do that. Gemma had a spell she could use. Claoigha."

Kenzie repeated the word in her head, not wanting to lose it. She was nearly to the street again, but she hesitated, torn between fleeing and running back to him for another stare-fest. *Dang, those stupid good looks. I gotta get out more.*

She turned and ran.

She knew people were staring at her, wondering what the rush was. But she didn't care. She wanted to be long gone, out of sight, far enough away to not be stalked or followed with superhuman speed. Her heart pumped a mile a minute, and even if she wasn't still scared witless, she needed to get all that energy out of her system.

Claoigha. Claoigha. Claoigha, she thought with every thumping step, committing the term to memory. If the spell worked, that could come in useful. She'd have to try it sometime—when she was far from home and had someone safe to contact. Okay, so that might be a while.

She began to sing softly between pants, the tune working to ease her nerves as the words of the spell scrubbed her scent from any stalking vampires. It was just a precaution, Gram's wards being enough to keep any would-be vampire invader out. Still, no sense leaving a bread trail to their doorstep—no matter how cute he was or sincere he seemed.

"Sweeph an bolladhá, sweeph an bolladhá, camdach, diúltidhá, sweeph an bolladhá." Kenzie breathed easy as she repeated the words of this spell, which was thankfully more forgiving than the binding spell she'd used on Leif.

Kenzie slowed to a walk, satisfied that the song was doing its job. At least, she believed so. She found the subway entrance and descended the steps, sending furtive glances to the shadows that lurked behind her. None seemed deep enough to hold a vampire.

Juliet

The night was filled with so much drama that Juliet actually couldn't wait to get back to the Dome where it was quiet.

Now that she'd gone to her first party, she thought staying in to watch a movie sounded much more appealing. The party started out pretty smoothly. There were the usual whispers about her presence, but they weren't as hateful as she was afraid they would be.

She floated around the party, pretty much invisible to the other phoenixes that were there. Myreen was right, though: the dark lipstick she put on got the attention she shyly craved from Nik. He offered to get her a drink a few times, which meant he kept his eyes on her, and that thought alone brought butterflies to take flight in her stomach.

Throughout the night she sometimes had to repeat a newer mantra to herself. *Breathe, keep your head high, and don't freak out.* No matter what happened, the last thing she wanted to do was let her emotions get the best of her and cause a fire. On top of the social fire that was already blowing up. She thought keeping a low profile would be in her best interest.

It took everything inside of her not to lose it when Trish started bullying Myreen and Kenzie. She set her drink down and felt her hatred toward the mean mermaids grow in the pit of her stomach.

She wanted nothing more than to set her fire free. Ever since the explosion with her father, she desired to feel that burning bond with the flames. And if it wasn't for Nik placing his warm hand on the lower part of her back, she probably would have broken her vow to herself and lit the party up. And not in a good way.

"Are you okay, Juliet?" There was obvious concern in Nik's eyes as he stared into hers. She was confused, because he would only be concerned if he cared... *Does he care?*

"Uh, yeah. Thanks. They're just so... mean. I don't get why they have to be that way." She tried to keep her peripherals open to the scene in the living room, just in case she did need to help her friends. But it was proving to be much harder as she got lost in Nik's dark ebony gaze.

"It wouldn't be a normal school if there weren't mean girls, right?" She could tell he was trying to make light of the situation.

"You wouldn't understand. Being best friends with the dragon prince doesn't exactly place you in the victim category." Juliet picked up her drink again, but Nik looked like her words actually bruised him.

"I would, as a matter of fact. You know, this isn't our first conversation. It shouldn't be hard for you to remember our last one." With a raise of his eyebrows he lifted his cup to her in a sort of cheers and wandered off. *What is he talking about? What conversation?*

Now completely preoccupied, she didn't know how much time passed before Myreen came looking for her.

"Hey, I— I need to get out of here. Kenzie is so upset and this party just... sucks. Care if we leave before it ends?" She looked frantic as she rambled on.

"Definitely, let's go. Are you alright, Myreen?" Juliet hooked her arm into Myreen's and led them outside. Myreen shook her head in disbelief.

"I just don't get it. Why is Kenzie and her kind so looked down on? Why won't anyone tell me anything?" Myreen put her face in her hands and Juliet could sense her frustration.

"I wish I could help you understand. I'm just hearing the word selkie for the first time. I can ask my dad and see if he'll spill anything." Juliet didn't like to see her friend so hurt.

"Thanks, J. That means a lot. I know things are rough with you two right now." Myreen's voice cracked, and Juliet could see tears well up in her eyes. But none of the tears fell, so her words must have helped, even if it was only a little.

They'd left the party early, but they were still going to be late for curfew. The thought of her father knowing she snuck out with Myreen to go to a party *after* the mess she made in the avian training room put enough fear into her. The last thing she wanted to do was get caught.

For the rest of the short ride, Myreen was so quiet in her own thoughts that it gave Juliet enough time to come up with a way to sneak in. It wasn't until they were waiting on the secret platform that led to the school that she told Myreen her plan.

"Okay, my dad should be off duty right now, but his second-in-command won't hesitate to snitch on us. So, when it gets here, we get on in the very back. Stick to the shadows and we should be fine." Hearing the shaky words come out of her own mouth made her realize just how nervous she actually was.

Juliet slipped the moment the train doors opened. As she scrambled to get to her feet to hide in the shadows like she planned, she couldn't hold back the laughter, and Myreen cackled as silently as she could beside her. But even through the laughing, she could still see the sadness in Myreen's eyes. She didn't blame her, though; it was a rough night.

They successfully made it past the guards and back into the silent and eerie hallways of the Dome. Afraid to make any noise, they removed their shoes to tiptoe their separate ways to their bedrooms.

Juliet threw herself onto her bed. Once her frizzy orange hair hit her pillow, sleep came easily.

Her eyes felt heavy, which came from doing more in one day than she'd ever done in her whole life. Not all of it was good, but it also wasn't all bad. The single thought of Nik and what he said to her echoed through her mind until her eyes fell closed. The last thing she saw before succumbing to the darkness was the late hour of 2 AM.

***

Three loud knocks woke Juliet up, causing her to groan loudly. As she looked over at the clock that sat on her desk, her lips pursed and her hands turned into fists. 6 AM? Who dared wake her up at this hour?

Groggy and now annoyed, Juliet drug her feet out of bed and to her door. Storming in and pushing right past her, her dad towered over her with his arms crossed over his puffed out chest. His eye twitched and his breathing was heavy. Like a slap to the face, she was instantly wide awake.

"I am beyond disappointed in you. After you ran out on me yesterday, I came back here to speak with you, and to my surprise, you were nowhere to be found. And neither was your new friend. Do you have any idea how worried I was? That you go out there without even telling me or anyone else? Especially with *her*. Who knows what danger follows her? And you accompany her to a party, of all places, missing curfew and sneaking in. You're lucky I waited this long to come in here." He paced the room in quick and frantic strides yelling at her through clenched teeth.

"I'm… sorry?" It was all she could muster up.

"Was that a question?" If smoke could come out of his ears, it would be. And maybe it was. The early hour and the lack of sleep had Juliet wondering if she was imagining this to be worse than it actually was.

"You know what? Forget it. If you thought you were off the hook for losing control in the training room yesterday, you were wrong. Get yourself together and be there in ten minutes. All the materials you need to clean up your mess will be waiting for you. Come find me when you're done."

Without waiting for a response, he slammed the door behind him, causing the entire door to vibrate.

At first, Juliet could only sit frozen in fear and shame. But she knew how serious he was when he told her she had ten minutes. Rapidly running to brush her teeth, she didn't even care to change into something more appealing than the thick, oversized sweatpants that she'd thrown on in her hurry to get to bed.

As soon as her fingers touched the doorknob, she remembered about the other students, who had to have heard her father's bellowing. She put her headphones on and ran out. *Head down, no eye contact, headphones on high, and keep cool.* It seemed she'd been repeating those words less and less as of late. Since Myreen had come. *What danger could dad be talking about?* The loud classical melody that tuned out everything around her couldn't tune out what her father said.

In just under nine minutes, she reluctantly walked into the charred room. Her shoes picked up the thick black ash that clung to the floor, leaving white footprints behind her. Juliet took a deep breath, inhaling the toxic fumes of the deep-rooted smoke. It was an attempt to prepare herself for what was going to be a dreadfully long day, but even she knew that nothing could prepare her.

If it wasn't for her music, the first two hours would have gone by excruciatingly slowly. The delicious smell of bacon and eggs wafted through the air, a nice change from the current smoky smell, and immediately Juliet spun around to see if she was hallucinating or not. She practically ran at full speed to her very own hero, embracing Myreen in a hug that almost knocked down the trays of food she was holding.

"Whoa there, killer. You'll knock down the coffee that we both so desperately need." Myreen set the trays down and did a full circle around the room. "Wow. You really did a number here. Your dad must have pushed your buttons, huh?"

"You have no idea. And this morning was worse. Except I didn't set anything on fire, but it sure looked like he was going to." Juliet stuffed the bacon in her mouth and buried her head in her hands.

"Yeah, the whole Dome heard him this morning. I thought I was dreaming. Then, when I went to find you for breakfast, someone pointed me in this direction. Sorry you got in trouble for going to the party. Even more so now because it was such a bust." Myreen looked down at her feet while she fussed with her fingers.

"It's okay. I guess this is something I'll have to get used to, being the daughter of a Lieutenant General. He's just so different than how my mom was toward me. He's so strict."

"Well, doesn't that mean he cares? If he didn't, he wouldn't give you so many rules. Trust me, he's just like that because he loves you." Myreen's eyebrows scrunched together and tears welled up again in her eyes.

But Juliet didn't want their day to be so somber. "So… Nik was nice last night." She knew it would be the perfect distraction. Boy talk, who could resist?

"Oh? How do you mean?" Myreen's eyes nearly bulged out as she leaned forward in her seat.

"I don't know, he refilled my drink a few times. And he said something to me before we left that I couldn't understand at first, but now I think I do." Juliet daydreamed about the moment he mentioned, and it brought a small smile to her lips.

"Well! What was it?" Myreen's impatience caused Juliet to giggle.

"When I first got to this school, everyone was too afraid to befriend me, either because of my dad or because of my uncontrollable situation. There were a few times that I just needed some space from all the whispers, especially from the other phoenixes. You see, my mother was human. So I'm only part phoenix. And I guess that's a big red mark to my name."

Myreen's head perked up like a curious cat. "Or maybe you're just unique and rare."

Juliet knew what Myreen was trying to do, but the memory was so thick that it felt like it was choking her.

"Well, one day, Trish was tormenting me about my mother, and when I ran off, Nik went to look for me. Of all people, the *hot dragon* went to see if I was okay. He told me about his own mother, who's also human. Back then, I appreciated his sympathy, but he was also popular. I mean, how could he understand what I was going through?"

"I would have thought the exact same thing." Myreen nodded as she finished her fruit bowl.

"So, I brushed it off and never had the guts to talk to him again. I never really gave him the chance to, either. Blocking myself from the world with my headphones was easier than actually facing the music. Then last night, he tried to level with me again, and I kept saying he didn't understand. But he does. And I blew my chance. I know it."

Juliet's eyes took on the same sullen and sunken look as Myreen's, which was the complete opposite of what she wanted.

"Maybe. Or maybe not. But girl, next time, try to be more open to the possibility. I knew that lipstick would work, by the way." Myreen gave her a smile as she stood with her tray.

"Thanks for breakfast. I definitely owe you one. I was starving. I should be done here by dinner. Do you want to meet in the Dining Hall?"

"Actually, if we *both* tackle this room together, we could be done earlier than that. I have nothing better to do; every mermaid hates me. And maybe we can help each other out with this whole boy stuff. After last night, I need all the help I can get."

Struck at how nice Myreen was to offer her help, Juliet almost cried. She knew being Myreen's friend was worth it. Even if Myreen came with baggage full of danger.

Myreen

The Dome was quiet as Myreen walked back from the training room after helping Juliet. It was Saturday. Everyone was probably kicking back in their rooms and enjoying a lazy day. *Or maybe some of them went home to their families for the weekend*, she thought, making herself cringe with envy.

She didn't like this empty day. She didn't like knowing that all that waited for her was an empty room and thoughts of her mother.

Deciding against dark and lonely, Myreen veered off and took a sidewalk that led away from the main building. She hadn't done any kind of exploring since she got here, only going to the places she was expected to be.

She followed the path, aimlessly looking up at the dome overhead, at the gorgeous deep blue that surrounded everything. When she looked back down at the ground, she saw that there was a garden up ahead. Large pink and sherbet-orange roses blushed at her as they peeked over their bushes.

As she came closer, the heady sweet aroma filled the air. Without the movement of a breeze, the smell hung around the garden as if glued to that patch of oxygen.

Myreen entered and inhaled the perfume, enjoying the tinkling sound of water spilling down the large fountain at the garden's center. She sat on one of the stone benches that surrounded the fountain and admired it. As with all the other décor at this school, the fountain was made up of different shifters, all climbing on top of each other, as if to escape the marble they were carved from.

"Pretty, huh?"

Myreen turned to her right to see Kendall stepping into the inner circle of the garden. After the way the party ended last night, she felt more than a little awkward around him. All the other mermaids had made it clear that she was not welcome in their presence. She hadn't stuck around to find out if Kendall felt the same.

"Yep," she said, turning her gaze back to the fountain, unsure of what else to say.

Kendall sat beside her. "I was looking for you in the common room. What have you been up to all day?"

"I was helping Juliet clean up a mess she made yesterday." She thought it best not to go into much detail; why give the rumor mill more fuel? "I know mermaids don't approve of befriending other types of shifters, but it's been pretty well established that I'm not your typical mermaid." She couldn't help but let the bitterness slip into her voice.

"Maybe that's what I like about you," Kendall said, putting his hand over hers. "Our people have it pretty much ingrained not to trust outsiders, not to trust anyone but their own. Mermaids have been hunted since the dawn of time, first by large aquatic predators, then by man and vampires, and even by other shifters. We're a proud and guarded people, and that pride tends to sour our hearts and turn into prejudice. But you… Your heart is open to everyone and everything. I haven't seen one inkling of judgment in you. You give everyone a chance, no matter their background and race. I admire that, even if I personally disagree with those you choose to open your heart to."

Myreen was taken aback. Put in that kind of light, Myreen could finally understand the mentality of those that hated her. It didn't make her any more okay with it, but at least she knew where it was coming from. And to know that Kendall wasn't with the other mermaids on his opinion of her meant the world to her.

"Thank you for that," she said, noticing that his hand was still on hers.

He nodded. "I was wondering if you'd like to take a swim with me."

She smiled wide, unable to hide her joy at his invitation. "I'd love to. But isn't the training room closed on weekends? Or is there another pool in the rec room?"

"Actually, I had something else in mind," he said, the corner of his mouth lifting in a secretive smile. "Come with me."

He closed his hand around hers and tugged her after him. They left the garden and headed for the corner of the main building where it met the bottom of the dome. Myreen wondered where he could possibly be taking her. Not that she had the map memorized, but she didn't remember seeing any other pools on campus.

As Kendall led her further into the corner, she saw that there was a door, somewhat camouflaged, right next to where the wall touched the thick glass. Kendall lifted a hidden metal flap on the wall to reveal the kind of retina scan that was on the entrance of the school. He leaned forward for the device to scan his eye, and the door unlocked and popped open an inch.

Kendall looked at her as he pulled it open the rest of the way. "Only mermaids can get in here." He held the door open for her, but she was hesitant to go in.

"What is it?" she asked, peeking in and seeing nothing but darkness.

"It's a secret exit that leads directly into the lake," he said, unphased by her hesitance. "Only a few of the Mer students know about it. And now you."

Her suspicion dissipated instantly, replaced by a humbling sense of honor. On the map, the only way in or out of the school was the front entrance from the subway. But as the Dome was built and funded by mermaids, it made sense that there would be an escape hatch only they could access. If something happened to the Dome, of course the mermaids would be concerned with saving themselves.

Myreen stepped into the small space, and Kendall closed the door behind them. As her eyes adjusted to the darkness, she could see that they were in a small room, about two meters wide and two meters deep. There was a flight of stairs directly in front of her that led to a room about the same size. A faint bluish glow came from the floor of the room at the top of the stairs, giving this moment an even greater sense of magic.

Kendall encouraged her up the stairs, where she saw that the glow was coming from a round portal in the floor that was completely open to the water of the lake. He pulled his shirt up over his head, showing the uniform swim top underneath, then took off his pants as well and sat at the edge of the portal. He stuck his legs in the water, and Myreen noticed that they didn't transform. His legs were still human legs— muscular, thick, nicely-tanned legs.

She gasped. "I can't go in there," she objected with a fervent shake of her head. "I don't know how to transform without salt water. And I don't have the first clue of how to swim without my tail!"

"It's alright, I came prepared." He reached into the pocket of his discarded pants and pulled out a vial of clear liquid, then tossed it to her. "It's salt water."

She caught it and looked at it, still unsure about this experiment. The pool in the training room was nothing but salt water, so she had no trouble staying in her mermaid form there. But this tiny amount of salt water?

"How long will it last?" she asked, pulse racing at the thought of returning to human form too far from the portal.

"You'll be fine," Kendall reassured her with an indulgent chuckle. "Once transformed and in the water, your body will have no reason to change back into a human form until your skin begins to dry. Many mermaids actually struggle to change back to human form in water, salt or not."

"Really?" she asked, a bit more confident. "Why would they want to?"

"Out in public, with humans, could you imagine accidentally letting your tail out because some water happened to splash on you? That would expose you, and our entire species. That's the whole purpose of our Transformation class, in fact. Every other species at this school takes that time to learn how to shift. We use it to learn how *not* to."

She nodded. It made sense.

She got ready to disrobe, but she didn't have her swim top; she was wearing a pair of jeans and a cute top she'd borrowed from Juliet.

"So you thought ahead enough to bring me a tube of salt water, but you didn't bring my swim top?" she asked, putting her hands on her hips in a playfully accusatory pose.

Kendall smiled in faux innocence and shrugged. "I guess I forgot."

Myreen frowned in obvious disbelief.

"Okay, I'll turn around while you get in," he said, standing up and turning around to face the dark wall.

She was pretty sure her entire body was blushing as she shakily pulled down her jeans. She had never been anywhere near this exposed in front of a boy—or anyone, for that matter—especially one she liked. As she prepared to quickly pull down her panties, she eyed him closely. Sure, he seemed respectful, but he was still a guy, and what guy wouldn't try to sneak a peek at a girl he seemed to like while she was stripping right behind him? Like ripping off a band-aid, she pulled them down as quickly as she could, then yanked open the little vial and spilled it onto her legs, rubbing it all over like lotion.

The reaction was instantaneous, and the emergence of her tail meant the removal of her legs, and as she literally didn't have a leg to stand on, she face-planted to the floor.

At the *thud*, Kendall spun around, then rushed to help stabilize her.

"Sorry," he laughed, "I should have warned you to sit down before applying the salt water."

Myreen was laughing too, both at herself and from embarrassment. "It's okay, I should've been smarter. Help me over to the portal?"

Kendall swooped his head under her arm and carried her to the portal, gently lowering her into it.

The cool lake water felt amazingly good on her tail, and she reveled in the feeling of her fins wafting in the mild current.

Responding to the partial-body submersion, the upper half of her body continued the transformation, and the searing pain in her neck meant that her gills had come out. She tried to take a breath, but her throat and lungs stung like they were on fire.

"Hurry. Get all the way in so you can breathe," Kendall cautioned.

Myreen let go of the edges of the portal and let herself fall in. When next she inhaled, water filled her open mouth, and the burn washed away. She could breathe. Relief flooded through her.

Kendall was beside her soon after.

"How do you feel?" His words came out both muffled and amplified as they moved through the water, but she could still clearly understand each syllable.

She swished herself around to let the sensations sink in. "I feel great!" Shock reverberated through her at the sound and feeling of her own voice in the water. It was the strangest thing she'd experienced yet, and that was really saying something after all she'd been through at this school. She looked down, and was relieved to see her form-fitting top was staying in place.

"Good, let's go for a swim." Kendall nodded toward the open, seemingly endless water.

Without another word between them, they swam side-by-side through the lake. This was completely different from swimming in the pool. Here there were no boundaries, no limits. She could move around as she wished without the worry of bumping into the wall, or another mermaid—besides Kendall, of course.

They swam everywhere, and Myreen was awestruck by the freedom of it. Schools of fish swarmed around them now and then, and it was amazing to see them come so close, like she wasn't a foreign intruder, like she belonged in these waters they called their home. One fish swam right up to her face, and she cupped her hand under it, inviting it to come as close as it wished. The little fish accepted her invitation and gently nuzzled across her cheek before rejoining its school and disappearing into the depths.

"I want to show you something," Kendall said.

Myreen nodded.

She swam beside him, letting the currents from his fins guide her. It was strange how easy it was to be in sync with him.

They dove deeper. The water cooled, though not enough to bother her. Myreen wondered how far she could dive, what limitations her mermaid body had. A large form loomed ahead, and Myreen's eyes widened.

"Where are we?"

"It's a shipwreck. There are tons of these things down here."

The body of the boat was still intact, a large water wheel resting next to it as if it had been leaned up against the side. There was something quaint about the construction, the railed deck, the tall stacks protruding from the top, though all of it was covered in a thick layer of grime.

"Tons of shipwrecks?"

"You'd be surprised just how much stuff is on the floor of the lake. Come on." Kendall slid through a window.

Myreen followed him, peering around the dark interior. It was as breathtaking as it was eerie. An old piano sat in one corner, and what must have been crystal chandeliers hung from the ceiling. Chairs lay haphazardly across the floor, all of it covered by a blanket of green.

"This is one of the better wrecks. Not too many lives lost. Others you're practically digging through bones."

Myreen shuddered. "There aren't any dead bodies here, are there?"

"No. I think they all washed away. But they left behind some pretty cool stuff. It's actually part of how we funded the school. The mer make great deep-sea treasure hunters."

She wiped away the slime from one of the drops attached to the chandelier, releasing a cloud of goo. Myreen coughed, the water rushing out of her gills. But a bit of the crystal shone through.

"Oh, watch yourself. We don't want to murk up the waters with algae too much."

Myreen nodded.

"Here." Kendall wrapped his hand around the crystal drop, carefully maneuvering it off the chandelier. "A memento of our time together."

Myreen blushed.

Kendall's smile faded. "We should get back to the school."

Myreen followed again, not realizing they'd angled up until the pressure around her began to ease and the Dome loomed big and round beneath her. She could see the entire school from this birds-eye view— or fish-eye view, rather. It looked so small from up here. The people walking along the sidewalks looked like ants crawling through a super hi-tech ant farm.

Kendall reached out to take her hand, and she let him. There were no words to describe the feeling surging through her. She was beyond grateful that he chose her to share this incredible secret with. She had never felt more at home anywhere in her life than she did floating in this lake. If she never went back to dry land, she wasn't sure she'd be too disappointed.

Kol

Whoosh. Whoosh. Whoosh. Whoosh.

Kol beat his powerful wings against the crisp night air until he managed to find an air current that flowed high above the lake. Stretching them out to their full span, he relaxed into a glide as his dark gray scales moved and adjusted. With the moon concealed behind a cloud, the lake was almost black, and even with enhanced vision, he still couldn't make out the Dome below the water.

But that also meant *he* couldn't be seen.

Still, dark gray scales seemed like the best color for the moment, orange or gold might've gotten him caught or spotted by a fishing boat. *"Flying dragon spotted over Lake Michigan"* was not the sort of thing Oberon would be pleased to be reading in the Chicago Sun Times or local twitter feeds.

So dark gray it was.

As it mostly was.

As it always was whenever he was close to the school.

There was only one other dragon—or person at all—who even knew about the uniqueness of Kol's scales besides his parents and sister. And that was only because of their trip to the Alps last summer. He'd dragged Nik on their annual family vacation for some company. His sister, Tatiana, rarely came anymore, and his mother had a charity event that prevented her from being around much. So "family" vacation was a loose term. It was more of a "trip with the general as he *schmoozes* dignitaries and expects his son to play Xbox all day in the hotel room."

Seriously, Brett would've been the perfect son for the General.

Nik agreed to tag along, and he and Kol decided to take a flight over the majestic peaks one afternoon. But being away from the school caused Kol to forget to keep his scales dark gray. His go-to *boring* dark gray that wouldn't draw attention. When they rested near the peak of Mont Blanc, Kol's scales should have stuck out as clearly as Nik's deep red ones against the white snow. Instead, he essentially disappeared as they adjusted to different shades of white and light gray.

They were like invisibility scales.

Kol didn't want to keep the knowledge of his chameleon-shifting ability from his friend, except for the insistence of the General. With Kol destined to be in the shifter military someday, his father worried what would happen if and when the information reached the wrong ears.

Kol knew it wasn't for his protection—which was wholly why his mother agreed and insisted that Kol keep his promise of silence—but his father was afraid if word got out while Kol was still young, that he could be persuaded to join the wrong side. And with the extra perk of camouflage scales, there would be bribes and fights to get him on all sides.

So Nik knew, but no one else at the Dome did. Not even Oberon.

And he had to keep it that way.

Kol pushed his right wing down to pivot and turn back the way he'd come. The cloud had moved and revealed the not-quite-full-moon, so his reprieve was over. After the party, Kol was wound up and angry about the entire Myreen-Kendall situation, and he hadn't had a chance to de-stress from it. Flying among the cold air was exactly what he needed. But it was time to get back. The waves glistened with the moonlight, sprinkled over their peaks. With his enhanced dragon eyes, he could make the faint outline of the half-spherical glass that housed hundreds of shifters like him.

Now that his thoughts were becoming clearer, he could see the beauty of it all.

On the other hand, it was also enough light that he feared being spotted. He was half-tempted to shift colors, but didn't dare risk running into another dragon—or Director Gryphon.

Plus, he knew it was getting late, and he had one more stop before going back to campus.

Less than ten minutes later, he landed among the underbrush of a small but dense copse of trees at a small park in the city. Using invisibility to get there without being seen was the only exception to his rule. It was better than landing in the middle of nowhere and needing transportation.

Kol stretched his neck out and shook his head, then flicked his scales to trigger his shift back to human. His wings shrank and formed into arms and hands, and his neck shortened as his thick, dark hair sprouted above his still-glowing blue eyes. Finally, the joints in his legs straightened, then bent the backwards as the scales on his feet rescinded to reveal the pink skin beneath.

Once upon a time, shifting had been uncomfortable and even painful, but now it was his escape from the dramas of being a *Dragon Dracul.* Well... and away from teenage drama. After the *Ken D0ll* run-in at the party, he needed the break.

But it was time to get back to reality.

He located his regular clothes underneath the bench where they were concealed, and swiftly pulled on his jeans over his *smart* shorts. One of the worst things about being a shifter was the nudity that was inevitable when going from dragon back to human. The smart clothing—the guys' version was similar to a wrestler's spandex—was better than the alternative. Kol yanked his t-shirt over his head as he walked out of hiding and back onto the sidewalk.

One more errand.

***

Kol gripped the paper bag tightly in his right hand as he ducked into the gardens. The fries were surely getting cold. He'd hoped to sneak back upstairs without being seen, but had narrowly missed being caught by two faculty members the moment he arrived back at the Dome and panicked.

His height was definitely an obstacle when it came to stealth missions. Being six-foot, six-inches didn't give him many hiding place options, at least nothing that would conceal him enough to sneak past anyone, let alone someone of authority. And unfortunately, his skin and clothing didn't have the same properties as his dragon scales. So, he did the only thing he could think of: *Step one*: hide out for an undetermined amount of time, and *Step two*: hope the teachers all went to bed soon.

The plan made him uncomfortable. Probably because it *wasn't* a plan.

It was late and Kol wasn't supposed to be outside his dorm, let alone just getting back to the safety of the school grounds. And the white bag with *Mack's Diner* printed in navy blue letters was evidence enough that he'd snuck out. But dumping the evidence wasn't an option.

Chili cheese fries were too valuable for that.

Kol had promised Nik and Brett to buy some after the party the night before and hadn't delivered. *Stupid Kendall encounter...* And a promise was a promise, and forfeiting a game of pool was the same as losing one. His friends had reminded him of that well past curfew.

So he owed them.

Tonight.

The fries were getting cold, but a few fireballs would remedy that if he could just get back to the common room without being seen.

If Kol had been smart, he would've worn all black to give him *some* chance of blending into the shadows while he waited, but he also hadn't planned on almost getting caught. Normally he *was* smart, so it made it that much worse that he hadn't thought about it and changed from his stark white shirt and faded jeans. Hopefully he wouldn't somehow glow under the dark blue-gray colors of the lake above the Dome. At least the almost full moon and starlight didn't penetrate this far below the water. So it wasn't imperative to wait for cloud cover.

As long as he kept himself under control, and as long as his fingers didn't light up or his eyes glow like a beacon in the darkness for any reason, he would stay hidden.

He hid on the far side of the fountain, breathing deeply to keep calm. If someone ventured out, they wouldn't see him right away. The rushing of the waters drowned out any movement as he crouched down and willed himself to be as small as possible. Which wasn't easy.

Several minutes passed with no sign of anyone, so he rounded the fountain slowly, but then frowned and ducked back to his hiding spot. There were two other students walking toward him.

What were they doing out so late?

Wait.

Blinking several times, he told himself that thick dark hair of the girl belonged to one of Trisha's minions, Alessandra, because he recognized the perfectly coifed wave of sandy brown hair on the male.

The same color as the Mattel dolls.

Ken-Doll.

But after the party, and after the *incident* with the fish, Kol knew Kendall was no longer dating Alessandra because he was interested in—

She laughed at something Kendall said, and Kol's blood boiled. He felt his own scales lift from his skin slightly, and he struggled to get his breathing under control again. Shutting his eyes tightly, he pushed them back down. It wouldn't be wise to show their current iridescence. Or his most likely still-glowing eyes.

Kol no longer cared about getting caught by teachers. He rose to his full height and waltzed right up to them. Kendall flinched at his approach. Myreen narrowed her eyes.

"It's past curfew," Kol said. Matter-of-fact.

Myreen covered her mouth.

Kendall scowled—clearly recovered from his immediate reaction to Kol. "Right," he said. "You don't turn us in, we won't turn you in." He gripped Myreen's elbow to lead her away.

Kol side-stepped to block their path.

"What do you want?" Kendall asked, injecting annoyance into his tone. "Can you believe this guy?" he asked Myreen, hooking a thumb in Kol's direction.

"Where have you been?" Kol asked, looking directly at Myreen. But making sure his voice said he didn't really care about her whereabouts. Like it was typical, small talk to meet in the gardens at midnight to have a chat. He knew he wasn't kidding himself, but was very practiced at sounding like he was indifferent.

She glanced at Kendall before opening her mouth to speak.

"It's none of your business where we were," Kendall cut her off before she could.

"I wasn't asking you." Kol seethed, but kept his cool. "Myreen can answer for herself."

She looked at Kendall again, who had moved a step ahead of her, putting himself between her and Kol.

"Kendall took me swimming," she said softly, not meeting his eyes. He noted that her hair was wet. And so was her shirt. Why hadn't she worn her smart clothes?

"I thought the pool was closed," Kol said. Myreen's eyes drift up toward the vastness of the gray-blue Dome.

Out? How did they get out?

"Mers gotta swim," Kendall said, shrugging his shoulders.

"So why are you out so late?" What was he doing? Why couldn't he let this go?

"Like I said," Kendall said, moving another step forward so he was only a foot away from Kol's white shirt. "We won't say anything if you don't." He poked Kol in the ribs, goading him.

Kol balled his fists, the paper of the bag crinkling in his hand. If he wasn't careful, he'd light it on fire. He could see the reflection of the blue glow of his eyes over Kendall's shoulder in the waters of the fountain. If he wasn't careful...

"Are you gonna hit me again, *prince?*" Kendall spat, jutting his chest out like he did that night.

Kol didn't have to look at Myreen to see the look of shock pass over her features.

"What is he talking about?" she asked.

"Didn't you hear?" Kendall spat, keeping his eyes trained on Kol's. "The *prince* has a fiery violent streak." To keep with dramatics, Kendall placed a palm on Kol's chest. "You'd better stay back, Myreen. I wouldn't put it past him to hit a girl."

Kol *wanted* to hit Kendall again. He deserved it. But it would only prove him right.

"I don't hit girls," he said, his voice low. "But I don't hit men, either."

Kendall scoffed.

"*Fish,*" Kol said, certain that Myreen hadn't heard him. He dared glance in her direction, but her eyes were trained on her fingers again. He was pretty sure she hadn't heard. And if she did, she had to know he wasn't talking about her.

Kendall calmed and stepped back, taking Myreen by the hand.

Kol glanced away. "I've gotta go," he mumbled and turned back toward the dorms using his long legs to put distance quickly between him and *them*. He was a glutton for punishment, and turned to look back, fully expecting to see Myreen and Kendall gazing into each other's eyes at the fountain's edge or engaging in a torrid make-out session.

But they weren't. They were heading back to their own dorms.

And he caught Myreen looking back at him, too.

Oberon

"You're lucky, you know?" Ren said as he kept pace with Oberon. It was Monday morning, an hour or so before classes began, and the duo were walking from the Grand Hall to their classrooms.

"And what makes you say that?" Oberon asked.

Ren snorted. "As a gryphon, you can just slip away like you did two nights ago and fly around in the sky for as long as you want, getting away from the claustrophobia of the Dome."

Oberon hadn't exactly been flying two nights ago. He'd been meeting with Leif Villers. And if word got out that he'd been communicating and plotting with a vampire—even one who had allied himself to the shifter cause—bad consequences would follow.

Any vampire was a threat in the eyes of the military, as well as every other shifter Oberon knew. Even if they claimed to be aiding the shifters.

"Sure, I can go up-top, walk the streets of the surrounding cities,"

Ren continued. "But I can't do so in my kitsune form without being spotted as a freak."

"You invented this place, Ren," Oberon said. "You took the possibility of this underwater school and made it a reality. And now you feel its walls closing in on you?"

Ren held a finger in the air. "Oh, I've invented lots of things I haven't liked."

"Oh, really?" said Oberon. "Name one."

"Easy. The tooth sealer device."

Oberon gave Ren a confused look. "Every dorm room has one of those, Ren. All of our students use it twice a year, and you've completely eliminated the need for dentistry in the Dome, allowing healers to focus on other things. It's some of the best preventative health machines you've ever created."

Ren looked about the empty hallway that ran between the Military Training Room and the Research Lab. "You want to know a secret?" Ren whispered. "I haven't used it in years."

Oberon snickered. "You probably have a mouthful of cavities."

"I'd rather take the cavities than have *everything* I chew on feel like it's made of rubber."

Oberon shrugged, shaking his head. "It takes a few days to get used to the extra bounce. But I don't even notice it now."

"It's wonderful to know you are so adept at… adapting," Ren said, stumbling over the impromptu tongue twister. "But me? I could never get used to that rubber feeling. And I won't lie, Oberon. I'm having a hard time staying confined to the Dome. I've been here for years. Don't get me wrong, this alliance of shifters is needed, and I'm grateful for it."

"You're wanting to leave?" Oberon discerned.

The kitsune bobbed his head from side to side. "Not *leave* leave. More of a change of pace."

"Like what?"

Ren stopped in his tracks, causing Oberon to do the same. He turned around to face the math teacher.

"I'm a master tinkerer and inventor," he said, as if it were something as easily worn as a pair of shoes. "I teach math."

"You're an invaluable resource in both capacities," Oberon agreed.

Ren shook his head. "It's not enough. I want more."

Oberon studied him for a few moments.

"Director?" he asked. "You want my job? Because it is all yours."

Ren's brow furrowed. "No, no, no. I don't want your job. I can barely direct myself, let alone an entire school."

"What is it you want?" Oberon asked.

Hesitating, Ren took a nervous look behind him. The hall was still empty.

Turning back to face him, Ren said, "Do you ever miss it?"

Oberon blinked. "Miss what?"

"The frontlines, Oberon. You're really going to make me spell it out? I miss the vampire fights. The need to protect our people."

"Ren, those days are long over." Oberon suddenly felt tired and old.

"Maybe for you," Ren replied. "And I understand your reasoning and your guilt."

Guilt?

Oberon set his jaw. Ren was referring to his broken promise twenty years ago. A promise he'd made to his wife, Serilda, to never leave her to go hunting vampires. A promise that, when broken, had resulted in her death. The ultimate consequence.

He was angry at such a comment. It felt like an accusation. Oberon wanted to put his life-long friend in his place—

"Look, all I'm asking is that you think about transferring me to the military. My team of tinkerers are more than capable of taking over the school's projects. And if you find the time to look at the schematics I sent you a couple days ago, you'll see that I'm the perfect candidate to manage the vampire tracking system for the military."

Oberon exhaled slowly, his teeth closed and his cheeks puffing out. He knew Ren hadn't meant to aggravate him. But the wounds produced by the loss of his wife were easily reopened.

"I went over the schematics last night," he said at last. "They look good, and I believe Delphine will be willing to fund the prototypes. But just because I approve of this, does not mean I will warrant a direct transfer to the military."

Ren frowned.

"You are too valuable to send out into the fight," Oberon explained. "And your tinkering projects are doing a lot more for our cause than you probably realize. Trust me, you're supporting the military just by staying here and giving them any technological advantage possible."

"I guess I get nostalgic about the days when me, you, and Jade were the shifter army," he said, half-grinning.

The mention of Jade brought on another wave of sadness. She'd been their friend back in the old school—a naga. The trio had studied together for years, being the same age and going through the same classes. They'd even graduated at the same time. But Jade had been killed in one of their fights against the vampires. Draven had taken her tail as a trophy.

"Back then, we were the only ones willing to fight," Oberon said. "And now, we've been able to train numerous others to continue what we started."

"I'm not twenty-one anymore, either," Ren added. "As much as I hate admitting it, I no longer have the youthful agility I once had."

Oberon chuckled. "That makes two of us." He placed a hand on Ren's shoulder. "The end of Draven is near. I can feel it. Stay here and invent. We need you."

Oberon's smart watch chimed, alerting him that a meeting was about to start.

"I've got an appointment with Myreen Fairchild. She's probably at my classroom door waiting for me."

Ren's dark eyes grew wide. "*The* Myreen?"

Oberon nodded, then turned around and headed for the nearby door that led to the hallway of classrooms.

"Do you still believe?" Ren called after him.

"Yes," Oberon replied without turning around. "I'll talk to you later, old friend."

He swept through the large entryway, his shoes tapping the smooth flooring. Following the curve of the Dome, he stepped past the first four classrooms. Sure enough, he found Myreen leaning against the closed door, facing outward. She was busy chatting away with another student—Juliet Quinn, one of the phoenix shifters, and daughter of Malachai Quinn, one of the school's greatest protectors.

"Forgive my tardiness, Miss Fairchild," Oberon said, interrupting their quiet conversation. "I was tied up talking with another teacher."

Juliet gave him a smile, then winked at Myreen. "I'll see you in class."

Myreen nodded and waved, stepping away from the door. "See you later."

Tapping his watch, Oberon opened the door to his classroom.

"Thank you for coming, Myreen," he said. "I'm glad to see you've been able to make some friends here at the school."

They stepped inside, triggering the sensor that turned the lights on.

"Juliet is great," she replied. "And it hasn't been easy, but I've managed to make a few other friends."

Oberon nodded as he sat down in his chair behind his desk. He powered on the tablet built into his desk and gestured at the chairs in front of him. "Please, have a seat."

Myreen pulled one of the chairs out from under the desk and sat down quickly.

"You're probably old enough to have experienced friends coming and going throughout your life," he said. "That is something that happens to everybody. Fortunately, some friendships last forever."

He thought briefly of Ren, how their lives had been forged together throughout the years.

Blinking, he noticed Myreen was waiting for him to continue.

A chuckle came from his mouth. "Forgive me. It's easy for me to get caught up in my own memories. Tell me, who else have you made friends with here at the school?"

Myreen shrugged. "Not too many others, really. The only mer who is willing to be friends with me so far has been Kendall. The other mer students have kept their distance from me, except for the ones who seem to hate me."

"I apologize for the difficult position you're in," Oberon replied. "I regret that we couldn't find you sooner. It would have helped in a lot of ways. But then again, your experiences growing up with the humans has made you the person you are today. Had you come earlier, you might not be the young lady you've become."

He hoped the words would give her some food for thought.

"Have you made any other friends with students outside of the mer?"

Myreen nodded, pointing her thumb over her shoulder. "Juliet has been a really good friend. She's… a lot like me. We've gotten along ever since we met last week."

Oberon was quite aware of the issues Juliet had been through. Her father, Malachai, had confided in him multiple times about Juliet's rough upbringing. The phoenix fighter had expressed how unfamiliar he was with parenting, and Oberon had struggled with giving him appropriate advice. He'd never raised any children. Serilda had been seven months pregnant at the time of Draven's devastating attack on the previous school. And she'd died, along with their unborn child, who would've been an adult by now.

He felt a stray tear trickle down his cheek.

"Director Oberon?"

He breathed deeply, wiping at his cheek. "I'm sorry. Our conversation has pulled on some tender thoughts."

He wondered what she was thinking, seeing the noble school director whimpering like an infant.

"It sounds like Juliet is a good friend," he said. "And more than likely, she needs you just as much as you need her."

"I've heard that around here, people kind of try to stick to their own kind," she said. "You know, mermaids with mermaids, dragons with dragons?"

Oberon smiled. "In terms of friendships, should we limit ourselves to just our own species? If I were to follow that line of thinking, I'd be one extremely lonely person. I am the last surviving gryphon, at least to my knowledge. My closest friend is a kitsune—Ren Suzuki, your math teacher. And I consider Delphine to be a close friend, too."

"And what about my friend Kenzie?" Myreen asked.

Oberon analyzed her for a second.

"You're referring to your friend who tagged along the night I brought you to the Dome?"

Myreen nodded.

"I must caution you about interacting with selkies," Oberon said solemnly. "They are magic users, and are quite mysterious. They keep themselves veiled, and so it is impossible to know what their intentions and motivations are."

"You want me to completely stop talking to her?" she asked with distress.

Oberon placed both hands on the table and leaned forward. "You are free to choose who your friends are. Nobody else has the right to make that choice for you. But history has shown how untrustworthy selkies are. I would urge you to stay close to the friends you've made here, and try to build new friendships with other shifter students. Particularly Kendall. He's a good kid, and I believe you will be able to learn much from him."

Myreen nodded, shifting a bit in her chair and struggling to keep eye contact. Oberon hoped that such advice wouldn't cause more problems for her.

"The real reason I asked you to meet me this morning was to find out how you're doing," he said, shifting the conversation. "How are your classes going?"

"For the most part, they're going well," she said. "There's so much to learn—everything is so new. It can be overwhelming sometimes."

"I imagine so," Oberon replied. "And I wish I could say it'll get easier soon, but I don't know how honest of a statement that would be. You have years of catching up to do."

Probably not the best thing to say to her, he told himself.

"But," he continued, "I believe out of any student in the school, *you* are the most capable of picking it all up quickly. Just make sure you're putting effort in. I promise you it will pay off."

"You really think I can do it?" she asked.

"I know you can."

She hesitated, then said, "I've been having a very hard time transforming at will."

He chuckled again. "There are a fair number of shifters who struggle with transformation in the beginning. Take your friend Juliet, for example. Sometimes these things take time. And at least you have water and buoyancy to help you out. Try being a gryphon with a father who tries teaching transformation by taking you a mile into the air and dropping you."

He raised one hand and slowly lowered it, matching it with a whistle that went from high to low until his hand smacked the table.

Myreen's eyes widened, more out of humor than surprise. "He really did that?"

Oberon smiled. "Multiple times. My mother was always there to catch me."

The memory of his caring parents threatened to force his emotions to resurface again. He kept talking to keep them at bay.

"My point is, keep trying. You'll get there, and it'll become second nature to you."

He saw confidence build in her sky blue eyes, and staring at them, he felt even more sure that this girl was the one. This was the siren. She'd figure things out in due time.

"Classes will start shortly," he said. "You better get going."

"Thank you. So much," Myreen said with a smile.

"You bet," Oberon replied. "And remember, my door is always open. If you ever need to talk, I'm here."

She nodded, then got to her feet, making her way between the desks and out of the classroom.

Oberon sighed heavily, tapping his tablet to prepare for another day of teaching.

Patience, he counseled himself.

Myreen

Despite the incredible time she'd had with Kendall in the lake over the weekend, and Oberon's advice that she should focus on that friendship, Myreen hadn't been able to get Kol out of her mind. The way that he had stood up for her at the party, when he *thought* Kendall had hurt her… She hoped it meant that he cared about her, more than just as a friend. He kept her at arm's length, and yet he kept butting in between her and Kendall. He was just acting straight-up weird. Was it too much to hope that maybe he couldn't get her out of his mind, too?

She understood that embracing Kendall was the smart thing to do. Never in her school life had such a good-looking, fun, and ambitious guy shown this kind of interest in her. And he had sway with the mermaids for some reason. If the two of them ended up dating, maybe the other mermaids would eventually accept her. It wasn't like she didn't have feelings for him, but that instant chemistry just wasn't there—not the way it was with Kol. And what a fool she was for letting that chemistry ensnare her, because he obviously didn't return those feelings, despite what Juliet insisted.

"What are you thinking about so hard?" Juliet asked as they walked to the dining hall for lunch after Myreen almost bumped into someone.

"Oh, uh, just how terrible I am at being a mermaid," she lied. "Mastery this morning was an epic fail. I can't make water do anything—aside from splash as I flail around hopelessly in it."

That part wasn't a lie. Mastery really had been a futile effort, and she presumed it would be for the foreseeable future. As connected to the water as she felt when she was swimming in it, water apparently did not feel the same way about her. Unrequited feelings seemed to be the theme of the day.

Juliet held open the door of the main building for her. "Eh, don't beat yourself up about it too much. I'm pretty terrible at being a phoenix, as you've seen for yourself from the mess you helped me clean up. I can't control the fire inside me worth a damn. At least you can transform, though. I still haven't been able to do that yet."

"But I can only transform as a reaction to salt water," Myreen corrected as they walked into the Grand Hall. "I can't shift at will, either."

"And that, my friend, is why we're the perfect match." Juliet winked.

"Exactly. If you were a guy, I would totally date you."

"If I were a guy, I would totally date you, too! As long as I didn't blow you up." They both laughed and got in line at the buffet station.

After they got their food, they scanned the tables for a pair of empty seats. Myreen caught sight of Kendall waving them over to his table, which was occupied by a few of his mer friends. She was grateful for his invitation, but gulped at the thought of intruding on the other mermaids. Juliet, however, wasn't shy about it at all, and eagerly went to his table.

"Hi ladies," Kendall greeted as they sat down.

Lenore and Helena took one look at Myreen and stood up, Lenore slapping Trevor's shoulder for him to follow.

"I'm still eating." He shrugged her off. Lenore narrowed her eyes at him for a moment, a "traitor" accusation in her glare. Then she and Helena walked away.

Trevor gave a curt nod to Myreen and continued to eat his food. She was grateful that at least one of Kendall's friends didn't hate her, or at least not enough to interrupt his meal.

"Sorry," Kendall said. "They'll come around. Just give them time."

Myreen nodded and sighed, then picked up her fork to start into her food. When she looked up, she saw Kol enter the dining hall with Nik and Brett, and her heart skipped a beat. She cursed inwardly, wishing that Kendall had that effect on her. She watched as he got into the buffet line and saw that everyone who had been ahead of him silently stepped aside to let him go in front of them. It wasn't the same thing as the way the mermaids at this table had treated her. Those students weren't moving away from him out of disgust but out of respect. Though Kol seemed perturbed by their action, he went ahead anyway and got his food.

"What is his deal?" Myreen couldn't help but ask, still watching him. She turned around to address Kendall and Juliet. "Kol, I mean. Why does everyone treat him like he's…"

"A prince?" Kendall finished for her with a sneer. Her attention to Kol hadn't been lost on him, and he felt a twinge of guilt for it.

She shrugged, feigning innocence. "Yeah. You said he was descended from dragon royalty, but why does that matter? He's not heir to some throne, is he?"

Kendall snorted a sarcastic laugh. "No, thank god. The Dracul family lost their throne centuries ago."

That name rang a bell. "Dracul? Why does that name sound

familiar?"

Juliet snickered behind a bite of pizza. "Okay, even I know who Dracula was."

"Dracula?" Myreen said a little too loudly, then markedly lowered her voice to continue. "Kol's related to Dracula? Dracula was a dragon? I thought he was a vampire." After all, now she knew vampires existed, so anything was possible.

Juliet laughed again and shook her head. "Nope, that was a rumor started by the vampires. Vlad Dracul was a dragon king, and his family fought off vampires for decades before he took the throne. That whole thing about mounting bodies on spikes? Those were all vampires. Impaling is one of the best ways to kill vampires, as long as you get them in the heart."

"Wow, I would have never imagined Dracula was a dragon," Myreen mused, stabbing at her tuna salad with her fork.

"You know the word Dracul means dragon, right?" Trevor asked in a snide tone. "It's not like it's that big of a stretch."

Kendall hissed at Trevor—a warning to be nice, Myreen assumed. Trevor rolled his eyes, but nodded his acceptance. Apparently, just because he didn't leave, didn't mean he didn't dislike her.

She tried to let his negativity roll off her. "Okay, so if Dracula was a shifter, why did the vampires start a rumor that he was one of them?"

"He waged a war against them," Kendall answered. "It wasn't public, though, that his enemies were vampires. Back then, humans were very superstitious, and I guess he wanted to protect his people from the truth of vampires, otherwise they'd freak out. So, the vampires used that against him. They started the rumor that he was a vampire so his own people would turn on him, and it worked. That respect for him turned into fear, and his campaigns on vampire-infested lands failed. His family had to flee and lost all respect of the humans they swore to protect."

"But even after they lost their crown, his family continued to fight for shifters," Juliet said. "And not just dragons, but every kind of shifter. That's why, to this day, they're still respected above all others. Kol's father is the general of the shifter military, ranked even above my dad. If he wanted to declare himself some kind of king of the shifters, I doubt there'd be anyone who would put up much of a fight."

It was Trevor's turn to snort. "I would follow no royalty but my own." He slapped Kendall on the back.

Myreen furrowed her brow at that, a question mark on her face as she looked at Kendall.

"Didn't you know, Myreen? Kendall is a mer prince," Trevor said. "Oh, of course you wouldn't know. You've got stars in your eyes for that dragon."

"Trevor, that's enough," Kendall cautioned with a note of authority, and Trevor's posture stiffened.

"Sorry," Trevor said, all traces of disdain gone from his voice. "I just meant that my allegiance is to your royalty, if I ever had to choose."

"Wait, you're a mer prince?" Myreen asked Kendall. "Why didn't you tell me?"

Kendall shrugged like he didn't care, but couldn't keep the proud smile from leaking through. "It's just not something I flaunt, that's all. And... I guess I wanted you to like me for me, not for my status."

She smiled. Could Kendall really be as good as he seemed? Not only was he a hot guy who liked her and *didn't hide his affection for her*, but now she found out he was a prince!

"Well, mission accomplished," she said, making him smile in a way that somehow made him look even more gorgeous.

"I understand that you mer just recently joined the rest of us shifters," Juliet said to Trevor, "but why are you all so against dragons? I mean, the Draculs fight for everyone, mermaids included. The least you could do is show a little respect."

"And what would you know about any of it?" Trevor retorted. "Either of you. You both only found out about shifters, like, yesterday. You weren't born into the world the rest of us know. So why don't you keep your opinions to yourself?"

"What's your problem, dude?" Juliet snapped, clearly getting her feathers ruffled. "It's not my fault nor Myreen's that we weren't raised in this world. We're both doing the best we can to catch up. But at least I know to respect those who made this life possible—who made this school possible. If it weren't for the Draculs, you mermaids wouldn't have had such welcoming shelter to come to on the surface."

"For your information, little bird, it was *mermaids* who funded this school," Trevor said, looking as though he was enjoying riling her up. "If it weren't for my people, none of you other shifters would have a shelter at all. You'd all be running scared as the vampires and hunters exterminate the lot of you."

Juliet's eyes were beginning to glow a threatening blue. If Myreen didn't do something to stop this argument now, they'd all be in danger of her unwieldy fire; although she didn't think she'd feel too bad if Trevor got a little singed.

"How about we all just agree that we owe a lot to everyone who came before us and just be grateful for this school?" Myreen said calmly.

"Very well said, Myreen," Kendall said. "Trevor, why don't you take a walk? We'll catch up later."

Trevor frowned, but he had too much respect for Kendall to argue any further. Without another word, he backed out of his chair and walked away.

Juliet was still breathing heavily as she watched Trevor exit the dining hall. "No disrespect to your people, Kendall, but some of your friends are real tools."

Kendall sighed and rubbed the back of his neck.

Before he could say anything to ease her frustration, Juliet stood up. "I think I'm gonna take a walk, too, before I explode all over you guys." Then she stomped away.

And Myreen and Kendall were left at the table alone. An awkward tension hung between them.

"I really am sorry about my friends," he said, looking conflicted. "Nothing would make me happier than to see them embrace you as I have. Not that I have anything against other shifters, but mermaids might be more willing to give you a chance if you took a break from Juliet. I know she's your friend, but she's pretty unpopular with everyone. Not just mermaids. Even the phoenixes keep their distance from her."

Myreen couldn't believe she was hearing these words come out of his mouth. "You're trying to tell me to stay away from the only person at this school who has never judged me? She's my only friend, Kendall."

"Look, maybe I said that wrong," he said, shaking his head. "I didn't mean don't be friends with her, I just meant you should branch out, is all. She's just not the easiest person to get along with. If other students see you hanging out with more agreeable people, they'll change their mind about you. Let them see you with the *right* people. The right person."

"Maybe mermaids are taught to pick and choose their friends based on status, but I'm not that kind of person," she said, her own anger spiking. "I'm not going to snub someone just because they're unpopular. And if that's the kind of person you are, then you shouldn't be spending so much time with me." She stood up and grabbed her tray, ready to go run after Juliet.

Kendall grabbed her arm. "Please, don't be mad at me. I really am just trying to help. Man, how did this conversation go so wrong? I was actually hoping you and I could… go out some time. Like, on a… date."

Was he really asking her to out after he just insulted her only friend here? He sure had the arrogance of a prince.

"What do you even like about me?" she asked. "You're a prince, and I'm an outcast. You could probably have any mermaid you want. What makes me so special?"

"I already told you," he said, an endearing vulnerability in his sky blue eyes. "You're different."

"And yet you're telling me to be like everyone else," she said. She pulled her arm out of his grasp. "I can't have this conversation right now. I need to go check on Juliet."

He stood up and followed her as she left the dining hall. "Myreen, wait."

She stopped and turned around.

"Would you just think about it?" he asked. "Us, I mean. I'm happy to keep tutoring you, even if you just want to stay friends. But I'd like to try being more. Just… think about it. Okay?"

She looked at him for a moment as they stood outside the arch of the dining hall. Part of her wanted to just say yes, to give this a try. He looked so sincere as he waited for her answer. Her lowered self-esteem—inflicted by the judgment of everyone else at this school—couldn't let her see why a guy like Kendall would like her so much. It didn't make sense. Kind of like her gravitation toward Kol.

She had allowed herself to get caught up in the drama of her romantic feelings for both boys, because it was a distraction from her sorrow over her mom. Daydreaming about them meant escaping her mourning and fear. But the reality was that she wasn't in the right place to go out with Kendall. Not right now. Especially when she had feelings for another guy.

Kendall was still waiting for a response, so just to end the tense moment, she nodded. That seemed to be enough for him. She turned around and went in search of Juliet.

Leif

Relief flooded Leif as he stepped off the airplane. He was a firm believer that humans and vampires were meant for staying on the ground. The sky was for shifters and birds.

Oberon had utilized school funds for the flight, and the entire way had been a cruel torment for Leif. He didn't know why he was so terrified—if the plane were to crash, the chances of him actually dying were extremely slim. Minus a decapitation, he'd regenerate with no problems. But he'd still feel whatever pain he'd incur from an unfortunate accident.

"The things I do for shifters," he mumbled.

A vampire trapped on a plane full of humans, he thought. *Like a snake in a box of mice. Except the snake is pretending to be a mouse.*

Leif could hardly believe he was back in the state of Washington. He'd had a direct flight to Wenatchee, and he'd purposely caught an evening plane.

He'd only packed a carry-on with clothing. There was no way that airport security would have allowed him to bring blood bags on the plane, so it was easy to pack light. Leif knew there would be plenty of blood options at Heritage Prep—the vampire school run by Draven. And honestly, blood was the least of his worries right now.

His chief concern at the moment was figuring out how he was going to convince Draven to let him rejoin the organized group of vampires.

Leif had spent a good portion of the flight running through different scenarios. In every case, he only saw the wrath of the vampire leader coming down on him like a slab of copper.

The other huge thing on his mind had been the girl he'd met in the alleyway back in Chicago. The selkie. She hadn't been Gemma, but she looked like she could be her sister. And she knew all about the old magic—had even used some on him. But he'd screwed up the conversation—he'd tried his best to be friendly. Even with the offer to help her get into Oberon's school...

"Hello sir," an airport employee said cheerfully, interrupting Leif's thoughts. "Welcome to Pangborn Memorial Airport. Are you in need of a ride? We have a few shuttles that can take you into town, as well as a cab service."

"I don't need a drive, thank you," he replied. "I can walk just fine."

"Forgive me," the uniformed man said. "I wasn't implying you couldn't walk. The convenience of a drive is something we're happy to provide."

"Trust me, walking is much more convenient for me," Leif said, dragging his carry-on right past the man.

"Of— of course," the man stammered. "Thanks for flying."

Leif didn't respond as he made for the automatic glass doors that led out into the cool Washington night.

Outside of the airport, he was happy to see just how not-busy the

244

place was. Only a few cars were out, either dropping off or waiting to pick up passengers.

Wenatchee got him relatively close to his destination. Heritage Prep was located within Cle Elum city limits, but a bit north in an outcropping of the mountains along the Teanaway River.

That meant Leif would have to cut southwest through some rougher terrain. It would be a difficult hike over the Columbia River and through the Wenatchee Mountains—at least for a human. Leif would have no trouble with the journey. His vampire speed would get him to Heritage Prep soon enough.

Pressing forward, he took long strides in the appropriate direction. Technically, he was in a neighboring city to Wenatchee, but it would only take him a half hour or so at top vampire speed to make it to Cle Elum.

He considered traveling down to Vancouver—it had been years since he'd visited where the Frost Boarding House had been. That was the only place he'd ever felt truly at home. Leif had run away from his parents in California at the age of fifteen, and the Frosts had taken him in, giving him room and board in exchange for him to manage their orchard. They had become like family, and he'd gotten particularly close to their daughter, Camilla. A sibling bond had formed between them. She'd become a sister to him, and he missed her dearly. He wished he could confide in her right about now.

But Vancouver was out of the way, and Oberon would have looked down on such an excursion. Perhaps after his rejoining of the vampires, Leif could make a trip down memory lane.

Drawing out the arm straps on his carry-on, he hoisted the bag onto his back. It was late enough in the evening that he didn't worry about being spotted. Leif would stick to the shadows in the city, and once he was to the mountains, he'd be free.

The sooner he got to Draven, the sooner he could finally be with

Gemma. That was the only thing that mattered.

***

Thirty minutes later, Leif was descending from the mountains, the towering gothic turrets of Heritage Prep pointing high into the air like spears. There were a dozen of them—all black—appearing to be connected to one big shadow in the night.

Leif came to a stop and set his jaw: this was the last place on earth he wanted to be. He thumbed Gemma's brooch in his pocket.

"Is this what I should be doing?" he asked her.

Sometimes he'd hear Gemma's voice in his head, answering his questions and guiding him. He knew that those thoughts were likely his own, a mask he placed on them to help him feel that she existed in some way. Leif would never believe she was completely gone.

But Gemma's voice didn't fill his mind. Only Oberon's promise did. The gryphon had proven himself to be a man of his word. Their alliance had lasted for fifteen years, and in that time, they had grown to trust each other.

Leif looked down and kicked at a few loose rocks, causing them to go tumbling down the mountainside.

"I'm doing this for you," he added, nodding his head. "I *will* bring you back. I promise."

He continued his descent, his perfect balance and superhuman speed moving him quickly down to the base of the mountain.

Finding himself at the foot of the grand staircase, Leif angled his head up. Fifty-four stairs ran up to an enormous doorway like a dark tongue hanging out of the maw of an enormous beast. And he was about to enter it.

Leif began the ascent, and as he drew nearer to the door, he found one solitary figure standing at the top, arms crossed, waiting for him.

Beatrice Morton. The woman responsible for making him a vampire over a hundred years ago. And just twenty years ago, they had worked as a team to search for the shifter school that had been located in South Dakota. Leif had known Beatrice since his first day at the Frost Boarding House, where she resided for a time.

It seemed as if heavy weights had been fastened to his legs as he continued to approach her.

"Well, well, well, look what the werecat dragged in," she said as he got closer.

"Good evening, Beatrice," he said calmly.

She had a band wrapped around her wrist, and Leif saw her push on the small screen with painted, black-nailed fingers. She was in her customary black jeans and black hoodie with her platinum blond hair streaming out like a budding flower—a poisonous one.

"Leif Villers, I can't believe you've returned," she said, shaking her head. "Is life on your own beginning to become too much for you?"

"Still as lovely as ever," he replied, not answering her question. His lying would start soon enough. But for now, he just wanted to get away from her. "I need to speak to Draven."

She grinned slyly. "Fancy that. He's on his way down to greet you personally." Beatrice's face grew serious. "You do know that Draven swore he'd personally rip your head off if he ever saw you again, right?"

Nodding, Leif said, "I'm sure he won't be as happy to see me as you are."

Beatrice snapped her fingers and pointed at him. "Bingo! The truth is, I've missed you Leif. Life is just not the same without you."

Leif made it to the top of the stairs, keeping a few feet between them. Easing over to him, Beatrice planted a kissed on his cheek. He had a sudden urge to push her away, but she wrapped her arms around his neck and brought her red lips close to his ears. Whispering, she said, "I'm hoping you've finally forgotten that selkie and have considered a proper relationship with me."

Leif gently took Beatrice's arms from around his neck, then held them between the two of them. As quick as he could, he grabbed her by the shoulders and made to trip her down the stairs. But she was just as quick as he was, and just as strong. She smacked his arms away, her leg speeding into a blurry kick aimed at his chest. He quickly blocked it with his arms, putting all his force into pushing against it. She spun from the velocity and his strength, and Leif took advantage of her unbalance by sweeping his leg into hers.

Beatrice went sprawling, and he grabbed her out of the air to launch her down the stairs. But she dug her fingernails into his arms as he went to throw her, locking her grip. He lost his balance, and they ended up tumbling down the stairs like wet clothes in a dryer.

Leif impacted at the bottom of the stairs with a hard *thump*, but felt no pain. His body rejuvenated quickly. What surprised him was Beatrice lying on top of him.

"Thanks for the dance, Leif," she said. Before jumping away from him, she pecked his lips.

Leif was infuriated by the kiss and leapt to his feet, spitting and wiping at his mouth. Throwing Beatrice a glare, he saw that she was grinning impishly.

"Are you two fools finished yet?"

Leif looked up to see the dark form of the vampire leader standing ominously at the top of the stairs.

"We were just catching up," Beatrice said, her hood down and her blond hair bouncing as she pranced up the staircase. "Leif stole my heart a century ago."

Leif began a slow ascent, allowing as much space between him and Beatrice as possible. "She never had one," he said loud enough for them to hear.

She snapped her fingers again. "He *stole* my heart and to this day he continues to *break* it."

"You two have the oddest relationship," Draven said.

Leif knew he'd encounter Beatrice again at some point. He just wished it would have happened after he met with Draven. This night wasn't going as well as he'd expected, and that was saying a lot.

At last, Leif stepped up to Draven. The vampire leader was wearing dark slacks and a pressed, lavender button-down shirt, pointy, polished shoes finalizing his outfit. His brown hair was styled perfectly, and his meticulously-groomed five o'clock shadow framed his face. He appeared as if he were about to go hit up the local Cle Elum pub.

Draven sized him up. "How long has it been, Leif? Ten years?"

Leif met his gaze. "Fifteen. But who's counting?"

Draven snorted. "Who indeed?" He wagged a finger. "I'll tell you what, you are one elusive vampire. I've never known anybody else who has been able to stay off the grid as well as you have."

With a shrug, Leif said, "We all have our talents."

Draven nodded. "So we do. Come in, won't you? There is much for us to discuss." The vampire leader turned around and walked through the massive threshold.

Beatrice nodded her head toward the entrance. "Better keep up with him. Despite his relaxed demeanor, he's furious with you. Better not keep him waiting."

Leif eyed Beatrice warily as he walked into the vampire fortress. The place looked the same as it had fifteen years before. The entryway was expansive, large blood-red banners holding a dark outline of a drop of blood hung near the ceiling. Underneath each drop was written *Heritage Prep.* The vampire fortress was also a school and recruitment center for possible vampires, called Potentials. Long ago, vampires didn't care necessarily *who* they bit to increase their numbers. Draven had taken a special liking to the most brilliant minds in the world. After all, what being of intelligence wouldn't want to live eternally?

Leif contained a shudder. He hated the dark feeling bouncing around the black walls, holding shadows that danced in the candlelight. He couldn't think of any other place in the world that had made him feel more unsettled. Except for maybe Beatrice's arms.

"So many memories, huh?" Beatrice said. "I can't believe you willingly left this remarkable place."

Leif bit at his lip, not wanting to say what was really on his mind.

She pointed to their left. "In case you missed it, Draven went into the trophy room. He's waiting for you there."

Leif bobbed his head in acknowledgement and stepped over to the open doors. The trophy room was a large chamber that was used solely for collecting rare objects—including fascinating body parts of shifters Draven had killed.

Walking through the large arched doorway, Leif saw Draven sitting behind a desk, his legs propped up and his arms behind his head.

"Take a look around, my friend," Draven said, admiring his ornamented walls. "I've increased my collection while you've been gone."

In sections based on different shifter species, Leif saw the long, lizard-like tails of several nagas. They ranged in an assortment of colors, as did the sections with mounted mermaid and kitsune tails. Displayed on the wall directly above Draven's desk were the two sets of gryphon wings the leader vampire cherished so much. There was empty space above them—a place to mount the wings of the final gryphon still alive: Oberon.

"Impressive," Leif said, the first of many lies he'd tell spilling from his mouth. Leif was disgusted.

Getting to his feet, Draven said, "It is far from complete. Throughout the years, we vampires have been successful in hunting down shifters who have joined together in schools and other groups. But this hidden academy we keep hearing about has been most elusive."

"They must be getting smarter," Leif replied.

Draven stared at him with piercing eyes, but Leif didn't shy away from his gaze.

The vampire leader began to slowly pace around the room, glancing admirably at his trophies.

"Indeed." Draven stopped walking and narrowed his eyes at Leif. "What shifter news do you bring from Illinois?"

And there it was. Leif figured Draven's network of spies would have discovered him eventually. The question was, how long had Draven known his whereabouts in Chicago?

Leif shrugged. "You know me. I gave up hunting shifters long ago."

Half smiling, Draven pointed a finger at him. "As elusive with words as you are with your place of residence. Perhaps a more direct question will provide more direct answers. Have you run into any shifters in Chicago?"

"The chances of *running into* shifters anywhere is high," Leif replied. "They're all over the place. But I haven't actively sought them out. Let me ask you something: How long have you known I've been laying low in Illinois?"

Draven snorted. "The prodigal son returns home and starts asking questions." Shaking his head, he said, "You don't have such privilege, Leif. Tell me. Why did you come back?"

The question hung like smoke in the air. It had been the one Leif had been dreading the most.

He kept his face solemn. "You know precisely why I've returned. To be honest, I thought I'd be fine in solitude again. I was wrong."

Draven crossed his arms and put a finger to his lips. "You desire to rejoin us, and yet you hate the idea of hunting shifters. I find that strangely paradoxical, don't you?"

"I don't revel in their deaths like most vampires," Leif said, being careful of his words, "but I've come to believe that while our goals might be different, they do intersect."

Shaking his head, Draven said, "You are still in pursuit of finding a way to bring back your selkie girl?"

Leif gritted his teeth at the loose mention of Gemma. She was a lot more than a *selkie girl* to him.

"You've got to stop living in the past, Leif. People die—every day, actually. And none of them ever come back. The magical power to bring people back to life is a fable to keep fools like you hanging on to a thread of hope."

"I can't let go, whether it be a rope or a thread," Leif said. "I will help you in your hunt if it means I might run into magic users."

A dark laugh erupted from Draven's mouth. "And will you kill them if they refuse to help you? Will you act as a vampire should?"

Leif didn't hesitate. "I'll do whatever it takes."

Their eyes locked and Draven stepped slowly to him until their noses nearly touched.

"No," Draven muttered.

Leif blinked. "'No' what?"

"No, you may not rejoin us. You abandoned us when we needed you. I should kill you now for your betrayal."

Leif wanted to lash out and kill Draven and do Oberon—and the world—a favor. But he knew he couldn't. His fight with Beatrice outside was proof enough that a fight between vampires was a lengthy task. Every vampire in the school would be alerted, and his life would be over in minutes.

"And you'd be doing me a favor," Leif replied.

Draven tilted his head back, his face contorting ever so slightly out of confusion. "You… would accept death with open arms?"

"I've been living half a life for over a hundred years. Death would bring me a freedom I've waited a long time for."

The vampire leader's eyes narrowed. "And you've come here purely out of selfish reasons? To hunt down a shifter or other magic user to aid you in your quest to bring back your long-lost love?"

Leif knew this wouldn't be enough for Draven, but he thought he'd start with it. "I have... other goals as well."

Draven's eyebrows raised. "Like what?"

"I seek to hunt down and eliminate the Dracul line of dragon shifters."

Leif still had a burning hatred for the royal dragon line, despite aiding the shifter world for the past fifteen years. The proud, sadistic look on Aline Dracul's face came to his mind. He realized that his last statement held more truth than he'd expected. He felt his rage build up for the dragon shifter who'd been living at the Frost Boarding House all those years ago. She'd somehow found out the secrets he and Gemma held, and Aline ended up murdering his love as a result.

He found his hands clenched, the muscles in his arms tight and his nostrils flaring. Of all the things Leif had been through, his life had changed for the worse because of Aline Dracul.

"Now that's the fire I needed to see," Draven said, taking a few steps back. "The passion and anger that invigorates the soul. If you can keep that up, you may rejoin us here at Heritage Prep."

Leif blinked, his eyes refocusing as thoughts of his past drifted away.

"That's it?" he asked. "I'm back in?"

Draven gave him a hard look. "That's the first step. But since I'm not killing you, you require *other* punishment for abandoning your brothers and sisters here. It will be a means of testing your loyalty to me and the vampire cause."

Leif had guessed there would be some sort of punishment. But he'd suffered more mentally than any physical ailment could even come close to.

"What will you make me endure?" he asked.

"Meet me at sunrise down in the dungeons," Draven said. "Your punishment will be analyzed by Potentials as well as other vampires who seem to have... issues being a vampire. As for what you'll be enduring? You will be going into it blindly. You might want to *fill your tank* with some human blood tonight. And you might want to get as much fresh air as possible."

These were hints to his future torture. Thirst was surely involved. But needing fresh air? That could point to several different outcomes.

"If you decide to make a run for it," Draven added, "I will send a team after you and they will see that your head and heart are removed from your body. Do you understand?"

Leif bowed his head. "Yes."

"Good." Draven gestured toward the door. "It's time for you to leave. See you in the morning."

Leif nodded once more, then turned to make his way out.

Back in the entryway, Leif was relieved to see that Beatrice was nowhere to be seen. He didn't feel thirsty after the conversation with Draven, but decided some fresh air would be nice. Tomorrow would come too quickly.

Kenzie

Kenzie lay in bed, unable to sleep as she took stock of her life. She missed Myreen, wondering how she was doing, what she was doing, and if she'd made any more friends. They hadn't really talked since the party. Kenzie had just sent a quick text to let Myreen know she'd gotten home safe. She assumed Myreen was busy, probably with all sorts of exciting shifter stuff. And Kenzie was busy, too, but if she was to be honest, she'd have to admit she was kind of grateful Myreen hadn't tried to contact her. The green-eyed monster was a nasty beast, and as much as she cared for her friend, being around her right now hurt. Besides, Myreen had friends at the school. She'd be fine.

And the vampire she'd met, Leif, wouldn't quite leave her thoughts alone, either. It didn't make sense for a vampire to have a grimoire, unless it was his. Could he have been a male selkie? They were rare, but not entirely unheard of. Becoming a vampire would destroy his magic, leaving him unable to open parts of the book. Still, he should know more than a couple of low-level spells. Of course, she hadn't even heard of that communication spell. Why bother with a cell phone when you had that? If mom or Gram hadn't taught that to her, chances are they didn't know the spell. Maybe his family was similarly strict?

Of course, there was always the possibility he'd killed a selkie to get the grimoire. Kenzie shuddered at the thought. Somehow, she didn't think that was the case with Leif, but still... *Don't assume that because he's good looking, he's a good guy,* Kenzie chided herself. She'd met enough ugly-hearted beauties to know there was a difference.

The sound of the front door opening and closing caught her attention. She tapped the top of the clock at her bedside, making the face glow. It was after one in the morning. She strained to hear the voices, her body tense. She relaxed as she recognized Gram's warm tones.

Curiosity grabbed hold of her, and sleep being as elusive as a cat, she crept to the door, prying it open just the tiniest of cracks.

Mom and Gram's voices drifted down the hall, but not nearly enough to make out the words. They laughed. Kenzie eased the door open and crawled down the hallway, stopping as soon as their conversation became clear. She sat on her knees, hoping she hadn't tripped any of Gram's spells. Although, maybe the woman hadn't bothered, it being so late on a school night and all. Still, experience taught her that the more distance she could maintain, the better.

"Not again! Mom, that's the third time this week." Kenzie's mom's voice came from the kitchen, pots and plates clanking. Why the woman would still be up doing dishes at this time of night, Kenzie had no idea.

"We can't afford to be picky. Besides, he pays good." Gram sighed. She sounded exhausted.

"But he's a vampire."

"And I've taken every precaution. Vampire money is just as valuable as shifter money."

Vampires? Kenzie thought they had no dealings with the other side, seeing how heavily their townhomes were charmed. But it would explain the late hour. And the weariness in Gram's voice.

"Not all vampires are willing converts," Gram continued. "Some have to leave behind homes and families. I'm there to help, if needed. That's all."

"But meeting them in the dark, alone? You don't know what could happen."

"I know that magic is a powerful currency. Selkies are few, and even fewer from such a strong bloodline as ours. It's in no one's best interest to kill me."

"Did you at least get the stuff for the poultice? The full moon is coming, and I want to be ready."

Kenzie stretched out so she was flat on the floor, giving her tingling legs time to recover. It didn't make sense that Mom and Gram still kept stuff from her. She was sixteen now. Practically an adult. And they'd denied her the magic she'd craved, saying it was for her own safety. Yet here the two women were, putting their necks on the line meeting with vampires and weres and who knew what else? If something happened to them, Kenzie would be defenseless. Well, mostly defenseless. She'd been able to take care of that vampire with the spell Gram had taught her. But it was a temporary charm, meant to give her time to escape. Not exactly a lasting solution.

Wait, was this the reason they knew so much about vampires? Not fear, but experience? Kenzie wanted to storm into the kitchen and demand answers. But she couldn't bring herself to start that fight. Not again.

Kenzie sighed, then stiffened.

Leif had offered her a grimoire.

Kenzie's body buzzed with the thought. If he wasn't lying, if he really *did* want her help, maybe she should just say yes. Of course, bringing someone back to life was crazy, but he didn't need to know that.

The grimoire was the key, really. A selkie was only as magical as the spells she could wield, and spells were tricky creatures. Some spells simply failed, while others could backfire if done wrong. Gram had told her of one selkie who tried to cast a protective ward, only to suffocate herself. It was probably true, though the thought had crossed Kenzie's mind that Gram had made it up to keep her from experimenting.

The magic in their line was dying, or at least locking up like Gram's arthritic joints, and mom and Gram were just letting it happen. That was the rub of it. Kenzie did her best to remember every spell she'd ever been taught, but the mind wasn't the most reliable piece of equipment. Stupid short-term memory. And Mom and Gram forbade her from writing anything down, probably afraid of losing a new grimoire.

The sound of movement sent Kenzie scrambling backwards. She wasn't about to get caught. She hadn't made that mistake in years. Not since the time she'd been whisked to the ceiling by Gram's magic, after trying to find out who mom was with behind the locked door of the home office.

She slipped back into her room, silently closing the door. Mom and Gram were still talking, though their voices had taken on hushed tones. More shifter talk, or maybe vampires, or magic, or any number of things they kept from her. Kenzie looked down, the soft glow seeping from under the door touching her hands, now balled into fists.

It wasn't fair.

And just like that she knew what she had to do.

Diving under the covers, her heart threatening to beat out of her chest, she spoke just one word.

"Claoigha."

Though spoken barely above a whisper, the spell reverberated in her head like a bell. She directed her thoughts toward Leif, unsure if she needed to speak his name or if the spell itself was enough.

"Who is this?" The tone was guarded, but it was definitely Leif. There was a certain roundness to his voice and the way he shaped his words that carried a vintage vibe.

She was smiling like a fool. The spell worked. "Kenzie," she whispered, unsure if she could talk to him with the magic alone. "I, uh, reconsidered your offer. I'll have a look at your grimoire."

"Wait, who?"

"Selkie girl? You attacked me the other night in Chicago... This is Leif, right?" Could he have forgotten her already? Maybe the offer wasn't on the table anymore, now that he wasn't trapped by her magic.

"Oh! Yeah, it's me. You said your name is Kenzie?"

"Mmhmm. Are you okay? I'm not... interrupting anything, am I?" Kenzie hoped he wasn't feeding. That would be awkward. This whole talking to vampires thing would take some getting used to. Assuming this conversation went well.

"No. You actually caught me at a good time. So you'll help me?"

"I'll try. But I can't guarantee that I'll be able to raise anyone from the dead." *Hopefully I won't turn them into a zombie, either.*

"I understand. Just... let me know as soon as you can if you discover anything?"

"Right. Yeah, of course."

The tension in the connection eased. "I had hoped you'd contact me. I left the grimoire in my apartment in Chicago. Can you get there?"

"Maybe this weekend? I've got school."

"That's probably for the best. I'll probably be... indisposed for a few days. You'll have to use your magic to get into the apartment. I don't leave extra keys lying around."

"I can do that. Where are you, anyway?" She couldn't help her curiosity.

There was a pause, and Kenzie wondered if she'd lost contact with Leif.

"I had to go out of town," Leif said at last.

Kenzie let out a breath. "Will you be back soon?"

"I should be. Where do you live?"

"Why?" Kenzie fired back, her nerves on end. Maybe this was a mistake.

"I'll want to get in contact with you when I get back."

"Oh." Kenzie cringed. She hated to lead him here. Shallow Grave or not, it was still her town. "You won't... eat anyone, will you?"

Kenzie could practically feel Leif grimace. "Not if I can help it. I've got some blood ba—"

"Okay. That's good. I'll take your word for it." Just the thought of blood gave her the heebie-jeebies. She didn't want images of Leif guzzling the stuff down dancing in her head. "I can give you my address, but you won't be able to come here. My place is pretty heavily warded against... your kind."

"That's okay. I can send you a letter when I'm on my way back to arrange somewhere more discreet to meet."

They hashed out the rest of the details, and Kenzie closed the connection, relaxing into her bed. Her throat was hoarse from all the whispering, but she didn't dare sneak out of her room for a drink. If her mom caught her, she might figure out Kenzie had been snooping earlier.

Kenzie felt the briefest pang of guilt. To go behind her mom's back to meet with a vampire and practice magic was so far beyond anything Kenzie had ever done. She could already feel her mom's steely gaze, displaying that patented look of disappointment, down to the crossed arms and tapping foot.

Kenzie pushed that thought aside. The vampire had a grimoire he couldn't use. And she was a magic user without a grimoire. Mom had always told her it wasn't safe to practice magic without a spell book to guide her. Well, now she wouldn't be guessing. Besides, Gram said not all vampires are bad. Maybe this Leif guy was a good guy in vamps clothing. Maybe.

The thought made her smile. Perhaps he wasn't such a waste of a handsome face after all.

Leif

"Kenzie," Leif whispered. Their connection of magic had just ended. It had caught him off guard: he hadn't expected the girl to reach out so soon—or at all, for that matter. It had been a century since he'd had a conversation like that. It had been with Gemma.

But Kenzie was not Gemma, and Leif had to force himself to keep the differentiation there.

She even sounds like Gemma.

But that could have been his mind playing tricks on him. Because he'd do anything to hear Gemma's voice again.

He wondered for a moment if there was any possibility Kenzie and Gemma were related. He wasn't entirely sure how many selkie families were in the world. Gemma was originally from New York and had fled to Vancouver, Washington, due to a bad home life. That's where he'd met her: at the Frost Boarding House. Was it possible that part of her family immigrated to Illinois?

He'd have to find out Kenzie's last name and see if it was all more than just coincidence.

Kenzie had traded addresses with him, and he took her warning about her home being guarded very seriously. Selkies were a cautious people. Their magical abilities could do extremely strange things. The last thing he wanted was to walk in and have his arm shift to his waist, or his eyeballs to go vertical. Or spontaneous combustion.

But in his desperation to get Gemma back, he'd alerted a selkie right to one of his most treasured possessions: Gemma's grimoire. One of two items he'd kept that belonged to her. The other object was the brooch she had worn every day. Leif felt the outline of it in his pocket. He always kept it with him—it felt like a part of her was still with him.

But her grimoire—that was a different story. It was heavy and old. Leif only rarely ever looked at it. There wasn't much purpose in doing so—he couldn't use the spells it contained. The bulk of it he couldn't even understand. Most of all, he didn't want to run the risk of damaging any of the pages. The massive book could very well hold the secret to bringing Gemma back.

And so, it was hidden in a lockbox mounted in the closet of his studio apartment in Chicago. Leif had given her the passcode: 2907. It was more than just a number. It was a date. The numbers symbolized the greatest day of his life. The twenty-ninth of July. Back in 1898, it was the day he and Gemma were engaged to be married. But to Kenzie, those numbers would be arbitrary, lacking any meaning.

Soon, it would be back in the hands of another selkie. And he hoped Kenzie would come through and help him. She was young, and he had no idea just how experienced she was with her magical abilities.

Leif knew her motivations weren't centered around helping him. Not directly, anyway. She wanted the grimoire, likely to learn ancient spells. But if trading the grimoire resulted in Kenzie finding a resurrection enchantment that would bring Gemma back from the grave, the trade would be more than worth it.

And if she couldn't end up helping?

That was why he was back at Heritage Prep. It was why he'd come back to Draven.

Rejoining the vampires was a backup plan now. If Kenzie failed, he'd have to rely on Oberon to help him. And he'd promised the gryphon he'd find out what Draven knew about the prophecy and the siren.

Sticking his hand in his pocket, he pulled out the brooch. It was leaf-shaped with five points. The base metal was green, and the veins were made of gold. The bottom held a pearl, and the diamond-studded outlines of the wavy points ran to the middle. At the center was the face of a woman gazing solemnly to the side.

Leif held it to his lips and closed his eyes.

"I'm coming for you, Gemma."

***

The crack of dawn arrived, adding to the renewed hope Leif now had. To any other vampire, the first rays of sun would scorch bare skin away. But not Leif. The enchantment Gemma had placed on him over one hundred years ago was eternal and unbreakable. His resistance to the sunlight was like two magnets with the same poles—or at least that's how he understood it. Honestly, Gemma had tried explaining it, but her language had been from another time. Basically, it wasn't quite reflection, and it wasn't quite deflection.

While the sun did shine brilliantly, it also cast a shadow on his mind. It was time to meet Draven and suffer through whatever the vampire leader had decided was appropriate punishment.

Fortunately, Leif had been busy with his conversation with Kenzie and the thoughts of Gemma that had followed.

He got to his feet and began the long walk up the stairs that rolled up into the fortress known as Heritage Prep.

It didn't take as long to make the climb this time around, and Leif figured that had something to do with the fact that Beatrice wasn't waiting for him at the top. The memory from the night popped into his head, and he found himself wiping his mouth with his hand, as if her kiss was still stuck on his lips. He couldn't stop the shudder that ran from his head to his toes.

The huge, dark, cast-iron doors were shut to keep the sun out. No doubt all the windows in the school would be shut, too. Except maybe for the rooms where humans were waiting. Humans who served as feeders for the vampires, as well as the ones trying to prove their 'vampire worthiness' to Draven.

Leif was familiar enough with the entrance to know how to get inside. A door within the door formed. It was wide and high enough to let him through. It was just another trinket of technology Draven had somehow come to possess over the years, but it did the trick—only allowing minimal light to enter the fortress.

Stepping inside, his eyes had to adjust to the darkness. Once they did, the familiar figure of Beatrice stood in front of him. His hands clenched into fists and his jaw tightened. He couldn't stop the scowl from forming on his face. She was the last person he wanted to see first thing in the morning.

She had her weight on one foot, her shoulders hunched a bit with one hand on her hip, dressed all in black as usual.

"Have a good night?" she asked warmly, but her words felt cold to Leif.

He nodded. "Actually, one of the best nights I've had in a long time."

Smiling, Beatrice said, "Must've been from our dance."

Another shudder trickled through his body. "That had nothing to do with it, actually."

She put her free hand on her chest. "Ooh, Leif, that hurts."

"I've said it before, and I'll say it again." Leif pointed between himself and Beatrice several times in rapid movement. "You and I? Whatever we used to have together, that happened a *long* time ago. And it predates both of us being vampires. Whatever relationship you are hoping for with me will *never* happen. Not after the events you set into motion by turning me."

Her grin only increased. "I can offer you an eternity of love. That selkie of yours would have died eventually, anyway."

Anger bubbled in Leif like boiling water, threatening to spill over.

Calm yourself, Gemma's thoughts surfaced just before he was about to strike out at Beatrice. *She is desperate for any kind of emotion from you. Beyond blood, feeding off emotion is the passion of vampires. You saw what happened last time. Do not give her that control again.*

His breathing slowed at the very sound of her voice in his head. It was so vivid, as if a part of her were still alive. And Gemma's voice was completely right.

"I have a date with punishment that I'd better see to," he said, moving past her.

At the last minute, she grabbed his arm firmly, stopping his progression toward the stairs that led to the dungeons below.

She stepped close to him, bringing her cold lips to his ear.

"I don't want to see what Draven does to you down there," she whispered seriously. "But whatever torment he puts you through, I want you to know I don't agree with it. If you survive, I will be here to help you recover."

He tore his arm free from her grip and continued on.

"Don't worry about me," Leif called as he walked to the top of the stairs. "If I live, I'll recover just fine on my own. If I die? Well, you can start looking for others to promise your undying, eternal love to." *Actually, you should do that whether I live or die.*

Leif took two stairs at a time, his body descending in perfect sync.

It wasn't that he was excited for what he was about to go through. But he did want to get away from Beatrice. And the sooner he started his punishment, the sooner he'd be done.

At least he hoped.

The dark stone stairway was lined with muted lights, which were embedded in the walls. Long ago, when the fortress was built, the vampire originators had relied on torches. Those had long since been replaced. Draven was a believer of finding and utilizing technology as much as possible.

Following the half circle, he jogged past the opening that led to the first lower level. Heritage Prep was a massive place, and far more than just a school. Draven's legion of vampires were housed in the same place, and the higher up the ranks individual vampires became, the higher up in the towers they resided. The lower levels were living quarters and classrooms for Initiates—humans desiring to become vampires. Some of them were sons and daughters to the vampires living in the school, waiting to be turned, others were willing volunteers. Draven himself had been a human Initiate—at least until he'd come of age—but he'd been bred for a much grander purpose.

When Leif first arrived at the school twenty-five years prior, he was taught about nobility among vampires. Draven's lineage was the oldest, going back thousands of years. Each successive male vampire in his bloodline would mate with a human girl every fifty years to produce a male heir. The strength and abilities compounded with each generation, giving Draven abilities and strength unlike any other vampire.

Leif knew he stood in status as a result, but such classifications never bothered him.

Most Initiates were the main source of blood for the vampires living in the fortress, but Leif knew that a fair number of vampires had a thirst for hunting in the nearby cities and campgrounds. Some believed that the blood from unwilling victims was more satisfying than the Initiates, just waiting to be gifted immortality by being bitten.

Leif could sense groups of the humans congregated close by, more than likely being instructed by vampire teachers. He realized he didn't take advantage of drinking during the night. He'd been too wrapped up thinking about his conversation with Kenzie, and his hope for Gemma.

His shoes tapped against the stairs, echoing in his ears and bouncing off the walls both in front of and behind him. Leif was surprised that he didn't run into any humans or vampires along the way.

Five levels down, the stairs finally ended, opening into a wide chamber that held a damp and musty smell. Leif had rarely ventured down to the dungeons during his time working with Draven, and now he remembered why.

There were dirty cages lining the walls, their iron bars painted black. Most of them were empty, but Leif discovered that a few held humans who were suffering from their own punishments. They made no noises; there were several vampire guards around who were strictly there to stop any whimpering or begging.

One of the guards saw Leif and approached him. "Well, well, well," the short, stocky vampire sneered. "Look, fellas. Leif Villers really has come back."

The other nearby vampires turned their attention to Leif, and he found he recognized a few of them. And he definitely knew the one who was now standing in front of him, tapping a metal club against his hand. The dungeon keeper had a receding hairline, and his spiky-gelled white hair shot out at random points.

"Hello, Rory," Leif said. "I see that some things never change. Like your status."

The vampire's sneer disappeared, replaced with a wicked glare that Leif had seen on multiple occasions.

Rory pointed his club at him. "We'll see how snappy you are after

Draven's through with you."

"I can hardly wait for the party," Leif replied. "Where is Draven?"

Scowling, Rory twisted about and pointed the opposite direction. "Thataway. Past the next rooms of cages. Madness Chamber."

A shock of worry made Leif twitch at the mention of the torture room, the nickname bringing back memories. It was one room he'd never actually been to. But he'd heard plenty about it. And he'd heard plenty *from* it.

"That excited, are you?"

Steeling himself, Leif said, "I was simply worried my punishment was going to be a lot worse: having to report to you down here for the next month. I'd rather be stabbed in the chest by a copper pole."

Rory moved with superhuman speed, swinging the club straight at Leif's face. His rapid reflexes were triggered, and Leif caught the top of the bludgeoning weapon with his hand, matching the strength of the dungeon keeper, holding the club above both of their heads.

Gritting his teeth at the strain, Rory said, "You never were one of us. And you never will be."

Leif wanted to agree with him. The dungeon keeper was right: he would never be one of them.

Instead he said nothing, just kept his eyes locked on Rory's with bold determination.

His attention was pulled as Draven strutted into the room full of cages.

"Rory, Rory, Rory," he tsked. "Will you please explain to me why you're keeping Leif from his duties?"

Duties. So that's what the vampire leader was calling torture now. It seemed a little too fitting a definition.

"The outcast started it," Rory whined, relaxing his arm. Leif let go of the club.

"There's no need for insults," Draven corrected smoothly, shifting his gaze from Rory to Leif. "He's come back home. And outcasts *don't* come home, do they?"

Leif knew the question wasn't aimed at Rory.

"No, they don't," Leif answered.

Tilting his head, the vampire leader looked back at Rory. "See? We're all on the same team here." Bringing his pale blue eyes back to Leif, he said. "It's time."

Leif nodded, stepping past Rory.

"See you around," he said with a nod, then walked by the rows of cages, feeling the fearful gazes of the human captives following him.

"Sorry you got held up by him," Draven said as they walked side by side through the next room of cages. The apology was insincere, only used as a formality.

Leif kept his gaze forward, not wanting to see the haunted looks of the caged humans.

"I expected nothing less," Leif replied. "Rory is a fool."

"A loyal fool," Draven added.

A short, awkward silence surrounded them. To anybody's eye they would appear to be friends, perhaps walking off to share a meal together.

They walked into the next room, more cages set into the walls. Leif's footfalls seemed to get heavier the closer they got to the Madness Chamber.

"I must admit, I'm still shocked you came back," Draven said, breaking the quietness.

"It had to be done," replied Leif.

"Indeed."

They were now in an area of the fortress that Leif was entirely unfamiliar with.

"I should probably prepare you a bit for what's about to happen," Draven said. Again, the insincerity of his tone wasn't hidden. It seemed as if he were gloating.

We must be approaching the Madness Chamber.

Clearing his throat, Draven continued. "Typically, in similar instances, the punishment for deserting occurs at the top of the center tower—my personal chambers. The betrayer is placed in a cell made up of tinted glass that blocks out *most* of the sun. But not all. The roof of the tower opens, and the punished then suffers a slow burn that can last for several days. It's excruciating, from what I've heard. If the deserter desires to shift his loyalties back to me, salvation is rewarded just before death."

Leif shuddered. It was a torture created specifically for vampires. Gemma's spell would protect him from that kind of torture, and Draven knew it. Being a daywalker had given Leif vast privilege during his first stint with the vampires.

"Nobody has ever betrayed me twice," Draven continued. "It's a tough lesson to learn, but it is effective."

Up ahead, Leif could see a small doorway that was bleeding red light. He forced himself to swallow.

"Since that method of punishment would do nothing to you, I've had to think outside the box."

Upon reaching the doorway, Draven gestured for Leif to go in first. Leif looked at him, not seeking forgiveness or a way out, but exuding determination.

"Whatever you have prepared, I will prove my loyalty to you." *For Gemma.*

Stepping past the threshold, he saw that the red room was about as small as his studio apartment. And it was full of vampires gazing at him curiously. They pushed to the sides of the room, revealing a plexiglass container that had to be at least ten feet high and ten feet wide. Some form of liquid was inside it—Leif didn't want to guess what. But the whole thing seemed like something that would be found in an aquarium.

271

Except it lacked fish.

"You might be wondering why such a crowd is here," Draven said as he made his way over to the tank. "These are brothers and sisters who have expressed doubts about the vampire cause. Keep in mind that they haven't deserted. Leif, you are about to become their greatest teacher."

The door shut behind them, a steel bar falling into place, locking them inside. Leif was glad Rory wouldn't be able to watch from the doorway. Whatever Leif was about to endure, he didn't want the dungeon keeper to have the chance to gloat at him.

Looking the tank up and down, Leif said, "Acid? Chemicals?"

Draven furrowed his brows. "No, nothing that intense." The vampire leader tapped a screen that was embedded in the wall, engaging a pulley system that lowered a large, round slab of metal Leif had originally mistaken for part of the ceiling.

"I'm assuming that's copper?"

Draven rolled his eyes. "We're not monsters, Leif."

I beg to differ, he thought.

Another few taps on the panel by the door caused the far wall directly behind the tank to pull out into two staircases that surrounded the tank.

Leif looked at Draven in confusion.

"Come." Draven said, walking to the left staircase and gesturing for Leif to go up the right one.

He did so.

The top of the stairs joined together, creating a landing. From this high up, Leif could see the other side of the flat sheet of metal. Just as Draven had said, it wasn't copper, but a solid steel which seemed to be a common theme in the fortress. Leif had never noticed that detail before.

There were no chains, no locking mechanisms. Just a big, round piece of metal.

A lid.

Understanding dawned on him like the sun he'd witnessed climbing over the mountains that morning.

"Drowning," he mumbled.

Draven nodded. "Very astute, old friend."

Leif considered this. In all his years, he'd never experienced drowning before. A vampire couldn't actually die from prolonged submersion, but his body still required air. Such an experience would not be pleasant.

"This is Leif Villers," he called out, addressing the group of vampires in the room. "He was born in the late eighteen hundreds and was turned close to the turn of the century. Fifteen years ago, he deliberately deserted Heritage Prep and the vampire cause, outcasting himself into isolation."

Murmurs arose among the observers, causing Draven to raise his hand. They quieted down instantly.

These vampires hold a spark of rebellion that is about to be put out, Leif thought, sweeping his eyes over them. *And right now, if they would stand together, their strength in numbers would be too much for Draven. We could kill him. He's locked any help out.*

The thought was pointless. These vampires were still at the school, which meant they still had loyalties—however weak—to Draven. But maybe, given time, he could plant enough seeds to form a rebellion. A group of vampires who were willing to stand up to Draven. Leif started memorizing faces.

The vampire leader continued. "Last night, Leif returned asking for pardon and desiring to re-enter our family. After some discussion, it was agreed that he will be allowed readmission to our group of vampires and forgiven of his desertion after an appropriate punishment has occurred. Only then will the slate be wiped clean. May this be a lesson for you who have concerns about what we are trying to build in this world, and how trying to *go-it-alone* does not work."

The room went quiet as all eyes stared at Leif.

"How long?" he asked.

Draven pointed back down to the touchscreen by the door. "After your punishment begins, your countdown timer will appear there."

Leif nodded.

Wonderful.

"In you go," Draven said, placing a cold hand on Leif's shoulder.

Leif inhaled and exhaled a few times, knowing he wouldn't get the chance to do so again for a while.

Gemma, be with me, he begged. *I need you now more than ever.*

At random, the melody of Claude Debussy's La Mer popped into Leif's head. The song was a similitude of ocean waves and falling droplets of spray. Although the water below him looked still like a sheet of glass, Leif wondered if Gemma had been the one to bring the melody to his mind.

Taking one last breath, he said, "See you on the other side," then jumped into the water. It was cool against his skin, red lights at the bottom lighting up, making the water look crimson, like blood.

Leif watched as Draven ran down the stairs and punched in the command for the lid to fall into place. As it did, he suddenly felt himself being pulled down to the bottom, near the bright lights. The lid somehow had the ability to make him sink—more of Draven's strange technology.

Already he felt the need for another fresh breath. The air in his lungs threatened to spill out of him at any moment.

The tank vibrated as the heavy lid sealed into place.

Draven stepped away from the panel, and the digits that popped up on the screen took the air right out of him, causing trailing bubbles to dance in the red light.

It read *24:00:00*.

One whole day.

Gemma, I need you.

The thought came as his lungs filled with water, and his mind sputtered.

Gemma...

Kol

Kol adjusted again on the faux-leather bench in the corner booth, making that embarrassing squeaking sound. The one that always drew the attention and side-eyes of every person at every other table within hearing range. Even though they all *knew* what happened when denim rubbed against the always cracking upholstery.

Restaurant benches were not generally made with comfort in mind for persons over six feet tall. Being well over that called for constant discomfort for someone of Kol's stature. Hence, the need to shift sitting positions often. And the noises were a natural result of it.

He tried not to care too much as he swirled his spoon around his mug of too rich hot chocolate. He actually liked the change of location. Usually he was summoned to an up-scale private club in the VIP section, or a private table at the Oriole restaurant, which meant he had to dress up for a conversation with his father that would last less than five minutes.

Kol's liquid chocolate had gone cold, but it hadn't been very appetizing to begin with. He wished he'd brought Nik or Brett with him to at least kill time, since the General *always* made him wait. But his father had been very specific in his instructions that he come to the out-of-the way, run-down diner—that was no *Mack's Diner*—alone.

Being high up in the military, one would think that Eduard would always be punctual for his meetings. And Kol was certain that he was for everyone else, but something about *teaching him patience* was always the first thing that flew from Eduard's lips if Kol mentioned the tardiness.

Which was always.

He'd learned early on not to mention it.

The King's *Hound Dog* played over the speakers when the chime on the door rang the announcement of another patron.

Kol didn't even need to glance over to know his father had finally arrived and commanded the respect and attention of every host, waitress, and customer in the entire establishment as their heads all turned toward him. If Kol didn't have his own, albeit different, respect for his father he might've rolled his eyes.

He might've rolled his eyes if he'd been a little bit less anxious, too.

He had an inkling about the reasons for the meeting.

"Malkolm," Eduard said in his commanding voice and slid into the bench opposite Kol. Two of his underlings occupied a table two spots over. Within eyesight. Out of earshot.

"Father," Kol said, looking his father in the eye. He knew better than to cower, even though he knew what was coming. "Did mom come with you?"

"She's shopping."

Kol's mood deflated even more. He knew the reason his father wanted to meet, but he'd hoped to at least see his favorite parent to ease the blow.

He almost *knew* she wasn't aware of the task Eduard had given

Kol. She wouldn't approve of another Dracul male treating a girl the way she'd been treated her entire life. Victoria would never admit that it was nearly the same, just that it was cruel.

Eduard moved the mug Kol still fidgeted with to the side of the table, then laced his fingers together and leaned on his forearms. "She sends her love," he said.

If Kol didn't know the words were actually true, there's no way he would've believed it by the tone of his father's voice. All Kol could do was nod. "So," Kol said, *might as well get this over with.* "Oberon's office wasn't available this morning?"

"It didn't seem prudent to risk another student eavesdropping."

That's never bothered you before, he thought, but didn't voice it. Kol resisted the urge to narrow his eyes. He knew when his father wasn't telling the whole truth.

"Besides, I was in the area for another meeting."

And there it was. No need to inconvenience himself by trekking all the way to the school when he could summon his son, day or night, to anywhere in the greater Chicago area.

"Is the new mermaid in love with you yet?" It wasn't small talk and Kol knew it. They weren't having a father-son bonding moment over Kol's *almost* new girlfriend.

Which she wasn't.

"No," Kol said slowly then leaned forward too. "There are… complications. But you told me to *befriend* her. And I've done that. We're friends."

"A *friend* isn't going to divulge the same information a love-sick girl might," Eduard said with a half-smile that was rarely a friendly one. "You're a *Dracul*, son. We're royalty. And with that, a good head on your shoulders, and a face that any girl would fall for, I don't see the problem." He leaned back with his arms crossed. "What sort of *complications?*"

Kendall's smug face flashed in Kol's head. He shrugged. "It doesn't matter," he said. "I can handle it."

"Good." Eduard unfolded his arms and tapped the fingers of his right hand on the table. "Because if you bring up some excuse about taboo relationships between dragons and mers, I'll yank you from that school so hard and slap you right into the military where you belong."

Kol's heart sped. "But school—"

"Nonsense!" Eduard said. "You're seventeen. You're of age. And Colonel Candida has been asking about you."

Kol knew better than to say another word.

"Do what I've asked," his father said, his volume lowered, "and we won't have a problem. You can stay in your little *shifter school* until graduation. Now…" he smiled. Another forced half-smile. "Just so we're clear, what is expected of you, son?"

Kol wanted to argue that his father really had only asked for him to befriend Myreen. But it was futile to have the same argument about the General's wishes again. If it sounded like an implication or suggestion before, it was clear now. "Make Myreen my girlfriend." In order to make his father happy and to get the information he wanted, it was non-negotiable that he *date* her. Seduce her. *Make her his girlfriend.* It was the only way to ensure he could spend enough time with her to find out if she was indeed the siren from the prophecy.

Eduard raised an eyebrow. It wasn't enough.

"Make Myreen my girlfriend and make her fall in love with me." The words left him a little breathless. In order to do the latter, his heart was in serious danger. But also, he absolutely could *not* fall in love with Myreen. All because of the damned Dracul curse. Any love would be unrequited. If he fell for her, she would never love him back.

Eduard smiled. Now it was enough.

At least he'd be shipped off to the military and would never have to see her again if he failed and fell in love with her.

He felt the weight of what the General wanted him to do. Of what he was being asked to risk. And mixed with the sugary chocolate in his stomach, he felt sick.

Eduard pulled an envelope from the inside pocket of his jacket and slid it across the table.

"What's this?"

"The itinerary for your date," Eduard said smugly.

Kol dared to peek. There were several large bills and a card with the information of a dinner reservation for Mastro's Steakhouse. He swallowed the lump in his throat. Mastro's was very high-end. Eduard wanted Kol to show off his wealth and status to help Myreen fall for him.

When he glanced back at his father, he managed his very practiced *royalty* smile. "Yes, father," he said. "Thank you."

***

Kol paced the Avian common room, wearing down the floor with his lazy shuffling. The envelope with the money and reservation reminder was hidden away safely inside his shifter biology textbook. The one he hadn't cracked open in over a year.

Luckily, Nik and Brett were in class, otherwise they'd be bombarding him with questions about what the General wanted. They knew the only thing that would pull Kol from the school at the beginning of a school day—and actually get approved the day of one of Ms. Dinu's epic transformation challenges—was a summoning from Eduard Dracul.

So far, Kol had evaded their questions about the reason for Eduard's visit the day Myreen arrived, but another one this soon after probably had them both chomping at the bit to get it out of him.

But class was almost over, so it was best to leave where he might be found and find this girl to start the wooing process. He had been pacing and stalling, as if he still had a choice in the matter. As if he was contemplating and weighing the pros and cons. But he didn't really have a choice. And if he did, he'd already decided to obey his father's command.

So, Kol rocked on his heels, as if the motion would help propel him forward a little faster, then left the common room to find Myreen.

He found her quicker than he was ready for, in the middle of the Grand Hall. But before he could chicken out by pretending he didn't see her or by being distracted or disappearing somehow, she caught his eye and he stared a little bit too long.

He swallowed the lump in his throat and took advantage of his long legs, striding right up to her before she had a chance to escape, herself.

"Hi, Kol," Juliet said. He hadn't noticed the fire-starter standing next to Myreen, despite her hard-to-miss orange hair and the headphones around her neck.

"Hello, Juliet," he said, and noticed she herself looked a bit distracted. She was looking around Kol as if searching for someone. He ignored it and turned to the person he'd sought out. "And hello, Myreen."

"Hi, Kol," she said.

Alright. This is it, he thought. *Ask the girl out. It's not like you've never done it before.*

"Look," she said, maybe seeing Kol's brief hesitation. "I'm not exactly sure what beef you and Kendall have with each other, but I don't want any part of it."

Kol opened his mouth to say something that was most likely stupid, but she cut him off before he could.

"I like you both…" She shook her head and closed her eyes.

Kol felt a jolt of… something.

281

"I mean, Kendall is a mer, like me, and frankly, he's the only mer who actually seems to sort of like me or even talk to me." She had opened her eyes again, but was staring off at the black polished floor as she rambled. "And I like him too, so I'm not just going to stop…" she closed her eyes again and took a deep breath. When she opened them again, her eyes looked up to find his. She took one more split second before continuing. "You and I became friends first," she said. "And even though you're a dragon and I'm a mer, I still want us to be friends."

That night in the kitchen when they became *friends* flashed in his memory.

"I mean, we *are* friends, right?" she asked when he didn't answer right away. "Or would you rather—"

"Do you have plans Friday night?" he interrupted.

Juliet had been shuffling uncomfortably as Myreen rambled, but she stiffened in sync with Myreen turning to stone.

"P— plans Friday after class?" she asked, her voice suddenly soft and airy.

Juliet nudged her, snapping her from her wordless state.

She shook her head quickly as her cheeks colored. "I don't have plans Friday."

Kol felt the heat in his neck. Now it was his turn. Asking about a girl's plans wasn't exactly asking a girl out. He cleared his throat. "Will you go out with me Friday night?" The wait for her answer was suddenly torture. He'd definitely seen her with Kendall on more than one occasion. Meeting them at midnight in the gardens looked like more than a simple friendship, and he realized he didn't even know if she was dating the fish. Or hoping to date him.

But the wait for her answer was less than a second.

"Yes."

Juliet

What surprised Juliet the most was that Myreen actually hesitated. Kol Dracul just asked her out, and she needed Juliet to remind her that he was waiting for an answer. Maybe she was just stumped by his good looks. Juliet would be, if it was Nik that asked her out. Not that it would ever happen.

She could already feel the ugly green monster try to work its way through her mind, and she tried to stop it from expanding into a mess of jealous over-thinking. She was thankful that they had to separate to go to their classes.

Myreen only just got to the school and she was already asked out by two of the hottest guys in the Dome *and* was invited to a were party. But then again, no one ever even spoke to Juliet before Myreen did. That thought alone pushed the resentful feelings away. She was happy for her friend.

Myreen deserved some luck after what she went through. Juliet just had to wait a while longer for her spark of luck to arrive. It wasn't easy, but it would definitely be worth the wait when it finally happened.

Now that Juliet had talked herself out of the lonely path she was on, it was easier for her to get to her next class. In that moment, she realized she was actually attending all her classes—without any fiery mishaps. In fact, she had only tripped over her own feet twice in the last few days. Myreen really had a positive effect on her. *How can Dad not see that?*

Juliet placed her headphones over her ears and searched for her easy listening playlist. *Bublé* always knew how to keep her grounded, with his deep, soothing voice. In her own bubble of musical safety, she almost didn't see Nik coming from the opposite side of the hall.

His dark eyes melted her instantly, and they were on her. Brett said something that made him smirk, which made his dimples show. That set her off completely. Juliet felt her cheeks redden, and she didn't care who saw it. Before, she would have simply continued walking, embarrassed and ashamed.

But now, she gave him a wave. It was progress.

Nik gave her a curt nod and a tight smile. Was he still upset from the party? She didn't stop walking, but did turn to get one last look. Brett was nudging Nik on the arm, teasing him. *Boys are so immature. I'm glad I can't understand them.*

But she couldn't help but wonder if he would've stopped or waved back if Brett wasn't with him. She saw Brett more than Nik, thanks to them both being phoenixes. And even with his childish behavior, he was a pretty skilled and popular phoenix. She wondered if he teased Nik because it was obvious that Juliet was smitten.

Jealousy over Myreen's popularity was coming back.

Her mood was getting worse by the minute, and it took everything inside of her not to turn around and go hide out in her bedroom. But she knew if she did, it would only trap her in a mental argument with herself. Besides, she had to meet Myreen later to study. She contemplated whether she should tell Myreen about the meager exchange with Nik, even though nothing really happened. So why did it feel like she just got punched in the chest?

"Headphones off, Miss Quinn. Please take your seat." Mrs. Candida, the art professor, crossed her arms and waited until Juliet was in her chair.

As if she wasn't already anxious about Nik, being in art made her nerves even more erratic.

It was his mother who taught the class. And even though Juliet knew Mrs. Candida didn't know about her crush on her son, she always thought the woman could see right through her. It was almost exhausting how hard Juliet tried to make a good impression on this particular professor.

She stuffed her headphones into her bag and moved her attention to the lesson. She loved art, but didn't attend very much because there were more avians in this class than any of her others. And avians judged her the most. They just couldn't understand how someone of their kind could be so naive about their world. What Juliet didn't get was how everyone would rather bully or ignore her, rather than actually try to help her.

It wasn't difficult anymore to see why she and Myreen clicked so well. She didn't need the others. Myreen's loyalty was way thicker.

On the bright side, the number of dirty looks were reducing. The less she lit on fire, the more they seemed willing to accept her. And if it wasn't for Myreen, who knew how many more fires she would have accidentally made?

Tuning into Mrs. Candida, Juliet learned that the lesson of the day had to do with layers. Knowing where to place the idea of the creation in the perfect position. Clay was the medium Juliet chose to work with. She figured it was the easiest to pair with the lesson.

Starting with the bottom, base layer she began to work her way up. Everyone was so focused on their project that the entire class was silent. But even with her concentration, her mind kept going back to Nik.

She compared the assignment to him, as she created her unexpected masterpiece. Just like every person, he had layers of himself, and Juliet wanted to know them all. The day that he tried to relate to her, she knew now that it was one of his deep layers. And the guy he had to be in front of his friends, that was an outer layer. *One he clearly cares about if he won't even stop to say hi.*

Since the party, it felt like anytime she tried to talk to him or stop him in the halls, he wouldn't get the hint. With Kol around, Nik was more willing to hold a conversation. But when Brett was around, he was way too cool to be seen talking to someone like her.

She could grasp why. Since meeting Myreen and Kenzie, Juliet found a part of herself that she didn't know she had. A courageous and self-confident side that she had been trying to embrace. Her new confidence had helped her think of actual conversations she could have with Nik. Them being half-human was their biggest common ground.

She was almost sure they were two of just a few in the school that were only half-shifter. Which maybe included Myreen. But no one really knew who her father was, or if her mother was even a shifter. She briefly wondered if there was some kind of shifter DNA test that someone could take if they didn't know what they were. She was sure that would be too easy. She made a mental note to ask the school's genius tinkerer, Mr. Suzuki, about the possibility of creating such a test.

Mrs. Candida clapped her hands to get the class's attention, and Juliet had to blink a few times to refocus her eyes.

"Ten minutes left, class. Wrap it up, then clean it up."

It took only a minute for Juliet to complete her subtle, yet not-so-subtle, self-portrait of herself. Or of what she would be if she actually shifted. A phoenix. It was beautiful and haunting, with large wings that looked as if a layer of fire blazed over them. The body was long and slim, showing off the ruffled feathers that would replace her skin.

Staring at her creation made her even more eager to transform.

And even though she knew patience was not something she possessed, for this, she had no other choice. Her dad continued to drill in her head that once she controlled the power within her, shifting would come with ease. But what him—or anyone who *wasn't* Myreen—couldn't understand was that it was so much easier said than done.

Juliet stood to place her phoenix in the shadow box under her name. She actually received approving looks from the other students. Even Mrs. Candida looked impressed, and that alone raised her spirits.

Even still, as she left the classroom, she slid her headphones right back on her head. No one ever had the guts to pull them off her head, so when someone behind her tugged them off, she immediately thought she was getting picked on. With a raised fist, she spun around, ready to ruin someone's face.

"Whoa!" It was Nik. Alone.

Breathe, chill out, be cool. "Sorry," she sheepishly said.

Nik handed her headphones back and nodded his head, indicating they should walk. He led the way toward the Main Hall, which surprised Juliet. She knew it would be hard on him if anyone really saw him talking with her.

"No need to apologize. It's good to be on your toes." He smirked, and his dimple dipped into his cheek. Any sliver of confidence that she thought she had faded away the second his dark eyes met hers.

"Because I'm prone to get in a fight?" Not intending to sound offended, Juliet continued without giving him a chance to respond. "I mean, with my dad being who he is. I'm not surprised I can kick some ass." Juliet playfully put up her fists to throw a few punches in the air. The sound of Nik's laugh smacked her right in the heart.

"So, I'm sorry about before. Brett can be…"

"Obnoxious?" She finished.

He laughed, and again her breath hitched.

"Thanks. And I'm sorry, too. For the night of the party. I didn't mean to be so judgmental." They stood off to the side, where it was darkened by a shadow.

"It's alright. I get it. Honestly, I was surprised that you were there at all. Or that your dad let you go."

Juliet snickered, anxiously playing with a piece of her hair. "He didn't. I was in deep trouble the morning after."

Again with the smirk. "A true rebel, huh?"

The blushing and clear swooning overpowered her will to respond, so they lingered there.

With perfect timing, Brett exited his class and walked their way.

"Well, I'll see you around?" Nik said.

It wasn't a request to go on a date, but it was enough for Juliet. He wanted to see her again. "Yeah." She tried to sound cool, but even she heard her voice shake through the one syllable word she choked out.

Nik left her with his signature smirk and caught up with Brett, who gave him a weird look. Juliet numbly walked straight to find Myreen.

She couldn't believe they actually spoke. He was even better than she thought , and a new spark of hope filled her heart.

She only wished that their next encounter would be sooner rather than later.

Myreen

Myreen bounced with each step as she walked into the mermaid training room for Transformation. The butterflies in her stomach were flying so high that they threatened to lift her clear up off the ground.

After all his weirdness, he'd finally asked her on a date! Why did Friday have to be three days from Tuesday?

She practically skipped to the locker room. But just before she went in, she caught sight of Kendall coming out of the boys' locker room. There was a hopeful question on his face when their eyes met.

A pang of guilt suddenly stabbed her. She hadn't seen Kendall since his poorly timed date proposal yesterday, and she knew that he was going to be hoping for her answer today. Right now.

She had decided so easily against going out with Kendall, but the instant Kol looked her way, she was ready to dive right in. It wasn't Kendall's fault that she liked someone else more, although it wasn't really her fault either. How was she going to let him down gently? Especially when he would no doubt find out about her upcoming date with Kol, one way or another. The dragon prince asking out the outcast mermaid was bound to be hot gossip fodder.

Ultimately, she decided that the best way to handle it was to just avoid it and be vague. Not the noblest course of action, maybe, but it would spare Kendall's feelings. At least for now.

She leisurely slipped into her swim top and strolled out of the locker room at as slow a pace as she could without looking handicapped. Luckily, before Kendall could approach her, Delphine came up to her, right out the door.

"Hello, Myreen," the stunning redhead greeted. "Now that you've had some time to get used to your sea legs, so to speak, I would like you to practice controlling the shift. See how quickly you can change back to human after leaving the water, then try to keep your legs from changing when you get back in."

"Okay," Myreen said, the butterflies in her stomach drowning.

With every other student in this class having already mastered transforming, pretty much from birth, she had Delphine's full attention, which was both a good thing and a bad thing. Myreen hated being in the spotlight, and having Delphine focus solely on her meant that everyone else could focus on her, too. All the better to shove it in her face if she failed. The pressure was on.

Stepping into the pool, the scales under her skin reacted instantly to the salt water. She couldn't imagine actually being able to stop the shift. Her tail was out in seconds, the sharp agony of the transformation mercifully brief. Delphine stayed at the edge of the pool, dangling her perfectly creamy and unshifted feet in the water to prove to Myreen that it was possible.

Myreen still hadn't quite figured out how to keep her gills closed and had to submerge her face after a few seconds so she wouldn't suffocate. She took a deep breath under the water and held it, so she could resurface and await further instruction.

"Having trouble breathing?" Delphine guessed at the look of Myreen's pursed lips.

Myreen nodded stiffly.

"Then we'll let that be the first lesson—keeping your gills closed when you want to breath above the water. Class won't be very productive if your brain is suffering from oxygen deprivation."

She giggled in an *I'm-laughing-with-you-not-at-you* sort of way, but Myreen still felt slightly mortified for it.

"First, exhale and let all the water out of your windpipe," Delphine instructed.

Myreen breathed out, feeling the water pour out of her gills.

"Good, now focus on your neck and command your gills to close. It can feel kind of like trying to make your ears move at first, like a muscle that just wasn't meant to move voluntarily, but once you've found those small muscles, you'll be able to control them with ease."

Myreen nodded and, still holding her breath, closed her eyes and focused on her gills. She concentrated on her neck, becoming very aware of the exact spot on her neck where the gills were slit open. They felt dry and parched, like lips that were chapped and needed constant licking. They stung from the open air.

She strained just about every muscle in her neck trying close them, until finally she had to take a breath and dunked herself under the water to inhale sharply. She coughed from the burning draught in her throat and gills, grateful that the cool water she filled herself with relieved it quickly. After she caught her breath, she inhaled deeply to resurface and try again.

She didn't know how many times they had gone through this exercise, but finally, she honed in on those tiny muscles and managed to close her gills. She let out the breath she'd been holding and let the naked air fill her throat. As she was still in aquatic form, the unfiltered air burned her throat, making her swallow several times to sooth it.

"Very good, Myreen!" Delphine praised. "The sting will take some getting used to, but after a while, you won't even notice it."

Myreen cleared her throat in vain. "It feels like I have strep." She grimaced as another swallow made her throat ache.

"I promise, it will get easier," Delphine said. "We'll take a short break and let you adjust before we start on controlling your shift."

Myreen nodded and allowed her breathing to return to normal. Her throat hurt so much that she wanted to chug the entire pool. But she was afraid that if she let her gills open, she wouldn't be able to close them again.

She looked around the room, and sure enough, at least half of the mer students were watching her like she was a reality tv show, some of them looking quite amused. She hated that she was so far behind them all, that she had to try to catch up while on display for all of them to witness and ridicule. She had tried so hard not to blame her mom for keeping her from growing up as a mermaid, but at this moment, she couldn't help but feel resentment, which only made the guilt that much stronger. Why couldn't her mom have at least told Myreen what she was? Whatever her mom was running from, Myreen could have understood, if given the chance. Why keep this whole part of who they were from her? It made Myreen angry, and yet so horribly conflicted.

"Feeling better?" Delphine asked.

Nope, not even slightly. "Yeah," Myreen lied. "Let's do this."

"Good! Okay, we'll take this slow. First, I just want you to practice changing your legs back as quickly as you can when you get out. Once you've shortened that time, we'll work on keeping them from changing at all."

Myreen nodded and lifted herself out of the pool, pretending that she and Delphine were the only two people there.

***

Not counting Myreen's meager accomplishment with closing her gills, the rest of Transformation went as expected—with no progress in controlling her shifting. She tried to remind herself that this was only her second time in Transformation class, that expecting herself to learn this stuff any faster was just setting herself up to fail. But it was hard to keep things in perspective when all the other mer knew how to shift or not shift at will, when all of them could manipulate water as easily as breathing. It was all just so frustrating. And she could tell that Delphine and Oberon expected her to excel at being a mermaid. She didn't want to disappoint them.

When the hour was over, Myreen sat on the edge of the pool, waiting for her tail to dry enough for her to get her legs back. She so wanted to get out of the room. As much as she loved swimming, the pool reminded her of every way in which she didn't fit into the shifter world. The degradation she received from every pair of eyes that passed was enough to make her want to fall back into the water, hide in a corner and never come up.

"Hey, how's it going?" Kendall sat next to her on the glossy tile floor.

Great. The last person she wanted to talk to right now. "As if you didn't see the train wreck that was me learning to be a mermaid." Just because she didn't like him *as much as* she liked Kol, she still liked him enough to be mortified that he'd gotten to watch her struggle.

"It wasn't that bad," he said, shrugging it off. "We all struggled at one point, you're just a little behind, that's all. You'll catch up in no time. And then you'll be bored in this class like the rest of us."

Kendall had no idea how much she hoped it would be like that. "Even if that does happen, I'll still be the outcast mermaid that nobody wants to swim with."

"That's not true. I'll swim with you any time. So hurry up and learn this stuff so we can kick back and float." He chuckled encouragingly, but Myreen didn't join him. "You know that was a joke, right?"

"Yeah, I'm sorry," she said, looking down at her slowly drying pink fins. "I'm just not really in a laughing mood."

"Well, why don't you let me cheer you up," he said. "Sneak out with me tonight and we'll see a movie in town."

There it was again—a date invitation without warning. He was so good looking, and so good for her in lots of ways, and yet, even considering going to see a movie with him felt like she was somehow cheating on Kol.

"I can't, not tonight," she said, brushing a dripping lock of hair behind her ear. "I have some more studying to do for Shifter Bio."

"Okay," he said, and she was relieved there wasn't a note of offense in his voice. "Would you like a study partner? I tested out of that class."

"I already have plans to study with Juliet today, but maybe some other time?" It wasn't a complete lie; she really did have plans to see Juliet later. They just probably weren't going to spend much of that time studying.

"Alright," he said with a curt nod. He started to get to his feet, then paused and hovered in a kneeling position. "Look, that stuff I said about Juliet, please just totally forget about it. She's a great girl, and a great friend. And you deserve to have a great friend." He smiled a smile that could melt a bra clean off, and her heart tripped over itself in her chest.

Why couldn't she just like Kendall one hundred percent? Things would be so much easier. As he walked away, she almost wanted to call him back and say yes. But she knew she would never forgive herself for not trying things with Kol. She had to see where it went. And if that turned out to be nowhere, then maybe, hopefully, Kendall would still be around waiting for her. Dang, did she feel like scum for thinking like that.

Finally, her tail had dried enough for her to retract her scales and begin the shift back to legs. The bones adjusted, drifted and separated, peachy skin replacing the shimmering pink scales until she had her pale legs back. She got to her feet and went into the locker room to finish drying off and get dressed in her uniform.

Before she could open her locker, an aggressive hand shoved her into the blue-painted metal.

"Stay away from Kendall." Myreen knew that voice. The self-absorbed tone of elitism, and with only half the venom of Trish. It was Alessandra.

Myreen turned around to face the raven-haired mermaid that could pass for her sister. Alessandra was glaring at her so fiercely that Myreen almost feared she might burst into flames. Luckily, only phoenixes and dragons had that power.

"Kendall and I are just friends," Myreen said in a voice that was just as assertive. "What do you care anyway? You two aren't dating anymore. Wait, did he dump you?" Myreen could feel the snide teenage girl in her coming out, wanting to pick a fight. She couldn't stop it.

"That's none of your business," Alessandra snapped. Clearly, Myreen had struck a chord.

"Yeah? And what your ex and I do is none of yours. So back off. I'm not in the mood to humor you today." Myreen turned her back on the privileged mermaid, almost daring her to continue.

"Don't turn your back on me." Alessandra grabbed Myreen's shoulder and yanked it to make her face her again. "You're not worthy of him. You can't even transform like the rest of us. You're not a real mermaid, and you never will be."

The insult sliced deeper than Myreen expected. Alessandra had just put into words the exact fears floating around in Myreen's mind.

"Girls, do we have a problem here?" Delphine entered the locker room and sauntered over with her arms crossed over her chest, her long red hair looking like a halo of fire around her head. As nice as Delphine could be, she could also be a strict disciplinarian, and Myreen was seeing that side of her very clearly.

"No, ma'am," Alessandra said, instantly straightening her back and putting her arms at her side. "Myreen and I were just reaching an understanding about boundaries, weren't we?" She sneered at Myreen, then spun on her heel and walked away, flipping her black locks over her shoulder.

As much as Myreen hated Alessandra in that moment, she knew she was right. Myreen would never be one of them. And not for the first time, she wasn't entirely sure she wanted to be.

Myreen

Friday can't come soon enough, Myreen thought as she left the mermaid training room late Thursday afternoon.

For the last three days, she had been taking one-on-one transformation lessons with Delphine, and she was no closer to being an expert mermaid than she was to being a rocket scientist. No matter how hard she tried to keep her scales withdrawn, as soon as her skin touched salt water, her tail came out.

Myreen wasn't used to not getting things she worked at. All her school career, she had been the student who studied hard and got good grades. She never failed at anything. Shifting at will was her first academic failure, and it made her both depressed and painfully frustrated. She couldn't not clench her fists every time she thought about it. If she didn't find a way to vent this frustration, she was going to implode.

Deciding against going to the main building to wait for dinner, she veered south toward the defense building. There shouldn't be anyone training right now, so she would have the entire space to herself. She didn't think of herself as a fighter, but punching something sounded like a really good idea right now.

When Myreen entered the gym, there were a couple of older students scattered on the workout equipment. She recognized them as Oberon's defense assistants, and they were all so focused on their treadmill jogging or weightlifting that none of them bothered to glance in her direction.

Good, I can be invisible.

She headed for an elliptical in the abandoned far right corner, set down her laptop bag and climbed onto it. Once she found her rhythm, the exertion began to soak up all that pent-up agitation burning a hole in her guts. With each cycle of her steps, each panting breath, each bead of sweat, her angst melted away, replaced by a bittersweet exhaustion.

After forty-five minutes, she no longer felt the urge to punch anything. She slowed to a stop and climbed down to get a drink of water.

As she unscrewed the cap on her water bottle, she heard a door close on the other side of the gym. She looked up to see a brawny guy drenched in sweat leaving what she knew to be the simulation room.

Myreen hadn't yet seen the inside of that room. She knew that it was used for testing skills to get out of Defense class, but clearly the guy who left wasn't taking a test. He seemed to just be using it for training. Her curiosity was piqued.

Slinging her bag loosely over her shoulder, she walked briskly across the gym. She looked over her shoulder. There were no rules posted anywhere that the simulation room was off-limits, or that special permission was needed, but she still felt like she was doing something she shouldn't be. No one in the gym was paying her any mind, though, so she turned the knob and pushed open the door.

To her surprise, the room was completely empty. Nothing but a very large box with four white walls, a white ceiling and a white floor. The white that shone on every naked surface was a stark contrast to the dark gray that covered everything else on this campus, making the room seem uncomfortably bright.

How could anyone train in this room? There was nothing here. Myreen didn't know what she'd expected, but she definitely expected more than *nothing*. Was she missing something?

The sound of mischievous giggles made her turn her head to the door behind her.

Trish, Alessandra and Joanna were hovering outside the doorway, Trish with her hand on some digital keypad on the wall.

"Have fun," Trish said, flaring one eyebrow. Then she slammed the door closed and locked it.

Myreen ran to the door. "Hey!" she yelled, wrenching at the door knob. "Let me out!"

The lights began to dim, and before Myreen knew what was happening, the white walls around her pixelated and were replaced by dark green shrubbery. Every inch of the room flipped square-by-square, the white floor becoming brush-covered earth beneath her feet, the ceiling turning into a star-spangled evening sky. The boundaries of the boxy room in which she'd been standing only seconds ago were gone, and she was now stranded in the middle of a dark forest.

For a moment, she panicked, and disorientation threatened her sanity. How could she really be seeing what she was seeing?

But then she remembered the purpose of the room she was in. *Simulation.* None of this was real. It was nothing more than a projection. Albeit, an incredibly realistic projection. The smell of pine was crisp and potent, so strong she could actually taste it in the back of her mouth. The chirping song of crickets came from all directions, which was impressive because she definitely hadn't seen any speakers.

Despite how authentic the forest appeared, she had to still be in the room—which meant the walls and door were here somewhere. She just had to find them.

She was yanking on the door just a second ago, so it had to be close by. Myreen took a step behind her, in the direction she believed the door to be. Dried leaves and pine thistles crunched under shoe. *Wow, this all seems so real.* She turned and reached forward, blindly feeling for the door knob that she knew had to be in that general area, but her hands touched nothing but air.

She took another step forward. And another. And another still.

By all logic, she should have bumped into the door by now. The room was only maybe ten yards by ten yards. She put her hands in front of her and walked forward, and when her hands made no contact with the wall, she broke into a run, dodging through the trees.

How was this possible? How could she be running in the same room and not have smacked into the wall yet? It made no sense! Could she have somehow gotten turned around and run in the wrong direction? Even if she had, she'd run at least the distance of the width of the room. It wasn't possible that she hadn't found any of the room's boundaries.

She turned around and lifted her foot to sprint in the opposite direction, hoping that she had somehow been confused and the door was the other way, that this was some trick of the mind, an optical illusion. But her foot caught the back of her other ankle and she tripped, flying forward to the ground. Her hands rushed forward to catch herself and met the leaf-littered floor.

Her heart thudded in her throat. Myreen could feel the crumbly brush under her palms. She got to her knees and inspected her open hands, the flakes and clumps of moist dirt clinging to her skin. She could *feel* all of it. She reached for a leaf and picked it up, its stem solid between her index finger and thumb.

Anxiety building, she stumbled toward a nearby tree and slapped her hand on its trunk. Sure enough, the rough bark scraped at her sensitive skin. *Is this real?*

"Alright, Trish, you've had your fun," Myreen called out, her voice echoing through the vast woods. "Let me out!"

Nothing changed. She might as well be talking to the trees.

Something whistled past the side of her head and lodged in the tree in front of her. An arrow.

"What the—?"

Then another one pierced the ground right next to her foot, narrowly missing her shoe.

"Oh, no!" she gasped. She jumped to her feet and darted deeper into the forest as a storm of arrows chased behind her.

The leaves felt real, the ground and trees felt real. Did that mean if she got hit by one of these simulated arrows, she would feel real pain? She didn't want to find out. Her legs moved as swiftly as they could, leaping and bounding over unearthed roots and randomly placed boulders, absolutely terrified of getting struck.

"You can run, but you can't hide, little fish," a male voice called out from the darkness of the forest.

Another whistle streaked through the air, and Myreen tripped on something and face-planted into the foliage. She rapidly looked down at her foot. An arrow had landed right in front of it. She was glad that the arrow had missed her, but now she had lost all momentum.

"Gotcha!" Strong fingers gripped the hair at the back of her head and yanked her off the ground. Myreen screamed and scratched at the fingers that sent fire into her scalp as the man turned her to face him.

He looked like a typical military guy—buzz cut, rough features, bulging muscles everywhere. And an absence of light in his eyes. He wore a thick black vest with shiny silver buckles all the way down his torso. The guns strapped to each side of his belt made her squeal.

"Any last words, freak?" the man hissed.

Myreen squeezed her eyes shut and braced for whatever this simulation was programed to do next.

Her hair was released, and she fell to the floor. When she opened her eyes, she was nearly blinded by bright white. She was back! Of course, she knew that she had never really left the room, but the simulation was off!

"Myreen, are you alright?" Kol stomped in and offered her a helping hand.

Without thinking, she leapt up and threw her arms around him. "Thank you, thank you, thank you!"

When his arms didn't close around her, she pulled away from him and cleared her throat. Kol looked confused, as if a hug from her was a foreign language he didn't understand. Maybe he just wasn't a physical guy? She already knew he wasn't an emotional one.

"Uh, a– are you hurt?" he stammered.

She shook her head. "No, I'm fine."

The awkward frown on his face was replaced with a stern brow. "What were you even doing in here?"

"I saw someone come out of this room and I got curious," she said, defensively. "I just wanted to see what all the fuss was about. But Trish locked me in and turned it on, and I couldn't figure out how to get out."

Kol sighed and looked to the floor. "I thought something was up when I saw her and her conjoined triplets leaving the building."

"They left?" she exclaimed, outraged. She had at least thought that they'd stick around to watch her struggle and get a good laugh out of it. But no, they left without a second thought. Trish was pure evil. "I can't believe they just left me in here to rot! I would've been stuck in here all night if you hadn't showed up."

"Not likely," Kol said, his mouth set in a firm line. "The sim stops when someone wins, either the participant or the sim itself. And you were dangerously close to losing."

The grim look on Kol's face made her gulp loudly. "It wouldn't have actually hurt me… would it?"

Kol met her fretful gaze, but said nothing. That was answer enough.

"Thank you, Kol. Truly." As if she didn't like him enough already.

"Come on, let's get out of here before we both get trapped," he said.

He opened his hand again, not in a gesture of assistance but one of comfort—or closeness. After his reaction to her hug, she knew his invitation to invade his personal space was profound. She slipped her hand into his and, savoring how good it felt, she let him pull her out of the room.

Oberon

The lights in Oberon's empty classroom dimmed as he adjusted the settings on his tablet. Delphine sat on the other side of his desk; classes had just gotten out for the day.

"I think you'll find Ren's schematics to be quite intriguing," he said, accessing the three-dimensional holo file that demonstrated the new vampire tracking system.

"Military tech has never been intriguing to me," Delphine replied critically. "Such things have always fallen under your umbrella."

Oberon couldn't argue with that.

"I think you'll at least find the science behind it interesting. Most of all, the military will be able to detect a vampire attack before it actually happens."

She lifted one of her eyebrows and ran a hand through her copper hair.

"That's a lot better than what we currently have. Let's see what

Mister Suzuki has come up with."

Enabling the holographic display, Oberon's eyes lit up, reflecting the neon green pixels.

"This is the actual size of the device," Oberon clarified as they observed the sphere, just an inch diameter. "But for greater study, we'll magnify." He tapped a zoom command on the tablet, and the 3D image grew to the size of a beachball. "How in-depth would you like to go into the schematics?"

"The basics, Oberon," Delphine replied. "Honestly, I trust your judgment on this. If you believe it's worth investing in, we have the finances to make it happen. If you're on the fence, maybe we need to talk to Ren about working on something else."

"Of course," Oberon replied. This was how their conversations generally went. Delphine didn't want to know how each little part of the machine worked. "Let me explain the design in the simplest form, so you have a basic understanding of how the device works. First of all, you'll notice that the shape of the system is actually similar to a golf ball. You can see the tiny divots encompassing it. Those are sensors that are ultra-tuned to a particular chemical—the same one that vampires generate when they're needing to fill their bellies again. Ren calls it *desidine*. The thirstier they are, the more desidine they put off, and the easier they are to track. And the amount indicates just how dangerous they'll be."

Delphine tapped her lip in thought.

Oberon manipulated the controls again, and the outside of the image shot out, as if it had been blown apart. "As you can see, within the device is a GPS unit, as well as a cellular chip for transmission. These GPS units will allow us to know right where the thirsty vampires are located. The cellular chip will tap into local services and transmit levels of desidine directly to the servers here at the Dome. The military will have live data to observe, and will be able to react accordingly. And of course, there is a battery powering it all inside."

"You're traipsing out of the 'basic' information zone," Delphine said.

Oberon half smiled. "My apologies. I guess even I get wrapped up in the technicalities of Ren's designs. Essentially, these devices will allow us to move from tracking vampire attacks to detecting actual vampires."

"*Thirsty* vampires," Delphine corrected.

Oberon blinked a few times. "Well, yes, I suppose that's right. Technically, we won't be tracking vampires, but their chemical releases. But that at least gives us a chance to prevent attacks, versus waiting for them to happen."

Nodding, Delphine said, "How many of these devices will we need?"

"I'd say one for every person in the military," Oberon answered. "We'll also want to have spares for sympathizers who are aiding us."

Oberon instantly thought of Leif as he said this, but he couldn't give a vampire tracker to an actual vampire. In fact, the trackers would put Leif at significant risk; at some point, Oberon would have to explain his dealings with the vampire and how much of a help Leif had been to them behind the scenes.

"Ren is widening his scope," Delphine said, her emerald eyes shimmering in the holo-schematics. At last she nodded. "Let's bring the necessary parts in and get these built and distributed."

Oberon's eyebrows shot up in surprise. "We haven't gone over cost yet."

"I don't need to see the numbers," Delphine replied. "I'm not worried about cost, as long as everything is accounted for in the end. And don't seem so surprised; if these devices will help us prevent vampire attacks, there's really no choice. We have to do it."

"I'll let Ren know," Oberon replied. "He'll be pleased to hear of your approval. And hopefully it'll give him more motivation to stay in his position."

Delphine tilted her head, her red hair angling to the side.

"Has Ren been complaining about his job?"

Oberon shrugged. "He expressed an interest in being transferred to the military, but I talked him out of it."

Blinking, Delphine said, "Ren? In the military? He'd get eaten alive—and not by vampires. Can you imagine him trying to stand shoulder-to-shoulder with Eduard Dracul?"

Oberon chuckled, wondering how the General would react to Ren's puns.

"Believe it or not, I've seen Ren in combat, and he's a force to be reckoned with," Oberon said. "He's knocked off his share of vampire heads in the past. But his talents are better spent here in the Dome. I'm giving him the responsibility of monitoring this new system, so he'll have contact with the military as data comes in."

"Hopefully that will be enough military involvement for him," said Delphine.

"Agreed." Oberon touched the tablet, causing the 3D schematics to disappear and the room's lighting to increase. "That's about all I have for you today. Is there anything else you wish to discuss?"

"Actually, yes there is," Delphine replied, rubbing her hands together. "It's about Myreen."

"Ah, yes. How is our little siren doing?" Oberon asked.

Delphine's lips thinned. "She's struggling with transformation."

Oberon nodded. "She told me so a few days ago. I'd asked her to meet with me, so I could check in on how her first week went."

"Her inability to shift at will doesn't concern you?" Delphine asked.

"She'll get it down, Delphine," Oberon replied. "It's been a little over one week. Myreen's entire world has been turned upside down. Between all the new experiences she's going through here at the Dome, as well as losing her mother, the stress she must be enduring could be limiting her abilities."

"But we have no basis for believing she's the prophesied mermaid," Delphine countered. "Besides finding her late, she hasn't shown any abilities out of the ordinary. In fact, as far as expectations go, she hasn't even come close."

"Again, it's been just over a week."

"I've begun one-on-one tutoring with her. The effort she puts herself through to shift is abnormal. Yes, such things take focus, but I know infant mermaids who have figured out transformation. For mer, these things come naturally. With Myreen, it seems foreign and forced."

"My recommendation would be to keep working with her," counseled Oberon.

"It could take a lot of time," Delphine said. "Of all people, I'd expect you to be the most urgent about seeing the prophesied siren take power."

Her words caught him off-guard.

Of all people?

She was referring to his past and the revenge he wanted to take on Draven. That had been twenty years ago. He'd changed since then. Oberon had invested his life in the school. Bringing down Draven was important to him, but there were other things that had superseded avenging his murdered wife and parents. Like the school and the future of shifters around the world.

He held his tongue; Delphine had always been blunt in conversation. He'd learned long ago that if he let his own stormy attitude come forth, they would clash.

"I think it's worth mentioning that when I found Myreen through vision, there were no fireworks or angelic voices indicating that she was the prophesied mermaid." Delphine leaned forward and rested her cheek on her hand. "I was hopeful then, because she was the first *stray* mermaid we'd found. But more and more, I'm thinking we need to keep looking."

Oberon narrowed his eyes. "You want to give up on Myreen because sparks didn't fly during the vision you found her in?"

Delphine partially smiled. "And the fact that she's been struggling with shifter basics for the past week. I understand that her life has been put in a whirlpool. But the qualities that would be expected of the prophesied siren... I'm not seeing them in Myreen."

Oberon sighed. "And so you want to continue your search for another stray mermaid."

"With your permission, yes," Delphine said. "If the siren is still out there, we're only hurting ourselves by focusing our efforts on Myreen."

He couldn't argue with that. Just because he hoped and believed Myreen was the siren, didn't mean that she was. And if the stray mermaid from the prophecy was still hidden, valuable time would be wasted.

"How would you feel about having one of the more advanced mer students take on her tutoring responsibilities?" Oberon offered. "That would free you up to spend more time searching for another stray mermaid."

Delphine considered his words for a few moments. "That might be very good for her. She's having a hard time fitting in with the other mermaids."

Oberon nodded. "I've heard as much. I know that she has been getting along quite well with Kendall Green. Perhaps he'd be a good tutor for her?"

"Kendall has taken a particular liking to her, despite how the rest of the mer students have been acting around her. But I'd like for Kendall to continue to focus on honing his visions. I think it would be wise to involve somebody else who has become quite skillful with their abilities. That way they can focus on more than just transformation."

"Who do you have in mind?" Oberon asked.

Delphine tapped a finger to her lips. "Trish would cause too much drama, I'm afraid. And so would Joanna." She pulled her hand away and sat up straight, snapping her fingers in the process. "Alessandra. She's an extremely gifted swimmer, and out of the rest of the mermaids, she's the best at water manipulation."

Oberon nodded his approval. Alessandra had been a good pupil in his history classes, and from what he'd heard from the other teachers, she was a well-rounded student in general.

"My biggest concern is how she will react to such an assignment, and how she will *act* around Myreen," Delphine added.

"Perhaps through tutoring, the doors of friendship might open?" Oberon said. Such was his hope. He'd certainly had his issues with Delphine throughout the years, but they'd been able to see past those differences and become good friends.

"I wouldn't expect it, but perhaps that will be the case," Delphine said. "Would you like me to take care of giving the assignment to Alessandra?"

"I believe that would be best," Oberon replied. "Being the director of the school gives me authority, but seeing as you're the head of the mermaids, I think she might take the assignment a little more seriously from you."

Delphine nodded. "I'll see to it at once." She got to her feet and pushed the chair back under his desk.

"One other thing on Alessandra," Oberon said. "Myreen has expressed to me how certain cliques have gone out of their way to be mean to her. Can you emphasize with Alessandra just how important this is to you and to me? Don't go into detail or anything. Just... help her to realize Myreen is a mermaid, too, and deserves to be treated like one. That will help her more than any tutoring could."

"Of course, Director," she said. "I'll let you know what comes of this. And in the meantime, I'll spend a little more time searching for other stray mermaids."

"Thank you, Delphine," Oberon said, opening the door for her from his tablet.

He watched her leave, then sat back in his chair.

"So many moving pieces," he muttered, his eyes zoning. "High winds, be with us."

Kol

Kol made some excuse about forgetting something before leaving Myreen, who headed off to dinner. He had too much on his mind. Eating in a room full of students and teachers was the last thing he wanted to be doing.

He needed to clear his head. Another flight would be ideal, since shifting into a dragon stopped him from thinking altogether and let his instincts take over. Calculus equations and facts about shifter biology and history—they were never the problem. He liked those. He would sometimes recite such knowledge and facts like a chant. Even in dragon form. Beating his wings among the clouds as he rattled off statistics and numbers was calming.

Drama about a girl, though? He needed something to temporarily erase that from his mind.

But he couldn't go for a flight in the middle of dinner without permission. Especially since it was still daytime.

The idea had crossed his mind to use his invisibility trick—after sneaking out, of course—but there was still a chance he would get caught. And he wasn't in the mood to risk it. Not after hearing and seeing everything that had just happened with Myreen.

He'd seen Trish and her two minions snickering amongst themselves as they left the defense training room.

"Seriously, that girl needs to know what's best for her," Joanna said.

"Yeah, if she really wants to be one of us, then she needs to stay away from him," Alessandra added. *"Seriously, he and I are on a break. Who does she think she is?"*

"No kidding!" Trish said. *"He's totally yours, Aless."*

"Yeah, and besides that, she can't even shift!" Joanna laughed.

"Right!" Alessandra said. *"Whoever heard of a mer who couldn't shift when they were like… two?"*

"Yeah, two months old!" Trish said.

All three girls laughed.

"Maybe she's a special *mer…"* Trish added, sarcasm lacing her voice.

"How do you think she'll do in the sim?" Alessandra asked.

"At least you set it to Beginner Level One," Joanna said.

Kol tuned them out after that and rushed to the simulation room, yanking poor Myreen out before that military sim took a chunk out of her. At least Trish had the sense to set it to the lowest level. It was the level they always used for brand new students to get the feel for what the simulations could do. But he'd never heard of a single student who couldn't beat the *human opponent* simulation on the first try. It was designed to be easy in order to build confidence. He'd heard his father and Oberon discussing that very purpose when the simulation room was first being designed, long before he came to the school.

Other students argued that Kol had the upper hand when he first entered that chamber as a new student—his father being who he was, and being so involved in the design and construction of it—but it was truly his first time experiencing anything like it. To beat Beginner Lever One, Kol didn't even feel the need to shift, and he only used one fireball to dispatch the opponent.

And to Kol's defense, he hadn't beat the sim yet. That shut up the students who used to claim *unfairness*.

But Myreen was about to get pummeled in there. He'd seen her through the two-way mirror before he shut the thing off, and she wasn't even *trying* to fight back.

That worried him for more than one reason.

Kol went back to the training room. Everyone was at dinner, so he knew he'd have the place to himself.

He plugged into his headphones and set the treadmill on a brisk jogging speed and focused on getting into the zone. He only lasted five minutes before his thoughts began to wander back toward the issue he'd been trying to run away from.

If the simulation incident wasn't worrisome enough, the things he'd overheard from Trish and her fellow evil step-sisters would've achieved the same goal: *Myreen can't shift?*

That seemed like a big issue. Especially since she was a mer, as they'd said in so many unkind words. Shifting usually came more naturally to mers than the other species, since they had the ability from *birth*. Sure, the problem wasn't rare in other types of shifters, weres specifically were known to struggle. Since a were had to be bitten by another were and weren't born a shifter, the abilities weren't in their blood—until it was. It didn't merely lie dormant in the genetic makeup until puberty, like with born-shifters. Unpredictable weres were actually fairly common.

But even born-shifters had their problems, such as Myreen's phoenix friend, Juliet, who was infamously bad at controlling her fire. Kol wasn't sure if it was just a rumor, but he'd overheard that she had an accident in the Avian training room recently.

And Kol even had an uncle who couldn't dragon-shift until he was in his early twenties—he also had other developmental issues since birth, so it wasn't a surprise or shock to anyone. And he was so beloved that no one cared, anyway.

But if Myreen was the mermaid from the prophecy, the one to save them all from Draven, something as simple as shifting into her dominant form should be second nature. She shouldn't even have to think about it.

Even if she'd never done it in her life.

And that was *very* worrisome.

If Kol overheard right—and he didn't doubt it after seeing her struggle in that simulation—Myreen was having serious issues.

He shut off the treadmill and walked over to the weights. Concentrating on his breathing as he did a few reps, he attempted to sink back into the heavy metal music that blasted into his earphones. Heavy metal wasn't his first choice most days, but trying to discern the different blaring instruments and the lyrics from the screaming lead vocalist was almost enough to distract him again.

Almost.

If Myreen can't even shift... he thought, and shook his head to banish what was coming next. But stopping thoughts was near impossible. *Then maybe the General is wrong.* Maybe she wasn't the mermaid from the prophecy.

Kol dropped the weights with a loud bouncing thud. The teachers hated it when students dropped them, but he didn't care right now. He stood still and took some deep breaths, seething. He was angry at himself for not yanking her from the simulation immediately. He was angry at his father for *assuming* Myreen was the mermaid from the prophecy and forcing him to become involved with her. He was angry at himself for not keeping his feelings as tightly to his chest as he'd like.

And he was angry at Myreen.

It was stupid, but he was mad at her for not being able to shift, for not fighting back in that simulation when it should have been instinct for her—he'd seen many mers beat Beginning Level One only using one hand, and one of the graduated mers held the record for quickest time until Kol beat it last year. She should have fought back.

He was angry at Myreen for not being the mermaid from the prophecy.

Like it was somehow her fault.

"Was that supposed to be like a mic drop?" Brett said loudly so Kol could hear him.

Kol yanked out his earbuds without bothering to turn the music off and turned to his friend.

"Because usually you do that when you've made a point," Brett teased. He motioned with his hands as if dropping a mic and made an explosion sound.

Kol wasn't following.

Brett pointed at the weights Kol had just dropped and the lightbulb finally went on.

Kol shook his head and ran a hand through his hair before plopping down on one of the plush benches.

"Everything okay, man?" he asked, widening his stance and putting both hands behind his back, just the way Kol always remembered Brett's dad doing when the conversation became serious. "You missed out on a mean meatloaf tonight… *yum!*"

Kol rolled his eyes. He doubted meatloaf was on the menu that night. And if it was, it shared no resemblance to his sister's meatloaf and was closer to gourmet.

A towel fell on Brett's shoulder and they both looked to see Nik had joined them.

Brett eased his stance and folded his arms. Nik must've felt the tension; he took a seat on the bench opposite Kol and waited for one of them to speak.

Kol looked at both of his friends. "How'd you know I'd be here?" he asked.

"I heard about the terrible trout trio locking Myreen in the simulation room," Brett said. "And turning it on."

Nik's eyes widened. "I just followed Brett," he said. "How is she not in the infirmary?"

Kol shrugged. "They set it to Beginner Level One."

Nik and Brett blew out a relieved breath in unison.

"Well, that was *kind* of them," Brett said. "I guess she would've experienced it in a couple of weeks, anyway. At least she got it over with, unless it didn't count."

"How long did it take her to beat it?" Nik asked.

Kol didn't answer.

"She beat your record, didn't she?" Brett teased. "That's why you're off here sulking."

"I had to shut it off."

"Wait, what?" Brett asked. He and Nik were both clearly confused.

"She almost landed in the infirmary," Kol said. "She didn't even fight back."

For the first time in as long as Kol could remember, Brett was silent. And Nik didn't say anything for several long minutes, either.

"What did your father want?" Nik finally asked, changing the subject. Another subject Kol wasn't in the mood to discuss, but Nikolai and Brett were his best friends.

"He threatened to yank me from school and slap me in the military early if I didn't do what he asked." He turned to Nik. "Apparently your father has been asking about when I plan to join."

Brett swore.

Nik kept his cool a bit better. "What did General Dracul ask you to do?"

317

Kol looked over his shoulder and scanned the training room to make sure they were alone before turning back to Nik and Brett.

And then he told them everything. About the prophecy. About the suspicion that Myreen was the mermaid from the prophecy. How Eduard wanted Kol to get close to her. How Eduard wanted Kol to get her to fall in love with him.

"*Whew!*" Brett let out a breath when Kol had finished.

Nik gave him a knowing look. Nik was the only person outside of his family who knew about the curse.

"That sounds… *risky.*" Nik said.

Kol ran both hands through his hair again, then kept his head resting on his palms. "You're telling me."

"I don't see the problem," Brett said. "She's a cute girl. I'd date her."

Kol glared at Brett and his smug face.

"I mean… I *won't.*" Brett held his hands up in surrender. "'Cause she's clearly *your* girl. I just don't see what the problem is."

Other than her not being able to shift? Other than the fact she didn't fight back? he wanted to retort, but didn't. And he ignored the part about her being *his* girl. She wasn't *his*. Not yet, anyway. And when she eventually became *his*. He could *never* be hers.

Because then he'd lose her.

"Do you like her?" Nik asked quietly.

Myreen's face ran through his head. From her thick dark hair weaved with the blue streaks, to her penetrating sky-blue eyes. The way she sometimes twisted her mouth when she was nervous. The way they'd talked that first night in the kitchen.

But he answered truthfully when he said, "I'm not sure."

Kol

Eduard had one of his cars waiting just outside the subway terminal, ready to take Kol and Myreen to *Mastro's Steakhouse*. That fact alone annoyed Kol to no end, but he ushered Myreen into the back seat, anyway. He'd been half-tempted to call for a cab instead and pretend like he hadn't seen the car. And even though his father was certain to see through Kol's B.S. and call Kol out on his *"unbecoming passive-aggressive behavior,"* he didn't care.

But he took the car for the same reason he decided to take Myreen to the place Eduard had reserved—or had one of his minions reserve. By following the General's orders exactly, by moving his pawn precisely the way the chess master directed, Kol could better keep his head clear and his heart locked away.

As long as the *date* felt like a *mission*—albeit tricky because he needed her to fall in love with him—there was minimal risk. And with Kol's analytical mind, he wasn't too worried about emotions getting the

319

better of him. *Mostly*.

The drive was at least twenty minutes in traffic, but they sat in silence. Kol made it a point to look out the window for the majority of the ride, to keep his eyes from straying to her pale blue dress and the way it somehow made her eyes that much more blue. If that were possible.

The original plan had been to meet in the entrance hall, then take the subway out together, but Kol decided to surprise Myreen by waiting in the mer common room—call it a romantic gesture or something. Mers didn't frighten him, so he didn't think it'd be a problem.

It was definitely a problem.

Even though he'd made sure the *Ken-Doll* was elsewhere, he didn't even make it to the door before being caught by none other than Trish for trying to sneak in. Kol felt himself stiffen and his pulse quicken being alone in the same air space as her, since they'd once made out in one of the greenhouses. The awkwardness was so thick, she didn't even have to scold him or threaten to report him to the faculty. Kol decided to rush out and wait for Myreen at the bottom of the stairs instead.

But that had been his second mistake.

He hadn't planned to facilitate a Cinderella-esque entrance for Myreen. But the instant she saw him standing at the bottom of the stairs in his dark, tailored suit, her face brightened, and she clutched the railing a bit tighter. Kol tried to keep his posture casual, but stiffened the instant he saw the way her calf-length shimmery dress caught the light with each step as she carefully walked down the stairs. The sleeves were short, and the neckline wasn't too low, but the pendant of her necklace pointed at the bit of cleavage that did show.

The dress was modest, which was both good and bad for Kol. Good because Kol was never attracted to girls who wore low-cut, *revealing everything* clothing. Those types were only worth wasting time with in the greenhouses. They rarely had anything interesting to talk about.

But it was bad because Kol was attracted to the ones who wore clothing that left more to the imagination. The ones who covered up because they had a different sense of self and other ways to draw attention.

So Kol watched the street lamps out the window almost hypnotically.

"Penny for your thoughts?" Myreen's voice sounded almost musical, like water trickling down a stream beside him.

"Huh?" Kol turned to her, making sure to focus his gaze on her eyes.

She giggled. "What are you thinking so long and hard about? You've hardly said a word."

"Oh," he said, looking down at his lap because—as it turned out—looking at her pretty blue eyes was perhaps worse than letting his eyes wander lower. "Just stuff with my dad. He gets in my head sometimes."

She nodded. "Do you wanna talk about it?"

"Not right now," he answered evasively. He could only imagine if she knew what was going on in his mind, and that thought brought with it a twinge a guilt.

"Alright," she said, then leaned back into her seat and looked out her own window.

They remained quiet after the driver pulled up to the curb. Kol offered his arm to Myreen to help her out of the car. Her eyes flew up to the large, lit sign above the entrance. The ambiance of the place permeated even to the sidewalk.

She was clearly impressed, but he never cared when people were impressed by his family's wealth. Which was probably why, under most circumstances, he would've refused his father's offer of the dinner reservation. Not because he was ordered to. But this wasn't most circumstances.

Maybe she was the type of girl who easily fell in love with the idea of money and power and high class and everything that went with those three things. He could only hope—he'd have no danger of falling for her if it were true.

They were seated in a private corner of the restaurant where they could easily hear the live jazz band playing, but still hold an intimate conversation. Myreen kept her hands folded in her lap and her eyes trained on anything except for Kol after they placed their orders. He knew her discomfort was his fault--he'd stared out the window the entire car ride.

If she was ever going to develop feelings for him, she couldn't be wondering why he had invited her and then ignored her for the duration of the evening. So he scrambled for a topic. Recent events didn't seem like the safest ones—what with her being locked in the sim room and the fact that she was struggling with shifting. He'd need to ease into the latter topic.

"I see you haven't taken my advice," he said.

"Hmm?" She turned to him, but stared at the table instead of actually looking at him.

He leaned toward her, the advantage of his height bringing his face closer to hers. "You ordered the filet mignon instead of the blackened salmon."

Her eyes finally found his. "You mean the fish?"

"Salmon are fish, yes," he said. "And mermaids need plenty of omegas in their diet." Part of him wanted to tease her more, to flash a smug look and watch her reaction, but the way her hair fell over her shoulder at that exact moment, the black and blue waves shining in the ambient light, nearly took his breath.

So his fact-spouting sounded just like that.

She gave him a half smile and nodded once, clearly not amused. He scrambled again. He wasn't about to cheat and use his dragon pheromone trick. The one that would instantly make Myreen respond the way he wanted no matter what stupid things flew from his mouth. He could do this. She wasn't the first girl he'd talked to. He'd kissed plenty. But she was the first he was trying to get to fall for him.

"You know, it's too bad mers can't fly," he said. "It's a clear night, perfect for flying."

She eyed him curiously, the way her left eyebrow rose defining the rounded edges of her face. "Now we're talking about the weather?"

Kol crossed his arms over his chest and sat back again. "Just making conversation."

She nodded, the stiff look on her face relaxing. "If mermaids could fly, I'd probably fail at that, too," she said with a sad laugh. "Can dragons swim? In shifter form, I mean. Obviously, you can swim. I mean, if you do know how. Sorry, I'm babbling." She frowned in a way that was simply alluring.

Kol gritted his teeth against appreciating her appeal, and in so doing missed an opportunity to charm her by assuring her she was doing just fine. So he averted his eyes when he said, "We can swim, but it's not really worth our time."

Myreen's cute frown deepened into one of disenchantment. "So swimming is beneath you dragons?"

Ugh, all he was doing was pissing her off. He had to stop fighting himself on this and be as charming as he knew himself to be. "Well, yes, obviously," he said, then smiled and added, "it literally is. You know, dragons fly over water?" He winked.

Another slow nod, this without even a fake smile.

What are you doing, Kol? Get it together.

"Alright," he said, annoyed, but trying hard not to let it leak into his tone. "What would you like to talk about?"

She crossed her arms and gave him a long look. "You're supposed to be a walking encyclopedia on shifters, right?" she asked. "Tell me something I don't know."

"Well that's easy—" he said, then caught himself, realizing too late how rude it sounded. "So, something you haven't learned in your few days of shifter biology?"

She nodded stiffly.

"Well, all shifters tend to have a personality directly related to the type of shifter they are," he said.

"Meaning?"

"Dragons are naturally charismatic and confident," he said, waving a hand at himself and winking. It wasn't actually true most of the time, in his case, but others still perceived him that way, so he attributed it to his dragon nature filling in that gap.

She didn't seem amused.

"Nagas are very vengeful and a little bit self-righteous," he said.

She shrugged her shoulders. "I haven't met any nagas yet."

"Okay, then take mers. They're all kind of stuck up and self-important because of their ability to shift from birth." He realized the stupidity of that the moment he said it, but didn't take it back. "Except for you, obviously," he amended.

"Yeah, 'cause I'm not a very good mer anyway," she said softly.

Ugh. Now I've hurt her feelings. Which seemed stupid because he'd just told her that she *wasn't* stuck up. "Don't be hard on yourself, you'll learn to shift."

Her cheeks reddened. "I didn't know you knew about that." Did her lower lip quiver?

"Hey, and next time in the sim room? Just fight back!" This was getting out of hand, but he couldn't stop it. "You'll be certain to beat Beginner Level One if you just try."

She narrowed her eyes at him. "I had no idea what was going on. I was tricked into that sim. Everyone else who goes into that thing, goes in knowing exactly what to expect. I would have fought back if I had known it was going to be so real. Excuse me for not living up to your expectations. And everyone else's."

He pressed his lips together, determined not to say another word. He did, however, nudge her with pheromones that would buoy her self-esteem back up.

"Do you have any idea how amazing it is to swim through the water—breathing and all—and see things that no other intelligent creatures can see?" she asked.

It worked.

"I may still be learning to shift at will, but I *can* shift," she said. "And I've seen the most amazing things just in Lake Michigan, already."

When has she been swimming in the lake? he wondered, but didn't ask. "It's the same being in the air. Above everything, looking down at the city. Seeing things you could never see by walking or driving."

"It's not just the water, though," Myreen said. "I really hope that I can develop my clairvoyance. Can you imagine being able to see what will happen in the future?"

He knew it didn't work exactly like that, and that all mers didn't have the gift, but he didn't correct her. "One word," he said instead. "Fire."

She opened her mouth to speak.

"And before you say *water manipulation,*" he cut her off. "C'mon! *Fire!*"

Myreen leaned forward and waved a hand as if conjuring it right then. "Water puts out fire."

He leaned closer, too. "Pheromone. Dispersion."

"What?"

"Dragons can manipulate the emotions of others by excreting certain pheromones."

"*Ew!*"

"It's not..." he shook his head. It wasn't worth arguing.

"Clairvoyance is way better."

"And there's that high-and mighty mer attitude!" he said, meaning to joke again, but it came out stiff and forced because she chose that moment to flip her hair back over her shoulder.

"At least I'm not a self-important dragon," she said. "A dragon who is *not-really* royalty, but likes everyone to pretend that he is."

She'd misunderstood him. And he couldn't blame her, because his tone had been all wrong. But that blow felt low, even for someone who wasn't informed.

"My family has done a lot for the shifter community."

"So I've heard," she said. "But that doesn't explain why you act the way you do. Cold one second, flirting the next! And I've heard the rumors about Trish!"

"You have no idea what you're talking about." Kol gritted his teeth.

"What, that you seduce girls to make out with them, then dump them the second you're bored?"

"Maybe you're more mer than I thought," he said. "I guess you can't change nature."

"What? Because someone actually called you on it? Just because you're charismatic and charming because of your *dragon nature*, doesn't mean that you can treat people horribly. Last I checked, we're all still *partly* human!"

"You are!" he nearly shouted. But at a look from the bartender across the room, he lowered his voice again. "You may be partly human, but I come from a long line of *dragons* on both sides of my family."

"So what does your family have to say about you going rebel and dating a *mer?*" She asked.

"You have no idea," he said, then switched the chemicals. Fortunately, he no longer felt at risk for falling for this ignorant, self-important girl. But she still needed to fall in love with him, so he put more energy into influencing than he ever had in his life.

Her blue eyes went glassy for a second and she reached forward for his hand with a frown on her face, like she was concerned that she'd angered him.

Good. It was working.

But she snapped out of it as quickly as she fell into it. "Are you doing that *thing* to me?" she asked, sounding disgusted.

Maybe a bit too much. But part of him wondered if he'd done it on purpose.

"I'm ready to leave," she said.

He waved a hand. "By all means. I'll message to have the car take you back."

She stood and stared him down. "How will you get back?" she asked, like she actually might care.

In all honesty, he'd probably call an Uber, but instead he said. "I'll *fly.*" He flashed one more smug look.

She stormed off.

Myreen

Myreen slammed her bedroom door and threw herself face first onto her bed. She was so frustrated that she again felt the urge to punch something, and she kind of wished that something could be Kol's stupid face!

How could she have ever thought she liked him? He was so damn arrogant. He walked around like he didn't care about his status, or ranks, or differences between the species. But underneath that handsome robotic exterior, he was every bit the dragon prince he was born to be. And he thought he was so much smarter than everyone else, and that what he believed was the absolute truth. She couldn't believe she had ever liked him!

At this moment, Myreen would be perfectly happy to never have to see him again. In fact, she was done with boys. Just done.

Knock, knock, knock.

Really? There were only two people in this wing that would knock on her door, and she was pretty sure it wasn't Delphine.

Rolling her eyes, she flopped off her bed and begrudgingly opened the door.

Kendall stood in the hallway with his hands in his pockets. She expected him to be mad, to come in and curse at her for leading him on and going out with his rival, in which case she was so ready to give him a piece of her mind. But he wore an uncertain expression, one that made him look even more cute and endearing. Was it humility?

They stood on opposite sides of the open door for a moment, Myreen debating whether to tell him to go away or let him in. "What's up?" she finally decided to ask.

"Delphine wanted me to give you a message earlier, but you were out," he said with a shrug.

"Oh." She stepped aside to let him in, then went to sit in her desk chair. "What's the message?"

"Delphine won't be able to tutor you privately anymore, due to some new business that has come up, so she's assigned another mer student to tutor you, instead."

From the tone of his voice, this did not sound like good news, and she could tell that it was not him who was given the task.

"Who's going to be tutoring me?"

Kendall twisted his lips to one side in an awkward frown before he replied, "Alessandra."

Myreen practically jumped out of her chair. "What? No! Why?"

Kendall shrugged. "My guess is because she's one of the fastest shifters, and she's the most talented with water manipulation."

Myreen began to shake her head repeatedly. This sounded like a death sentence.

She went over to her door and pulled it closed, then leaned up against it almost protectively. "It can't be Alessandra. She locked me in the sim room just yesterday. She pretty much tried to kill me."

"Wait, what?" Kendall gasped.

"Yeah, I would've been destroyed by the military guy in the sim if Kol hadn't showed up and turned it off," she said, throwing up her hands. "Why can't you just be the one to tutor me?"

Kendall sighed and shook his head. "Delphine wants me to focus on my seer abilities. She really wants me to be her apprentice after I graduate."

Myreen slumped onto her bed and groaned. This news was the cherry on top of a horrible evening. "With Alessandra coaching me, I'll never learn anything. She hates me."

"I wouldn't be so sure," Kendall said. "If she was given a task—by Delphine herself—she would do everything she can to succeed. Failure is not a word in her vocabulary."

Myreen shook her head, wishing she could just fade into nothingness for a while. How could things at this school possibly get any worse?

"So… you and the dragon prince, huh?" Kendall asked in a casual tone that attempted—in vain—to conceal his disappointment. "I heard that you two went out."

Myreen let out a sigh that sounded like a growl. "Doesn't anyone at this school have anything better to do than talk about each other?"

"Whoa, I'm sorry," he said, holding up his hands. "I didn't come here to make waves. If you like him, that's your business, and… I think you should go for what you want—"

"Well, you can rest assured that Kol is *not* it," she said, crossing her arms and looking away. "He showed his true colors tonight. There's nothing between us."

The room was silent for a moment.

"Oh," Kendall said, nodding slowly. "Are you okay?"

"Yeah, I'm fine, just in a bad mood," she said. She glanced sideways at Kendall, and the hopeful smile she saw on his face made her once again feel a confusing mixture of resolve and guilt. "Look, Kendall, I know you like me, and I'm sorry I didn't tell you about the date with Kol before. Things have just been... complicated. But tonight has made me realize that I just really don't want to date anyone right now. I need some time to find out who I really am before I can let anyone else in. And, if that's not okay with you, then I'll understand if you don't want to hang out anymore—"

"Hey, don't put words in my mouth," he interrupted softly. "I do like you, Myreen. And whether it be as a friend or something more, I'll take what I can get. I'm happy to just hang out with you, maybe even help you figure out who you are."

His smile practically twinkled with sincerity, and it warmed her recently chilled heart. She couldn't help but smile back. "Thanks. I could definitely use a guide."

He smiled even wider. "Well, if you're not too tired after your terrible date, you can tell me all about it. We can girl talk and maybe play cards?" He took a beaten up box of cards out of his pocket.

"Girl talk?" Myreen asked, raising one eyebrow and grinning. "You're really fighting hard to land yourself in the friend zone, aren't you?"

He shrugged and they both laughed. They plopped in the middle of the floor to play a game. Once the cards got dealt, and the conversation started flowing, Myreen felt so comfortable in Kendall's presence. He really was the perfect guy friend.

They played a few different games and talked late into the night, Myreen sharing stories from her childhood growing up in the human world, and Kendall telling her all about what it was like to grow up as a mer prince, half in the water and half out. His life sounded like a fairytale, and as she listened, she felt the slightest prick of jealousy.

She hadn't realized that she had started to fall asleep until Kendall nudged her awake and whispered that she should get to bed. Ever the chivalrous gentleman, he scooped her up into his arms and lay her on her bed, even pulling her blanket over her.

"Goodnight, Myreen," he said before he left her room.

"'Night, Kendall," she whispered sleepily back.

As she drifted off, now more than ever, she could see the two of them having a future together. She could see them growing up, getting married, having little mer children, their family frolicking in the endless blue of some ocean. Maybe someday. For now, she was just happy he was her friend.

***

The next day was her first training session with her arch nemesis— Alessandra. How Delphine thought it was a good idea to stick the two of them together, Myreen would never understand. She wasn't looking forward to what was sure to be a torture session. So much so, that she dragged out every minute she could before arriving at the mer training room.

She also felt a bit jilted by Delphine, as if by not having time for Myreen, she, too, was rejecting her. Delphine had clearly had expectations of Myreen when she first came to this school, and Myreen had definitely not lived up to any of them. She felt like having to endure Alessandra's presence one-on-one was a sort of punishment for being a disappointment.

Alessandra was already in her swim top when Myreen entered the mer training room, and the snobby brunette rolled her eyes when she saw her come through the door. Myreen mimicked the gesture and went to the locker room to take her time getting into her own swim top. She heard the door open behind her.

"Look, neither of us wants to be here, so can we just get this over with?" Alessandra said with a snide tone.

"Wow, something we actually agree on," Myreen said. "Fine, what great things do you have to teach me?" Myreen didn't try to conceal any of the disdain that laced her words.

Alessandra flipped her hair off her shoulder as they went back out into the training room. "Plenty. Not that I expect you to pick up any of it."

Myreen clenched her fists, fantasizing wrapping her fingers around Alessandra's little bobble-head neck. The wound to her pride from the sim room incident was so fresh it burned, but Myreen knew that someone had to take the high road here. And it wasn't going to be Alessandra.

"If this tutoring thing is going to work, we have to put our personal feelings aside and be professional about this," Myreen said. "So how about we leave our mutual hatred at the door—only for as long as we're in this room."

Alessandra looked at her sideways under thick black lashes, then shrugged. "I guess that sounds reasonable. Besides, if I can't turn you into a true mermaid, what does that say about me?"

Myreen rolled her eyes.

Alessandra gracefully lowered herself to sit on the pool's edge, positioning herself almost as if she were posing for Vogue Magazine. It made Myreen sick. Until she realized why. Alessandra's feet and legs slowly and elegantly merged into a beautiful, dark green tail.

Myreen watched with admiration, in awe of how easy Alessandra made it look. It still hurt Myreen every time to transform, the popping and adjusting of the bones causing her to perform what had to be a very unappealing dance in the water. But Alessandra made no movements whatsoever, like the transition was as simple as breathing. And what was more, Alessandra wasn't even wet! She had shifted completely dry.

Smoothing her face to hide her respect for Alessandra's skills, Myreen asked, "How do you do that?"

"It should be a simple thing for all mer, really," Alessandra said in an airy tone.

Myreen narrowed her eyes and cleared her throat loudly, and Alessandra rolled her eyes again and sighed.

"Yes, yes. Well, I guess I've never really thought about it," Alessandra said. "Mermaid is the form we're born in. Human is the form we shift *to*. I think your problem is that you have it in your head that your legs are the real you, but they aren't, and you're fighting yourself. Try thinking about it like your fins are your true legs, like your scales are your true skin."

Myreen raised her brows at Alessandra's attitude adjustment. What she said was actually *helpful*.

She sat down next to Alessandra, adopting the same pose, closed her eyes and tried to focus. Of course, she would think her legs were her real form. She'd had them under her all her life. But she couldn't deny how natural—how *right*—it felt to be in the water.

Be the real you. Be the real you. She chanted in her head, over and over.

She imagined herself in the lake again, surrounded inside and out by the cool blue water. In her mind, she twisted about in it, feeling her tail bend and curl, feeling the water flow around her fins. She felt at peace.

But nothing happened. Nothing changed.

"Hey, that's a start." Alessandra's voice made her open her eyes.

"Huh?"

She looked from Alessandra's face to her own legs. To her surprise, the skin of her calves and shins were covered in a thin layer of shimmer. Her scales had started to come out!

Myreen gasped with her mouth wide open.

"Don't get too excited just yet," Alessandra said. "It wasn't a full shift. You still have your legs out. But if we keep at it, we might make a real mermaid out of you. Eventually."

The small hint of encouragement in Alessandra's voice was almost impressive, and Myreen couldn't help but feel a twitch of gratitude that her tutelage had produced real improvement. She still hated Alessandra for what she'd done to her, but maybe the mermaid wasn't a completely horrible person.

"Thanks," Myreen said.

Alessandra eyed her for a moment, as if that was the last thing she'd ever expect to come out of Myreen's mouth. "Yeah, well, don't mention it. Seriously. Don't. I can't have my friends thinking I'm helping you. Unless you begin to excel, in which case, I taught you everything you know. Got it?"

Myreen shook her head and chuckled. "Whatever you say."

Juliet

One thing Juliet learned over the years was that rumors were always far from the truth. Or, in rare moments, they were spot on. It was fascinating how fast word traveled. One peep from one bird and suddenly the flock was in disarray. Myreen and Kol's date was already the hot topic of the day. Whispers were everywhere. Loud enough to be heard, of course.

Juliet couldn't wait to see Myreen, just so she could hear what really happened. One group said that they fought so bad, Kol shifted and nearly burned Myreen. Another group said that they couldn't keep their hands off each other. And the best rumor yet was that Myreen threw her drink in Kol's face, then made him walk back to the Dome.

Juliet didn't see Myreen for breakfast, and assumed that she was hiding out in her room to avoid the inevitable chatter. But the last thing she wanted to do was go and check on her, because Trish and her minions guarded that wing like a three-headed mer-dog. Even if she was eager to hear the truth, she wasn't going to willingly venture into their lair.

Deep down, Juliet wanted rumors of her and Nik floating around. Whether they were true or not, the thought of their names being in the same sentence was a fantasy. Juliet felt selfish hoping that Myreen's date went alright, because if it did, she would see Nik more, and in a closer setting.

As she walked into the dining hall, she looked for Myreen to be sitting with the guys. But when she spotted the back of Myreen's head, it was far from where Kol sat. *I guess it didn't go well.* Juliet sulked over to her friend and plopped down in the seat across from her.

"So, you look… like you need some coffee." Juliet didn't want to sound hungry for date details, so she tried to ease her way into it.

"Thanks?" Myreen sighed. "You just don't even want to know," Myreen said in a low and melancholy tone.

"Aw, sorry. Guys suck. Do you want to talk about it?" Juliet got up to move to the seat next to Myreen.

"Not really. I just know that it'll never happen again. He and I are *not* on the same page. About anything." Juliet sensed Myreen's frustration growing.

"Well, you're right, then. You shouldn't go out again. You deserve someone who wants to understand you and accept you for who you are." With a small smile, Juliet decided not to pry further. "Anyway, I missed you for breakfast. Did you pull one of my signature moves, hiding out in your room?" She chuckled and nudged Myreen in the side.

"I wish. I spent my morning with *Alessandra.*"

"Um, yuck! Why on earth would you do that?" Now Juliet was getting frustrated.

"I had no choice. She's my new transformation and mastery tutor."

"That is so unfair. So… how was it?"

"Not as bad as you'd think, I guess. I'm just… not getting the hang of this. And I can tell how it's disappointing everyone. Which is weird. Like, why does everyone care so much?"

Myreen hung her head in her hands.

"That's a crummy situation. Nobody should be put under so much pressure. Especially when you only just learned about this world. They all need to seriously back off."

Myreen didn't move.

"If it makes you feel any better, remember that I'm nowhere close to shifting. At least you've been able to see your tail. My dad keeps saying that patience is the answer. But how annoying is that? Who has patience anymore?" Juliet was grateful to see a small smile, at least.

Myreen nodded at the lunch line. "Let's eat."

As Juliet followed Myreen, she couldn't help but sneak a peek at Nik. It was easy to pick him out of the crowd, and not just because he was sitting next to Kol, who towered over everyone. She liked the spirals etched into his haircut, and thought he pulled off the look so well. And his inky eyes matched his hair color so well. But his best asset was his smile—the wider it was, the deeper his dimples popped. Juliet's true weakness.

He faced Kol and Brett, and it looked like they were having an important conversation. But to her surprise, as she and Myreen walked past their table, he lifted his eyes to meet hers, as if knowing she was staring.

Kol must have noticed, because he turned to see what had caught Nik's attention. But he saw right past Juliet. His back straightened as he watched Myreen walk by. A hint of sadness roamed over his face, like a dark and gloomy shadow. It made Juliet wonder what actually happened on their date.

When the girls returned to their seats, Juliet tried to be nonchalant about taking the seat next to Myreen instead of across. It gave her a better view of Nik, even if she only saw half of his face. She would catch glimpses of his smile and it brought one to her face every time.

"Seriously? Would you like me to get a slice of him for you? I mean… you're drooling."

Juliet had no idea she'd been so obvious. "Um… I don't know what you're talking about." If Myreen could tell she was ogling Nik, could he? Fear ran straight through every cell in her body. "I gotta go. Training with Dad. Talk to you later." Before Myreen or anyone could stop her, Juliet walked briskly away.

She heard Myreen call her name, but she acted like she didn't, succumbing to the comfort of her headphones. Juliet never felt so embarrassed. Myreen was her closest—and only—friend. She didn't understand why she felt so ashamed for having her eye on a guy she was crushing on.

And yet, she practically sprinted to get to training with her dad—and sooner than she had to. Maybe it was just because she was caught by surprise. Or maybe it was because she couldn't pry her eyes off Nik, even if she wanted to. Admitting that would be far too much for Juliet, so she did what she did best: she ran.

***

"Juliet, focus. You're not concentrating. Do I really have to rile you up whenever I want to see your fire?" Malachai rubbed his closed eyes.

For the last hour, he had simply asked Juliet to summon a fireball. But with her mind somewhere else, it was proving to be much more difficult than either of them wanted.

"Again. You will not leave this room until I see at least one fireball."

"Wow, Dad. Thanks for the pep talk." Juliet knew there was really no reason to give him attitude, but he wasn't the only simmering inside. And those emotions were tenfold with the constant reminder of embarrassing herself at lunch.

There was a couch in his office that Juliet favored, because the leather seat cushions were long, not allowing her feet to touch the ground. She chose the couch rather than the large, grandiose chairs that sat in front of his desk. That was where he lectured most of the Phoenix students. But she was supposed to be comfortable while searching for her power, so she sat back against the leather with her legs tucked underneath her.

Malachai clapped his hands loudly in an attempt to get her out of her own thoughts.

With the sharp look she was giving her father, Juliet thought at any moment, a fireball was exactly what he was going to get. But the thought of him upsetting her purposely blocked her anger. *Could he be trying to set me off just for the lesson?*

She was full of mixed emotions, and it made her feel lost and alone. Anger was not what Malachai would be getting from her today.

He must have noticed her inner turmoil because he walked to sit next to her. Malachai took her hand and enclosed it within his large, burly, warm ones.

"Look, I know you've had a tough time here. And the last thing I want is to be a part of any negative experiences for you. I just want you to understand that it's not as difficult as you're making it out to be. I know things were never great with your mother, and you've had years to learn how to build walls. But now you're here. With me. You don't need those walls anymore, Jules. Once you open yourself up, I promise it will feel exhilarating. Like nothing you've ever felt before."

His proximity made Juliet uncomfortable, but she realized that was exactly what he was talking about. Her first instinct was to cut people off and crawl into her own dark hole. If she wanted things to change, it had to start with her.

Juliet wiped away the stray tears that fell from her eyes and straightened her back.

"There we go," Malachai encouraged. "Now, remember those times when your temper brought out the flames? Did you feel the connection afterwards? The sense of security? Or feeling invincible from the heat?" As he waited for her answer, she could feel the warmth in her bones. With only a nod of her head, he smiled.

"Good! That's great! That means that you've already cemented your bond with your gift. And by the looks of it, you have massive fire power. But I can't say I'm surprised: you are a *Quinn.*" Whenever he spoke about their lineage, he had an almost arrogant air around him. It both made Juliet want to laugh and roll her eyes at the same time.

Malachai took Juliet's hand and opened it again, palm up. "Alright, that feeling that you get, I want you to think of it. Close your eyes and picture how your flames made you feel. *What* they made you feel. For me, it's an electric warmth. Like lightning hitting solid ground. Forget that your brain was telling you to feel anger, and remember your heart was telling you to feel acceptance, relief, pride. Now, try to remember. Bring forth that feeling again."

With her eyes closed, Juliet did exactly as her dad said. Picking out that feeling was easy, because it was probably the best thing she'd felt in her entire life. Her body reacted to the fire each time she set it free. She remembered the embers dancing along her arms and the comforting sparks that grew with every flame that left her fingers.

"Yes! Jules, yes! Keep your eyes closed and think of wrapping your flames into a ball. A simple sphere. Roll it around in your head and command it to obey you. Use force. You have it within you, I can feel it."

Now this was a pep talk Juliet appreciate. She took his words and followed each direction. It was like a dream. Her inner phoenix was responding to her call. It was addicting. She wanted more.

"Open your eyes," Malachai whispered.

The moment she saw what she created, all she wanted to do was jump for joy. A beautiful orange-and-red ball of fire was floating above her open palm. She watched the flames dance within the closed circle. It had her hypnotized. She'd never been so proud of herself.

Her excitement grew so much, that the fireball multiplied. By the time she tried to shut it off, the fireballs had found their way to one of the chairs.

Malachai jumped up and swiftly put out the fire with one of his smart extinguishers.

Juliet felt ashamed.

But Malachai was still beaming. "That was incredible! Progress, Jules. Progress! You did that without losing your temper, and you did it well! Get that pout off your face and go get an ice cream to cool down. I'm proud of you. We're getting somewhere. Now, go. You get an A for the day."

With a new sense of pride, Juliet left the room, feeling intoxicated and dizzy. Even if it was for only a moment, she'd done it. She'd controlled her fire. And with time, she knew would live up to all that the Quinn name stood for.

Kenzie

Kenzie sat on the L train, heading toward Leif's apartment. She twirled her thumbs, one knee bouncing as the cityscape sped by. She'd been on the Green Line for nearly ten minutes, but still saw no sign of L Boy. What was his name?

Wes.

Kenzie half smiled at the thought. No, she didn't really expect to see him, but it would've been nice. Traveling through Chicago on her own was a little intimidating, especially after running into Leif last time. Sure, he was the reason she was here now, but that didn't make their first encounter any less nerve-wracking.

She thought about trying to meet up with Myreen—even going so far as to tell her mom that's what she was doing—but decided against it. Myreen had her shifter life and shifter friends. She probably didn't want to see her selkie outcast of a friend, anyway.

Kenzie knew that wasn't fair, but she wasn't ready to see Myreen yet, and she wasn't sure she was ready to share Leif and his grimoire just yet, either. Part of her wanted to tell someone—anyone—but another, more insistent part, feared she would lose the grimoire and any chance at deepening her magic if she did.

So here she was, alone, twiddling her thumbs, feeling excited and guilty and lonely.

The train hissed to a stop, and she followed the passengers exiting to the platform. She looked over the railing at the street below, watching the flow of vehicles and human bodies as they bustled to their many destinations. A few moments later and she was down the stairs, tugging on her backpack as she joined the stream of humanity.

She squinted against the bright sunshine, taking on an air of confidence as she made her way past the various shops. The oddity of a convenience store tucked into a soaring tower made her smile. The familiar aroma of cooked meat and warm grease mixed with the pungent rubber and asphalt, and a moment later she spotted a McDonalds, completely without a drive thru. Kenzie laughed. The city never ceased to amuse her.

When she reached Leif's building, she craned her neck to take in the skyscraper. Tier after tier of shiny windows stacked on top of each other, framed by semi-ornate stonework that looked both ancient and modern. She wondered briefly how many people might live in a place like that. It looked nice enough from the outside.

The double glass doors slid aside as she approached, sending a cool rush of air through her hair. Inside, she found herself gaping at the sleek lobby. It looked like a fancy hotel—cozy, elegant. Chairs and coffee tables sat in inviting clusters and an upscale restaurant stood beyond an arch to the right. The murmur of conversation filled the air, along with the faint clink of fine china and champagne glasses. Kenzie's eyes nearly bugged out of her head. This place was *way* above her mom's pay grade. It made her home look like a hovel.

The guy behind the concierge counter tipped his head as she approached. "Anything I can help you with?" he asked.

"No. Just visiting a friend. Thanks."

"Of course. Elevators are to the left."

Kenzie smiled and made her way to the elevator, the blood beginning to thunder behind her ears. Leif's description of the location was accurate, if a bit sparse. "Nice" didn't quite cut it. If it weren't for the lack of a check-in desk, she'd think she'd walked into a hotel rather than an apartment complex.

She felt a little self-conscious in her jeans and t-shirt, with its blurred, rude gesture print. If anything went wrong today, she wanted to die in her favorite shirt, but now she felt like it made her stand out too much. At least the concierge hadn't looked surprised. Maybe it wasn't as bad as she thought.

The floors dinged by, finally depositing her on the eighth floor. She got off, following the signs until she stood in front of room 823.

Kenzie took a deep breath.

This was it. Either Leif was lying, and this was some sort of trap, or she'd find the grimoire, tucked inside his hidden safe, just like he said. She'd done her best to avoid any doubt during her trip here, but now that she was standing outside his door, she couldn't push the thoughts aside any longer. She mentally checked her meager list of spells, wondering if she should start the vampire binding one, but decided against it. If this really was a trap, chances were her reflexes wouldn't be enough to keep her safe.

She hoped her mom wouldn't have to pick her up in a body bag, or worse, lose her only child to the dark underworld. Would her mom even want to have anything to do with her if she was turned?

Kenzie shook her head, rolling her shoulders. She could do this. And she didn't think Leif was a bad guy, even if he was a vamp. Why would he make up a story like that? Besides, the chance to have magic, to grow her power, was too tempting to ignore.

Kenzie looked both ways down the hall, checking for any signs of people. When she felt comfortable she was alone, she put her hand on the knob.

"Díghlisál," she muttered, slipping through as soon as she heard the telltale click. She quietly shut the door behind her, locking it back in place.

"So far, so good." Kenzie turned around, getting her first good look of the place. It was nothing like she'd expected.

Floor-to-ceiling windows stretched above her, lined by heavy white drapes. The view directly out the window was of the building across the way, but as she neared the sill, she could see down to the street below. Her sneakers squeaked against the glossy, dark wood floors as she continued to explore. The kitchen was gorgeous: ebony cabinets contrasted white marble counters, which looked untouched. She doubled back to the entrance, noting the closet where Leif said the safe would be, and then peeked her head in the opposite door. There she found a bathroom that looked like it was made to match the kitchen. It boasted more sleek flooring and cabinets, with a large white tub and countertops. Kenzie let out a low whistle. This place was gorgeous.

The one thing that stood out, though, was the fact that there was no furniture. Well, almost none. One chair sat in a forlorn corner of the living room. It was old, and it bore a metal plaque on the back that said FROST BOARDING HOUSE. Kenzie reverently traced the well-worn wood as she neared it, wondering what stories it could tell. And tucked into other corner of the living room sat a glossy black baby grand piano.

Kenzie lifted a brow at the majestic instrument.

"Cliché much?" she said aloud, her voice bouncing off the bare walls. The space felt so empty, she almost had to speak in order to fill the void. "Bet he plays Clair de Lune, too." She chuckled.

For an apartment, it didn't look very lived in. Kenzie wondered what Leif did with himself when he wasn't... hunting. Or maybe this was a decoy apartment. Although, who would spend money on two places, especially since this one was so nice? Surely he could find someplace cheaper.

"Or maybe he's loaded."

She ran her finger across a swatch of the smooth marble countertop, then inspected it. "Maybe he spends all his spare time cleaning," she said, staring in disbelief at her unsullied finger.

Weird.

But what was even weirder was that the place had no bedroom. She looked back through the tiny apartment, but still didn't find anything. "Not even a coffin to lay his head." She chuckled. "At least I know I'm alone."

She went back to the closet, depositing her backpack on the floor and opening the double louvered doors. A few coats and some clothes hung there, though it still looked awfully meager, even for a vampire who only needed to occasionally blend in with society. Kenzie thumbed through the garments, all of them dark, most of them pure black. "I'm gonna have to get you a t-shirt with a kitten and a rainbow on it." The man needed some color. And irony.

She pushed the garments aside, revealing what looked like an electrical panel. She hesitated a moment longer, her nerves back on edge. This was what she'd come for, but now that she was here, it kind of frightened her. What if she couldn't read it? Or she found out she wasn't powerful enough for the bigger spells? Or the book was set to destroy anyone magical who dared open its pages who wasn't of the bloodline who created it?

Kenzie took a deep breath. "Only one way to find out."

She opened the aluminum panel door, revealing warning stickers, some switches, and a set of dials. She focused on the dials, entering the code Leif had given her. *Two-nine-0-seven.* Her fingers shook as she grabbed a switch and began pulling. The inner door opened easily, and she let it swing wide.

The smell hit her first, bearing the distinctive scent of aged paper and leather. There was almost a sweeter scent beneath it all, like peach or apple juice had been dribbled on it at some point. She reached a tentative hand in, as if the book might grow fangs and bite her. When she made contact, she jerked her hand back, a strange zap tingling in her fingertips. *Static electricity*, she tried to reassure herself.

Blowing out a deep breath, she plunged her hand back in, snatching the book out before she had the chance to freak out again.

Kenzie took the heavy tome to the kitchen counter, wishing she had a barstool or something to sit on. She cast a glance at the chair in the corner, but decided against it. There was no way she was gonna risk breaking that thing.

She needed a moment to take this all in. Who knew what she'd face when she got back home? There was no way she'd be bringing this out in front of her mom and Gram.

The cover looked fairly typical of old books, somehow both simplistic and ornate at the same time. There were no words on the front, nothing visual to mark it as a book of spells, but Kenzie could feel that it wasn't ordinary. It was almost as if the book called to her, and she found a strange comfort in the feel of it.

She cracked the book open, pages rustling, a fresh waft of ancient dust filling her nostrils and flavoring her tongue. Right away she recognized some of the words. Whoever had written in it last must have been using English, though the phrasing seemed too formal to be anything recent. She thought again of Leif's accent, and wondered just how old he was.

She turned a few more pages, gaping at the drawings and descriptions, the spells and potions. This book was a treasure trove, and she intended to soak up as much of it as she could.

Another turn of the page and her eyes lit up. "You can change the color of fire?" She had no idea what selkie had come up with that idea, or why. Not exactly a practical spell. "I *have* to try it."

Kenzie read over the word for pink a few times, letting the consonants and vowels roll around in her head until she was sure she had it. She licked her lips, then held out her hand in front of her.

"Mádearg dóicheáhn."

Bright magenta flames flared from her fingertips, casting a pink glow on the marble countertops. Kenzie released the magic and shook her hand out.

Greedily, her eyes roved over the page until she spotted a spell for green flames. A smile spread across her face. "Harry Potter, eat your heart out. Viás dóicheáhn. Ack!"

The green flames jumped from her hand, skittering across the wood flooring until it touched the long drapes. Kenzie's eyes widened as the fire took to the fabric, starting to lick up the edge.

"No! No, no, no!"

Kenzie looked around the kitchen, but there wasn't anything—not a bowl or ashtray or vase—to gather water in. She flung open cabinets, casting backwards glances at the growing fire. The green had faded, but the curtains were still burning. She wanted to turn to the book for a new spell, but she had no idea how long it would take to find what she needed. So she kept searching, but the place truly was barren.

"Think!" She hit her head, then glanced at the fridge. The drawers. She could pull one of them out to fill it with water.

She pulled open the door, but the sight that greeted her stopped her in her tracks.

Blood bags.

The red liquid inside was dark, and the plastic frosted as the apartment air hit them. Kenzie gagged. She averted her gaze, and yanked the drawer out, slamming the door closed. It hit and slowly eased back open. Kenzie didn't wait to watch a second time.

She ran to the sink, filling the drawer with water. "Come on, come on, come on!" When she had what she hoped was enough, she dashed to the other side of the room, throwing the contents on the flames. They sizzled and smoked, but the flames went out.

Kenzie sighed. "Thank the fates for flame retardant material." She cast a wary glance at the ceiling, praying the sprinklers there wouldn't go off. After a few tense moments she decided she was in the clear.

Kenzie dropped to the floor, laying on her back with her arms and legs spread. "Great. I have the book for one minute and I'm already burning places down." Her eyes rolled to the white curtains—and the large, black burn spot. Kenzie groaned.

A beeping noise cut through the silence, and Kenzie sprang to her feet. The fridge. Ah, she'd forgotten about that popping back open. She covered her nose and mouth as she neared, hoping to keep the contents of her stomach right where they were. She hated blood, the sight, thought, and even smell of the stuff. Thankfully, whatever was sitting in the fridge wasn't emitting a smell, though she still felt the need to breathe through her mouth. She nudged the door closed, letting out a long sigh when the seal finally took.

She glared at the book, sitting so innocently on the counter. "This is your fault."

She slammed the grimoire closed, loaded it in her bookbag, and opened the door leading back to the hallway. She took one final backward glance, grimacing again at the curtains. "At least it wasn't the piano. Here's hoping he doesn't fire me the moment he gets back from wherever he went."

She locked the door behind her and scurried out of the building, keeping her gaze on her feet. It occurred to her that she might be able to repair the curtains with a spell, but the book was big, and after that last fiasco, Kenzie wasn't sure magic was her best option. For now, anyway.

She had a lot of work to do.

Leif

An early spring breeze sent a chill down Leif's back, reminding him that winter hadn't completely given up yet. It was morning—an hour or so after sunrise—which was the perfect time for quiet contemplation.

Taking his pruning shears, Leif snipped another branch. There was a hidden comfort in helping a tree grow straight and true. He wondered if trees felt pain as rogue limbs were cut, or if they were grateful to not have so much to nurture. The tree would be able to focus on growing in the *right* places, instead of spreading itself too thinly, and weakening its core in the process.

The lesson applied to life.

Growing up in California, his parents expected too much of him. It hadn't mattered how much Leif had done to please his father—it was never enough. But the Frosts had taken him in, and he'd been able to focus on the important things.

Snip. Snip. Snip.

As Leif clipped branch after branch, he wondered at the irony of creating scars to make perfection. There was probably a lesson in that, too.

The orchard was already starting to blossom, the promise of a great apple harvest whispering in the leaves.

"You have no aversion to mornings, do you?"

Leif nearly fell off the ladder he was pruning from. Catching his balance, his sheers fell to the wet soil below.

"Camilla, I did not hear you approaching," Leif said, his heart pounding against his chest. "You very nearly killed me!"

She laughed. "That would be a pity; Father's orchards would soon follow, no doubt."

Camilla's brown hair was newly curled, and it spilled over her shoulders. She was wearing a violet jacket over a practical, pastel-purple dress. She was holding a tray of steaming food.

"I brought you some breakfast," she continued. "Hot oatmeal and toast."

Chuckling, Leif said, "Very humorous, Camilla. You are lucky you are wearing such a beautiful dress today, otherwise I would pour that oatmeal all over you. But why are you up so early?"

She looked at him in confusion. "I always bring you breakfast when you are working in the orchard."

Leif's eyes narrowed at her seriousness. Something didn't feel right. "You used to, back before I was a vampire."

Camilla gave a nervous chuckle. "A vampire? What are you going on about?"

Yes, something was definitely wrong.

Looking around quickly, he said, "Wait. How did I get here?"

"In the orchard?"

Leif shook his head. "No, the boarding house. I wasn't here before."

"Leif, you are beginning to scare me," Camilla said, taking a few steps back.

She was the scared one? Moments before this, he'd been trapped in a tank of water, drowning over and over again.

"This isn't real. None of this is real."

He ran his fingers through his hair and hunched over, pulling hard. He felt the pain—it was as real as his drowning had been.

Out of the corner of his eye he saw Camilla drop the tray of food.

"Stop this, Leif," she cried, running to his side.

He fell to his knees. "Draven! What have you done to me? Draven!"

Burying his face in his hands, he found himself sobbing. This trap inside the past was worse than drowning. The orchard had felt real. Camilla had felt real.

"Leif?"

The question of reality faded away like steam in winter. He knew that voice, and it wasn't just in his head.

Looking up, his eyes caught sight of Gemma, red hair bouncing as she raced toward him from the boarding house.

"Gemma," he whispered, new hope driving him to his feet. Leif didn't care which reality he was in. Gemma was here.

He sprinted for her, his legs filled with adrenaline, his heart beating with eager love that threatened to explode out of his chest.

But something was wrong. No matter how hard he ran, the distance between them didn't shorten.

"Leif!" she called to him, her voice traveling the distance that their legs, for some reason, couldn't. She came to a stop and reached a hand out. Leif did the same.

"Gemma! Please, come to me!"

"I can't!" She shook her head sadly and dropped to her knees, her green dress melding with the grassy lawn.

Quite suddenly, the morning sky turned overcast, and cool

raindrops began hitting him.

"She'll never come to you," another voice said, whispering in his ear. "But I *am* here."

He hadn't heard Beatrice approach, and as he looked up at her, he found her pale, smiling face framed by her platinum blond hair.

The falling rain fizzled out and the orchard disappeared. Leif found himself kneeling behind iron bars, staring up into Beatrice's icy blue eyes.

"I've *always* been here," she said softly, reaching a hand through the bars, waiting for him to take it.

Her face changed for a moment to Gemma's, and he blinked a few times to see if his eyes were playing tricks. Gemma stood before him, hand still extended. Without hesitation, he took her hand in his, placing it against his cheek and closing his eyes.

"What is going on?"

Leif's eyes snapped open, and he turned to see Draven walking toward them. Gemma removed her hand from his hold. He looked back at her in anguish, stumbling back and slamming into the bars behind him. Gemma had been replaced with Beatrice once more.

A wave of nausea struck him as he recalled just pressing his cheek against her cold hand. The visual trick made him feel violated.

"Leif's finally regaining some coherency," Beatrice said. "He's not all the way there, but getting closer."

Draven threw a thumb over his shoulder. "Out. I'll take it from here."

"You sure you don't want me to stick around?" she asked, turning back and giving Leif a smile. "A woman's touch can be extremely helpful."

Leif gritted his teeth. "He said get out. So get out!"

Beatrice looked as if she'd been slapped, and Leif felt no remorse for it. She looked at him for several seconds, then sped away.

Draven turned and watched her leave. They were in the dungeon, but Leif was the only one locked up in this particular room of cells.

"Now *that's* the Leif I remember. Passionate and cold, knowing just what he wants."

Leif grunted. "What did you do to me?"

Draven stepped to the cage and squatted down, matching Leif's level.

Cocking his head to the side, Draven replied, "I gave you an appropriate punishment. Something we agreed upon."

Leif pointed a shaky finger at his own head. "What did you do up here?"

A sly smile grew slowly on the lead vampire's face, and he got back to his feet. Walking back and forth in front of the cage, he said, "I watched you drown over and over again for an entire day. Six times per hour. That means you drowned one hundred and forty-four times. But that was four days ago."

Leif looked down at the concrete flooring. "Four days? I have no recollection of the other three. Except for... vivid dreams about my past."

"Oh, yes, we know that much." He tapped a device on his wrist. Leif heard his own voice echoing in the empty prison room.

"Camilla, I did not hear you approaching. You very nearly killed me!"

There was a pause.

"Very humorous, Camilla. You are lucky you are wearing such a beautiful dress today, otherwise I would pour that oatmeal all over you."

Another pause. The nauseating feeling he'd felt with Beatrice crept its way back into his stomach and climbed up his throat.

"You used to, back before I was a vampire."

Draven tapped his watch again. "We've been analyzing your... conversations over the past three days."

Leif put his head in his quaking hands.

"There is *much* more than what I just played for you," Draven continued.

"That tank of water," Leif started. "It wasn't just water, was it?"

Draven snapped his fingers and pointed at him. "Right you are."

"So much for 'not being animals'." Leif brought his angry eyes up to Draven.

"You must understand that I had the interest of all vampires in mind," the vampire leader said. "You have been off the radar for fifteen years. The hallucinogens I placed in that tank of water were put there so you would spill information that could be beneficial to our cause. And if you had ulterior motives, those secrets would present themselves in your... conversations."

Leif had no idea what he'd said over the past three days. Could he have revealed his true purpose for returning to Draven? Had he spilled the beans about Oberon and the school? What about Kenzie and the grimoire?"

"It seems you are still very much attached to your past," Draven said. "Most of what we recorded were conversations with your precious Gemma. But Camilla and her parents seemed to make an appearance from time to time." Draven smiled wickedly. "And a surprising amount of Beatrice. She was thrilled."

Leif shuddered, not wanting to know what happened in those hallucinations.

"Fortunately for you, you passed the test," Draven said, slipping a key into the lock on his cage. "If you've had shifter dealings over the past fifteen years, they haven't been important enough for you to hallucinate about."

Thank you, Gemma! he thought. His dealings with Oberon were pretty important, but he believed that it was Gemma that had kept him from revealing anything about his mission here.

356

The heavy lock clanged to the ground and the door swung open.

"Come along," Draven said, gesturing to him. "We have much to discuss now that you've rejoined us."

Leif got to his feet, and was glad to find that the shakiness was wearing off. He hoped that was an indicator of where the hallucinogen level in his body was at.

Keeping pace with Draven, they walked out of one room of prison cells, only to step into another. Leif hated that the dungeon of Heritage Prep was littered with so many cages. He had to find out why their number was so high—and why they were mostly empty.

"The first thing we'll do is assign you an Initiate," Draven continued.

Leif grimaced. He was getting pushed down to the bottom of the vampire ranks.

"You really think that's necessary?" Leif asked, knowing he was taking a risk speaking to Draven in such a way. "I want to be back out on the frontlines. I have work to do."

"You're not ready," Draven said evenly. "I need to know you're back in for good. You have proven your intent to rejoin us, but now I need to confirm your loyalty. You will take on an Initiate, and we will see where things go from there."

They made it to the staircase, passing a sneering Rory, and began the long climb.

"You're likely thirsty," Draven said.

And he was. Leif could sense the humans on the floors above them, their blood calling to him.

"Your Initiate will be your blood source," he added. "You'll find no blood bags here, and if you're caught sneaking any inside the school, there will be consequences."

Leif kept his gaze on the stairs. He *loathed* drinking straight from a person. It was too intimate of an experience, and even though fresh blood was more potent, he felt dirty every time he'd had to do it in the past. Animalistic.

"Very well," he said with forced-pleasantness. Remembering Oberon's wish to find out Draven's knowledge of the prophecy, Leif shifted gears. "I've been out of the loop for quite some time. What news can you tell me? Anything you think I may need to know about?"

Draven nodded. "We find shifters frequently, but never in large groups. Nothing that would equate to a school."

Shrugging, Leif said, "Perhaps they learned their lesson after what happened in South Dakota." He hoped his tone didn't reveal the lie.

"No, those animals can't stay apart for extended amounts of time," Draven spat. "And we've caught plenty who have witlessly revealed such information. We've just been unable to find out *where* they are."

"So, there is a school out there," Leif replied with feigned ignorance. "I don't know your sweeping strategies, but the shifters must be hidden well if you haven't been able to catch them over the past fifteen years."

"It appears they've finally learned their lesson," Draven said. "They aren't hiding in plain sight. My guess? They've rallied the selkies and wherever that school is, it's being hidden by concealment enchantments."

How wrong you are, Leif thought, stepping past the bottom level of Initiates.

"I thought the shifters hated selkies," Leif said.

"Who knows what kind of alliances have been created among the shifters?" Draven said.

He's accurate as far as alliances go.

They made it to the first floor of Initiates, which meant Leif was getting one of the more promising humans assigned to him.

"Here we are," Draven said, letting Leif move into the room first. As he passed the threshold, he found that he was entering a common room. Luxurious chairs and sofas were placed in perfect symmetry, not one piece of furniture off. Dark, hardwood floors ran the length of the room, along with equally symmetrical, extravagant, blood-red rugs. In the center of the room was a long table made of solid wood.

Several Initiates were sitting down, having quiet conversations. Others were standing and talking. But as he and Draven entered, the room went entirely silent.

"Good morning, most-favored Initiates," Draven said melodiously. "Today will be a great day for one of you: another vampire is ready to have an Initiate assigned to him!"

Leif looked around and found one thing in common among all the humans' faces: hope. They were all hoping for an assignment. It was the final step in proving their readiness to be turned.

And their eagerness disgusted him.

Leif had never wished for immortality, and believed that any human that did had selfish motivations. No human-turned-vampire had ever set out to spend eternity ending world hunger or reversing climate change. Vampires had only ever wanted power and domination.

"Would Piper Adams please step forward?"

From the left side of the room, a tall, gangly woman stood up. An inch or two taller than Leif, she looked to be skin and bones. She had sandy-blond hair, and freckles speckled cheeks and nose. Her almond-brown eyes were slightly magnified by golden-framed glasses.

Leif could see the excitement in her countenance as she took long strides toward them. She was wearing a charcoal skirt that came up to just above her knees with a matching suit coat. Underneath was a simple white button-up shirt.

"A girl?" he muttered to Draven.

"A girl who double majored at Harvard in molecular biology and electrical engineering," Draven clarified.

"So, she's overconfident?" he whispered.

Draven sighed. "She's a genius."

The girl stepped directly in front of Leif. The space between them made him uncomfortable, but he held his ground and looked up into her eyes.

"Piper, meet Leif Villers," Draven said. "Leif, meet Piper Adams."

Even though Leif's hands were at his sides, Piper grabbed one and squeezed overzealously.

"This is the greatest day of my life," she exulted.

Leif's eyes widened, and he shot Draven a worried glance.

She laughed, but the sound resembled a pig's snort more than anything. "I've been waiting six months for this, Mr. Villers. Six. Whole. Months."

Leif scratched awkwardly at his head with his free hand, wondering when Piper would let go. "I don't know exactly how I'm supposed to react, but one thing we are going to start with—don't call me 'Mr. Villers'. Leif will do nicely."

Her eyes filled with wonder. "I can call you by your first name?"

"Um, of course?" Leif muttered. "That's what everybody else calls me."

Out of the corner of his eye, Leif saw Draven bring a hand to his forehead.

"You see us as equals," she said, her amazement increasing.

"Far from," Draven said. "You're an initiate. Leif is a century-old vampire. You have much to learn and master before you are even close to being on the same level as he is. His preference in how you refer to him has nothing to do with your status."

She bowed reverently. "Yes, sir. Pardon my assumptions. It won't happen again."

"Excellent," Draven said, giving her a look as if she were the scum of the earth. "You two will be working with each other for the next six months. A review will then begin to see if Piper is ready to be turned. If it is decided that she is worthy of it, Leif will be the one to take that action."

Leif would do everything in his power *not* to. He'd made it this far in his long life without turning any human, and he wasn't about to start. Even with a willing victim. Which meant he needed to extract the information from Draven as quickly as possible and desert this cursed place once and for all.

"If she's found unworthy, Leif will drink every last drop of blood flowing through her body," Draven said carelessly. "Now, I will show Leif to his new quarters. When he is ready, he will come down for you, Piper."

Again, the Initiate bowed. "I will wait patiently for him, sir. Thank you for this opportunity."

She gave Leif an excited look, then stepped back to the chair she'd been in, picking up the tablet she'd left there and sitting down.

Draven turned around, and Leif followed him out of the Initiate common room and onto the staircase heading back up to the main floor of Heritage Prep.

"I thought you said she was smart," Leif said.

"Don't label her quite yet," Draven said. "Her excitement masks her intelligence. This is every Initiate's dream. You'll see just how smart she is as she gets used to shadowing you."

Leif detected the warning in his words. Draven may have assigned him to Piper for a reason, but he knew that the vampire leader had assigned Piper to him for other reasons.

"Sounds like she'll keep me on my toes," he said.

"Indeed."

They passed the main floor and continued through the main staircase, making their way up the front tower.

"There are many projects going on, and many teams of vampires and Initiates are working hard to increase our rightful dominion over the world. You and Piper have an important assignment."

Great. Leif would have to get his hands dirty. He abhorred the idea of increasing vampire dominion. He stopped himself from showing any form of annoyance, although his emotions threatened to betray him.

"What would you have me do, Draven?"

The vampire leader came to a stop between floors.

"We have been experimenting," he said, drawing his blue eyes on Leif. Set in them was exploratory awe, which deeply disconcerted Leif.

"On what?"

"Hybrids," answered Draven.

Leif felt a developing knot in the pit of his stomach. "Hybrid *what?*

"Vampire-shifters," Draven said, raising his arms to the side. "Our glorious future."

"But that's impossible," Leif said. "Any shifter that a vampire has tried to turn has ended up dying. Vampire venom and shifter genomes don't mix."

"But we are on the verge of figuring out the final pieces of making it happen. Which is where you and Piper come in."

Leif withheld a gasp. This was terrifying information. If Draven was successful in figuring out how to make vampire-shifters, nobody would be safe. Too many powers mixing together. It would create an uncontrollable abomination.

"Do you not share the vision, Leif?" Draven asked. "You seem forlorn at this grand announcement."

Leif realized his misstep. "To be honest, I'm shocked," Leif said. "I never thought such a thing was possible. And if this is what you want me to do, I'll get with Piper today and we'll start figuring it out."

Draven smiled. "Then I'll show you to your quarters and get out of your hair. Welcome back, my friend."

They continued their ascension, but Leif felt his spirits drop. Was this information worth contacting Oberon about? Or should he continue working on Draven about the prophecy? It was, after all, the information Oberon had requested.

Not yet.

It was Gemma's voice in his head again, and he'd learned to follow it long ago.

Myreen

"Can you believe it's almost Thanksgiving already?"

Juliet pointed to one of the banners hanging in the dining hall that read: THANKSGIVING FEAST TONIGHT. The two of them were supposed to be studying Shifter History, but Juliet kept getting sidetracked.

"I feel like this semester has taken a really, really long time," Juliet went on, "but somehow, I still can't believe Thanksgiving is tomorrow."

"I know what you mean," Myreen said. "It definitely doesn't feel like a holiday's coming up." But it wasn't for the reason Juliet was implying. Knowing that a holiday was around the corner made her mom's absence that much more tangible.

"It's nice of the school to do this feast thing the night before, though, to get us in the mood," Juliet said, idly flipping the pages of her history book with the pad of her thumb. "Are you going home for the long weekend?" Juliet asked

The word "home" made Myreen's heart ache. She swallowed before shaking her head and saying, "Nope."

Not for the first time, she considered opening up to Juliet about her mom's death. Juliet was her closest friend at this school and still had no idea. But Myreen didn't want her friend to look at her differently. She didn't want to see the same pity in Juliet's eyes that she saw in Kendall's and Delphine's and even Oberon's. Juliet was a fun person, and Myreen liked being able to rely on that fun when she was around her.

"What about you?" Myreen asked, quickly getting the subject off herself. "Spending Thanksgiving with your dad?"

"Unfortunately." Juliet sighed and leaned back in her chair. "He wants us to 'bond'" —she air quoted with her fingers— "in a non-school environment. But I'm all free on Black Friday! Want to join me in the craziness of pre-Christmas shopping?"

Myreen smiled. "Yeah, that sounds like fun!" Yep, she could always count on Juliet. She looked at the nearest clock on the wall. "We'll talk about it later. I gotta go. Alessandra is *not* a patient tutor."

"Oh yeah, how's that going by the way?" Juliet asked, closing her history book as Myreen stood up.

"Honestly, not horrible."

It had been almost a week that Myreen had been practicing shifting and water manipulation with Alessandra. After the first few minutes of each session where they still remembered they hated each other, things progressed pretty well—when Alessandra wasn't being a nasty, conniving sea witch, she was actually quite helpful. She had a very technical view of her skills, so she was able to explain tasks in a very clear, easy-to-follow way. Myreen had fully shifted outside of water for the first time yesterday; it didn't last long, and Myreen had to get in the pool to keep her tail out, but they both considered that a win.

Now they had to focus on water manipulation, which was their goal for tonight's practice.

"I'll see you at dinner," Myreen said as she waved to Juliet and headed out of the Dining Hall.

She hurried to the training room, passing by students who were all excitedly chatting about their Thanksgiving plans. Myreen really had no idea what she was going to do. She had no home outside of the school, but the idea of being the only student in these empty halls for four days straight sounded beyond depressing.

Kenzie had invited her to her family's dinner, which was quite tempting. Myreen liked Kenzie's mom and grandma. They were sweet ladies. But the last time she had seen them, she didn't know they were selkies and they didn't know she was a mermaid. Things might be different now. And if they didn't know she was a mermaid, what if they found out during dinner and kicked her out? Her heart couldn't take anymore rejection.

Maybe it was just better to stay here. She could curl up on the couch in the mermaid common room and have the TV all to herself for the long weekend.

Walking up to the training room entrance, she decided to turn off those thoughts. She opened the door and went in.

"We're going to have to make this quick, today," Alessandra said, rolling her thick black hair into a bun. "I'll be leaving early tonight to catch a plane home. Mermaids don't exactly celebrate Thanksgiving, but my parents relish any mandatory days off from school to spoil me."

The way Alessandra said that last part stoked the fire of Myreen's dislike for the girl. She knew that Alessandra was a spoiled brat, and it made sense that it must be her parents' fault.

Myreen's mom might have kept secrets and dragged her all over the country, but at least she taught Myreen how to be a decent person. Myreen had to earn things she wanted, and she couldn't be more grateful to her mom for teaching her the true value of things.

I miss you, Mom…

Rather than responding to Alessandra's comment, Myreen just went to change into her swim top. When she came out, Alessandra was floating in the pool, making the water jump into the air and twirl around like a ribbon. It was beautiful to watch, but Myreen was a bit irked by Alessandra's showing off.

"You gonna teach me how to do that today?" Myreen asked as she padded barefoot across the tile toward the pool's edge.

Alessandra snorted. "Not likely, but all I can do is try my best."

Myreen gritted her teeth, thinking it best to ignore the snide comment and get as much as she could from this lesson.

She lowered herself to the floor, ready to slip into the pool.

"Uh-uh, transform first," Alessandra said. "Until you can shift at will perfectly, you need to practice *before* getting in the water. Every. Single. Time."

Myreen sighed but did as Alessandra instructed. She put herself in her mental happy place—deep in the heart of a dark blue ocean of her own imagination—and willed herself to become what she was really was. She imagined the water lovingly caressing her arms and cheeks, filling her lungs as if filling her heart.

And then it started. The bones of her ankles and knees popped and twisted as her legs morphed together, the pain of it forcing her to grimace. Without the aid of the salt water, transforming dry took much longer, and was therefore more painful. She urged her body to change faster so the pain would end, pinching her face as she concentrated. It was excruciating.

But the pain caused her to lose her focus, and her legs began to separate.

"Alright, just get in," Alessandra said, with no small amount of irritation.

Myreen plunged into the pool, and the transformation continued

367

through to completion. She was so relieved to be away from that pain, but disappointed that she got into her head and kept herself from finishing without the water.

When Myreen's face surfaced, she could tell that Alessandra had a few belittling things she wanted to say but was holding her tongue, which was actually a pretty impressive feat for her. The closer Myreen got to being a real mermaid, the closer Alessandra got to being a slightly less horrible sea witch.

"The key to controlling water is to visualize it as an extension of yourself." Alessandra got right to the point. "If you want to will an ounce of water out of the pool, imagine it's connected to a limb that you just can't see. Like an extra hand. Try it."

Myreen had tried and failed at water manipulation time and again, so she didn't expect this afternoon would be any different. But she closed her eyes and imagined that her hands formed a cup in the pool in front of her, filling with the water. In her mind, she lifted her hands out of the pool, still holding the water, not a drop spilling out.

She peeked through one eye to see if anything was really happening.

The only thing Myreen saw was Alessandra's barbie face scrunched in a dubious frown.

"Were you even trying to do anything, or are you, like, having some kind of seizure or something?" Alessandra asked, her arms crossed under her chest.

Myreen dropped her shoulders and sighed. "A seizure? I'm not mentally handicapped."

"Well, it would sure make a lot of sense," Alessandra grumbled under her breath.

Myreen scowled.

"What were you visualizing?" Alessandra asked. "Tell me exactly."

"I was picturing holding my hands in front of me and forming a cup in the water, then lifting that water out of the pool," Myreen explained.

Alessandra scoffed. "Ugh. Why can't you follow simple directions? I said imagine the water *is* a limb, not that limbs you already have are influencing it. You can't see the water as something that is being affected by you, it won't work that way. You have to see it as if it *is* you. Try again."

The trout triplet was certainly in a rush today. Though she did let slip the occasional insult during sessions, her attitude today was excessive. Myreen was getting ready to say to heck with it and walk out. Let the sea witch run off to her fancy, enabling parents.

But she wanted to get this right. She didn't want to kick off the next four days of solitude with more fuel for self-deprecation.

Myreen closed her eyes and tried again. How was she supposed to make herself believe the water was a part of her? This pool was enormous. Not that she had any kind of weight sensitivity, but being the size of this pool would make her way beyond fat. That wasn't a picture she wanted floating around in her head—her self-esteem was low enough already.

Then something occurred to her. She didn't have to imagine that her body was literally the size of the amount of water she was touching. What if her soul just extended beyond her physical self to also inhabit the water? She definitely felt connected to water, and the part that hadn't clicked until now was that it was a connection beyond the physical.

She imagined herself as her soul just floating in her body, imagined it radiating beyond her bones and skin and flowing into the water around her. She imagined feeling the water with her soul and not her physical senses, and the thought sent a ripple through her.

Concentrating on just the water directly in front of her, she reached her soul forward and upward. A gentle gurgle and splash of water made her eyes pop open. The surface of the water in front of her was waving and rocking.

"All that effort for a tiny water bubble?" Alessandra asked. "Well, at least you accomplished *something*."

The burst of joy sputtered out at Alessandra's derisive words.

"What is your problem today?" Myreen asked. "This is the best I've done in any of my tutoring sessions, and all you can do is shut me down. Don't you get that the closer I get to figuring this stuff out, the closer you get to not having to do this anymore?"

Alessandra's brows rose, and she looked a bit stumped.

"I get that you're happy to go home, but why is that making you even nastier than usual?" Myreen went on.

Alessandra looked away. "You wouldn't understand."

"You're probably right," Myreen said. "I don't understand how someone who has everything she could want can still radiate misery and hatred."

Alessandra shook her head. "I don't have everything."

Myreen frowned at her. "What, *don't* have—the newest iPhone?"

"I don't have Kendall." Alessandra said it so quietly that Myreen almost didn't hear it.

"What?" Myreen asked after a moment.

"See, you wouldn't understand," Alessandra said, pulling herself out of the pool. "Because you have Kendall following you around like a little guppy fish, and you don't even care."

Myreen watched with a stumped expression as Alessandra stomped into the locker room. This was the first sign of vulnerability Myreen had ever seen in the conceited mermaid, and for a moment, she could almost believe that Alessandra had feelings.

She lifted herself out of the pool too, and willed her tail to transform back to legs as fast as she could. Then she rushed into the locker room.

"Look, I don't know what you and Kendall had before, but I had nothing to do with it ending," Myreen said to Alessandra, who was changing.

"The hell you didn't," Alessandra snapped. "The day you showed up was the day Kendall dumped me."

Myreen's brows shot up. That was not something she expected to hear.

"That doesn't mean it had anything to do with me," she argued. "I'm sure it was just a coincidence."

Alessandra shook her head after pulling her shirt on. "Let me tell you something. When I first started here two years ago, Kendall was just as into me as he seems to be into you. He was so sweet and charming, and it was clear he was trying really hard to get with me. He told me that he dreamt about me, that we were destined to be together. And because he's such a gifted seer, I believed him. He told me we were going to change the world." She actually looked pretty as she stared off into the distance, reliving her story. Not the plastic pretty she always was, but true pretty, in a girl-next-door kind of way.

But the dream in her eyes faded and she narrowed them at Myreen. "Then you showed up, and suddenly everything we had together meant nothing. He said he was wrong about me. That I wasn't the girl he thought I was, and that it was over. I didn't understand it— not until I saw him swooning over you the next day. You ruined everything."

Alessandra stormed out, and Myreen sat on the bench to process what she just heard.

So that was why Alessandra and her friends hated her so much. It was absurd. Sure, Kendall had been interested in Myreen from day one, but that didn't mean he would end a two-year relationship because a new girl showed up—one that he didn't even know. That made no sense.

Even though she knew Alessandra's perception of the situation was distorted by pain, something about this left Myreen with a strange sense of unease, like there was something she should be aware of, but was just missing. But then again, that was true of just about everything in her life. There were loads of things she should know that she just kept missing.

So rather than dwelling, she decided to get herself dry and dressed and go to the Dining Hall to stuff her face with whatever comfort food tonight's feast had on the menu.

Kol

"Heading out?" Kol asked Brett, barely looking up from his books. Everyone was leaving for Thanksgiving now that the feast was over, but since Kol's family wouldn't be home anyway, he opted to stay at the school. He looked forward to the next four days without distraction, and planned to get a head start on his end-of-term essays and possibly make time to dive into a few books.

"Please tell me you don't plan to do homework all weekend?" Brett said, then slung is bag over his shoulder.

Kol laughed, but still didn't look up. With Nik and Brett gone, there would be no dragging him off to stupid parties, or talking him into an all-day-and-all-night virtual zombie raid in front of the flat screen. He was looking forward to it.

"Seriously." Brett plopped next to Kol on the couch in the Avian common room. Most of the students had left already, but a few still trickled out. "Find something fun or time-wasting to do."

Kol put his book down to look at his friend and smiled. "Time-wasting, huh?" Okay, so a zombie raid wasn't completely out of the question.

Brett held his hands up in surrender and looked like he was about to leave when a rare expression flashed on his face. "Have you told the General about the Myreen thing and you giving up?" he asked.

Kol cringed at the memory of his and Myreen's epic fail of a date. The whole thing had blown up in his face. Not only was Myreen *not* in love with him, he doubted she'd ever speak to him again.

"Here's the thing," Brett said when Kol didn't answer. "It's not like I was there or anything, but from what you've told me, and from the gossip in the halls, I think you really like the girl."

Whoa! This conversation had taken a complete one-eighty. And in a direction Kol never would've thought Brett would venture. Nik maybe, but not Brett. "You think I *like* her? She called me a '*self-important dragon*,'" he said.

"So? You've been called worse."

"She called me cold and calculating... or something. She had the nerve to bring up Trish and she wasn't even there!"

"Well... you did kinda play the girl."

"Urgh!" Kol growled, frustrated. "Whatever lies Trish has been spreading... *never mind.* Of course she lies."

"You can't hold that against Myreen."

"True."

"What's the issue then?"

"I..." Kol paused. "I'm not exactly proud of the things I said to Myreen, either. I pushed her buttons. I said things I knew would insult her. I'm pretty sure I hurt her feelings. I was such a *blue tail!*"

Brett dared let his smug look emerge.

"Spit it out, Claude!"

Brett laughed at the usage of his last name. Kol only did it when he was pissed off at him, and he knew it. So Brett pushed a bit more. "*Methinks thou dost protest too much...*" he sang.

"Since when did you start quoting Shakespeare?"

Brett stood. "You like the girl, Kol," he said. "This isn't just some stupid assignment from your father anymore."

Kol flashed his deadpan look before speaking. "Are you hearing what you're saying? I was rude to her. I insulted her. I freaking told her I'd *fly home* to make her even madder!"

"Exactly my point. You are sabotaging your *fake* relationship with her, because you have *real* feelings for her."

"Brett, you're an idiot."

Brett laughed, then left Kol to wallow in his thoughts.

Instead, he poured himself into his homework. And finished it.

Then woke up the next morning with nothing to do.

He considered conducting an all-day-and-all-night virtual zombie raid, and take Brett's advice to waste time, but it didn't sound as appealing, knowing that he wouldn't have anyone to play with. Not even online, since everyone in the US—and therefore everyone he knew—were all stuffing their faces with turkey and dressing and pumpkin pie for the duration of the day.

He went to the kitchen to find a quick breakfast, hoping that some spark of inspiration would come to him while he ate his Cheerios. Maybe he'd go for a flight. It had been a while since he'd taken one that lasted several days. And now would be the perfect opportunity to do it, since no one would be missing him.

Kol had all but decided to do just that, and rinsed and washed his dishes with the intention to grab his smart shorts and head out immediately, but right as he finished wiping his spoon, the kitchen door opened.

And the black-haired beauty—who had a way of infuriating him to no end—hesitantly walked in.

Kol immediately wanted to put his wall up. Despite what Brett said—that he was absolutely denying—there was no point even pretending to like the girl anymore. But something about the way they were suddenly caught alone in the place they'd first met, immediately extinguished any and all animosity he had toward her.

"You didn't go home, either?" he stupidly asked. "I mean, right," he amended. "Of course, you didn't go home. I'm sorry I even asked." He wasn't in any mood to see the look of hurt or anger he most likely just caused, so he didn't even look at her face as he made his way out of the kitchen.

"Why didn't *you* go?" she asked before he could make it to the doors. Her tone surprised him. It was soft and held no ounce of anger or hurt. His eyes immediately went to hers—again, the stupid words that came out only seconds ago apparently had no effect on her, at all.

He tried but failed to stop his brows from furrowing. "Hmm?" What had she just asked him? Was there some sort of magic in the kitchen? He was half-tempted to look for signs of a selkie spell.

"Why didn't you go home?" she repeated, heading toward the cupboard with the cereal boxes. "For Thanksgiving?" She pulled out the same box of Cheerios.

"My family isn't home," he said, injecting as much nonchalance as he could into that statement. Which wasn't hard, since his tone normally sounded that way. But since Myreen didn't go home because she had no one to go home to, he couldn't act like it bothered him in the slightest that he couldn't see his family on the holiday. At least he still had a family. Albeit dysfunctional.

She poured herself a bowl and he took her silence as his cue to leave, but she stopped him again.

"Off to do homework?"

He should've lied and said yes to prevent another fight, but instead he said, "A flight, actually."

Kol could practically feel her eyes boring through the back of his skull, and like the glutton he was, he turned to see it. But it vanished. Or maybe it was never there. But it must've been there, since it was the last thing he'd said to her on their date.

"My homework is done," he said and shrugged, like that made it better.

Myreen nodded and took another bite of her breakfast.

"Are you doing homework today?" he asked, unable to hide the evident hope in his tone.

She mimicked his shrug and after swallowing said, "Probably. I don't really want to, since everyone else is off having fun."

He didn't have to go for a flight.

"Wanna see me beat the sim room?" he asked.

Her eyes widened, and a smile split her perfect face. She nodded quickly.

Kol let a small smile emerge, then nodded once. "I'll go get my gear while you finish," he said, telling himself that he needed the practice anyway, if he was ever going to beat the thing and test out of class. "Meet me in the defense training room when you're finished."

She nodded again and Kol left.

***

"So… how does it work?" Myreen asked as Kol finished his stretches.

He started his routine, pre-simulation stretches before she arrived to calm his nerves. He'd already planned to run Intermediate Level Ten—which he beat last year—because it was one of the more impressive ones that was easy to show off in. At least for him. But despite that, he still had a knot in his stomach. The thought of her observing him, watching him shift into his dragon form to battle the simulation enemies, added another level to the whole experience.

"I heard you test out of class if you beat it," she said when he didn't immediately answer.

"Yes," he said between breaths. "That is the goal."

Her pause was heavy. Like she was carefully choosing her words. "Why haven't you beat it yet?" she finally asked.

"Ha!" he said, chuckling. "It's not that easy."

"I— I just figured since you seem to be so…"

Kol stood to his full height and watched her, waiting for her to finish her sentence. Was she trying to insult him? But the expression on her face showed total ignorance on the issue.

"The simulation is a complex and intelligent program," he said. "Each one is designed specifically for each shifter, to push them to overcome whatever their greatest weakness is in battle."

"Greatest weakness?" She pondered. "That guy in the simulation I was stuck in seemed… *human*. I would have thought something like a vamp—" Her words cut off with her breath.

She's probably thinking of her mom, he thought. "The simulation you were stuck in was one of the practice ones," he said, not drawing attention to the fact that he noticed her break in emotion. "There's an extensive series of practice levels that assist in getting you ready for the one you'll be tested on. Kind of like video games. Except each level starts the same, then adapts to whatever maneuvers you're favoring to force *you* to adapt."

"Do you have to go through *all* of them?" she asked, her eyes widening.

"It's not required, but it is suggested," he said.

"Okay. Are you attempting to beat it today?"

"Oberon has to be present for a testing, so no. I'll show you one of the levels."

"Which one?"

"Intermediate Level Ten."

She nodded, like she wasn't sure if that was impressive or not. "Which one was I in?" she asked.

He'd been avoiding telling her, but couldn't avoid it now. "Beginner Level One."

She nodded again, and Kol ended the conversation by getting her settled in the observation room, then left to face the white blankness of the simulation room.

He entered the code and readied for shifting as the room disappeared, icy arctic cliffs revealing themselves. As many times as he'd been in the room, it always felt as if he were being transported somewhere else in the world, not within the walls of the school's high-tech simulation chamber. Snow blanketed everything, and ice dripped down from the cliffs and rocks as Kol blew out a visible breath before bending his knees in a crouch. He closed his eyes to begin the shift.

Kol had the ability to explode-shift--transforming in the blink of an eye—but he drew it out instead. *Maybe it'll help her in her own shifting, if I show her in slow motion,* he told himself and figured he had about thirty seconds before the first simulation enemy appeared. He started with his feet, shifting the skin to his go-to dark gray scales and claws, then moved the scales up his legs. They flipped outward before settling, like the shuffling of cards. He took the longest to fling out his wingspan, pushing the air around him as they grew to their full length. But when he heard the cry of the simulation dragons in the distance—their high-pitched shrieks penetrating the air, vibrating the ice crystals until they sounded like glass wind chimes—he quickly moved through the rest of his shift. He changed his dark hair into scales, then pushed out a long snout and grew out his tail.

He couldn't see Myreen's reaction, but could only imagine the awe on her face as he pumped his wings and took flight to meet the simulation enemy dragons.

They were all slightly larger than Kol, and their bright red and green colors helped them stick out against the pale sky with ease. He'd learned early on that their agility was no match for his own. Kol weaved in and out of their formation, flying above, then below each of them, to force their open jaws and flame-throwing onto each other.

Bank right, fly up, half turn.

A sim dragon screamed.

Hairpin turn, veer left, tuck wings in and plummet.

Emerald green flashed past him, plunging to the icy cliffs below.

He had the beginning memorized, it had taken him so long to beat it. Now he anticipated when the sim dragons went from predictable, robotic entities—like the zombie sims in Brett's games—to the more life-like and reasoning ones when the computer began anticipating Kol's moves. Normally he could strike down at least a half dozen before the computer caught on.

In his peripheral, he caught another flash of green to his right—one he hadn't anticipated—and made his own calculations to bring it down. He bent into a nose dive, but immediately switched directions again to come up from below the beast and trap its left leg in his powerful jaws. Instead he got a mouthful of tail. The tails were thinner so there wasn't as much to bite down on, but he was able to sink in with two teeth—causing the dragon to let out a screech—then proceeded to swing it around like a catapult, releasing with precise force and trajectory.

The dragon hit the side of the cliff with a crunch, then plummeted unconscious—or dead—to the rocks below.

Instantly, he caught another one in his peripheral to the left. He went up instead of down, since the simulation would anticipate him using the same moves. He was about to clamp down on the bright red wingtip, but sharp teeth sank into his left foot, and he jerked away.

The bite only lasted an instant, but when he turned to go after his attacker, he didn't see another dragon. All he saw was the icy air and wispy clouds above. Scanning left and right, up and down, all the remaining dragons were fleeing in all directions, already at least a hundred yards away.

Weird.

This was not how the level was supposed to be won. It was required that he incapacitate or kill *all* the sim dragons. They'd never given up before, so why now?

Planning to land and regroup, he headed toward the nearest peak, when a searing pain shot through his right wing—right at the shoulder, and going straight back, like something was attempting to cut it off. He couldn't see the wound, but he was certain it was badly burned by dragon fire.

He let out a beastly dragon cry and blew out his own fiery breath into the air, but again, he couldn't see his enemy attacking.

When more teeth sunk into his left wing, and twisted like it *was* trying to rip it off, Kol realized he was dealing with a sim dragon more like himself.

One that had the ability to become invisible.

He didn't have time to panic, but that's exactly what happened. *Who changed the code? Who put an invisible dragon inside the simulation? Who even knew such an ability existed?*

Kol couldn't help but think that someone who had access to the simulation room knew about Kol's secret. And they somehow knew he'd be running this exact level today.

If he'd been alone, his first instinct would be to turn himself invisible as defense, then find another way to take this enemy down.

But Myreen was watching.

If he did it, she'd know a secret only his family and Nik knew about. A secret that could be used against him if the information got into the wrong hands. And though a big part of him trusted Myreen, another, more reliable part of him didn't trust anyone. Especially a mer who *just* showed up and strangely didn't know she was a mer.

Kol flapped his free wing, trying to shake off the enemy that still had a firm grip on him as he decided what to do. He succeeded, but was left feeling more exposed than he ever had. He had no way of shutting off the program, and with everyone gone for the holiday, he couldn't afford the simulation doing any more damage. So he did what he would've done if he didn't have an audience.

And went invisible.

The invisible dragon stayed close as they fought for what felt like hours. They tumbled through the icy air, back and forth, getting mouthfuls of scales—by sheer luck, at times. The dragon was determined to keep track of Kol's position, to end him, but that also kept the dragon within Kol's striking range. He managed to bite down more than once, disembodied cries confirming the damage. At one point, when the sim dragon had the upper hand—and Kol's leg in its jaws—they fell to one of the lower cliffs with a loud crash. The imprint of large wings and claws hitting the ice and snow, mixed with the splattered *not invisible* blood, which didn't look like enough to have come from Kol's injuries, gave him added courage.

When the beast flew off, Kol went still and silent. He waited, listening for beating wings, watching for visible breath. His patience was rewarded several minutes later when he heard and felt it fly close enough for Kol to aim a blast of fire.

It was a lucky hit. And hot enough to scorch a jagged line of scales. The damage voided their invisibility, turning them into charred blackness that could easily be seen.

The final blow was simple from there. Kol waited until the blackened scales settled on a lower cliff, moving up and down as the injured dragon attempted to catch its breath. Then Kol silently soared, wings outstretched, and glided until he was close enough that the sim couldn't escape. He bit down on its neck hard enough to hear a loud snap.

He quickly pushed the limp body over the edge, then lay panting on the ice and snow as he waited for the sim room to return to its normal, white walls.

He'd tired out more than he had in a long time. *Who reprogrammed it?* he wondered, a little bit panicked that someone had discovered the secret he'd held close for so long. And worse than that, now Myreen knew he could change the color of his scales.

Kol waited several moments after shifting back before rising to meet Myreen. He wondered what he could say to make sure she didn't reveal what she saw.

When he waltzed out to the defense room, he plastered a stoic expression on his face, pretending like everything that had just happened was normal, and not something that terrified him.

"That was intense," she said, sounding concerned.

He forced a shrug. "Do you see why the actual test simulation is hard to beat?"

She nodded.

"Look, what you saw in there?" he asked. "Could you... *not* tell anyone that you saw more than me beating the mountain dragons?"

"What do you mean?"

Do I tell her the truth about my ability being rare and secret? Or bank on the fact that she's essentially ignorant about what's normal in the shifter world? He only dithered for a second before deciding on the latter. "Just..." he flashed a Brett-worthy smirk at her. "If Nik and Brett found out it took me that long to beat it this time..." He let her fill in the rest.

"Ah, so your ego depends on it?" She smiled.

He hid his relief and just hoped that she would keep the promise. "Something like that."

"Sure. Are you hungry?"

"Actually, I think I'm gonna go crash for a while." He felt his knees buckling, and he hoped she didn't see the teeth marks on his feet and arms as he rushed back to his room.

Juliet

Thanksgiving was never really celebrated in Juliet's house. The big fancy dinner, the sappy speeches, even the cliché family drama was something she always wanted to experience. Before her father had to leave, her mother actually liked to cook. And as she was Indian, the food was usually so flavorful and spicy.

But Juliet was too young to really appreciate the taste. Or the simple fact that she cooked.

After he left, they went from home-cooked meals to delivery and take-out. Juliet and her mother made a sad tradition of pizza—popped in the oven, since all the restaurants by them were closed for the holiday.

But this year, Malachai was back in the picture. And just as Juliet thought, it was awkward. Almost like the dinners she had with her mother, except he looked uncomfortable because he didn't know what to talk about, not because he didn't want to be there.

Malachai took Juliet to a surprisingly crowded restaurant, the only one open in town. It wasn't the thanksgiving that Juliet expected. But she sensed that he really was trying to rekindle whatever relationship they'd had when she was a kid. And this was the closest she'd gotten to a Thanksgiving dinner in ages, so she smiled and was on her best behavior. Even if she ordered the most expensive items on the menu.

And while she was actually enjoying herself, she missed Myreen. She could hardly wait to go shopping with her the next day.

"So, remind me of your plans for tomorrow?" With raised eyebrows, Malachai tried to be stern about the question, but he'd waited until Juliet was happily stuffing her face with the double chocolate cake that she ordered for dessert.

"Shopping." She knew her answer would displease him, because it was so short and abstruse. So she smugly enjoyed watching him squirm in his seat.

"Juliet." It was the only word he said, but it was enough to make her roll her eyes.

She filled her fork with a massive piece of the cake and shoved it in her mouth.

With a full mouth, Juliet listed her plans. "We're shopping on a strip by the L. Going to the mall down the street. Eating. Then going back to the Dome." When she finished, she gave him a wide grin, knowing that chocolate covered her teeth.

Malachai practically spit out his espresso with a hearty laugh.

It triggered something inside of her.

She didn't know she remembered that laugh until just now, and it shook her to her core. Standing abruptly, she ran to the bathroom.

She squeezed her hands on the sink, her knuckles turning white. She tried to regain control over her emotions, so she stared at her reflection.

Breathe, Juliet.

The last thing she wanted to do was ruin Thanksgiving for any of the other families because she couldn't control her fire. She forced her eyes shut and tried to release the resentment she held toward her father. His laughter should bring her comfort, not bitterness.

As she walked back to their table, she saw that he had paid the bill and was gathering his things. By the sad look on his face, he knew exactly what happened, and it made him just as wearisome.

Which was not how Juliet wanted to end their dinner.

"Thank you for dinner. It was nice. We should do it more often." His eyes grew with shock and gratification, and she knew it was the perfect way to end their night.

During the ride home, he had a smile so wide she thought his teeth would fall out. It was something Juliet wanted to see more of.

Beneath his fierce demeanor, he was warm and kind.

Just like she remembered from her childhood.

***

Black Friday was the real holiday. Juliet's mom would always finagle herself a discount at the liquor store, and that was when she really stocked up. Satisfied with her booze haul, Malina would throw cash at Juliet just to get her out of her hair. Juliet never cared that her mother never wanted to shop with her. She knew the woman would rather be drinking.

So, she spent half of the amount on her music collection and the other half went into a shoe box under the bed. She swore that the day that she turned eighteen, she would leave. And she wanted to be prepared for it. But those plans all changed when she found out she was a phoenix.

Now, as she got ready to leave with Myreen, she was glad this was her path. She had a friend, and a parent that actually cared about her.

And she had a new world of possibilities. For the first time, Juliet appreciated her life. And for the first time, she was going to spend her black Friday money on Christmas gifts for those who were close to her.

Juliet waited for Myreen by the door to the platform. She was early because she knew Malachai would be there to send her off. He worried about her leaving the Dome alone, but she was clear to remind him that she had pretty much always been alone, and that she knew how to defend herself if she had to. That was the real seller. Still, something rubbed him the wrong way about Myreen.

"Just get there and back safely. That's all I ask. I know you're smart, so if anyone or anything looks suspicious, get back here immediately." Like a normal dad, Malachai had a tormented look in his eyes. But after Juliet repeated her defense strategy to him, he finally let her go.

"I'll be fine. And I'll be back soon. Want me to stop in when I do? So you know I'm back?" Myreen had turned the corner, and Juliet wanted her dad to leave.

"No need. I'll know." With a look of certainty, he spun on his heel and marched away.

Myreen walked up to her with a smile on her face, but Juliet could tell that she looked troubled. *Nothing a little shopping can't fix.*

Myreen had enjoyed the strip where Juliet's favorite clothing store was, so she was happy to tell her friend that they were heading there before going to the busy mall. That got a small smile from her. But the walk from the subway to the strip was silent.

"Are you okay, Myreen?" Juliet asked, beginning to worry.

"I'm fine. It's just… This is the first holiday without my mom." It was all she had to say.

Myreen hadn't said much about her home life, but Juliet knew that if Myreen was staying at the school for the holidays, home life couldn't be good. She just hadn't asked because she didn't want to pry.

387

"You never talk about your mom," Juliet said slowly. "What happened to her?"

Myreen looked off in the distance, obviously trying to elevate her face to keep the tears from falling. "She was killed the night I was brought to the Dome. Vampires got to her. If Oberon hadn't showed up, they would have gotten me, too."

Juliet pulled Myreen in for a hug. She knew exactly what Myreen was feeling—although, Juliet was perhaps better off without her mom. But she could tell that wasn't the case with Myreen.

"I know it's hard. I'm sorry." Juliet pulled away and hooked her arm in Myreen's, leading them to the first visible store.

"Memories are the real treasure in life. If you have memories of happy holidays with your mom, then you should relish them. Remembering the past is a fight that we get to cherish as long as we keep them fresh in our minds. We live up to the traditions and we keep them going. Because life has to go on."

Myreen's mouth opened in shock. Juliet didn't know if she had overstepped or crossed a line in their friendship.

"Sorry. I was trying to cheer you up. This is my first Thanksgiving without my mom, too. But my memories of her aren't great. So I focus on the good part of this holiday, like when she would give me money to go shopping so I could leave her to drink in peace." Juliet shrugged and looked down at her feet.

Myreen placed her hand on her shoulder and tugged her in for another side hug. "No, Juliet. What you said helped. Thank you for that. You're absolutely right. My memories of her are all that I have left, and I want to keep them alive. And sorry about your mom. But now you have me. And your dad. And Nik." Myreen winked, giggling when Juliet's cheeks turn red.

But Myreen still looked like she was having a hard time, her lips still stuck in a frown. Juliet took her hand and ran across the street to a coffee shop. They picked up some fancy caramel blended shakes, then squeezed around the tables to an empty corner by the window.

"Wanna talk about it?"

Myreen sighed. "Everything just keeps reminding me of her today. We used to love the holidays—the lights, the music, everything. Now it just feels... empty. And there are still so many unanswered questions. I just can't get over not knowing. I want closure, but it's almost impossible when I feel like I'm not being told the whole truth."

Juliet was relieved that Myreen opened up so easily to her. "Have you revisited that night with anyone?"

Myreen shook her head.

"I haven't either." Juliet got lost in her own thoughts as she remembered the morning of the incident. Her own guilt and heartbreak made her mouth feel dry. "I can go first if you want." She said it so low she was surprised when Myreen nodded.

She took a sip of her cold drink and inhaled deeply. It felt like all eyes were on her, and she had to reassure herself by looking around the room.

"It was my birthday when she died. She had already started drinking early that morning, so when I woke up, she was not in a celebratory mood. I had to remind her that it was my sixteenth birthday. And not once did she wish me a happy one. Instead, she used it as a countdown for two separate occasions. One, was how many years had passed since dad left. And two, how many more years until I could move out."

Myreen's eyebrows shot up, and there were already tears in her eyes. It made it even harder for Juliet to speak around the lump in her throat. She took another look around and another deep breath before she continued.

"I, uh, upset her, and she threw her almost empty bottle of liquor at the ground where it broke into hundreds of pieces. As I was cleaning it up, she was on her way to go upstairs. Well... she was saying some really harsh things under her breath. It broke me, more than I thought I could handle." One tear escaped, but Juliet caught it before it could fall.

"I didn't know that I was a phoenix then, and I didn't know that I could make fire come out of my body. Her words just... paralyzed me. Before I knew what was happening, it was too late. The entire downstairs was lit with flames. I heard the bottles in her liquor closet crashing to the floor and I knew it was going to blow. I walked out of there without a scratch, without a single burn, without my mom. When I went outside, my dad was just pulling up. I passed out, and only woke up as we were getting to the Dome."

Myreen wiped away her own tears and stood to give Juliet a hug.

"J, I am just so sorry. No one deserves to go through what you went through. I hope you didn't have to deal with that all the time." Myreen took her seat again.

Juliet squeezed her lips in a tight line, nodding to sadly confirm the worst. "Dad left when I was four. My mom didn't take it well. At all. It took a year for her to completely hit rock bottom. I guess I could say I'm lucky, because I learned how to take care of myself so young. I mean, I know he had to leave. The school's safety is important. I know that now. I just wish I knew that growing up, too. He speaks so highly of our *Quinn* lineage, like it's enough explanation. I want to forgive him... it's just hard."

Juliet felt a weight lift off her shoulders, and relief rushed through her. She always thought speaking of it would make her feel worse, but instead, she felt at peace with the incident for the first time since it happened.

She wanted her friend to feel that same freedom.

Myreen gave Juliet a half-smile. "I want to apologize for what you went through, but I know that won't help. All I can do is appreciate you. I'm thankful that you're here with us. And even though your dad gives me the evil eye, I can tell how much he loves you, and how sorry he is. Second chances are worth it."

Juliet's tears were on the verge of pooling out of her eyes, so she pushed her palms into them until they began to diminish. With another deep breath, she pulled her hands away and placed them on her cold drink.

"Thanks, Myreen."

"Guess it's my turn." Myreen looked around the room just like Juliet did.

"The last time I saw her alive, I fought with her. We moved around *a lot*. I've seen so many places. But it gets tiring. I never allowed myself to get too close to anyone, because I knew at any moment we would be leaving again. She wouldn't let me get on social media, and I had an embarrassingly strict curfew."

Myreen's eyes were glued to the floor. "So... the night that she died, I was invited to a school party." Myreen cleared her throat, refusing to make eye contact.

"I made it a big deal that she never let me do anything or go anywhere. And I was just so... mean. Rude and disrespectful. Which is not at all how our relationship was. She was my best friend. We never fought. I loved her so much." Myreen's tears cascaded down her flushed cheeks, but she kept her voice low. Juliet handed her a tissue and placed her hand on Myreen's, which was shaking.

"I went with Kenzie to the party, even after my mom begged me not to go. She looked scared. Like she was sure something bad would happen. And she was right. Kenzie and I went back and found her. She was just lying on the ground, not breathing. And she had bite marks on her neck." Myreen's eyes squinted, as if she could still see every vile detail.

"Before I could call the police or do anything to try to help her, Oberon showed up. He was stunned that I didn't know what I was.

And he told me *vampires* killed her." She said the last sentence in an even lower whisper.

Juliet covered her mouth as it flew open.

"I just don't get why she wouldn't tell me. I never learned how to swim, I couldn't be anywhere near the ocean. I didn't even take baths. She never even hinted that I was special. And I was born with a *tail!* I want to understand why it was such a secret. And I can't even ask her." Myreen was spiraling, so Juliet tried to think of something to distract her.

"What about your dad?" *Maybe that was too distracting.* She didn't want to sound rude, but she also needed Myreen to know that she cared.

Myreen shrugged. "I don't know a thing about him. Mom never liked to talk about him, so I stopped asking. For a while I thought it was him that we were running from. But now, I guess I'll never know." Myreen's tears dwindled.

"What about Oberon? Has he mentioned anything?"

"No, never. But they have to know, right?" A spark of hope flashed in Myreen's eyes.

"They can't withhold that kind of information from you. And it doesn't hurt to ask. I'll see what my dad knows about vampires. He's probably going to freak, but you deserve to know." Juliet worried she might be adding fuel to a fire she did not want to ignite, but her friend deserved a little hope.

They made a trip to the bathroom before they started their shopping, cooling their blotchy eyes after all the crying they didn't plan on doing.

Surprisingly enough, their shopping was even more fun after they had their heart to heart. Starting in a candle store and ending in an old vintage shop, their hands were already full of bags.

They swore to make the mall trip a quick one, so they could get back to the Dome. Juliet knew her father would be pacing, waiting for her arrival. But as they stepped off the escalator, a familiar voice shouted behind them.

"Myreen!"

"Kenzie!" Myreen's breath hitched, and she ran right into a hug. Juliet noticed that Kenzie flinched, but that was something she would be keeping to herself.

The last thing Myreen needed was to lose someone else close to her.

Kenzie

Kenzie looked through her bags one more time, trying to make sure she had everything she wanted. Christmas gifts for Mom, check. Christmas gifts for Gram, check. A little something for herself in case everyone else's gifts tanked, check. And she'd even gotten that kitten shirt for Leif. Although, if she didn't hear from him soon, she might just use it, herself.

It had been weeks since they last communicated, and it was his turn to make a move. She watched the mail come in, day after day, hoping to see something from him, but still no word. She hoped he hadn't been killed or something. Or maybe he'd come back to his apartment to find that nice burn hole in the curtain and decided she wasn't worth his time. But he'd probably want his book back if that were the case.

Kenzie sighed. She wanted to get into the holiday mood, but with everything going on—or not going on, in her case—she was teetering on bah-humbug. Even shopping hadn't improved her mood, and this was a tradition she always looked forward to.

She stepped into a space on the escalator, heading down to the main floor. The smell of grilled meats and warm fries came up from the food court, and Kenzie's stomach rumbled. As she descended, she spotted a head of black and blue hair just a little way down the escalator, bobbing next to a bright flame of orange hair.

"Myreen!" Kenzie shouted over the din, earning some glances from the other riders in front of her. She smiled and rose on her tiptoes, waving her hand wildly in the air as she repeated, "Myreen!"

Myreen's head whipped around, and she returned Kenzie's smile, tugging on Juliet's hand. The girls stepped to the side at the bottom, letting numerous shoppers past. Kenzie tapped her foot on the step of what felt like the slowest escalator in the world. When she reached the bottom, she jumped out of line and threw a hug around Myreen's neck. She pulled Juliet in for a hug next.

"What are you guys doing here?" Kenzie asked.

"What do *you* think?" Myreen held her own bags up in reply, but her smile faded a little. She exchanged a knowing look with Juliet, and Kenzie felt a pang of jealousy.

"Have you two had lunch yet?" Kenzie asked.

"Not yet," Juliet replied, glancing again at Myreen.

Kenzie hitched a thumb over her shoulder. "Wanna grab something from the food court? I'm buying."

The girls looked at each other again, and Myreen nodded. "Yeah. We can do that. It'd be good to catch up."

They settled on burgers and fries. Kenzie had Juliet and Myreen grab a table and guard the bags while she ordered. She couldn't help but look back once or twice, watching as Juliet rubbed Myreen's back. Kenzie was missing out on so much, not being in that school. She wondered again about Leif's offer, if that was even still an option. And again, that was assuming he was alive. The urge to try out her magical call spell was strong, but she pushed it down. Now wasn't the time. Besides, she could be patient. Maybe.

When Kenzie brought the food back to the table, the girls all dug in. But silence hung between them, thicker than the throngs of people milling through the mall today. Kenzie began to wonder if it was her, if everyone she met in the shifter world was destined to despise her. It hurt when Myreen turned down her invitation to Thanksgiving. It had taken a lot for her to push past her own selfishness and invite her friend over.

But maybe she hadn't done enough to clear the air.

Kenzie swallowed her bite of burger, washing it down with some soda. "I wanted to apologize. I— I shouldn't have run out like that, at the party. That wasn't fair to you two. And I'm sorry I screwed that up so bad."

Myreen shrugged. "There's nothing to apologize about. I'm sorry I outed you to everyone."

"And I'm sorry the girls you were befriending were mer-jerks," Juliet added, waving a fry around.

Kenzie smiled. "Thanks. So... how was your Thanksgiving?"

"Quiet," Myreen said, taking a sip of her drink.

"Yeah. Everyone went home for the holiday, so the Dome's pretty much empty," Juliet added.

"Oh." Kenzie sat a moment, pondering that bit of information. She tried to see it from Myreen's perspective, her not having a mom now. It didn't completely make sense, her turning down Kenzie's Thanksgiving offer, but then again, she couldn't imagine trying to celebrate the holidays without Mom and Gram by her side, no matter their differences. "Are you okay?"

Myreen nodded, but her eyes glistened. "I tried shopping today, but it just reminded me..." She sighed. "I'm sorry I didn't take you up on your offer for Thanksgiving. I'm not sure I made the best decision."

"Except you got some time to hang with Kol," Juliet said, nudging Myreen with her elbow.

"Kol? You mean Mr. Tall? A-k-a Hotty McSmugface?"

Juliet and Myreen both burst out laughing.

Myreen wiped at her eyes, her giggles subsiding. "Yeah, I guess you could call him that."

Kenzie leaned forward, her elbows on the table and her head in her hands. "So, are you two, like, a thing?"

Myreen rolled her eyes, but Juliet answered, "Not exactly. They've been doing this dance for a while. They had a date—finally!—and he totally botched it."

Kenzie folded her arms, a crooked smile on her face. "Too bad. He's certainly gorg. Maybe a little too stiff, though."

Juliet giggled.

Myreen threw Juliet a sidelong glance. "He's not stiff, exactly. He's... complicated."

Juliet let out a huff of a laugh. "Aren't all boys?"

Kenzie thought of Leif and nodded. "Yeah, I'm beginning to think so." She bit her lower lip, wondering if she should mention him, but decided against it.

"Speak of the devil," Juliet said, patting Myreen's arm.

Kenzie turned in her seat to see Kol heading straight toward them, a storm brewing in his scowl. She turned back so he couldn't see and said in a conspiratorial tone, "My, isn't he just a ray of sunshine?"

"What are you doing here?" Kol asked, his gaze focused solely on Myreen.

Myreen's brows rose into her hairline. "Well, hello to you, too."

Kol took a deep breath, looking at the trio, but he finally settled back on Myreen. "This is the *selkie* you brought to the party, isn't it?" His volume dipped on the word "selkie," as if he was worried someone would overhear.

Myreen's brows raised further. "Yeah. So?"

Kol leaned forward and put his hands on the table, bringing his height to almost average level. "So, hasn't anyone told you that it's not a good idea to hang around with them?" His eyes darted around the Christmas throng for a moment.

Kenzie snorted. "What is everyone's problem with selkies, anyway?"

"You're not—" Kol paused, pressing his lips together. "They can't be trusted."

Kenzie leaned back. That's basically what her mom had told her, but to hear it straight from a shifter was somehow worse. Did he even realize he was being prejudiced? Why did everyone assume all selkies were alike?

"What're you doing here, anyway?" Juliet asked Kol, waving around another fry.

"My mom asked me to pick up— That doesn't matter. What *does* matter is that you stay away from people who can use magic if you don't want a wound that never heals." Kol spun on his heel and marched off, his abnormally tall form taking forever to disappear into the crowd. And she was sitting down. It took everything Kenzie had not to ask him how the weather was up there. Oh well, maybe next time.

The girls looked at each other, puzzled.

Kenzie leaned back in her chair. "Well. There you have it."

"Whatever that meant," Juliet said.

"I wish he'd just be real for once!" Myreen said, throwing her fry onto the tray. "It's like there's this brick wall he keeps up, and every time I think it's coming down, he throws it back in my face again. Seriously, what is his problem?"

Kenzie sat up straight. "I don't know, but I have just the cure." After a moment of rummaging, she pulled one of the shirts she'd bought for her mom and Gram out of the bag. She held it so they could see the front, which was printed with a giant pixelated picture of Kenzie's head.

Myreen and Juliet stared, their faces a mix of quizzical and confused.

Kenzie turned it around so they could see the "I'm with this girl" printed on the back, adding, "After the reaction I got at the party, these are sure to jet-rocket you up the social ladder."

Myreen burst out laughing, and Juliet caught on a moment later.

Kenzie rolled the shirt back up and stuffed it in her bag. "Just kidding. These are for Mom and Gram." She thought about showing them the shirt for Leif, but decided the irony would be lost. And she felt strangely protective of that information, anyway. If anyone would understand, it would probably be these girls, but Kenzie just couldn't bring herself to tell them. She didn't know Juliet well enough, and besides, Myreen's mom was killed by a vampire. If Myreen knew Kenzie was working with one...

"Oh, Kenzie, I missed you," Myreen said after catching her breath.

Kenzie grinned. "I missed you, too."

"It's too bad you can't come to school with us," Juliet added, bouncing in her seat as a hopping Christmas tune started to play over the speakers.

"I've decided not to give up on that," Kenzie said. "At least, not yet."

"What plan is that crazy mind of yours hatching?" Myreen asked.

"*Moi?*" Kenzie asked, her hand fluttering to her chest in mock shock. "Why, I don't know *what* you're talking about."

Myreen shook her head.

"Well, if there's anything we can do to help, just let us know," Juliet said, and Myreen nodded along with her.

"Thanks." Kenzie gave them a half smile. It about killed her to not tell the girls about Leif, but what else could she do? Everything was still so new, so untested.

It took her ages to crack open the grimoire after that first day, afraid of starting another fire. But when she looked at the spell again, she realized her mistake. She'd mispronounced the word for green, which had obviously destabilized the spark. It made sense, and all, but she couldn't risk that kind of mistake if she was practicing at home. There would be questions. And consequences. And she couldn't lose the book.

There was something comforting about the ancient tome, like it was a long lost relative or an old friend. She kept it safely hidden under the head of her bed, only taking it out late at night to sneak a few pages in. Part of her wanted to rush through it, picking up only what she needed, while another part of her wanted to savor every page. All that magic, all those years of spells and knowledge. And it was all hers.

She couldn't risk losing it.

And Leif. His handsome face swam in her mind, a little fuzzier than the last time she'd thought of him. She wondered when he'd come back, and if he'd be the same. Gram had told her about vampire bloodlust, how it stripped them of every last semblance of humanity. She hoped to never meet a vampire in that state. Especially Leif.

"Well, we should probably get back to the Dome," Juliet said, looking at her phone. "If we don't get there soon, my dad is gonna freak."

Kenzie nodded. "Right. Yeah, I should probably go see if Mom and Gram are ready to go."

Myreen raised a brow at her. "You're out here shopping with your mom and grandma?"

"Not with. And yes, that makes it difficult to keep presents a secret. It's a recent tradition. We're still working out the kinks. But that *also* means I can sneak a peek when they're not looking." Kenzie flashed a cheeky grin and rubbed her hands together. Myreen and Juliet chuckled.

They all stood, taking care of the trash and gathering up their belongings. Kenzie threw hugs around Myreen and Juliet's necks. "It was good seeing you both. And I know I'm stuck in Shallow Grave and all, but if you ever need anything, don't hesitate to call."

Juliet raised a questioning brow. "Shallow Grave?"

Myreen smiled. "It's her nickname for Short Grove."

"Oh! Where's that?" Juliet asked as her brief epiphany settled back into confusion.

Kenzie shrugged. "About an hour west. You won't find it on any map, and for now, it looks like I'm stuck there."

Myreen put a hand on her shoulder. "But not forever. I'm sure of it."

Kenzie smiled. "Thanks."

She watched Myreen and Juliet leave, the sense of glum that they'd chased away settling back over her. What kind of a best friend was she, keeping secrets like she was? *I'm protecting her,* Kenzie assured herself, though she wasn't convinced. She looked down at the bags in her hands, and thought about heading back into the stores to pick something up for Myreen and Juliet, but decided against it.

If I'm doing this, I'm doing this good. She'd buckle down on that grimoire and start unlocking its secrets. She'd prove Kol wrong. She'd prove all of them wrong. And she'd do it with the best dang magical present a selkie could give—whatever that might be.

And as her thoughts turned once again to Leif, she wondered if there really was a way to raise the dead, because returning Myreen's mom would be epic.

If it didn't go horribly wrong.

Myreen

Bang, bang, bang!

Myreen jackknifed in her bed, startled out of a sound sleep by a loud banging on her door. Heart pounding in her ears, she struggled to rouse out of the confusion that resulted from waking up mid-dream.

She looked at the red numbers on her digital clock, then wiped her hands down her face. Why would anyone be so mean as to wake her up before six o'clock on the first day back to school?

The rude fist banged on her door again. Growling, she yanked off her covers and stomped to the door, ready to yell at whatever mer had come back early from vacation with a bone to pick with her.

The fire-haired phoenix was standing in the hallway of the mer wing, looking incredibly out of place, wearing an anxious expression.

"Juliet? What are you doing here?" Myreen asked, surprised and confused to see her phoenix friend in the mer hallway. Only a few of the mer students had returned yesterday evening, but not-a-one of them would have allowed an outsider into the dorm—especially not Juliet. "How did you get past the mermaids?"

"Everyone's too distracted right now to care. I slipped right in." Her voice was excitable, but Myreen didn't think it was about something good.

"Distracted? Why, what's going on?" Myreen yawned and leaned forward into the hallway to try to catch a glimpse of whatever might have the mers preoccupied.

"There's been a vampire attack on a student!" Juliet burst.

"What?!" Myreen was suddenly very awake.

Juliet came into the room. "Some students found her mangled body on the secret sub platform. She was almost completely drained of blood, and she just barely made it past the security door. It was amazing that she didn't lead the vamps right to us!"

"Oh no," Myreen gasped. Memories of the night she found her mom's body on the kitchen floor flashed in her mind in bright technicolor, just as painful as when it actually happened. "Do we know her? The girl who got attacked?"

Juliet nodded grimly. "I don't know how you're going to feel about this... but it was Alessandra."

Myreen's heart plummeted to the bottom of her stomach with a deep *thud*. Juliet was right. Myreen didn't know how she felt about the news, either. As much discord as there was between the two mermaids, Myreen would never wish ill on her. And after the way Alessandra's confession had sort of humanized her during their last tutoring lesson, Myreen felt somehow closer to her.

The news of her attack was frightening on several levels.

What if someone else had been coming to the Dome at the exact same time? What if Kendall had gotten attacked? Or Juliet, or Kol? Myreen was aware of how similar she and Alessandra looked—they could be sisters, if one squinted really hard. That could easily have been

Myreen, which in itself terrified her. Myreen couldn't even beat Beginner Level One in the simulator. If she came up against one of the vampires from the night of her mom's murder looking to finish the job, she wouldn't stand a chance. Especially if someone as skilled in mer abilities as Alessandra couldn't.

"Is she okay?" Myreen asked, instantly feeling stupid when the words left her mouth. "I mean, is she…?"

"Still the reigning wicked sea witch?" Juliet asked in a hushed but guiltless voice.

"*J*," Myreen scolded quietly. She didn't feel comfortable talking that way about someone who had gone through such a terrible ordeal, no matter how wicked they were.

"Yeah, she's still holding on," Juliet answered. "They rushed her to Ms. Heather's office this morning."

"What? She needs to go to the hospital!" Myreen was suddenly outraged at the treatment of someone who, up to this point, had been nothing but horrible to her.

Juliet snickered. "Ms. Heather's a harpy, and the school's lead healer. Trust me, her office is ten times better than any hospital."

Myreen did remember from her studies that harpies had the ability to heal wounds. She had learned in Shifter History that many of the supposed sightings of angels throughout history had likely been harpies visiting the sick and wounded. It made her feel a little better about Alessandra's care.

"I don't understand," Myreen said as she sat on her bed, Juliet following her lead. "Why are vampires so dead set on wiping out mermaids? First my mom, now Alessandra. Who's next?"

"Vampires are dead set on wiping out all shifters," Juliet said. "Vampires want us all eliminated so they can take over the humans with no opposition."

"Maybe, but they seem especially interested in getting mers out of the way," Myreen pondered out loud. "How many attacks have you heard of lately on any other types of shifters?"

Juliet shrugged. "I guess you have a point there." She dangled her feet off the bed as she thought for a moment. "Maybe vampires hate the elitist mer attitude as much as the rest of us?"

Myreen gave Juliet a sidelong frown. "That might make sense for Alessandra, but my mom was as far from elitist as a mermaid could be."

Juliet's face saddened, and she looked down. They sat in the room for a silent moment, the thoughts in Myreen's head louder than the backstage of a rock concert.

"I want to go see Alessandra," Myreen decided.

"What? Why on earth would you want to do that?" Juliet asked.

"Well, for one, I need to make sure she's going to be okay. I wouldn't say she's my favorite mermaid in the world, but we have sort of bonded since she's been tutoring me. And two, maybe she can give me some clue as to why the vamps attacked her. If there's any connection that could explain why my mom was murdered... It's just too big of a coincidence."

Juliet nodded, her brows furrowing. "Okay, let's go to Ms. Heather's office."

It was surprising to see the common room so empty after hearing the other mer students trickle in throughout the day yesterday. No wonder Juliet had been able to enter without a problem.

When they got to Ms. Heather's office outside of the Avian wing, Myreen saw why. Dozens of mer students were gathered outside the door. Some of them conversed in concerned whispers, and some of them openly wept. But, as so often happened when Myreen entered a mer-populated area, all voices fell silent, and all eyes narrowed at her. She ignored them and tried to push her way to the door.

"What the hell do you think you're doing here?" Trish's voice cut through the silence like a knife, and she inserted herself between

Myreen and the office door.

Foolishly, Myreen hadn't expected a confrontation here, now. "I–I just wanted to check on her."

"Why? So you could finish the job?" Trish shouted, her voice shrill with grief.

"What?" Myreen was taken aback.

Juliet stepped to Myreen's side, her hands balled into fists.

"I knew there was something suspicious about you the minute you got here," Trish went on. It was only as Trish leaned closer that Myreen could see the tears trailing between her waterproof-mascaraed lashes. "First you take her boyfriend, then you snake your way into studying with her, then you try to kill her. Well let me tell you, you may look like a downgraded version of her, but you will *never* replace her. You'll never be half the mermaid she is!"

Kendall exited the office just as Trish was finishing her little slur, and he pushed himself between them. "That's enough, Trish. Come on, Myreen."

"But I wanted to see Alessandra," Myreen said.

Kendall wrapped his hand around her upper arm and tugged her away. "Now isn't a good time."

"How can you still defend her when Alessandra is dying just behind that door?" Trish shrieked at the back of Kendall's head. He only walked more quickly.

"Wait, am I missing something?" Juliet asked as they rushed down the stairs and out of view of the hateful eyes of the gathered mer students. "Why does Trish think Myreen had anything to do with what happened to Alessandra? Doesn't she know her friend was attacked by a *vampire*, not a shifter?"

Myreen watched Kendall's face. His expression was stony, but his eyes were a storm of puzzlement and fear.

He knew something.

They walked out of the door of the Grand Hall and came out onto the sidewalk. The exterior walkways were a ghost town. They were completely alone.

"Kendall, what's going on?" Myreen pressed when Kendall didn't answer.

He pursed his lips before speaking, as if trying to find the best words. "Yes, Alessandra was definitely attacked by a vampire, there's no question of that. But…" He slowly lifted his gaze to meet hers. "She keeps saying your name."

Myreen's eyes widened, unsure how to process that. Now more than ever, she suspected that the vampire attack on her mother wasn't just about taking out shifters. There was something bigger going on here, she just couldn't see it.

"Did she say anything else?" she asked. "Did she say why they attacked her?"

Kendall shook his head. "She's in and out of consciousness. She hasn't said much of anything. Except your name, over and over."

Myreen was stumped. Why would Alessandra do that? Unless maybe she was dreaming about their tutoring sessions. But that seemed a stretch.

"So because of that, Trish thinks I was somehow involved? If it's clear that vampires got her, how could I be?"

Kendall averted his gaze. "There have been instances in the past when shifter individuals have allied themselves with vampires."

Myreen and Juliet both stared at him in shock.

"So they think that Myreen's a spy for the vampires?" Juliet crossed her arms over her chest.

Again, Myreen looked at Kendall's face for any signs of his opinion. Unfortunately, she only saw questions there.

"Kendall, that's insane," she said, her voice rising in pitch. "You know what happened to my mom. You know I could never be in league with the people who killed her!"

His brows rose, and he instantly put his hands on her shoulders. "Myreen, I don't believe what they're saying. I know it's not true, or even possible. You're no traitor. I just can't figure out why Alessandra... It's just very confusing."

Myreen nodded slowly, then took a deep breath. As if things at this school couldn't get any worse, now all the mer thought she had tried to kill Alessandra.

"Is she going to be okay?" Myreen asked.

"She lost a ton of blood," Kendall replied, rubbing his chin. "Her broken bones are easy for harpies to heal, but replacing her blood will take time. And she got a pretty hard hit to the head. Even once her body is healed, her head may not be. Another thing that isn't so easy for harpies to fix."

Myreen let out a heavy breath, somehow feeling even more weighted down. She needed Alessandra to wake up, and soon. Not only to help her solve the mystery of her mom's death, but also to stop these horrible rumors before they spread out of control.

Kol

Though the Avian common room held the normal buzz of activity after a long holiday—mostly dreary looks about being back—there was a frantic, panicked energy in the halls of the Dome.

Kol walked slowly as students turned to each other in hushed whispers. A lot of girls were crying and hugging each other, pointedly ignoring Kol's presence. Since Nik wouldn't be back for another hour, due to a delayed flight, and Brett was still in his room, probably asleep, he couldn't ask either of them what the apparent mass hysteria was about.

Fortunately, Miss Dinu rounded the corner and was heading his direction with her head down. "Hannah," he said, using her first name without thinking. He blamed his informality on the circumstance and his reason for speaking with her, and hoped that since she was a relative, she wouldn't mind.

But she didn't seem irked or otherwise when her glistening eyes met his. She'd been crying, too.

"What's going on?" he asked without pretense.

She swallowed hard and blinked a few times before adjusting her frames and tucking a piece of her short hair behind her ear. "You haven't heard?" she asked.

He shook his head.

"There was a vampire attack on a student."

Kol's heart sunk into his stomach as she explained what she knew. A girl had been found on the secret subway platform leading into the Dome, almost completely drained of blood. He barely registered the words, because he had to know the answer to his next question. "Who?"

The brief pause before her answer felt like a hundred years. Was it a were? Another avian? Though he didn't think a dragon would allow a vampire to get the jump on them very easily, it wasn't completely unheard of. And Nik wasn't back yet.

"It was one of the mers," Miss Dinu said. "*Alessandra?* I think is her name."

"You think?" He didn't mean for it to come out as a snap, but it only took him the split second that Alessandra's face flashed in his head, and the hesitation in her voice, for him to fear that she said the wrong name. That maybe it wasn't Alessandra, but *looked* like Alessandra.

She leveled her gaze on him with her head slightly tilted. Her emotions didn't show, but Kol suspected she was curious about his reaction.

"Was it Alessandra?" he asked, forcing his tone to steady. "Or… someone else?"

"It was Alessandra," Oberon said, coming up behind Kol.

Kol closed his eyes momentarily to calm the rising flood of… *whatever.*

"If you would please excuse us, Kol," he said. "I must speak with Miss Dinu."

"Of course," he said and waved a quick goodbye before heading down to breakfast.

Kol spotted Trish and her entourage—minus Alessandra, obviously—coming from the nurse's station before he entered the dining hall. His first instinct was to ignore the group, but thinking about how he would feel if it were Nik or Brett who had been attacked prompted him to say something. Especially given his and Trish's history.

"Trish," he said, pulling her from the group.

The other mer eyed her, silently asking if she wanted them to leave. She nodded, and they left the two alone.

"I heard about your friend," he said, awkwardly placing a hand on her shoulder, then quickly removing it. "What happened to her was atrocious."

She stared him in the eyes, in that penetrating way that showed her dominance, but then her expression softened, and she nodded.

"I wouldn't wish that on any shifter," he said. "No matter our differences." *Not even someone who thought locking a defenseless mer—her own kind—in a simulation against her will was okay,* he wanted to add, but didn't.

"Thank you, Kol," she said.

"How is she?"

"I think she'll live." By her tone, Trish didn't sound so sure.

"Did she say anything about the vamp that did it?"

Trish shook her head, then uncharacteristically stared at the ground. But then her head snapped up as a thought occurred to her and she landed her gaze back on Kol. Her expression was masked innocence, but he'd been acquainted with the manipulative mer long enough to know it was just a mask. "She keeps saying *her* name over and over."

"Her name?" He knew who she meant by *her,* but needed to hear the words.

"Myreen."

"Why is she saying Myreen's name?"

Trish shrugged and resisted the smirk that threatened to emerge. "Who knows? Maybe it was Myreen's fault?"

Kol wanted to call her BS, but even though her motives weren't the most sincere, he could tell that it was the truth. Alessandra *had* been saying Myreen's name. But why?

The dining hall had the same nervous buzz as students got their breakfast, but Kol didn't see many of them actually eating. He quickly grabbed something that resembled edible meat without really looking at it—his dragon side craving the protein this morning—and headed toward his usual table.

He hadn't realized he'd been scanning the crowd as he walked until he noticed the familiar black hair pulled into a ponytail that showed off the blue streaks. Fortunately, she had her back turned toward him and was speaking with her head lowered and tilted toward an almost identical tied up mess of orange hair. Myreen's friend, Juliet. He skidded past them without so much as a glance, willing Brett to actually hear his alarm and get down to breakfast, or for Nik's plane to have landed early.

He couldn't talk to her. He couldn't speak to her. He almost tripped when the image of Alessandra—sprawled on the cold concrete, face deathly pale and body nearly drained of blood—intruded his thoughts... and then her face morphed into Myreen's.

Speaking with Trish was different because he didn't... it was just different. He briefly wondered if Myreen knew Alessandra was saying her name, but decided she could find out that information from someone else.

Then, like the glutton he was, Kol sat at his table so he was facing her, and studiously avoided looking across the room at her face. He swore he felt her gaze fall on him more than once, but without his wingmen to verify, he couldn't be sure. He told himself that he couldn't have her sneaking up on him, that by knowing her position in the room, he could rush off if she approached.

Kol dug into his breakfast, eating quickly and barely tasting any of it with the plan to escape as soon as he'd finished. He felt guilty. He should've walked right over to Myreen as soon as he spotted her. He should've made sure she was okay—that she and her friend were okay after hearing the horrific news.

But knowing how Myreen lost her mom. And that this was an attack on another mer. Could—

"Didya hear?"

Kol nearly jumped from his chair, choking down the food in his mouth before it was thoroughly chewed. "*Damn it*, Brett!" he said, grabbing a fistful of his own hair and yanking it, then ran his fingers through it before glaring at his friend.

"Sorry, man," Brett said with a tiny shrug. "I guess we're all on edge." He sat down, the same mystery meat on his plate.

Kol calmed himself, but had lost his appetite and pushed his plate away. "Yes, I heard."

"Why do you think it happened?" Brett asked with a mouthful. "Oh, and before you freak out on Nik the way you just freaked out on me, he's back. He's just dropping his stuff and will be down in a sec."

Kol nodded, "Does he know?"

"He doesn't know details, but he knows something happened."

"Well, to answer your question," Kol said. "You probably know as much as I do."

Nik showed up in the cafeteria, but stopped at Myreen and Juliet's table first. Kol's guilt intensified. Nik was clearly consoling them while Kol had ignored them. Ignored *her*.

They filled Nik in on the details of the incident when he joined them. Kol was right; he and Brett had heard the same story. Minus the part about what name Alessandra was saying. He kept that part to himself.

Nik ran his fingers over his head, indicating his nerves. "Kol, do you think...?"

"Does he think what?" Brett urged.

"Do you think these vamps targeted her?"

"What would vamps want with a teenage mer?" Brett scoffed. He was trying to play up that he wasn't affected but the whole mess, but Kol knew better when he, too, pushed his plate away—half-eaten—and leaned back with his arms folded. "It must be a coincidence."

"On the secret platform?" Kol asked. "Doesn't seem likely."

"Does that mean they know the location of the Dome, then?" Brett asked.

Immediately Kol's thoughts flashed to the invisible dragon in the sim room. Had the vampires found the school? Had they already infiltrated its walls, sneaking in forces to form an attack?

"I was actually wondering if they targeted her specifically," Nik said. "And yeah, they probably wouldn't target some random teenage mer," he glanced at Brett. "But if what Kol told us is true..." He looked at Kol. "About that prophecy."

Kol put a finger to his lips and leaned into the table. "That's not common knowledge, and if my father found out I'd told you two morons, he'd ship me off tomorrow."

"But you said the prophecy is about Myreen, not—"

"Actually, I'm not so sure the prophecy *is* about Myreen," Kol blurted out. He hadn't meant to say it aloud. When Nik and Brett stared at him with all but gaping mouths he quickly amended. "I mean, that doesn't really matter. But what if those vamps attacked Alessandra because they were wrong about the prophecy too, and because she *looks* like Myreen?"

Again, Kol kept what he'd learned from Trish to himself.

"Do you think they know about the prophecy?" Nik's eyebrows were pinched in concern. "The vampires?"

"I hate to say this, but maybe you need to call the General, Kol."

"I think you're right," Kol said, then pushed up and out of his seat and left to contact his father.

***

"We are aware of the situation, Malkolm," Eduard said when he picked up.

"So what are you doing about it?" Kol leaned against a bookcase in the human world history section of the library. Even if the entire school wasn't still freaking out in the Dining Hall, the chances of someone catching him there was very slim.

"We're looking into it, but it seems to be an isolated incident," he said. "A random act by one vampire."

"Random act? Edu— Father," Kol caught his almost-slip. "She was attacked outside the secret platform."

"Yes, and she must've been followed. To the vampire, it must have looked like she was entering somewhere the public didn't have ready access to—which is the truth—and followed her."

"Look," Kol said, running a hand through his hair. "I should've told you sooner, but I don't think Myreen is the mermaid from the prophecy, but still I think she's being targeted."

"What information did you acquire that led you to believe that?"

"The fact that this mer, the one that was attacked…" he paused. "…looks a lot like Myreen and has been saying Myreen's name over and over since it happened."

"No, what information did you acquire that led you to believe Myreen is *not* the siren?" Eduard didn't sound mad at all, which surprised Kol at first, but then he realized that his whole mission was to

415

find out whether or not she was. There would never be any repercussions if the information he received proved that she wasn't.

"Well, for starters, she's not a very good mer. She's having a hard time shifting. And she can't even defend herself in a simulation." He had to quit bringing that up—Myreen had been caught off guard—but he still felt that even a mermaid caught off guard would've done *something* in there. The sim was a human, for harpies' sake.

"Well, if these vampires are targeting her, if they attacked a mer who looked like her, then they must have some information about her importance."

"Do you think *they* know about the prophecy?" Kol tried not to dwell on the fact that his father was actually speaking to him like an equal. He hadn't been berated for anything, at all, in the entire conversation.

"It's unlikely," Eduard said. "But they certainly know something."

"So you'll investigate?"

"I already have some men on it."

"Good," Kol said, suddenly relieved. His father might be a hard man to like, but he was very adept at his job. If Eduard said he had some men on it, he mostly likely had more than *some*, and had hand-picked the best men and women he had available. "And thanks," he added.

"But Kol?"

Kol groaned internally. He knew that tone. He braced himself for the scolding or lecture he was about to get.

"You're not relieved of your mission," he said. "Even if you don't think this girl is the siren, we don't have concrete proof yet."

"Yes, sir."

"Stay close to the girl."

"Yes, sir," he repeated, then hung up. He hadn't realized until that moment that the reason he hadn't updated his father on the Myreen situation and his suspicions about her *not* being the siren from the prophecy, had nothing to do with disappointing Eduard. As he'd just proved, Eduard didn't care either way, he just wanted the truth. But Kol hadn't told him because if Kol's information was enough and his father *had* relieved him of his mission—freeing him from ever speaking to Myreen again—he wouldn't have the excuse to keep seeing her.

He didn't *want* his mission to come to an end, and against his better judgment, he prayed that she was the siren so it never would.

Oberon

"High winds, blow me away," Oberon murmured.

He was in Maya Heather's office, the school's lead healer. Alessandra was nearby, lying on a small bed just off the ground. The mermaid's eyes were closed, but her body fidgeted continuously.

"I can heal her wounds, sir," Maya said as she pushed her silver-framed glasses higher up on the bridge of her nose. The large lenses magnified her blue eyes, and her frizzy blond hair curled about independently, going every which-way. "But her mind? It will take time for her to overcome the trauma she's been through."

The healer's words triggered Oberon's own traumatic memories involving the vampire attacks he'd suffered through. They flashed through his thoughts like a strobe light, and he closed his eyes as he was hit with a wave of nausea.

He saw the deformed body of his naga friend, Jade, as he and Ren had found her, her tail removed. He saw the old school director,

Zabrina Slegr, bones and body broken, a vampire standing over her. He saw his mother and father, their gryphon forms ruined and stripped of their wings. He saw his pregnant wife in human form, lying in a pool of her own blood…

"Myreen!"

Oberon opened his eyes, the memories disappearing like a light being turned out, along with his nausea.

Looking down, he saw Alessandra stirring under the white sheets. "Myreen. Myreen. Myreen."

He couldn't take his eyes away from the mermaid.

"That's all she's been saying since I've been able to stabilize her, Director," Maya said.

High winds, he thought, setting his jaw.

"I know it isn't my business sniffing about like a hound," she said, "but why would she keep saying the newest mermaid's name?"

Oberon sighed heavily. He knew the answer to that now, and he found his mind beginning to spiral.

"Keep doing your best with her," Oberon said, his breathing increasing as his heartbeats followed suit.

"Is there *more* I can do, besides healing her wounds?" she asked.

Oberon shook his head quickly, opening the door to leave. "That is precisely what I need you to do. Thank you, Maya."

"Myreen!" Alessandra called out again. "Myreen, Myreen, Myreen—"

He quickly stepped out of the room and shut the door, afraid that students nearby would hear Alessandra. The last thing they needed right now were more rumors about Myreen flying around the Dome.

He found Delphine and Ren waiting for him just a few feet away.

"How is she?" Delphine asked, the worry on her face seeming to age her.

Oberon shifted his eyes around the room and saw several students

419

about, awkward, not speaking to one another, pretending like they weren't by Ms. Heather's office for the sole purpose of eavesdropping.

"As good as can be expected. Her wounds are all but healed, thanks to Maya's incredible care." He stepped closer to Ren and Delphine, then whispered, "Walk with me."

He hoped his anxiety wasn't too transparent. He was the school director, and everybody here—teachers and students—would be looking to him for guidance and comfort. And if he was honest, he could use some of that right now, himself.

Speed-walking through the halls, he made for his classroom. It was the one place he was hoping he'd be able to get his bearings to think this situation through. Ren and Delphine kept up, talking behind him.

"The copper alloy lining the exterior of the trains likely deterred the vampires from pursuing the poor mermaid," Ren said quietly.

"A precaution I'm glad we put in place," Delphine replied. "One of many obstacles I hope will keep the vampires at bay, rather than draw attention."

They continued chatting, but Oberon's troubled thoughts caused him to tune them out.

Alessandra couldn't stop saying Myreen's name. Oberon had enough experience with trauma to form an educated guess as to *why*. The poor girl's attackers had mistaken her for Myreen. The girls did have physical similarities. But they'd been wrong, and probably knew it. This pointed at the vampires' knowledge of a girl named Myreen. It also indicated that they knew of her importance, which only validated to Oberon that Myreen was the siren from the prophecy. But that meant that the vampires, likely, somehow knew of the prophecy.

Draven is aware of Myreen and *the prophecy.* He'd been dancing around that thought since he'd first heard Alessandra say the mermaid's name. And finally acknowledging it, he realized the mistakes he'd made.

"High winds," Oberon muttered again. He'd sent Leif off to

Draven to discover this very thing. And he hadn't heard back from his vampire ally since he'd left weeks ago. For all he knew, Draven had killed him.

What made matters worse is that Leif's eyes were sharp, and he was extremely good at keeping tabs on vampire activity close by. He could have potentially stopped the attack on Alessandra. But then they would have been at square one—they wouldn't have learned that Draven knew about the prophecy and Myreen.

"I hate to point out the obvious, Oberon," Ren said, "but you're walking extremely fast."

"If it's too difficult for you to keep up, phase through the walls and meet me at my classroom."

"I'm always up for a brisk walk," Ren replied. "I'm more concerned with how you are feeling, my friend."

Oberon stopped, anger bubbling inside of him. "One of our students nearly died! This school was founded upon several ideals, one of which was a promise of protection for every shifter who attends. What *are* we if we can't even protect our own students?"

Ren threw a glance at Delphine. Oberon saw the kitsune's Adam's apple bob down, then come back up like a bouncy ball.

"We're almost to your classroom, Oberon," Delphine said, glancing over her shoulder. "We should go there before we start talking."

Oberon didn't see anybody—teacher or student—nearby, but didn't argue. He turned back around and continued through the arcing hallway, passing classroom after classroom until he reached his door.

He smashed a finger against his watch and the door slowly swung open. With long strides, Oberon entered his classroom and headed straight for his desk.

He wasn't prepared to spill all his thoughts, particularly about Leif. Nobody else knew that he'd been dealing with a vampire, even one who had been helping the shifters for the past fifteen years. But Leif had been involved with the destruction of The Island; and Ren and Oberon had fought him in a convenience store just as the school had been attacked.

Tapping his tablet, he locked them inside the classroom.

"I'm not going to draw out what needs to be said," Oberon said, giving Ren and Delphine a hard look. "Draven knows about Myreen, and he's hunting for her. He knows she's the stray mermaid from the prophecy."

Delphine narrowed her emerald eyes and crossed her arms. "That's impossible. How could Draven even know about the prophecy?"

Oberon shook his head. "I don't know. But Alessandra has been saying nothing but Myreen's name since she got here."

Ren looked at Delphine, obviously wanting to say something but not feeling comfortable enough to go through with it.

"You're allowing your thoughts to spiral out of control, Oberon," she said with a motherly tone. "Alessandra has been tutoring Myreen for the past little while. She could be rattling off Myreen's name for no reason at all."

Oberon's pride caused her words to ruffle his feathers. "Do you honestly believe that? It's too coincidental. The vampires are looking for Myreen." He glanced at his kitsune friend. "Ren, you understand that, right?"

Ren bobbed his head back and forth. "Well, it's a possibility I don't think we should toss right out the window. But on the other hand, you do have a way of..." He paused, spinning his hands around each other in front of him, then opened them up. "...blowing things out of proportion when you're emotionally invested."

Oberon blinked. He couldn't believe what he was hearing. "You think I'm overreacting?"

"Until we can get more information from Alessandra, we can't assume the vampires know anything about Myreen," Delphine said, sidestepping his question. "But if we find out otherwise, we'll have to take precautions."

Running a hand through his hair, Oberon said, "You want to pretend like none of this happened? The vampires attacked a student right at our front door!"

Delphine's lower jaw shift to the side, then straightened out. "I think you need to tell the school that an unfortunate vampire attack occurred with one of our students off-campus, and that the Dome is the safest place for our students to stay. We should also ask for more military eyes to be on the lookout."

"That's a good starting point," Ren agreed.

"Please remember, Oberon," Delphine said, "that while Alessandra's attack was horrific, shifters out in the world deal with these kinds of attacks daily."

That was a true point, which helped pull Oberon away from his reeling thoughts. He rubbed his eyes. He wasn't physically tired, but this whole situation had been so draining.

"Let's set up a live announcement," Oberon said. "As part of this all, I believe a cancellation of today's classes are in order. Heaven knows how much learning would actually go on if we tried to hold them. Ren, can we broadcast from my tablet?"

The kitsune whipped out his phone from his pocket and punched in a few commands, letting his thumb hang in the air. "Just say when, boss, and your beautiful face and charming voice will flood every screen and speaker in the Dome like the President of the United States playing on his PA system."

"That wasn't funny," Delphine said.

Ren wagged a finger. "You say that now, but wait until Oberon starts talking. I have a module enabled in the software that will turn his glorious speech into a rickety-rockin' rap."

"You do?" Oberon asked.

Ren flashed a smile. "I can…"

There was a moment of silence, then Delphine laughed. "I'm not going to lie. That would be brilliant, Ren."

The kitsune bowed low. "I live for the laughs, my dear. Life's too vanilla, otherwise."

Oberon groaned. Removing the embedded tablet from his desk, he held it up to his face. "Normal settings. None of this flippity-floppin' crap."

Ren's smiled broadened. "That was *almost* a joke, Oberon! Good job!"

"Ren," he said dangerously.

Looking at himself in the screen, Oberon realized just how old *he* looked. He shouldn't have been so quick to judge Delphine back in front of Maya's office.

"Are you ready?" Ren asked, his smile fizzling out like a phoenix diving into water.

Nodding, Oberon cleared his throat.

Ren's steady thumb tapped the command, overwriting every screen's status in the Dome. Oberon remembered how such announcements used to make him uncomfortable. It wasn't that way anymore. He'd grown accustomed to such things as director.

"Good morning, students and teachers," he said, staring into the little camera attached to his tablet. "Pardon this short interruption. Last night, one of our—"

"Whoops!" Ren said, fiddling with his phone. "Sorry, I forgot to connect to the transmission signal. But you sounded really good. Nice warm-up."

"I thought you were going to say that you *accidentally* turned on the rap setting," Delphine said with a chuckle.

Winking at Delphine, he proudly said, "I'm saving that one for later."

"Are we going to do the announcement *today*, Ren?" Oberon asked.

"The transmission signal connection has been established," Ren said. "Just say the magic word and I'll give you hundreds of faces. Well, hundreds… of the same face."

Oberon rolled his eyes, then held the tablet up, resting his elbows on the desk. "Do it."

Ren tapped his phone and nodded at Oberon.

"Good morning, students and teachers. Pardon this short interruption, but as many of you have likely heard, last night one of our students became the victim of a vampire attack. The student was not within the protective walls of the Dome when the attack occurred. We are saddened by the event, but are glad that the student survived and is recovering. Due to this event, the school administration feels that it would be best to cancel classes today. I urge you all to do your best to focus on your studies, either on your own or within groups.

"I cannot begin to emphasize how important it is for everyone who makes the conscious choice to step outside of the school to take proper precautions to stay safe. Don't go out alone. Watch your shadows. Try to put yourself in public places where a lot of other people are around.

"I will also take this time to remind you all that the Dome is a refuge from the storms outside. The vampires can't hurt you here, and they never will. The safest place for you is here, in the school.

"If any of you feel the need to discuss the safety and protection of our school, please speak with the heads of your houses. Thank you for your time."

Ren waited a few more seconds just to make sure Oberon was done, then cut the transmission connection.

"You know," Ren said, "I prefer your scripted announcements

much more. You're far less emotional when you read the words on your screen."

"I'm sorry for your discomfort, Ren," Oberon said without any ounce of apology.

"You do get a kind of *my-eyes-are-piercing-yours* vibe when you improvise," Delphine said.

"Good," replied Oberon. "I hope that means everyone understands the seriousness of what I said."

"You got the point across extremely well," Ren said.

Delphine nodded in agreement. "I've also been thinking that perhaps we should modify our curfew rules."

"That would be very appropriate, and I believe most of the students will be eager to follow it after what happened to Alessandra. How early do you think we should have the students back here at the Dome?"

Ren shrugged. "We probably don't need to set a time. I'd just say before sunset. We could even feature a tagline: *Vampires are up when the sun goes down.*" The kitsune held his hands together, then spread them out as he said it.

Cheesy, but it got the message across well enough.

Oberon nodded. "Why don't you take care of that, Ren? Distribute it on my channel, and send it to the devices of all students and teachers." He tapped his tablet and the classroom door opened. "And you'd better get back to your appropriate wings, both of you. You'll be needed to help keep order around the Dome."

"I will do that, and will also keep tabs on Alessandra," Delphine said. "As soon as she is speaking again, I will notify you, Oberon."

"Thank you," he replied. "Hopefully it won't take her too long. And one other thing, Delphine. Could you have Myreen come and see me right away? I should address the situation with her personally."

Oberon watched as she hesitated a moment.

"You aren't going to tell her about the prophecy, are you?" she asked.

"She isn't ready for that," Oberon replied.

"So what will you tell her?" Delphine asked. "We don't know why Alessandra keeps saying Myreen's name yet."

Oberon nodded. "I want to find out if *she* knows anything. And if she doesn't, then great, we'll wait until Alessandra is able to tell us."

"I'll send for her at once," replied Delphine, then left the room, leaving Ren behind.

Ren was staring at Oberon, his head tilted.

"You should probably head to the dorms and see if you're needed," said Oberon.

"I want to make sure you are doing okay first," Ren replied.

"I'm okay, Ren," he said.

Ren exhaled. "I was there, too, remember?"

Oberon looked down, not wanting the painful memories to be drawn out again.

"Just... I'm here for you. I always have been, and I always will be."

Oberon nodded, forcing himself to bring his eyes back up to his friend. "I know that, and I appreciate it. But I'll be okay."

Ren stared at him for another few moments, probably waiting to see if Oberon would budge. He didn't.

"I'll see you around," the kitsune said, then left Oberon to himself in the empty classroom.

Oberon popped the tablet back into the desk. He breathed in and out, trying to give his mind something other than vampire attacks to think about. In the end, he mashed his fists onto his hardwood desk, sending spikes of pain shooting from his hands up to his wrists.

He was tempted to call on the military to make an assault on their towers in Cle Elum. Leif had divulged that bit of information, but a direct assault on the vampire fortress would be a suicide mission.

Draven had obtained technology that rivaled the work of Ren, most of it having been tweaked to hunt shifters. Twenty years ago, Oberon had been shot with an odd device that Draven had called a *hookshot*. The tip was made of gold, and had pierced his wing, his weakness to the metal prohibiting him from flying. But that was old tech now. The abominations the vampires controlled these days were terrifying. The military took the brunt of such attacks, but every day, shifters around the globe were suffering, too.

"Director Oberon?"

He wiped the disgust from his face as Myreen poked her head in.

"Come on in, Myreen," he said, gesturing for Myreen to sit.

She stepped forward, wearing a baggy, long-sleeve shirt and jeans. Her dark hair with blue streaks was pulled back in a messy bun. She quickly pulled one of the chairs out from under his desk and sat down, resting her hands in her lap.

"It's been awhile since we've talked," he said.

Nodding her head, Myreen said, "It has, but that's okay. I wouldn't want you to feel like you have to meet with me all the time."

"And I wouldn't want you to feel that way, either." He cleared his throat as she waited for him to continue. "I'm assuming you watched my announcement?"

She nodded her head again.

"Have you heard who was attacked?"

Another nod. Oberon knew the conversation would likely be one-sided, but Myreen's lack of verbal communication surprised him.

"Who?" he said, trying to get her to speak.

"Alessandra," Myreen said.

Oberon tried relaxing himself, hoping that such a cue would help Myreen. "Have you heard anything else about Alessandra?"

Myreen swallowed. "Yes. She keeps saying my name."

"Do you have any idea as to why that is?"

Her eyes widened. "Sir, I swear, I didn't do anything. Sure, Alessandra can be a jerk sometimes, but I've never wanted her to get hurt. I would never do anything to her."

Her exclamations set Oberon aback. "I'm sorry, I didn't intend on sounding accusatory," he said, waving a hand in front of him, as if his fingers were erasing that notion, like the wipe of a whiteboard. "I believe the reason Alessandra keeps saying your name is that she's giving us a warning."

"A warning about what?"

Oberon leaned forward. "I know very little about you and your mother. Forgive me for bringing her up, but I must know if you have any idea why the vampires tracked your mother down."

Her eyes almost instantly got wet with tears as she shook her head. Through quivering lips, she said, "I don't know."

"Did your mother have any involvement with them? Did she do anything that would draw vampires to her?"

Quiet, whispery sobs came from her mouth, and Oberon felt a pang of guilt at reopening such a deep wound.

"Again, I'm sorry to bring this up," he said sorrowfully. "I know how painful and raw it can be."

She shook her head and shakily inhaled. "I don't think so. She never went out at night, or let me go out at night. But If she had anything to do with vampires, she never talked about it. My mother didn't tell me anything."

"And you know nothing about your father, or if he might be involved?"

"No."

So that was the answer. And he already knew it, but he had to be sure. He couldn't bring himself to tell her that he was convinced she was being hunted. That wouldn't help anything right now. She was already sad. Telling her that vampires were trying to track her down would only add fear to the mix. She'd never leave the school again. Perhaps that would be a good thing, though.

Oberon opened one of the drawers in his desk and brought out a portable package of tissues. He slid it over to her.

"I don't know what the future holds," he said. "I'm no seer. But I urge you to keep working hard on your studies and practicing your abilities. They will help offset the pain you're feeling."

She sniffled while nodding, snatching the package of tissues. "Can I leave now?"

"Of course," Oberon replied. "Thanks for being willing to talk."

She got up from the desk and walked briskly out of the classroom.

He sighed heavily. "Too many questions, not enough answers."

Myreen

How could things possibly get any worse?

As Myreen walked back to her dorm from Oberon's office, she felt as if a chunk of iron was lodged in her belly, simultaneously weighing her down and crushing her from the inside out. Already, students were whispering that she was behind Alessandra's attack. Considering the gossip factory that was Trish and her minions, Myreen had been expecting that. What she didn't expect was suspicion from the teachers as well. Even Oberon thought she was somehow responsible. Maybe not directly, like everyone else did, but he thought that by association, Alessandra had been targeted because of her.

And now he was implying that her mom had ties with vampires, and that's why they killed her? Myreen couldn't believe it. Vampires would explain the reasoning for rule number one, but Myreen couldn't imagine her mom ever being in league with vampires. Could it be possible that her mom had pissed off one of them by accident? It was obvious to her now that her mom had been running from someone or something all those years. Could that someone have been a vampire?

And to make matters worse, it was obvious Oberon knew no more about her father than she did. She wondered if she'd ever discover the truth of it all.

Myreen crept into the mer common room, keeping her head down and trying not to attract attention as she grabbed her bag and headed off to class. But when she got to her room, Trish and Joanna were standing in front of the door like a barbie barricade. Her laptop bag was at their feet, with the few articles of clothing she'd acquired while at the school messily stuffed into it and spilling out.

"What are you doing with my stuff?" Myreen demanded, feeling violated, which was just the cherry on top of the other horrible things Trish had made her feel this morning.

"Taking out the trash." Trish crossed her arms and kicked the bag so that it fell over, causing one of the shirts Myreen had borrowed from Juliet to fall out.

Myreen knelt to gather her things, the lump in her throat momentarily keeping her from verbally defending herself.

"Nobody wants you here," Joanna hissed. "You're no longer welcome in this wing."

"You're not even a real mermaid, anyway," Trish added.

Myreen hugged her belongings to her chest and swallowed the lump that constricted her voice, determined not to let Trish hear the misery she felt. "You can't kick me out. Delphine would never let that happen."

Trish narrowed her eyes and stalked closer to Myreen, like a predatory shark on a weakened fish. "Well, Delphine isn't here right now. She's too busy taking care of the mermaid you almost got killed."

"I already told you, I had nothing to with that!" Myreen was seconds away from exploding molten crazy all over the hallway like an undersea volcano.

"Save it." Trish made a closing motion with her fingers and thumb. "The truth will come out eventually, and when it does, *no one* at this school will want you."

Myreen struggled for a moment just to get her breathing under control. Though she didn't have it in her to hurt Alessandra, she damn sure was furious enough to lurch at Trish and rip all her perfect blonde hair out right now. But a fight would only make things worse. She knew she had to get out before she lost control, so she stormed out of the common room without another word.

Hot, angry tears blurred her vision as she trod through the hallways. She didn't exactly know where she was going. She considered tracking down Delphine and telling her about what Trish and Joanna did, but she knew that wouldn't fix anything. Honestly, it wasn't worth the constant fight. The mer didn't want her there, with the exception of maybe Kendall.

She found her legs carrying her toward the Avian common room. If there was only one person at this school who wanted her around, who would let her bunk with them, it was Juliet. And if anyone at the Avian wing had a problem with it, they wouldn't dare risk triggering Juliet's fiery temper.

As she approached the Avian wing, fewer eyes were on her. Avians didn't care too much about the drama the mer caused, so they usually bought into the gossip the least of all the primes. She had made the right choice.

"Um, you're not supposed to be in here," a bespectacled harpy girl said to her when she entered the common room. The girl looked more puzzled than territorial.

"Oh, er," Myreen hadn't quite figured out what she was going to say if someone tried to stop her.

"It's okay, Leya," Nik said, getting up from one of the couches and coming to Myreen's rescue. "She's just here to see Juliet."

The meek harpy merely nodded and carried her books off to another part of the large room.

"Thanks, Nik." Myreen was grateful for the save. If the Avians had barred her from their wing, she didn't know what she would have done. "Is Juliet around?"

"Uh, no, I think she's training with Mr. Quinn," he said. His eyes lingered on her in a way that said he knew about the rumors and didn't believe them. "But you're welcome to wait here for her, if you want."

Myreen nodded. "Thanks." She looked around the common room, fingering the strap of her bag.

Nik put his hands in his pockets and rolled his shoulders. "I don't know if you're into video games, but Brett and I are about to kill some zombies. Want to play?"

Myreen looked at the couch Nik had risen from and saw Kol and Brett sitting there. Brett already had a controller in hand.

"I'm not much of a player, aside from phone games. But I can watch."

"Sure, we don't mind an audience," Nik said. "Do we, Brett?"

"Not at all," Brett called back. "You're the one who's gonna lose. Now get your butt over here so we can start."

Nik chuckled and nodded at the couch before jogging over and reclaiming his seat beside Brett. Myreen followed and sat on the armchair catty corner to the couch, next to where Kol was sitting. She set down her bag as the boys dove into their game. Gunfire and splattered blood lit up the big screen TV in front of them.

Myreen watched with mild interest, distracted by the street warfare that was going on in her mind. She considered trying to find Kendall and getting him to talk some sense into Trish, but the mer wing really was the last place she wanted to be. Maybe tomorrow she would do it. For now, some space from her kind was what she needed. She had never felt like one of them, anyway. Maybe a permanent removal from the wing was best… Or maybe a removal from the school completely. It wasn't like she was excelling here. Maybe she was better off not being at the school, just as Trish had said. But she had no guardian, no money of her own, and nowhere else to go. What would she do with her life if she left?

She had to get off this train of thought; it was just too depressing. She tried to get into the gameplay, but the killing and gore only made her more uncomfortable. Her eyes wandered over to Kol, who had been very quiet all this time. His chin rested on his hand, his jaw clenched. His eyes were fixed on the screen, and she got the impression that he was purposely avoiding looking at her. Not for the first time, she wondered what was going on in that brooding mind of his. Did he believe she was allied with vampires? Was that why he was shutting her out? Or was she just imagining things?

She leaned forward and in a hushed voice said, "So, I'm sure you've heard about Alessandra."

He nodded without looking at her. "The whole school has."

She nodded and looked down. "Then I guess you've also heard the rumors Trish started. She blames me for what happened, which is just insane. You don't… believe it, do you?" Her eyes found his face again, almost begging him to give her the right answer.

He shook his head and pursed his lips in a noncommittal expression. "Everyone knows Trish is hateful. Whatever she's saying will blow over in a day or two."

Myreen kept her gaze on him, not missing the fact that he still hadn't let his eyes slip in her direction. *Come on, I know you're not that interested in this stupid game. Just look at me!*

She wanted to push the issue, to make him give her a real answer. Because from the way he was acting, she definitely got the feeling that he blamed her for it, too.

"Myreen?" Juliet's voice called her attention away from Kol's stony face and toward the entrance. Juliet rounded the couches to come to Myreen's side. "What's going on?"

Myreen considered pulling her aside to talk in private, but she figured if she was going to have to stay here indefinitely, everyone might as well know. "I was hoping I could bunk with you for a while. Trish booted me out of the mer wing."

"She did what!?" Kol snapped, suddenly unable to pull his wide eyes off her.

"That witch! She can't do that!" Juliet's anger was in full heat. "Did you tell Delphine?"

"No, and right now, I just don't care," she said. "I really just want some space from them. So... I was hoping you wouldn't mind letting me stay with you until this whole Alessandra thing blows over."

Juliet's fire cooled and her face smoothed into a pity pout. "Of course. You can bunk with me for as long as you need to. And if anyone has a problem with that, they can take it up with me." Juliet narrowed her eyes at everyone around, and no one said anything. "Come on, let's get you settled. Then we'll steal a tub of ice cream from the kitchen and we can talk."

"Thanks." Flushed with gratitude, Myreen threw her arms around Juliet.

They hugged for a moment, then excused themselves from the common room and headed for Juliet's room. Kol stood and stared at Myreen as she left, an apology in his amber eyes, and a building rage behind them.

Just once, she wished he'd let her in, give her a glimpse of what was going on behind that guarded façade. Maybe now with her staying in the same wing, she had a chance.

Juliet

Juliet's head spun in fury over Myreen's situation. The whispers and gossip were rude, childish, and severely infuriating. Not one of those students actually knew Myreen enough for them to make such false accusations.

Myreen had been through enough. And here she had nobody. Kenzie wasn't allowed at the school, so Juliet knew it was up to her to remind Myreen that she wasn't alone. And she was proud of her friend for having the strength to hold her head high for so long, but she was worried that Myreen might break down at any moment.

Juliet knew firsthand how damaging it was to bottle up emotions. And she knew what it felt like to think that there was no one to talk to.

So they met up as often as they could, like between classes and mealtimes.

And as they got ready to walk out of Juliet's room for lunch, she made sure to put her mean face on. She decided they'd had enough of everyone's idiocy.

Juliet was just finding control over her power, but she almost lit two classrooms on fire that morning because nobody would stop pointing the finger at her friend.

If it wasn't for the warning that Malachai gave Juliet, she would have initiated a fight long ago. She was lucky that people kept their distance from her, because otherwise, she would be like a rocker in a mosh pit.

She turned the knob and walked out first, just so people knew she was not in the mood. And by the way students quickly spun in the opposite direction, she was confident that her looks of fire were effective.

The best part was that it got some giggles out of Myreen. Juliet didn't intend to make her laugh, but she was glad she did. It was enough to remind her that she still had to remain relatively calm, for Myreen's sake.

The walk to the Dining Hall was weird, because everyone stepped out of their way. With the dirty looks she gave everyone, it wasn't surprising that they backed away. It was like they had their own lane.

It made her feel powerful, but also undeniably on edge. She could only imagine how Myreen felt.

They quickly got their food and took their usual seats across from each other. Juliet was even more jumpy than normal, so much so that she almost lost it the minute she heard a deep voice speak from behind her.

"Well, well." The male voice was familiar, but Juliet spun around with her fist in the air.

"Whoa!" Nik threw his hands up in surrender and walked around their table to take the seat next to Myreen. Juliet numbly retracted her fist and slowly retook her seat.

"We're going to have to stop meeting like this." Nik graced her with his heart-melting smirk.

Juliet's stomach sank, and she felt like she'd seen a ghost. Was he flirting with her? She couldn't move, she was so frozen in shock. Myreen gently kicked Juliet underneath the table to try and wake her up from her stupor, but it only caused Juliet to flutter her eyelashes.

Nik looked Juliet directly in her eyes. Even if she'd wanted to, she couldn't pull them away. "So... I know my timing couldn't be worse, but if I don't do this now, I don't know if I'll ever find the courage to again." He cleared his throat, clearly flustered, and Juliet just stared, confused. She saw Myreen try to hide her smile and so she turned to the side, just a little.

"Um... so Juliet, I was wondering if you would like to... go out sometime? Like on a date... with me?"

Juliet felt her entire world crash. And in a good way. Her heart raced, and all the blood rushed to her cheeks in a crimson blush.

Juliet blurted out her answer before he could change his mind. "Uh, for sure!"

Nik's eyes grew wide, and as she saw them light up, her heart jumped with joy.

"Wow. Thank you." For the first time, his smile looked shy, but as it grew wider his dimples came out on full display. *Breathe, Juliet.* "So, it'll have to be during the day because of the new curfew. I hope that's okay?"

Juliet practically swooned, and all she could do was rapidly nod. He gave a light chuckle then ran his hand over the back of his neck. Was she really making him just as nervous as he was making her?

"Perfect. Meet me in the common room this Saturday. Around noon?"

Again, all she did was nod. She thought he would get up to leave, but instead, he shifted in to face Myreen. "How're you doing?" Genuinely concerned, he looked down at his hands, as if ashamed of the behavior of the other students.

"I could be better. Thanks." Myreen shrugged her shoulders. "Of course, if it wasn't for Juliet, I would be far from okay. But she really is wonderful." Juliet and she felt her cheeks heat up all over again as Myreen continued eating her lunch.

"I can see that." Nik flashed his sultry smile at Juliet and her knees weakened, even while sitting down.

Myreen snorted, only slightly bringing Juliet down from her cloud. It was when Nik stood to leave that she finally awoke from her daydream.

"Well, keep your heads up. This will pass. See you Saturday, *Juliet.*" Her name sounded like a soft melody when Nik said it. And with a final wave, he was gone.

But Juliet was still dizzy over the way he said her name. Her mind spun in circles as it echoed his voice over and over.

Myreen waited until he was out of earshot to finally react. "Oh my word, J! I am *so* happy and excited for you. I thought that you were going to faint when he asked you. You're still pale as a ghost."

They laughed, and Juliet realized that the world was still moving around them. Nik was right, this *would* pass. And even though her mean demeanor had been working for them, entertaining the onlookers was not worth it. Smiling and continuing to enjoy themselves was what really mattered.

"I feel like my goosebumps won't go away," Juliet said as she buried her face in her hands, embarrassed and excited all at the same time. "Ah! I cannot believe that just happened. If you weren't here, I would so think I was in a dream." She wanted to scream, but she knew it would be a bit dramatic.

Instead, she stomped her feet briskly, then took a deep breath to calm herself. "The only thing that could make this better is if you and Kol came with us," Juliet blurted out before realizing it was insensitive.

"You mean like a double date?" Myreen said, the words slow and steady.

"Well, yeah. It would be much more fun with you there. But I totally get why that would be uncomfortable for you." Juliet didn't want Myreen to feel like she was obligated to go.

"Who knows. Maybe? I wouldn't mind if we went just as friends. But I wouldn't count on it. Our last date was a wreck. Something I'm sure neither of us wants to repeat." Myreen pushed her food around on her tray.

"It really is too bad it didn't work out for you two. I could have sworn I saw some kind of spark between you guys."

"I thought so, too. So much can change in such a short amount of time." Myreen stood to empty her tray and Juliet followed her lead. She swung her arm over Myreen's shoulder and squeezed for a quick hug.

As they made their way to their classes Juliet thought it would be the perfect time to ask for advice. "So, you've actually been on a date. Do you have any pointers? I could use them all. I don't know the first thing about dating. And the last person I want to ask is my father. Could you just imagine the look on his face if I went to him with questions about dating?"

The girls giggled.

"Honestly, I'm not the person to ask. I've only ever had one date, and it ended horribly." Myreen brightened as she added, "But one thing I *can* help you with is getting ready for your date. The dark lipstick worked so well for you at the party."

Myreen winked, but then sobered. "Speaking of your dad, how do you think he's going to react to you and Nik going out? I'm sure he'll be hearing about it shortly from the rumor mill. We all know how fast that goes."

Juliet didn't know how to respond, but only because she never thought she would actually be in this situation. "Good question. *I* might need to be the one to be prepared with one of Ren's extinguishers this time. Maybe I should tell him before he hears it from one of the other students. I can already hear him yelling my name through the halls."

With nerves causing her stomach to sink, Juliet stayed silent until Myreen's classroom came into view. "I'll see you after class, okay?"

"Okay. Good luck with your dad." With a tight smile, Myreen turned on her heels and went in.

Juliet felt a wave of worry as she pictured students bullying Myreen. Myreen could probably take care of herself, but Juliet still wanted to pummel anyone who tried to hurt her friend.

For now, she just hoped time would go by fast. And for a second, she didn't know if it was for Myreen's sake or for her own. The conversation she was about to have with her dad was something she was not ready for.

Knock. Knock.

"You may enter," Malachai's rough voice sounded through the door

Juliet almost turned the other way and ran. As she slowly pushed the door open, she tried to steady her breathing.

"Ah, Juliet. Our session isn't until later this afternoon. Is everything okay?" He seemed open to whatever she had to say, so she sat down and took the plunge.

"I was asked out on a date today—I said yes—I just wanted to tell you before you heard it from someone else," she blurted out.

"What? Who? When!?" His voice became louder with every question, causing Juliet to sink into her seat.

"Um. A date. Nikolai Candida. This Saturday afternoon." She wanted to sound stronger, but he looked as if he was ready to murder someone. His pale skin deepened to a fiery red, and Juliet could swear she saw smoke coming out of his ears.

"I already said yes and I'm not changing my mind. I didn't come here to ask for your permission. I came here so I could be the one to tell you. That's all." Juliet made to leave. His response had her temper rising, and the last thing she wanted to do was have another fiery mishap in his office.

"Juliet Quinn, sit down. I realize that I wasn't there for you growing up, but I'm here now. I appreciate you coming to me with this, but you can't expect me to be completely okay with it. I'm your father. This kind of news is never really welcomed."

Malachai regulated his breathing and his color was back to its pasty white. Juliet crossed her arms.

He hung his head and dragged his hands down the front of his face. "But I know I can trust you and I know you can beat anyone in a fight if you needed to. I want whatever makes you happy." Malachai took the seat next to her and took her small hand in his oversized one.

Surprised, Juliet nudged him gently with her elbow. "Thanks. Right now, I am happy. Now promise me you won't call him in here to give him the third degree."

Juliet raised her pinky and waited for her father to take it with his own. He stared at her hand in confusion, but then grabbed her pinky with his pointer and thumb.

Before Juliet could tease him for it, his reply shut her up.

"I will make no promises."

CHAPTER 50

Kol

It was late when Kol returned to the Avian common room Wednesday night. He'd been in the training room since finishing dinner to clear his head. Myreen hadn't spoken to him since Monday night, when she tried to talk to him after being kicked out of her room by the self-absorbed carp couple who blamed Alessandra's attack on her. And though he feared there was a connection, Myreen was not to blame.

And he should've acted like she wasn't to blame, instead of being quiet and distant. But in his defense, having her sit next to him in *his* common room had left him a little out of sorts in a completely different way.

So he'd run seven miles on the treadmill after inhaling his food, wishing he could escape to the skies instead. He was angry at himself, he was terrified for Myreen's safety, and he hadn't heard back from his father since pleading for the help of the military. But with the mandated curfew Oberon put in place, there wasn't an excuse in the world he could use to escape and fly away.

Kol could've immersed himself in a simulation, practicing so he could finally beat it, but after the *invisible dragon* incident, he hadn't even so much as glanced at the room. It was another thing that weighed on his mind.

But he stopped dead in his tracks when, after walking into the common room, all hot and sweaty from his workout, he spotted her— Myreen—sitting right in the middle of the couch with Juliet and some of the other Avian girls. They were watching one of those sappy, gag-worthy chick movies.

All the girls looked to see who had come in, but his eyes were already trained on Myreen's and locked for a full second—longer than he was comfortable with. He almost took the cowardly way out and headed off to shower, since she was in a room full of girls, but instead he nodded toward the hallway, hoping she understood the gesture.

Myreen's eyes widened slightly and she excused herself, ducking beneath the screen to minimize blocking any of the other girls' views.

They walked partway into the hallway, so they could still see the common room but were out of earshot. Kol kept several feet between them—he didn't want to scare her away with his stench—and leaned against the opposite wall. Her hair was up in a high ponytail and she folded her arms casually, but in a way that put a different sort of distance between them.

"I wanted to apologize," Kol said.

Myreen immediately unfolded her arms. She wasn't expecting an apology.

He twisted the edge of his shirt, unwilling to meet her eyes. "I shouldn't have been so quiet after everything happened. I shouldn't've have treated you like..." he couldn't find the words.

"Like it was my fault?" she prompted.

He shook his head. "I never thought it was your fault. I mean it." He paused. "I— it terrifies me to think that the attackers thought

Alessandra was you, but I never— I could never blame you for what happened."

"So, I don't know, Kol." She sounded exasperated. "One second you're all flir— like a good friend to me, and the next you're acting like I'm some stupid, stuck-up mer who you want nothing to do with. Like Trish."

"You are *nothing* like Trish—"

"Well," she cut him off. "I just figured since you made out with her and all that..." she trailed off.

He didn't like what she was implying. "You are *nothing* like Trish, and you mean more to me than she ever would. We're friends remember?" He winked at her, but he was certain he imagined the sudden pink in her cheeks, because she seemed skeptical. "I'll even prove it to you," he blurted out.

She raised an eyebrow. "You'll *prove* what?"

"That I'm really sorry and that I want to make up for being a stupid guy... and that we're friends."

"*Friends,*" she said, like it was a foreign word.

He took a step back, realizing in his declarations he'd drawn closer to her than he was currently comfortable with. If she noticed, she didn't mention it. Satisfied that he'd said what he wanted to, he took another step further into the hallway. "Well, I'm gonna shower," Kol said, hooking a thumb over his shoulder. "Stay on your toes, Myreen," he teased.

"Actually," she said, stopping him. "Since we're *friends*, could I ask you something?"

He turned so he was facing her full-on again.

"Nik asked Juliet out on a date today," she said, and this time he knew the blush in her cheeks wasn't imagined. "And Juliet asked if you and I..."

"If we would double?" Kol finished.

"Yeah," she said, a little sheepishly—in that way that erased all his maneuvering to get back to the friendship level. In that way that made him want to take her in his arms right now—to hell with the way he currently smelled—and make her exclusively his.

He ran a hand through his greasy hair. "Let's do it." He tried to sound casual about it. That they were doing a favor for their friends by joining. But even he heard the quaver in his voice. "When?"

"Saturday," she said. "Sometime during the day because of the curfew."

Kol nodded once, then turned his back before he did something his heart would murder him for. "Later, Myreen." He wanted to make one more joke about her watching out for what he had planned, but no longer thought he could say it in a way that wouldn't give away his true feelings.

***

"You know this could get you suspended," Brett hissed early the next morning as he, Kol and Nik snuck into Oberon's private office. The empty space certainly had a different feel than when his father had procured permission to discuss the very thing that had turned his life on its head. Eduard's assignment for Kol to *befriend* Myreen. It felt like a lifetime ago.

And here he was again for the same damned girl.

"Oberon won't suspend *Malkolm Dracul*," Nik teased. He seemed less broody and... more responsible since the morning before. After speaking with Myreen last night, Kol finally knew why. Nik had asked out her phoenix friend, Juliet, yesterday morning. "Nobody suspends the *dragon prince.*" Nik said, using a bellowing announcer voice.

"Nik!" Brett hissed again. "*Shut. It.*"

Nik rolled his eyes at Kol when Brett's back was turned. Kol just

447

shrugged, still surprised by Nik's recent behavior.

"Why don't you just ask the girl out?" Nik asked, while Brett searched the drawers for Oberon's tablet.

"Oh, the way you asked out Juliet yesterday?" Kol teased.

"H— how did you—?"

"Myreen told me," he said. "And if you remember, I did ask the girl out. It was a disaster."

"Right," Nik said with a nod, suddenly sobering to his default-self.

But Kol missed the old Nik. "Myreen actually asked me out last night to double with you and Juliet."

"Found it!" Brett said, pulling the tablet out and swiping the screen to wake it. He then began his attempt to hack in. Kol still doubted his friend could do it, and was working on a contingency.

"She did?" Nik asked.

"I hope it's okay if we come along?" Kol asked.

"Yeah!" Nik said, sounding a little relieved. "Actually, that's probably good, since it's my first date with Juliet. And she'll be glad to have her friend there, too."

"You really like her, don't you?" Kol asked. The thought hadn't occurred to him until he saw the knowing look on his best friend's face.

He nodded a little sheepishly. "Yeah," he said quietly. "I do."

"In!" Brett shouted in his hiss-whisper. "Okay, are you ready Kol?"

"How'd you do it?" Kol asked, a little bit in awe. He was suddenly nervous, and so used the questioning as an excuse to stall.

"Katya Sayuri," Brett said as if that answered the question.

"The kitsune?" Nik asked, sounding as confused as Kol felt.

"Yep," Brett said, then brushed his fingers on his shirt. "She has a crush on me."

Kol rolled his eyes. "Let's get this over with."

"Why are you doing this, anyway?" Nik asked. "You just told me she asked you out again. Why do you need to make a fool of yourself now?"

"Who says I'm making a fool of myself?" Now his nerves had skyrocketed.

"For the record, I told you it was a bad idea," Nik said.

"Then why did you come along?" Brett asked. "Kol and I could've handled it."

"Because I'd never hear the end of how I missed out," Nik said. "Plus, I still think Kol might chicken out."

Kol hit Nik on the shoulder with the back of his hand. "Thanks for the confidence, *Brett 2.0.*"

"Now or never, man," Brett urged, ignoring the slight. "Oberon doesn't use this office much, but someone is certain to notice we're all missing from class."

"Right." Kol wiped his palms on his jeans. "Let's do it." He looked at Brett for the go ahead.

Brett pointed at the button on the screen for Kol to push.

He cleared his throat, then tapped it with his finger.

"Good morning shifters!" he said in a voice that even *he* didn't recognize. "This is Malkolm Dracul, and I have a very important announcement." Kol glanced at Brett who circled his hand, indicating that Kol needed to speak quickly because now the time was ticking. From the corner of his eye, he noticed Nik move closer to the door to stand watch. "The incident with Alessandra was unfortunate and we are all upset that *any* student had to go through something so horrible. But…" Kol paused for effect. "Myreen Fairchild is not to blame for these actions. Myreen has *nothing* to do with what happened." He suspected that part might not be entirely true, but it wasn't something the entire school needed to be privy to.

"So stop treating her like a pariah!" He continued. "She's a mer, just like the rest of you stuck-up, conceited mers, even if she didn't have the privilege to be raised like one. Myreen did not deserve to be kicked out of her room—yes, I'm talking to you, *Trish and Joanna."* He imagined the looks the fish were getting at that exact moment and resisted the urge to smile and ruin the whole thing. "And she *will* be allowed to return to it and be treated with the respect she deserves." He leaned closer to the camera and narrowed his eyes. "I'm sure Delphine will make sure of that."

He leaned back again and flashed his best princely smile. "Myreen Fairchild is my *friend,"* he said, giving a smirk for Myreen, even though whoever was watching also saw it. "She is my friend, and as a friend of a *Dracul,* she has the full protection and respect of *all* the Draculs." Kol leaned close again. "So if *any* of you have a problem with that, or think it's a good idea to mess with Myreen Fairchild again, you will have myself and the rest of the Draculs to answer to."

Kol clicked the button to shut the transmission off, feeling very proud of his performance.

"Ha!" Brett said, staring at his phone.

Nik and Kol looked at him expectantly.

"It's Katya," he said. "She just texted and said we could've done all that from our own devices. We didn't need to break into Oberon's office." Kol threw something at Brett's head, but he ducked.

The three of them walked out of the office with their heads high.

Kenzie

Kenzie arrived at Leif's apartment building on another sunny Saturday. The wind howled through the streets, whipping at her hair, but she hardly felt it. The bookbag hung heavy on her back, and she pulled at the shoulder straps for the millionth time as she made her way through the sliding glass doors.

She was better prepared this time, throwing on one of her nicer sweaters with some dark jeans and chunky heels. And she wore a smile as she walked through the swank lobby, heading straight for the elevator.

Before she knew it, she was in front of apartment 823, her heart thudding just as hard as the last time.

She raised a hand to knock, but hesitated. She had no idea if Leif was back yet. He hadn't contacted her, and she still wasn't sure if she should contact him, so they were at a bit of a stalemate. But she had nowhere else to go. Shallow Grave was too small a town for privacy.

Even if she could find a warm enough place to practice her magic—some abandoned building or shed, maybe—chances were someone would see her go in. She couldn't risk it.

So here she was, risking her neck in a whole different way.

She stood silent a moment longer, waiting to hear some sort of movement from inside. The soft ding of the elevator let her know that someone else was coming, so she grabbed the doorknob, the decision made for her, and said, "Díghlisál."

The faint click had no sooner sounded than she was inside, easing the door silently closed. She stilled her breath as footsteps tapped down the hall, but they stopped long before they reached this particular apartment. Kenzie let out a breath, sagging against the door.

She turned around, taking in the apartment. "Hello?" she called, holding still as she waited. If Leif was back, or he'd lost this place, she didn't know what she'd do next. But the apartment was exactly how she'd left it, the partially burned curtain unmoved. The only difference from last time was the fine layer of dust that graced everything.

"Yeah, definitely not back," she muttered.

A thread of worry worked through her. What was taking Leif so long? If she were being honest, she had kind of hoped he'd be here this time. He'd invaded her thoughts with his mysterious request and handsome face. She wanted to know more. And she wanted to talk to him about this magic stuff.

She was about filled to bursting with this little secret. Not being able to tell people she could do magic was one thing when she knew next to nothing about how to wield that power, but it was entirely different now that she had a grimoire full of spells and potions to unleash. Leif was the only person she knew that she didn't have to hide that from. And he was missing.

Kenzie sighed.

She pulled the bag off her back and unzipped it. The first thing she pulled out was a small blanket she'd packed for just this reason. It was easier than bringing a chair—and she was definitely *not* sitting on the one he owned, *or* the piano bench—and this old thing wouldn't be missed around her house if she left it.

Next, she pulled out the shirt she'd bought Leif and hung it up in the closet. The note she'd written, complete with his name on the front in the most artistic penmanship she could muster, went on the countertop where he could immediately see it. *If he's not distracted by the curtains.* The note just basically caught him up on what she'd been doing. And briefly explained the curtain. More or less.

Finally, she pulled out the grimoire, as well as a Ziploc bag filled with dirt and dried flowers. She opened the baggie, setting it up so it wouldn't spill its contents. The earthy aroma hit her first, followed by faint traces of rose.

The flowers were wild roses, given to her by a boy back before she became the town pariah. When she brought them home to show her mom, blushing and giddy, mom had instructed her to lay them flat in a book so she could keep them. Weeks went by, and the flowers were forgotten, until recently, when she was looking through her room for something to experiment on. A quick glance through the grimoire revealed a regeneration spell specific to plants. Apparently, someone in the book's history really loved plants, because there were several of those kinds of spells.

This particular spell wasn't the most intricate one she'd seen, but it *was* the most complicated spell she'd ever attempted on her own. And she didn't have Mom or Gram to make sure she stayed within the lines.

And the spell had particular importance. If it really could bring back a dead flower, maybe she could find something more powerful.

Something that could maybe bring a person back from the dead.

Kenzie flipped the grimoire open to the page she'd bookmarked, nervously reading through the spell again, even though she'd memorized it. She'd been practicing for days, writing it down (and then erasing everything so that her mom and Gram wouldn't find it), silently running through every syllable of every word. After her last fiasco, she was a little hesitant to pull the trigger. Still, she was reasonably sure she was ready.

And so she was here.

But first, her nerves needed a distraction.

She made her way to the black piano, swiping at the dust coating the keyboard cover. It fluttered through the air like magical motes. Kenzie sneezed. She opened the cover, just for a peek. The alabaster white keys stood in stark contrast to the smaller keys between, and to the body of the instrument. It kind of reminded her of Leif, his dark clothes and hair contrasting with his incredibly pale skin. Maybe this was his version of getting a dog—they said pet owners tended to pick pets that looked like them.

Kenzie's mouth pulled up into a half-smile. She let her fingers pluck out a few notes. She was a disaster with instruments, though she loved the idea of them. She'd even tried her hand at violin when she was younger, but gave up when her mom declared it sounded like she was strangling a goat. She gently closed the cover, wondering what she'd do with her time if she had an eternity to fill. Learning piano would probably be high on the list. Maybe that's why this was here. Was Leif learning, or was he experienced with the instrument? Just one more mystery surrounding the vampire.

Returning to the blanket, Kenzie took off her heels and sat down, crossing her legs.

Time to focus.

She took a deep breath, staring at the spell as she began to speak. "Leathra, kruthitheoirha, goraih maigh a   agaht."

The tips of her fingers grew warm, and she smiled. She retrieved the dried flowers out of the bag of soil, rubbing her fingers gently along the brittle petals. The spell called for a focus of nurturing, and she thought of kittens, their cute little furry faces making her want to spout baby talk. When she felt she'd done enough, she turned her gaze back to the book. This next part would take all her concentration.

"Guinle chashaidha guin, mo bhron antas druil."

A tingling feeling spread through her body, the energy crackling and snapping. Her heart beat faster, and her hair moved as if in a gentle breeze. The light in the apartment seemed to dim, despite it being daylight outside. But Kenzie refused to look around. She stared at the book, seeing the plant begin to sparkle, the color becoming vibrant, the stem and leaves plumping.

"Dághéin!" she shouted, roots sprouting from the cut end of the flowers. She planted the roots in the soil and finished the incantation. "Leathra, kruthitheoirha, goraih maigh agaht."

She closed her eyes for a moment, letting the magic drain and settle. When she dared open her eyes again, the apartment was once again brightly lit, and a smile broke out on her face.

The roses stood tall and strong, roots woven through the soil. A bit of a glow still kissed the petals, though even as Kenzie watched, it faded. It was perfect, probably even better than new. In the right container, it would put even the fanciest of floral arrangements to shame.

Kenzie stared in silence for a moment. When she couldn't contain it any longer, she got to her feet. She jumped off the blanket before it had the chance to slip from under her and ran to the bathroom.

"I did it!" she shouted as she stared at herself in the mirror. "I did iiiiiiit!"

She did a little dance, then screamed and grabbed her hair.

This. Was. It.

"I have magic. I have magic!" She felt her face and arms. "And I'm still alive."

She broke into laughter, then ran back into the apartment, heading for the chair—the only thing in the place that looked remotely lived in. "I have magic!" she yelled at the chair.

Suddenly weary, she made her way back to the blanket and collapsed on top.

The bag knocked over, and Kenzie scrambled to get it upright again, pushing the dirt back inside. She zipped up the sides a little to help hold things in place and pushed it off the blanket.

"I have magic," she whispered, laying down on the blanket, careful to keep clear of the dirt remnants.

She knew just who to give the roses to. Myreen. It would be her Christmas present, a hope for things to come.

Because if she could bring a plant back to life, there was a good chance there was magic to bring a person back to life.

Kenzie closed her eyes. *Just for a minute,* she thought, as her mind drifted to thoughts of the grimoire and all the endless possibilities it held.

Kenzie started when the edges of a dream gave her the sensation of plummeting through the floor. She pushed herself up, unwilling to succumb to sleep, but collapsed again. She took a moment and stared at the ceiling.

This can't be right.

She rolled onto her side and forced herself into a seated position, squinting at the writing around the spell she'd just done. There was some handwriting there, personal notes someone had left behind that were hard to make out. Super fancy cursive, it looked like. The page was torn in the middle, further obscuring one of the words.

"Uses *something* essence," she muttered. But what was the something? That blank had been bothering her for a while. She flipped the page, and saw a little of the torn area had been bent back. She tugged gently at the edges and found an L, an O or an E, with maybe an

I or a T or H between. Kenzie decided the middle one was an I and the end was an E, making it L-I-blank-E. "*Something* essence, *something* essence."

Dread ran her blood cold as she stared at it again, realizing what it was saying. The spell used *life essence* to revive the plant. It would explain her fatigue. How much time did she lose? Was the life essence something that regenerated, or was it something you could use up? And if it took some to revive a plant, how much more would it take to revive a human?

"Maybe there's a work-around." Kenzie flipped through the pages, but she could only get so far before it felt like they were sticking together. She'd encountered this before, but hadn't paid it much attention. But now, she needed more info, she needed to dig deeper. But the grimoire wasn't going to yield its secrets so easily. She had to be careful, trying to get past the wards. Selkie curses were notoriously horrible.

But despite the dangers, Kenzie found the thought of cracking this thing open exhilarating.

"I should call Leif." Screw waiting for him to contact her. She'd been patient enough. Besides, he'd said to let him know as soon as she'd discovered anything. This had to qualify.

"Claoigha," she said, before she had the chance to chicken out. The familiar ringing sensation prompted her to conjure thoughts of Leif. She smiled as she thought about how he'd react.

"Leif, it's Kenzie," she said as she felt the connection take. "Selkie girl?"

"Kenzie?" Leif swore under his breath, though the words still carried through the connection clearly. "Where are you?"

"Oh. Um, at your apartment?" Maybe this was a really bad idea.

"Fine. Stay right there."

"Okay." She closed the connection, then panicked. How long did he mean for her to stay? Was he coming there? And during the day?

"Crap, the curtain!" If he was upset that she was *in* his apartment, then he'd be pissed to find that she'd ruined one of the few things he owned. She'd meant to try to fix that, anyway, but had forgotten amid the excitement of the roses.

"Come on, come on, come on!" she muttered as she flipped through the pages of the grimoire. "Ah!" The spell for mending cloth came into view, and she put her finger on the spot to help guide her through the incantation. She ran through the word once in her head, just to make sure she had it right.

"Sewansuás." The hole in the curtain came together, but the sides weren't even, so it puckered. "No! Not like that."

She scanned over the page again, and found the one for patching holes, hoping it would fix it rather than making it worse. "Séadach mende— ack!" The door opened before she could finish the spell, and her lack of concentration sent the fabric to puckering further, the spot turning a bright green color that started bleeding up the curtain like a vat of dye.

Kenzie stepped in front of the curtain, her face burning as she faced Leif. "You got here quick."

Leif raised a brow. "Vampires are known for their speed."

"Right." *And for being incredibly attractive.* He was even more handsome than she remembered from their encounter in the alleyway. And thankfully, he didn't look thirsty. Kenzie shuddered, trying to block out the memory of the blood bags sitting in the fridge.

"You shouldn't be here," Leif said, grabbing the note from the counter.

"Sorry. I just, I don't really have anywhere to practice at home. I thought—"

Leif put the note back down, unopened. *Not even a peek?* "That's fine, I meant you shouldn't be in Chicago. There are vampires."

Kenzie put her hands on her hips. "You think? There's one standing in front of me right now."

Leif barely batted an eye. "Can you get back home before dark?"

"Of course! Don't you want to know why I called you?" Kenzie's threw her hands in the air, letting them flop back down to her sides.

"Yes, but quickly, though. I don't want anyone to know about... any of this." Leif went to the fridge, and Kenzie put a hand over her mouth, hoping, praying he wasn't about to open it.

"Ooookay. See the roses?" Kenzie said, her voice muffled by her fingers.

Leif turned, brows furrowing as his gaze rested on her. "Yes. Your point?"

"They were dried." Kenzie gagged when Leif opened the fridge, nonchalantly moving the bags into the freezer compartment. "For the love of cheese, finish up already!"

Leif wore a smirk as he closed the doors. "Squeamish, are we?"

Kenzie gagged again, then nodded. *Think about something else. Think about something else.*

"So about these dried flowers." Leif walked to where the bag sat on the ground, dropping into a squat that looked worthy of a magazine cover.

Kenzie managed a half-smile. She had his attention now. And he definitely had hers. *That's right. Think of the beautiful man in front of you and not the stuff he drinks.* Kenzie almost gagged again, but managed to hold it together this time. Working with a vampire was *not* going to be easy.

Leif examined the flowers with a delicate touch. It was strange how he was both coarse and soft in the same breath.

"Can the same spell apply to a person?" Leif asked, really looking at Kenzie for what felt like the first time since he entered the apartment.

"No." As Leif's face fell, Kenzie pointed at the roses and added, "But if I can find a spell to do that, it's not impossible that there might be something to do what you're asking."

"Good. Go home and keep looking." Leif stood and headed for the door, and Kenzie's heart dropped. This wasn't the big congratulations she'd hoped for. And certainly not the conversation about magic she'd been dying to have.

"Wait!" she called, hoping for just a little more time with him. "Do you have any more information about the selkie who owned this book?"

Leif stilled at the door, his hand on the knob. "Why?"

"Because of the locking spells. I can't get to the really good stuff unless I know how to unlock it. What were they like? What did they do? Something that would help me figure out what they used in their spells. Maybe that trinket you have of hers?"

Leif sighed, his free hand going to his pocket. "Give me some time to work on it."

"And now's a bad time because?" Kenzie probed, pushing her luck as far as she could.

"I'll tell you that if you tell me what happened to the curtain."

Kenzie stood there, mouth open but unsure what to say.

And then Leif left.

"Well, fine then," Kenzie said to the door.

She pouted as she packed up her stuff, even taking the blanket with her, though she happily shook the dirt onto the floor. But she was careful with the roses. Hopefully she didn't kill them before Christmas. If she did, though, she knew she could revive them again, and mostly-dead roses couldn't require nearly as much life essence as long-dead roses. Right?

Myreen

Myreen stood in front of the mirror, turning this way and that. She wore a blue knit sweater that brought out her eyes, and skinny jeans with knee-high boots. She left her hair down, but kept pushing it behind her ears.

"Are you sure this looks okay?" she asked Juliet, who was laying on her bed flipping through a magazine while Myreen put on her finishing touches. Juliet already looked like a rock star in her off-the-shoulder white sweater dress and mint green leggings. Her legs were swinging to the beat coming out of the headphones draped around her neck.

Juliet smiled at Myreen. "You look great! Kol's gonna die when he sees you."

Myreen's shoulders slumped. "We're just going as friends. I don't want to look like I'm trying too hard." Even *she* knew that was a lie.

They were so far from being just friends.

Kol's impromptu announcement over the PA system had caused quite a stir around campus. The mer bullies had stopped pestering her, although that probably had more to do with Delphine's enraged lecture at the entire mer wing than fear of upsetting the dragon royal family. But the look of reverence that replaced the smug suspicion on the faces of all the other students was directly out of respect for the Dracul protection that had been placed on her. Kol had gotten into a lot of trouble for that stunt, as well as Nik and Brett. A gesture like that was not something one would do for just a friend. She wanted to show him how truly touched she was by what he'd done.

She went back to the closet and started looking through. There was no way she was braving a dress like Juliet. The Chicago days were getting colder and shorter, and the city of wind really lived up to its nickname. But nothing in the closet was jumping out at her.

Juliet smirked and shook her head. "Right. Friends. Well, *friends* or not, you can still knock his big ol' socks off."

Myreen sighed and went back to the mirror to look herself over once more. This would have to do. They were meeting the boys at noon, and it was already nearly a quarter to.

"I still can't believe he went on the intercom for you," Juliet said, and Myreen could hear the smirk in her voice. "That was super romantic, I gotta say."

Myreen blushed and continued to ignore Juliet's insinuations. As much as Myreen wanted to dwell on that notion, there were other things weighing on her mind.

The thought of going outside the Dome made her a little nervous after what happened to Alessandra. She still hadn't had a chance to visit the mermaid laid up in the nurse's office. Despite Delphine's intervention, Myreen was still wary of purposefully going anywhere the mer were if she didn't have to, and she was afraid Trish and Joanna would be standing guard over their fallen friend. Delphine had insisted that Myreen come back to her room in the mer wing, but Myreen had asked if she could remain with Juliet—at least until Alessandra got better. Delphine had agreed, but she wasn't happy about it.

"I think I'm going to swing by the nurse's station to see how Alessandra's doing," Myreen decided on the spot.

Juliet's face scrunched up. "Really?"

"Yeah. Things have died down a little. I just— I feel like I should visit her." Myreen still couldn't shake the feeling that it should've been her lying in that bed. But maybe the harpy nurse had been able to make some progress with her healing. It would help to get some answers.

"Want me to come with you?" Juliet asked, tossing the magazine aside and sitting up.

Myreen shook her head. "Nah. I'll be fine. It'll just be a quick visit before we meet the guys."

"Okay. But you better be in the common room at noon." Juliet gave Myreen a firm stare, then melted into smiles. "I need my wingman. Or girl. Or should it be fin-girl, since you're a mermaid?"

Myreen laughed. "Let me know what you come up with."

Juliet saluted as Myreen slipped out the door.

The halls were abuzz with students enjoying their day off. A few guys emerging from the were prime complained loudly about having cabin fever. The new curfew meant there was little daylight left once classes were over, so there was no sense going out on weekdays. Myreen didn't see what the big problem was, but she didn't have to shift every full moon, either.

She stopped just outside the nurse's office, hesitant to go in. Trish and her gang had been merciless last time, and if they were in there, she'd have to leave without seeing Alessandra—again.

But it was quiet. Myreen entered, wondering if maybe Alessandra had miraculously recovered, but she was still there, her eyes closed, looking pale. The bandages around her neck were the worst, though, as they reminded Myreen of her own mom, seeing her with those two small holes in her neck, her eyes vacant. It was almost enough to make her turn and leave.

"Myreen!" Alessandra said, her head thrashing back and forth, and Myreen's eyes widened.

Ms. Heather dashed past Myreen in a blur of blonde frizz. She put her hands on either side of Alessandra's head and spoke in a soothing tone.

"I'm sorry," Myreen said, turning to leave.

Ms. Heather spoke over her shoulder. "No need to be sorry. It's gotten less frequent, though I think she still dreams about what happened. Might do her some good to hear your voice."

Myreen took a deep breath and approached the bed as Ms. Heather stepped away. It took a few moments for words to come to Myreen, as she stared at Alessandra, looking so small and frail in that bed.

Myreen dug the toe of her boot on the tile, feeling weird and out of place. "I'm sorry. I hate that this happened to you."

Alessandra moaned, but she didn't start thrashing again. Myreen took that as a good sign.

"I know we've had our differences, but I hope you get better soon. I almost miss your, um—" She glanced at Ms. Heather, who had her glasses low on her nose as she looked over some paperwork.

"—your motivational speeches."

Alessandra moaned again, her fingers curling into the sheets. She began to whisper, and it took a moment for Myreen to catch what she was saying. "Looking for you. Looking for you. Looking for you."

Chills ran up Myreen's back. She looked to Ms. Heather for her reaction, but the nurse didn't seem to notice. Maybe it wasn't that unusual.

Myreen glanced at the clock. She had five minutes to get back, and for a moment, she almost didn't want to go. But Juliet's hopeful face popped into her mind. And it was her decision, not Kol's, to set up this double date in the first place.

"Alright. Well, I have to go. Get better soon." Myreen nodded at Alessandra as she turned to leave.

"Take care, dear." Ms. Heather's gaze flicked to Myreen for a moment, and she smiled before turning her attention back to her paperwork.

Myreen moved swiftly through the halls as she headed for the avian common room. Her heart was racing, and even though she wasn't really alone, she couldn't wait to get back to her friends, where she felt the safest.

Nik, Kol, and Juliet were all in the common room by the time Myreen arrived. She was a little out of breath, and Juliet raised a brow.

"Are you okay?" Juliet asked, handing Myreen her coat.

"Yeah. Sorry, I just lost track of time and had to sprint back here." She gave everyone a nervous smile, willing her breathing to slow. She wanted to get the subject off her. "How was detention with Ren?"

As punishment for Kol and his friend hacking the PA system, Oberon had sentenced them to weekend detentions with Ren Suzuki, the math teacher and school engineer. He seemed like a funny guy in Algebra, so she imagined that detention with him couldn't be too bad.

Kol gave her a small grin. "It was fine." He shrugged.

"No it wasn't," Brett called from the couch. "It was torture! He made us scrub tiny nuts, bolts and tubes, *then* he made us put them together! My fingers hurt so bad I don't think I'll be able to play all weekend. How the heck am I supposed to entertain myself with you four shacking up?"

The four of them smiled, and collectively deciding to ignore Brett's whining.

"So, what's the plan?" Myreen asked.

"I was just saying we should go see a movie before we go to Mack's Diner," Nik said, bobbing his head at Myreen.

"Do we have time for a movie?"

Nik grinned. "Of course! I've got it all mapped out. There's a sub entrance right by Mack's that'll get us back here quick."

Myreen nodded, but the butterflies just wouldn't leave. Although at the moment, she couldn't tell if they were from the idea of being out too late, or the way Kol's chest looked in that black sweater.

"We can't decide," Juliet said, taking Nik's hand. "Should we see Always for You or Into the Dawn?"

Myreen bit her lip as she took a moment to think about it, but Juliet's weight had definitely been on the first option. She thought she remembered seeing something about that movie. She was ninety-nine percent sure it was a romantic comedy, which both intrigued her and made her grimace. She wasn't sure that was really friend-date material. But it wasn't her and Kol's date, it was Juliet and Nik's. Myreen and Kol were just along for the ride.

"I've heard Always for You is a good one," Myreen said at last, and Juliet pumped her fist.

Myreen flashed an apologetic grimace at Kol, who nodded once. It looked like he was okay with that. Or at least as okay as a guy watching a rom-com on a friend-date could be.

They made their way to the exit, but when they got near, they found a line of students waiting to get out.

"What's going on?" Kol asked.

A guy in front of them turned around. "Extra security. You guys have your smart clothes on, right?"

Everyone nodded, except Juliet, who paled. She shrugged. "What? It's not like I can shift."

"They don't just keep you covered, you know," Kol said, his tone matter-of-fact.

Juliet groaned. "Fine. I'll be right back."

"Hurry!" Nik called after her, smiling as he watched her run down the hall.

Myreen crossed her arms, directing her attention to Nik. "I guess this is the moment I'm supposed to tell you that you'd better not hurt my friend."

Kol raised a brow. "I think Juliet's the more dangerous of the two of them."

"Hey, she's doing great with her fire... stuff." Myreen wasn't sure what the official term was.

"She's only dangerous if you get her fired up." Nik's grin was far too wide, and both Myreen and Kol groaned. "But she's in good hands. Gentleman's honor." He held up his hand, an earnest look on his face.

Myreen smiled.

The trio shuffled forward with the slow-moving line, and soon Nik began tapping his foot, casting backwards glances.

A few more students piled behind them before the sound of shoes pounding on tiles announced Juliet's arrival. She skidded to a stop, taking deep breaths.

"Just in time," Nik said, draping his arm around Juliet's shoulders.

Her already red face flushed brighter, and she beamed at Myreen. "Sorry. That thing's not easy to get into when you're in a rush."

Their group was next, and as they stepped forward, Mr. Quinn crossed his bulging biceps. Nik removed his arm from Juliet's neck, giving Mr. Quinn a curt nod and a smile. Juliet clenched her jaw, a warning in her eyes as she tried to stare down her father.

"Going out, are we?" Mr. Quinn asked.

"Yeah," Nik said, standing a little straighter. "Movies and dinner."

Mr. Quinn's hard gaze stayed on Nik a little longer than the rest. "You all have your smart clothes on?"

Everyone nodded.

Mr. Quinn sighed. "Make sure you're back before sunset."

"Yes, sir," they all mumbled.

Mr. Quinn softened a little as he turned his attention to Juliet. "Be careful out there, okay? Stay together. Be smart. There are monsters lurking everywhere."

They all nodded again, but Myreen's heart rate spiked as they were waved through. *We'll be back before sunset,* she reminded herself. But she couldn't quite shake the ominous feeling hanging over her.

They piled into the train with the other students. The car was crowded, and Myreen realized this was the busiest she'd ever seen it. The doors hissed closed, making the many conversations even louder.

Myreen and Kol grabbed one pole, while Juliet and Nik held onto another one, the seats all being taken.

Myreen could feel Kol behind her, his breath warming her hair. She almost wanted to lean into him and have him wrap his arms around her. *We're just friends,* Myreen reminded herself.

She looked over at Juliet and Nik, who were doing just that. They looked cozy and happy, wrapped up in their own private world. Myreen was happy for Juliet, though she felt a pang of jealousy. She and Kol just didn't work as a couple. That much was perfectly obvious after their last date. Sure, he looked like he was chiseled straight from one of her fantasies, but it had to be about more than that.

But even that wasn't quite enough to distract her from the ticking clock she had going on in her head.

She watched the water slide by as the car sped toward the secret platform. *The place they found Alessandra.* Myreen shook her head, trying to dislodge the image filling it. Alessandra almost looked like she was just sleeping in the nurse's office, moments ago, but that didn't keep her mind from creating the blood and bruises she was sure Alessandra had come in with, as bad as she'd been beaten. To distract herself, she began counting the hours it would take to do everything Nik was planning. It didn't help that the extra time it took to get out of the Dome had pushed their plans back even further.

Myreen couldn't shake the feeling that going out was a bad idea, Mr. Quinn's admonition echoing in her head. *I'm just nervous about the date*, she told herself, though even she wasn't convinced. But there was no sense getting worked up about monsters, when they only came out after dark.

And they'd be back well before dark.

CHAPTER 53

Juliet

As if Juliet wasn't already overwhelmed, throwing embarrassment on top of that was almost disastrous. She intentionally didn't put on her smart clothing. She wasn't even close to shifting yet, so she was sure there was no need for it.

But she didn't want to be the reason that they couldn't leave.

Pulling her tights off then on again almost made her frustrated enough to call the date off. But she quickly remembered how handsome Nik looked, and it brought warmth to her cheeks and fire to her determination.

And Juliet made it back to the group in record time.

The look on Nik's face when he saw her again made her forget about the three times she'd tripped, trying to make it back so fast. She wasn't familiar with dating, but the way he looked at her made her feel like he was her future.

And then there was her dad. Juliet put all her focus into the death stare that she tried to give him. And in her mind, it worked, though she was sure she would hear him complain about something when she returned.

Malachai warned her about *monsters* that were out there, and if it were any other time, she would have happily ran back to her room to hide from them. But she was too giddy with excitement over her date with this *dragon* to care. Besides, she felt safe enough with Nik and Kol around.

It wasn't until the guys had bought the tickets that Juliet realized how much of a chick flick the movie was. While Nik looked like he could care less, Kol looked like he was walking into a funeral.

Rom-com movies were Juliet's favorite kind. Probably because she thought she would never be lucky enough to experience it for herself. But now, as she sat next to her date, she thought she might actually get a chance at a storybook romance.

Sandwiched between Myreen and Nik, Juliet couldn't be happier. She shoveled the messy, buttery popcorn into her mouth as she laughed along with the movie. She was so into it that she didn't realize how much popcorn she actually went through. Embarrassed, she wanted to hide it from Nik. Juliet tried to subtly place the nearly-empty bucket of popcorn on the floor by her feet.

But Myreen took it. She placed it on her lap and reached her hand in, her entire forearm disappearing into the box. Myreen tried to hide her smile as she shook her head.

Juliet cleaned her hands off and chugged her drink until she heard a slurp. She thought for sure that she was failing as a date.

But as she leaned back in her seat, Nik moved closer and closer until their shoulders touched. She felt fidgety. She liked his closeness, but she couldn't bring herself to sit still.

She moved her hand to rest on her knees to try to stop them from bouncing. But it wasn't her hand that stopped them. It was Nik's. He tried to be delicate, but his hand was heavy and slightly clammy. It made Juliet smile.

But she was still anxious—anxious enough to make her fire emerge. She tried to stop it from happening, but it was already too late. She felt it in her stomach first, like a swarm of butterflies dying to escape. Then it flowed into her arms and straight to her hands. Nik pulled his hand away from the burn and shook it. Juliet looked at him with wide eyes.

But Nik slowly and gently placed his hand over hers again.

After the initial shock, all her worries went away. He kept his hand on hers for the rest of the movie, which made her feel like she was floating on clouds. She was so caught up in his warmth that she almost didn't notice when everyone stood up to leave. While the credits rolled, they followed the line of moviegoers to the exit.

"I'm shocked to say this, but think I actually enjoyed it." Kol sipped on his drink as they walked out of the theater, free-throwing the empty cup into a trash bin.

Everyone agreed. It was still light outside, but Myreen and Juliet couldn't take their eyes off the bright and colorful string of lights that hung in every store window.

Flashing lights snaked up light poles and met in the middle of the street where the word JOY sparkled its red and green spirit. Juliet knew it would be brighter, and therefore more magical, when it was dark. But just because the new curfew prevented her from enjoying that, didn't mean she couldn't cherish this festive moment.

"I love Christmas." The words slipped out of Juliet's mouth as she spun in a circle.

Nik caught her hand and twirled her back in his direction, right into a hug. They were so close that she felt his rugged breathing underneath his chest. If it weren't for Kol clearing his throat, she would have stayed there the entire night. Kol and Myreen walked ahead toward the diner, making sure to keep a comfortable distance from one another, while Nik stayed back, with Juliet. He tangled his fingers with hers, and her breath hitched.

"So, is Christmas your favorite holiday?" he asked as he looked down at their intertwined hands.

"No, but I love the meaning behind it. My mom didn't exactly celebrate it, so the movie marathons that they play on TV were all I had. I'm looking forward to this year, though. There are a lot of new people in my life and shopping for them is… different. But good different." Nik chuckled, and Juliet realized she was rambling. "Sorry. Guess I'm excited."

"No, don't be sorry. I like you this way. It's nice to see you like this… with your guard down." He looked worried, like he might have offended her, but she understood what he was saying.

"I have to be guarded. I'm small and I'm not exactly the phoenix everyone expected. You know, being a *Quinn* and all." But she didn't want to turn this night into a pity party. "Actually, Halloween is my favorite holiday. You get to dress up as anything you want. And you get *candy*! Plus, scary movies are the best. What about you? What's your favorite holiday?" She couldn't believe how easy it was to tell Nik about her life, things she'd kept to herself until Myreen came along.

"That's a tough one. I'd have to say New Year's. There's so much hope and courage in people when they're ending one year and start an entirely new one. Their ambition, their goals and resolutions. It's just… inspiring."

Juliet thought her knees were going to buckle right out from under her. If he wasn't holding her hand, she probably would have fallen. She just adored this sweet side of him.

"I can see why it's your favorite." They started moving toward the diner again, keeping a slow pace. Juliet knew their hands would have to separate at some point, but they were clicking so well.

"I'm really glad you agreed to come on this date with me." He kept his eyes on the ground, but held on tightly to her hand.

"I know exactly what you mean." Juliet couldn't hide her smile, even if she wanted to. There was nothing that could ruin her mood.

They stepped into the retro-styled diner, filled with red seats on white-and-black checkerboard floors. A juke box lit up the room with its inviting selection of music and bright colors. The restaurant must have switched out their records for holiday tunes, because a catchy song about a red-nosed reindeer filled the air. Juliet bounced and sang along as the waitress brought them to their booth. The guys took their seats across from the girls. Juliet liked that it gave her a better view of her date.

"This place is awesome! I'd like to come here when they have their regular records in there. I can only imagine what classics they'd have."

Nik smiled. "I've always wondered what you have playing in those headphones."

Juliet's smile grew as she caught on to the fact that he'd been curious about her. "Depends on my mood. I have a playlist for everything. Even one I made for the day that I test out of defense. But I enjoy doo-wop most. I just love that era."

"Wow. That's impressive, and not at all what I expected. Glad this is the place I brought you to, then."

Juliet was so lost in Nik's dimples that she hadn't realized how silent Kol and Myreen were. And now that Juliet assessed her friend, she could tell that something wasn't right. She didn't want to push. They could talk about it later. And this night was important to Juliet, which Myreen seemed to understand. If not, she probably wouldn't be on another date with Kol. And for that, Juliet would always be grateful.

But deep down, she wanted the two of them to hit it off. And not even for her own selfish reasons of dating best friends. She thought they were good for each other, that perhaps she could tone down his rough exterior, and he could be a light to her darkness.

It was better than her and *Kendall* being together. He rubbed Juliet the wrong way half of the time, which she blamed it on his mer DNA. Although maybe she couldn't say that about mers anymore, because Myreen was far from their usual, stuck-up nature.

Juliet cast another worried glance at Myreen. She looked a little jittery. Juliet didn't want to take her eyes off Nik, but she couldn't just ignore Myreen's discomfort.

"Order us a couple of milkshakes. We'll be right back." With a subtle nod of her head, Juliet gently pulled Myreen out of the booth. They walked into the bathroom and stood by the floor-to-ceiling mirror.

"What aren't you telling me?" Juliet didn't want to sound stern, but she didn't like to see Myreen so on edge.

Myreen looked at the floor. "Nothing. It's just… It's weird. I thought I could handle it—being out on a friends date with Kol—but it's just confusing me. The movie was easy because there was no room for conversation. But now… it's just weird." Myreen looked less stressed, but Juliet could tell there was something else.

Juliet pulled on one of her curls. "It was unfair for me to ask you to come with us. I just needed your help. I didn't think I could get through this alone."

Myreen half-smiled. "Trust me, you're doing just fine. Nik is into you, girl. You didn't need me at all." Myreen nudged Juliet, who blushed.

She shook her shoulders and took a deep breath. "Okay. Well, thanks. But don't think I don't know you're still keeping a secret. I want you to remember that I'm here for you, whenever and however you need me. Whenever you're ready, I'll be here to listen." Juliet squeezed Myreen in a side hug.

When they got back to their table, the milkshakes were waiting there for them, along with a large plate of chili cheese fries.

"You've got to try these," Kol said as he grabbed a fry from the goopy mess. "They're the best."

Nik nodded, his eyes searching Juliet's. She shrugged as she sat down, Myreen already helping herself to a fry.

"Oh my gosh," Myreen said around her bite, holding her hand in front her mouth. "These really are good."

Juliet made sure to engage Myreen and Kol in conversation after that, so it wasn't as awkward for them. It helped, but they both still looked ready to head back to the Dome. And as much as Juliet didn't want the date to be over, she knew her dad would be pacing the floor awaiting their arrival. Her eyes met Nik's as she took a sip of her milkshake, his dimples making an encore appearance.

This curfew sucks.

Myreen

As they waited for the check to arrive, Myreen's legs bounced under the table. She was eager to get back to the Dome—and not just because of the new curfew.

Even after their disastrous real date weeks ago, Myreen wanted to give their friendship a try, dating clearly not being in the cards for them. But for whatever reason, she was drawn to Kol. And keeping things platonic was a bit difficult when his black t-shirt hugged his perfectly-muscled physique so nicely.

And when Juliet and Nik were radiating sexual tension like a contagious disease.

If Myreen didn't create some distance between Kol and herself soon, she would fall right back into the *I-like-him* pit, and who knew how long it would take her to get out again? If she ever did.

Finally, the check arrived and the guys stuffed bills into the booklet, freeing up the four of them to leave.

When they stepped out onto the sidewalk, the sun's sherbet orange glow barely clung to the edges of the scattered clouds above.

"We'd better get moving," Kol said, looking up. "It's almost curfew. We don't want need anyone getting into any more trouble."

They all hustled to the nearest subway station so they could hop trains to the secret platform.

"Closed for maintenance?" Juliet complained as they stopped in front of the closed-off entrance.

"Ugh, we don't have time for this," Kol grumbled.

"Too bad it's not darker out, or the three of you could just fly back." Myreen smirked at Kol, hoping the reference to one of their earlier arguments would make him laugh.

The comment seemed to catch him off guard, and she was momentarily afraid he was going to get upset. But then a small smile spread across his chiseled lips, and for a brief and wonderful moment, they were on the same wavelength.

"Or we could all just jump into Lake Michigan and you could swim us back," he quipped, making her grin even wider.

"Yeah, I'd prefer not to do either of those things?" Nik interjected with a note of confusion in his voice.

Kol chuckled. "Alright, we'll just have to call an Uber and have them take us right to the platform."

"On it." Nik pulled out his phone and started tapping.

In less than five minutes, a blue sedan pulled up and they all got in. It looked like they were going to make it, and with time to spare. There was no official time to which they had to be back, but she figured as long as there was *some* light in the sky, they were safe. Although, she wished they weren't cutting it so close.

After idling in the same place for several minutes on the Clark Street Bridge, it was clear that something wrong.

"Any idea what's going on up there?" Juliet leaned forward in the back seat to get closer to the driver, who looked like he moonlighted as a café barista.

"How should I know?" he replied, seeming more irritated by the traffic than they were. "Probably an accident. Stupid drivers."

Myreen sighed. "We're so close to the station. This could *not* be worse timing."

Kol looked out the window at the darkening sky. Then he looked at them. "We'll just have to get out and run on foot. It's only a few blocks. If we take some of the backstreets, I'm sure we can make it at least inside the platform before curfew, which'll hopefully be good enough."

They scrambled out of the backseat and filed through the motionless vehicles to the walkway on the outer edge, where they made a run for it.

The farther they ran, the darker it got. The street lights turned on, competing with the already-glaring Christmas string lights on every storefront. It soon became clear that they weren't going to make it anywhere by sundown.

Urgency and dread filled Myreen's stomach, pushing her even faster. She didn't need any more heat coming down on her right now. She didn't know what Oberon would do to her for breaking curfew. He might place her on house arrest—or go the other direction and kick her out. Of course, she knew that was ridiculous, but the thought of leaving the only place she could call home flushed hot panic through her veins, causing her feet to stumble.

Luckily, Kol was right next to her, and with quick reflexes, he caught her upper arm before she could fall. As they ran, though, he didn't let go. He moved his hand to her forearm, his way of tugging her after him as he pushed ahead. He was running like his life depended on it, and Myreen realized he was doing it for her. That realization warmed her chest, easing her fret ever so slightly.

As they rounded a corner to cut through an alley, Kol slowed his pace. His tightened grip set off alarms in Myreen's head.

"What's wrong?" she asked.

"Look at the ground," he said.

She looked down at the cracked pavement of the alley on which they ran, but she didn't see anything amiss. She turned back to him and shook her head in a silent question.

"There's a street light right at the start of the alley," Kol said. "And we aren't casting any shadows."

Myreen looked briefly over her shoulder at the yellow light hanging on the corner, then back to the alley in front of them. Kol was right: none of them had a shadow.

Myreen frowned. "Huh, that's weird."

"No," Nik said, his voice grim. "It's vampires."

Vampires? What do shadows have to do with vampires?

Behind them, the sound of smashing glass pierced the air, and the whole alley fell into darkness.

"Very astute, my boy," a voice said, sounding as though it was coming from the darkness itself.

The four of them stopped running and instinctively pulled tightly together, angling their backs toward each other.

"Someone give him a gold star," the same voice said, and a figure emerged from the darkness at the other end of the alley.

His skin was pale white and smooth as marble, heavily contrasted by his tailored black suit, manicured black hair, and short goatee. His ice-blue eyes locked onto Myreen's, ensnaring her. It almost made her blind to the handful of other pale, inhumanly gorgeous creatures that slowly appeared behind him as the darkness seemed to roll back like fog.

Myreen knew without question that the man, who stared at her like a lion at his prey, and the pretty people that now surrounded them were vampires. She knew they existed. She knew that they killed her mom, and attacked Alessandra, and had taken millions of lives throughout history. But having a distant concept of them and actually seeing them standing a few feet in front of her? That was two very different things.

She was terrified.

But not for herself. Kol and Juliet were two of the only people she had in the whole world, and the thought of losing them to vampires, like she'd lost her mom, was soul-wrenching. She kept trying to put herself in front of them, but Kol's large hands and feet kept pushing her back.

"Hello, Myreen," the black-haired vampire said, taking a step toward them. He was clearly the leader. "At last we meet."

What does he mean? How does he know my name? "Who are you?" was all she was able to say.

He smiled, looking horrifyingly beautiful. "I am Draven, the ultimate Denholm Heir and Vampire Unifier. I have been looking for you for a very, very long time, my lost little mermaid."

Draven? Myreen knew that name. He was the most feared vampire in the shifter world. But why had he been looking for her?

Kol pushed ahead of Myreen, edging her behind him. "What do you want with her?"

Draven turned his icy gaze to Kol, scanning him up and down. "Stance of royalty, air of self-righteousness, stench of smoke. You must be the latest Dracul progeny. You look just like your father."

"Answer the question," Kol demanded.

Draven laughed, and his vampire subjects encircling them chorused in laughter as well. "You don't get to order me around, boy. I give the orders." His lips curled wickedly. "Fetch her," he said, tipping his head toward Myreen.

Panic flared in her chest as one of the male vampires behind Draven dove toward them in a blur of speed.

481

"No!" Kol shouted, then hurled a ball of fire at their attacker.

The vampire dodged the fireball and tackled Kol, Myreen only just getting out of their way. The vampire thrust Kol up against the brick wall of the strip mall that lined the alley. Kol bared his teeth and began to change. Ash gray scales popped up on his arms and traveled the length of his neck as his body expanded, stretching his t-shirt and jeans until they ripped. His hands turned into claws, and wings sprouted from his back and spread, pushing him away from the wall. The vampire now looked like a small child up against Kol's dragon form.

The transformation ignited a free-for-all. Draven's other vampires closed in on them, eyes aimed at Myreen. Nik shifted into his dark-red-scaled dragon form, and he and Kol clawed and bit and spit fire at the vampires, fighting off three or more at a time. Juliet put those martial arts moves she'd been honing in gym class into action, fighting off any vampire that managed to get through Kol and Nik.

And all Myreen could do was squirm and flinch, standing there with frightened, doe eyes, and arms hugged against herself. She'd never felt more useless in her life. Her friends were fighting for their lives, and she couldn't do anything to help them. Why hadn't she tried harder in Defense class? Why hadn't she trained as hard as she could?

A female vampire flipped over Kol and Nik like an acrobat, landing right in front of Myreen. She grabbed Myreen's arm and, flaring her brows, said, "Gotcha!"

"Oh, no, you don't!" Juliet yelled, and a blast of fire flashed on the vampire's back.

The vampire shrieked and spun on Juliet, wrapping her in an embrace from behind and sinking her teeth into Juliet's neck faster than Juliet could retaliate. Juliet screamed.

A flip inside Myreen switched. She was not going to let anyone hurt her friend!

Myreen hurled herself at the vampire woman, wrenching those

stony arms away from Juliet with a strength Myreen didn't even know she had. The vampire was so surprised by Myreen's ability to bend her arms like they were noodles that she retracted her fangs from Juliet's neck, and gasped.

"Leave my friend alone." The command that left Myreen's mouth was not in her normal voice. The sound was deep and resonating, almost song-like.

To her amazement, the vampire froze, a sort of fog glazing over her eyes. Juliet didn't miss her opportunity, wriggling out of the vampire's clutches.

"Well, now isn't this a pleasant surprise?" Draven said, standing in the same spot as before, watching all this with amusement, like a spectator at a sporting event. "I never dreamed you'd be a siren, too. You are proving to be well worth the wait."

"A siren?" she and Juliet parroted.

Dragon-Kol roared in pain, and the vampire that had slashed at his abdomen zoomed at Myreen and swooped his arm around her waist. White hot fear shot through her, and all the strength she'd had a second ago vanished. Her captor leapt to the wall, quickly climbing upward.

"Juliet!" Myreen yelled, stretching her hand toward her friend. Juliet jumped, but their fingertips barely grazed.

Myreen was being taken too far, too fast.

No matter how hard she hit the vampire or struggled against his grip, she couldn't escape. And even if she could get out, she worried about plummeting to the alley floor. She was trapped.

It was over.

They had her.

Juliet

Ever since Juliet learned she was a phoenix, her first instinct was to try and bury the power she felt. But now, as she watched the vampire take Myreen, she knew she needed to do the exact opposite.

She focused on her fury and the fear of losing Myreen, and embraced the simmering heat within. Blazing balls the size of marbles escaped her fingertips, shooting like a machine gun. It shocked her so much that she almost lost control of the direction they were going. So she put all her focus into aiming them, before she knocked out a window or something.

Targeting the vampire engaged in a fight with Nik, the balls entered the vampire's body. He fell to the floor, frantically rolling on the ground as the pain burned him from the inside out. Nik's eyes grew as he stared at the damage that Juliet had just done.

Three more vampires appeared, blocking her path to Myreen. But Juliet was on a vicious rampage—one she wasn't about to quench. She stopped in her tracks and closed her eyes, drawing confused looks from the vampires. Combining her hands, she willed her fire power to her fingers, focusing on creating a rope of thin lava.

It happened quickly. Juliet swung her hand over her head, and used the lava strand like a whip. She lassoed it around the ankle of the far vampire. The others tried to jump out of the way, but it was too late. With one slick wave of her hand, Juliet caused the lava rope to flare into a wall of fire, torching all three vampires to a crisp.

But there wasn't time to relish her small victory.

Juliet caught sight of Myreen being dragged over the edge of the roof. It sent grief through her entire body. An ice cold chill started from her head and seeped down to her feet. She felt her heart beat slower and slower—so slow that she thought it would fail her.

Was it the pain of losing Myreen, or did she just give up on the idea of getting her back? Every cell in Juliet's body seemed intent on shutting down, and she fell to the ground. Her heart thrummed its last beat, nothing but searing and burning pain lingering in her chest. She thought she'd be stuck in the blackness of her own comatose mind forever.

But before the darkness consumed her, a spark, like a firework, exploded in her brain.

What had felt like hours was only seconds, the fight still raging around her, Myreen's foot just disappearing.

Juliet rose to what seemed like a dream, dark ash appearing at her feet. Her vision was enhanced, focused and tunnel-like. Every fiber of her flickered like the wick of a candle, succumbing to the heat that enveloped her soul.

And as she tried to stand, she couldn't move her feet, because her feet were no longer there.

She stared in awe as she tried to balance on rose-colored talons, which radiated a pearly sheen.

She flailed her arms, but quickly realized they were gone as well. In their place were large, red and orange wings that draped behind her like a veil. She sucked in a breath as she got lost in her golden-yellow feathers, which sparkled in the shimmering firelight that consumed them.

She flapped her wings, a clumsy and disoriented flail. She moved her head from left to right, hypnotized by the waves of fire encasing her body. But it was the smoke trailing from her that calmed her enough to steady her new wings.

She didn't have time to waste.

Another batch of vampires circled Kol and Nik, whose fierce glares didn't flinch at being outnumbered. The dragons fought back-to-back, annihilating one vampire after another. Juliet was relieved. They'd be okay.

She just had to get Myreen back.

Two vampires raced toward her, large weapons strapped to their backs. She'd seen something similar on a pamphlet in her dad's office. She didn't know what they did, but they stood out, because they looked like miniature cannons or bazookas. It didn't make sense why a vampire would need such a weapon.

One of the vampires disengaged the weapon from the strap on her back, and her partner stopped to assist.

Juliet glanced to where Myreen had just disappeared. She needed to get to her friend. But she was still trying to adjust to her new body. She had to get it together.

The first vampire pulled back on a piece on top of her armament, firing it directly at Juliet. Like a dance, Juliet gracefully avoided the pellets it spewed. *Heh, not so bad.*

The vampires were getting more and more frustrated with every bullet that zipped by.

Juliet was done with this. She opened her sharp, shiny beak to let out a shriek, and with it came a wave of fire.

Juliet flapped her wings with as much strength as she had. She was shocked when her body shot up into the darkened sky. With her magnified vision, she looked back. The two vampires and their weapon were incinerated.

Her attention went to the vampire that had Myreen. They'd only made it one roof over.

She tucked her wings behind her back and dove. She let out another one of her shrieks, but this time there was no fire with it. The vampire carrying Myreen looked back, his eyebrows pushed together in shock and confusion.

Seeing Myreen so close boosted Juliet's confidence. She could get her friend back. She'd had plenty of defense training—though that was in her human form. Hopefully it would still prove to be effective in her phoenix form.

With another strong and heavy beat of her wings, she ducked and prepared to crash.

A grunt came from the vampire—and Myreen. But she'd hit her target. The three of them rolled in different directions. Juliet was back in the air in seconds. The vampire stumbled as he tried to catch his balance.

Juliet inhaled deeply and blew out, focusing on the fear that had coursed through her when he'd taken Myreen, and she breathed fire.

The vampire let out a brief wail as he turned to ash.

"J– J– Juliet?" Myreen said, her brows pinched, the glow of flaming phoenix reflecting in her eyes.

Juliet gave her a nod, and swept down, gently hooking her talons—the only part of her not on fire—around Myreen's shoulders—then took off.

Now that she had Myreen back, she had the chance to savor her phoenix form. Everything she'd heard from the other students about shifting was right. It *was* freeing and magical, and just plain satisfying. She reveled in the way the whirling wind felt beneath both feather and flame of her wings.

But a loud roar snapped her back to the danger still at hand.

Again, Juliet dropped her head and swooped toward the ground. But she wasn't familiar enough with her phoenix form, and holding Myreen didn't help.

The girls crashed into a pile of garbage bags just a few feet from Nik and Kol. Juliet's head hit the nearby trash bin. It pulsed with pain, and her vision blurred. Myreen groaned next to her.

Instinctively, Juliet reached up to rub her head—and immediately realized she'd shifted back. She looked down and was relieved to see she wasn't naked. *So glad I had to put on my smart clothes.* But when she pulled her hand away from her face, crimson blood puddled in her palm. She tried not to panic—there were bigger things at stake.

"Myreen!" Juliet scrambled to her friend.

There was a large gash on the back of Myreen's neck, and blood dripped out of the open wound, filling the air with its thick, metallic odor. Juliet was afraid the vampires would smell it, and immediately felt guilty for hurting Myreen. If she'd just stuck her landing, they wouldn't be injured.

Plastic bags rustled behind them, and her rage swelled.

Slamming her fists on the ground, she heard a sizzle, the acrid odor of burning plastic and food filling the air. With one fluid movement, Juliet swung around, her leg in the air. Her foot made contact with the jaw of the approaching vampire, and she heard a crack that she knew was a broken bone. The vampire with the broken jaw crouched down with his head in his hands.

With a sinister sneer, she turned and prepared to fight the rest of the vampires circling her and Myreen. Two vamps were trying to inch their way closer to Myreen. Juliet spun and spread her arms, blasting two large balls of fire directly at the heads of the encroaching vamps. *Two down, two to go.*

The first vampire, the one she'd cracked the jaw of, was back up. He joined the remaining vampire as she turned to fight Juliet, rather than attempting to take Myreen. Juliet smirked. That was exactly what she wanted.

They charged at her with the speed of a bullet, but Juliet was still buzzed from shifting, her senses still enhanced. As if they were moving in slow motion, Juliet ducked out of the way.

Snarling, they turned to strike again, coming at either side of her. Juliet jumped and spread her legs in a perfect, symmetrical split kick. Both vampires fell to the ground, wounds on their heads.

Juliet formed the same rope of fire, slinging one strand around each of the two vampires. She squeezed her hands into fists, and they screamed in agony as the ropes tightened around their torsos. Their bodies tore apart, snuffing out the vampires simultaneously.

Juliet raced back to Myreen, who watched in shock. Turning Myreen's head to reevaluate the gash on her neck, Juliet stared. It didn't look nearly as bad as she remembered. In fact, it looked like it was almost...

BOOM! BOOM!

A loud blast exploded, causing the ground to vibrate. Juliet looked around frantically, in search of the noise. Three groups of vampires stood directly in front of Nik. He was surrounded.

His red scales flashed in a panic, and Juliet's heart sunk to her stomach. In horror, she watched the closest vampire pull back on the top piece of her cannon-like weapon.

At any moment, Nik would be blasted. She couldn't leave Myreen, but she couldn't watch Nik, so defenseless and exposed.

Juliet squeezed her eyes shut. Pulling on her fear and rage, she took a deep breath and opened her mouth to send her shriek of fire to every vampire there.

BOOM! BOOM!

She screamed. But she was too late. Her fire had defeated several more vampires—enough to dampen their attack. Through the thick smoke, Juliet watched as Draven and what was left of his cronies fled to the darkness, another form joining them.

Juliet pulled Myreen to her feet, and they ran toward where the guys were, her heart broking into millions of pieces.

"Breathe, J. He's going to be okay." Myreen's gentle voice helped keep her steady, but she was still so afraid.

As their bodies came into view, Juliet's heart beat faster. She ran the rest of the way, then froze in her tracks.

The bloody body she was staring at wasn't Nik's.

It was Kol's.

Juliet stared down at Kol's limp, human form, and a lump balled in her throat.

She felt angry at herself for feeling relief that it wasn't Nik, lying there, blood pooling around him.

She felt grief because she knew Kol didn't deserve this—none of them did.

And she felt panic, because the Dracul Prince was probably dead.

With his head on his knees, Nik trembled. Juliet wanted to console him, but the grim remains of the fight were all around them. She wouldn't know where to start.

Juliet went to Nik, hoping he was okay enough to help her figure out their next step.

"Why did he do that?" Nik moaned. "He didn't have to do that! He shouldn't have saved me. He shouldn't have!" Nik's frantic shouts pierced Juliet.

Myreen threw herself on the ground by Kol's body, tears flooding down her cheeks. When Myreen shouted Juliet's name, Juliet ran to her side, thinking nothing but the worst.

"Look!"

Juliet and Myreen watched as an open wound on Kol's face shrunk. Juliet frowned at Myreen, who looked just as confused.

Kol sucked in a shuddering breath, then groaned.

"He's alive!" Myreen cried.

They needed a way to get back to the Dome… but how?

Kol

BOOM! BOOM!

The blast shook the buildings and reverberated through the ground. Kol braced himself against the impact, then whipped his tail to knock out the two vampires behind him. The vampires thought they were catching him off guard, but he'd known about their position ever since they left the others. They were attempting to surround him, but Kol would never allow himself to be in that position of weakness—not as skilled as he was.

Their entire attack was well executed. The vampires had effectively separated Kol and Nik from the girls, occupying them with a barrage of constant assaults. But he knew that a couple of teenage dragons weren't their target. His fears were confirmed when one of the vampires snatched Myreen and took off with her.

Instinct instantly took over, panic flooding beneath his scales and enhancing his senses exponentially. He tried to jump away in flight, to go after her and save her from the blood-sucking, mer-killing monsters. But he was immediately pinned down by three more vampires. He couldn't break away unless he wanted to be seriously injured—or worse. And he would've done it, but the constant defense and pre-emptive offense kept him moving at a neck-snapping pace. He couldn't find a chink in their armor to exploit.

Kol hated that he couldn't go after Myreen. It would break him if something happened to her.

But he couldn't think about that.

He almost missed the metal object that nearly impaled him when he saw the phoenix screech and go after Myreen.

Juliet.

It had to be. He'd never seen her shift—didn't even think she could—but he knew Brett couldn't have known about the attack. And besides, the bird was slightly smaller than Brett, and more orange-colored. So, it definitely wasn't him. Or any of the others.

It had to be Juliet.

Deftly, Kol was able to dodge another weapon, snapping the neck of the vampire wielding it before moving on to the next five that were already attacking. He couldn't think about Juliet's abilities, and just hoped she could save Myreen without getting them both killed.

If she couldn't… *nope.* He was *not* going to think about *what if's.* Not now.

Nik's deep red scales flicked, flipping up then settling and reflecting the streetlight like an old-fashioned disco-ball. Nik was panicked, and it was his way of distracting the enemy while simultaneously drawing Kol's attention.

Nik was surrounded. Kol didn't even realize they'd been separated.

Kol rushed forward, not bothering anymore to find a weakness in his attackers' ranks. In less than a second, he clamped his jaw around one near him—after blasting fire at three others—and tossed the limp

493

creature into the side of a building before bracing to jump to Nik's side.

That's when he saw it.

Time seemed to slow as one of the vampires pulled back some sort of switch or lever on the top of what looked like a very high-tech weapon. Whatever it was, it was going to kill his best friend.

And he could *not* allow that.

Without thinking, Kol rushed forward, putting the entirety of his gray scales between the unknown weapon and Nik.

Fire seemed to envelope them right before—

BOOM!

. . .

. . .

. . .

Kol tried to fight against the unconsciousness, though his eyelids felt like lead and his entire body burned from the inside out. He should give into it—extinguish the wretched burning that wasn't coming from his own, familiar flames—but they weren't out of danger yet.

He needed to shift again and drive the vampires off.

He needed to contact Oberon.

He needed to get everyone back to the safety of the Dome and regroup.

A strange feeling cooled against his cheek and his eyes flew open as he gasped for a breath.

The pain intensified, causing a groan to escape without permission. It was everywhere, burning, aching, stinging and raw. It was scattered in pockets the shape of marbles, though smaller in size, all over his body. What had those vampires had done to him?

Kol attempted to calm his hitched breaths, willing his enhanced senses to dull to more human-like and force his over-active nerve endings to quiet. As he did so, he no longer felt the edges of the wounds—they lost their roundness and coalesced into spilled blood, collecting in rivulets as it spread. And the pain spread with it, but it faded just enough to keep him conscious. Fortunately, his pain threshold was high, adrenaline still coursing through his veins.

Myreen and Juliet hovered over him, tears streaming from Myreen's clear blue eyes, and Juliet with a frown on her face as she looked back and forth between him and Nik, who was a few feet away.

Nik. He was okay. From where Kol lay, it looked like he hadn't been hurt. Nik shot Kol with a guilty, but furious expression. Kol didn't want to see it, didn't want to deal with Nik's anger, so he quickly looked away as Juliet jumped up to join her boyfriend.

It felt like something was stuck in his side, like he was being jabbed in the ribs, and so he turned to his side to feel for it... and felt the wound there. Refusing to allow the panic to set in, Kol reached in with his finger—his vision flashing with bright lights and color as the sharpness of the pain intensified—to remove the pellet-sized ball of lead.

He knew it was lead because it scorched his fingers, and he dropped the shrapnel like it was on fire.

Any attempts to calm his breathing became futile as he realized that his body was probably riddled with small lead pellets just like it—the wounds he'd felt before he dulled his senses were the correct shape and size. But there were too many to count in his current state. It was all he could do to keep from hyperventilating as his breathing became heavier.

There would be no shifting now. And if he didn't get help soon, he might be a goner.

But he couldn't think about that just yet. He needed to save the others. He attempted to sit up, but Myreen pushed him back down.

She pushed him down! When he needed to get back up to defend them!

"What are you doing?" she asked, looking confused and panicked and angry all at once. Then she began to cry again, a bit hysterically. "You nearly *died,* Kol. You need to… don't move… you need help," she said, then hiccupped. He could barely understand her.

Kol frowned, furrowing his eyebrows. "Myreen,*"* he said softly. If she wasn't such a mess, he might've shouted at her for being so naïve about the shifter world and its dangers. "We're being attacked by vampires. I need to get up."

"We *were* attacked," she said a little clearer, and sounding weirdly annoyed with him. She swept a piece of her hair away from her face. Even wild and tangled from being hauled off by that vampire, her hair still looked soft. Kol felt the sudden, strong urge to touch it. "But they're gone."

He blinked at her. Surely she lied. Surely they were trapped in a single, small glimpse of a moment that would be popped any second now, when the vampires decided to finish them off.

Surely she was wrong.

But that seemed absurd. There was no way that any of them would be left alone for even a few seconds the way those vampires had fought. They had been relentless, but he hadn't seen a single one since he'd opened his eyes.

She had to be telling the truth. Otherwise they would all be dead now.

The relief sank into his muscles. The danger was over. They were close to the subway station. If he could just rest a few moments, they could get safely back to the Dome. Certainly Oberon would insist on retaliation, and Kol would be the first to march up and volunteer. A quick fix by Miss Heather and he would be as good as new.

Yes, just a moment to rest.

His eyelids became heavy again, but then the pain set in with force.

"Oh Kol! Y— you could've… please be okay!" Myreen surprised him by reaching for his right hand and pressing the back of it against her jaw. He could feel the wetness on her skin as she began to sob again. A tear escaped and splashed on his knuckles, still pressed against her face. She closed her eyes for a moment. Her eyelashes stuck together in places from their wetness as they rested against her cheeks.

He watched her, a little bit confused. He looked over at Nik who was holding Juliet, both wearing only their smart clothing, with their heads turned away from him and Myreen. Clearly Nik was too distracted to help him decipher this situation. But when Kol looked back at Myreen, an overwhelming feeling barreled over him, too. The words Myreen just spoke was the anthem of exactly how he felt.

Wincing against the pain, Kol moved to prop himself on his free elbow. He hardly noticed the roughness of the pavement—in fact, it probably would have hurt a little if he weren't already fighting against the intense, radiating pain that spread out like wildfire from every single point of injury—but he barely noticed the tiny pricks of the gravel as they imbedded into his skin. He nearly collapsed again, he felt so weak, but she looked so small, so fragile and frail as she clutched his hand. His hand that could easily swallow hers. So he fought through it and remained upright.

Myreen's eyes snapped open, a flash of furrowed brows and tight lips—anger that he knew was directed toward him for daring to sit again—flitted across her face. "What are you doing? Lay back down!"

But he ignored her. She released his hand, but he left it near her face and turned it slowly, so he was cupping the soft skin along her jaw and beneath her chin. She held very still at his touch. Tears still streamed down her face, creating black streaks of mascara along her cheekbones. He absently moved his thumb back and forth, but stopped when he noticed the goosebumps rise along the curve of her neck.

"I don't know what I would have done..." Kol's voice cracked, so he trailed off and swallowed, pushing the emotions—and the blood—down. "If Juliet hadn't saved you," he whispered.

Myreen's forehead creased. He wanted to smooth away the concern, but didn't want to remove his hand. Unfortunately, he had to because his left arm was giving out and he needed both arms if he was to remain half-sitting. So he let go and braced himself against the concrete with his palm. It was taking a lot of willpower to keep himself partly vertical.

She must've seen his struggle because she didn't look disappointed that he'd stopped touching her. Or maybe she didn't feel that way about him, and was only concerned for a fellow shifter. Maybe she'd barely noticed the sudden distance between them. Maybe she'd do the same and feel the same if she were in a similar situation with Nik or Brett... or *Kendall.*

But her eyes softened as she watched him—perhaps trying to discern his thoughts?

Myreen finally averted her eyes and looked down at Kol's chest, but saw something there that caused her pain and so looked back at his face. He managed a smile because all that mattered was that *she* was okay. That Myreen was safe. That Myreen was here.

A determined look crossed her face, maybe in response to his expression, and she reached out to touch his face, stroking her thumb against his cheek. Maybe she did feel the same. She had to care about him at least a little, right? Otherwise she never would have asked him out on a second date.

But his arms were spent, and Kol collapsed again onto his back with a grunt. A high pitched sound came from Myreen when he fell back. He fought the blackness again as the pain increased. He winced against it and hissed until it ebbed like the tide and faded.

When he opened his eyes all he could see was Myreen. She was looking up, shouting something as she hovered over him. When her eyes met his, bearing the color of the sky and glistening with tears, she asked him something he couldn't register. Her hair fell like a waterfall, cascading around his face. There were creases in her forehead that he desperately wanted to smooth away. She should never have to have such worries in this world.

He cut off her words—words he wasn't comprehending anyway—and reached forward with his left hand to draw her nearer to him. He twined his fingers through her tangled hair and closed the canyon-sized gap between them… and kissed her.

She didn't respond at first. Perhaps she was stunned. Perhaps the kiss was unwanted. But it only took a second before she kissed him back. Her fruity lip gloss mixed with her salty tears and his tangy blood. She leaned her body into his, but it was a direct hit to the injury in his ribs where he'd extracted the lead only moments ago. He cried out, breaking the kiss, breaking the spell, breaking the moment.

"Kol I—" her hands flew up, waving over his body like she wanted to help, but didn't know how to without touching him. Finally, she dropped them again along with her expression. "Kol, I'm sorry," she said.

But she shouldn't be. He'd kissed *her*.

"Oberon!" He heard Nik shout.

"Don't apologize," Kol said to Myreen, allowing a small smile to form on his lips in assurance. But he was spent and fell back again. His eyes slammed closed.

"Oberon! Ren!" Juliet choked. She sounded like she was crying. "We're here!"

Kol just smiled and hoped that he'd get another shot at kissing that girl again.

Oberon

Oberon could see his breath steam in the cold evening air. But the outside temperatures weren't what chilled him to the bone.

He was bent over Malkolm Dracul, whose body was lacerated in hundreds of places, wearing nothing but his smart clothing, which also bore countless holes. The dragon prince was moving with a wounded slowness in a pool of his own blood.

"High winds, what did they do to you?"

Kol groaned, as if attempting to respond. But his eyes were closed. Oberon knew the boy didn't have much time left.

"We have to get him back to the Dome," he said, setting his jaw as he tried to think of the best way to transport Kol.

Ren bent over and grabbed something small that shimmered dark silver with moonlight. Sniffing at it, he said, "Lead." Looking around, the kitsune picked up several more identical pieces off the ground. "Lead pellets. Dozens of them."

Oberon felt lightheaded as he realized what that meant. All the little lacerations on Kol's body weren't cuts at all. They were wounds where lead pellets had struck him.

"You don't have any healing elixirs in your bag, do you?" he asked.

Ren shook his head. "I haven't carried those since the Island. Their healing properties wear off and become less and less potent the longer they go unused."

Oberon sighed. "We've got to get him to Maya right away. If the boy's body is full of lead, he won't live much longer."

Nearby, Myreen wept bitterly, pulling Oberon's attention from the dragon prince. She was shivering in the cold. Her friend Juliet Quinn was close by with Nikolai Candida keeping a comforting arm around her. Nik and Juliet were in their smart clothing, showing that they'd shifted to face the vampires in battle.

"Are you three hurt?" he asked, knowing just by their postures that Kol had suffered the worst from the fight.

Myreen didn't respond—likely couldn't. Her eyes were trained on Kol as she cried.

"He saved my life," Nik said distantly. Oberon had been in enough fights to understand how easy it was to relive violent memories. The distant look in the boy's eyes disappeared and he looked back at Oberon. "Kol dove in front of me when they shot their cannons. He shielded me."

"Cannons would be too bulky to carry around in public without drawing unwanted eyes," Ren said. "Probably some sort of scattershot. Wide spread, by the looks of it."

"Once we get back to the Dome, I'll get reports from each of you," Oberon said. "But we can't linger. The vampires could return at any moment."

Ren filled his trusty backpack with the pellets, then ran down to where larger, discarded objects were.

"You guys go on ahead," Ren said. "I want to collect as many samples as I can before this all gets swept away."

"I'm going to need your help hauling the boy," Oberon replied. "Vampire trinkets mean nothing right now."

Ren grabbed whatever it was he'd gone to retrieve, then sprinted back, his backpack jingling with metal pieces. The kitsune threw the item into the mix and pulled the drawstring.

"You want his legs or his shoulders?" Oberon asked.

"The boy is a tank, and unfortunately, I am not," Ren said. "You take his shoulders."

"Why did I even ask?" Oberon mumbled, getting to Kol's bleeding head.

"Hey, exercise is your hobby," Ren said. "Tinkering is mine. But give me just a moment. I'm sending a message off to Delphine to have her get a gurney to the front entrance of the Dome. I'm not carrying this kid all the way to the infirmary."

Oberon ignored him, placing his hands under Kol's back. "I'm sorry, kid, but this is probably going to hurt."

Angling the boy's back up, Oberon scooped his hands under Kol's arms. Kol groaned at the movement, and his head lolled backward, the whites of his eyes showing before they closed.

Ren grabbed onto Kol's battered legs.

"On three," Oberon said, heart pounding. He knew that moving an injured person was extremely dangerous, depending on what kind of wounds had been inflicted. He hoped they weren't causing any more damage—at least nothing irreparable—but they didn't have any other choice. "One... two... three!"

Together, they hoisted Kol up. Oberon had anticipated the weight of the boy—Kol was well over six feet tall and was quite muscular from the different exercises and defense trainings his father had put him through since he was a child. But still, Oberon's own muscles shook from the effort.

"This kid's gotta cut back on his meals," Ren said with a grunt.

Nik moved to help him.

Oberon was grateful they were near the subway entrance, but as close as they were to the Dome, time was running out.

***

They made it back to the Dome without incident, but the subway ride seemed to take forever, and Kol was unresponsive the entire way.

Oberon's back and arms flared with exhaustion from carrying Kol—they didn't really have anywhere appropriate to set him on during the sub ride, and Oberon didn't want to risk the strain of lifting him again, both for Kol's sake and his own. He gritted his teeth and kept his fists clenched as they made their way into the school's entrance, Juliet and Myreen bringing up the rear.

Thankfully, Delphine was waiting for them with a wheeled bed from the hospital wing. The worry on her face turned to shock as they came into view.

"Is that the Dracul boy?" she gasped. "What happened to him?"

"We'll find out the details soon enough," Oberon replied quickly. "Hurry, Ren, Nik. Up and onto the gurney in three."

He counted off, and they gently raised Kol onto the bed.

"Delphine, please keep wandering eyes away," Oberon said, tapping at the touchscreen controls on the gurney. He sent the command for the bed to propel itself to the infirmary. "We'll follow the gurney to the hospital wing."

Delphine nodded, looking down the hallways. Oberon knew that the assignment he gave her was a tough one, but he really wanted to limit Kol's visibility to the other students.

Keeping pace with the gurney, Oberon's watch buzzed as an emergency message displayed.

Attention students: Tonight's curfew requires everyone to go back to their respective common rooms and dorms for the remainder of the evening. Any students caught outside of their assigned wings will undergo daily sim room detention for the rest of the year.

-Miss Delphine Smith

"Thank you, Delphine," Oberon whispered.

Before he knew it, they had reached the hospital wing.

A mao student was walking out, holding an ice pack against her head. It fell from her hand and she gasped as she saw Kol's gruesome form.

"Out of the way, child!" Oberon yelled. His urgency and anxiety removed any filter he'd kept on as director of the school, but he didn't have time to regret his exclamation.

Fortunately, the girl did move away, but she rubber-necked until they burst into the infirmary.

"Good gracious, what happened?!" Maya asked, completely stunned.

"Another vampire attack," Oberon said, panting from the exertion. "Kol needs your aid thirty minutes ago."

"Right," Maya replied, pushing her ever-falling glasses higher on her nose. "Put him right here."

With the gurney now immobile, Oberon pushed it to an open part of the infirmary where curtains had been parted—next to the still slumbering Alessandra. It was likely where the medical bed had originally been before Delphine brought it. Tapping the controls on the display, Oberon locked the wheels in place.

"Multiple lead pellets are embedded in his body," Oberon said, getting out of Maya's way so she could see to Kol. "Worst of all, he's lost a lot of blood."

Maya shook her head, feeling at Kol's neck. "We've got to get both under control. His pulse is weak. His chest is barely rising." Maya tapped the display screen attached to the bed and began to work.

Oberon heard sobbing coming from behind him, and he turned about to find Myreen and her friends still standing there. His heart plummeted as he realized he'd forgotten they were still there.

"Ren," Oberon said. "Please escort Nikolai and Juliet to my office and get them some clothes. I will return there with Myreen shortly."

The kitsune nodded. "Of course."

"And don't pester them with questions, please. They should only have to explain what happened once."

"Understood." Ren gestured to Nik and Juliet. "Come along, you two. Let's go."

They stepped out with Ren, who turned around at the threshold and gave Oberon a serious look, then continued out.

Oberon placed a hand on Maya's shoulder. "Keep me apprised, will you? I know you will do your best for him."

Maya nodded. An x-ray image of Kol's body filled the screen she was staring at, indicating just how many pieces of lead were embedded in his body.

"I'm going to send for a few other harpies to come and aid me," she said, handling the urgency with calmed determination. "We need to work quickly."

Oberon patted her shoulder. "Do what you need to do."

He turned again to Myreen. Her hair was askew and her eyes red. Oberon approached her, and her gaze met his.

"I'm so sorry," she mumbled through quivering lips. "I'm so sorry, I'm so sorry."

Oberon brought her into a fatherly embrace, and she rested her tear-stained face on his shoulder. "Hey, you have nothing to be sorry about, Myreen."

"We tried to get back before curfew, but there was traffic, and the subway was blocked off." Myreen's words were rapid and hard to understand.

"It was a coordinated attack," Oberon said. "I have no doubt about that. But like I said, it wasn't your fault. You should not be apologizing."

He swallowed, realizing he could no longer keep things hidden from her. Keeping her in the dark was no longer serving her higher interest. "There are a few things I've been meaning to tell you. And you deserve to know them."

She didn't pull away from him, but her silence indicated that she wanted him to continue to speak.

Oberon felt comfortable talking about this, even though Maya was in earshot: the lead healer was aware of the prophecy. And Kol and Alessandra likely wouldn't hear or remember anything he said, anyway.

"Last time you came to my office, after the attack on Alessandra, I wanted to explain why that attack happened, but was afraid of how you would react. But after tonight, you must know: the vampires are hunting you."

At this, she pulled away from him and looked into his eyes. The sadness on her face framed a deep fear he understood all too well.

"Why me? I'm a useless mermaid."

Oberon shook his head. "You are much, much more than that. Which brings me to the other bit of knowledge I feel like I must confess to you."

She rubbed at her nose, swollen eyes looking at him while she waited for him to continue.

"What I'm about to tell you is extremely confidential, Myreen. I would impress upon your mind that you will be better off not disclosing such information to anybody else."

She nodded, an eagerness stirring in her countenance.

"Delphine is the greatest seer in the world. Her clairvoyance goes beyond the skill of any other mermaid that I know. Years ago, she received a prophecy about a stray mermaid. This prophecy states that a stray mermaid would be a siren, and would be the one to bring an end to Draven and his group of vampires."

She stiffened at his words, her eyes widening.

"Siren?" she whispered.

Oberon looked at her in confusion. Out of that entire declaration of the prophecy, she had pulled the word *siren* out of it?

"Yes, a siren," he said. "I believe that siren is *you.*"

He felt relief at finally telling her the truth, as if a great weight had been taken from his shoulders.

"That's what he called me," she murmured.

Again, Oberon gave her a confused look. "Somebody called you a siren?"

She nodded quickly, looking down at her feet. Anxiety replaced his short-lived relief.

"Who? Who called you a siren?"

"Draven did," she said softly, bringing her gaze back to his.

Oberon licked his dry lips as she said the vampire's name.

"Draven was involved in the attack?" he asked. "And he called you a siren?"

She stiffened again. "Something happened... During the fight. Something weird happened with my voice."

Oberon's heartbeat increased. "You must tell me."

"It's hard to explain," Myreen said, her fingers finding the edge of the curtain partition she stood next to. "Juliet was in trouble. A vampire had her. And I told the vampire holding her to leave her alone." Her eyes distanced, just as Nik's had, as she recalled the memory. "My voice was different, though. It was still mine, but it was a deeper, fluid sound. Almost like I was singing, even though I wasn't."

She was a siren! *The* siren! His eyes widened, and his mouth opened ever so slightly as she spoke.

"And the vampire holding onto Juliet went quiet, and still, like I hypnotized her or something. That's when Juliet escaped. There must have been some kind of magic in my voice to make her freeze like that."

"You're *the* siren," he said as he stared at her with increasing awe. "I have always believed, but now I know it."

"But if I'm this siren from the prophecy you've talked about, that means I'm supposed to kill Draven, right?"

Oberon nodded, not knowing how else to directly answer her question. That was a heavy weight for anybody to bear. He'd failed in killing Draven twenty years ago. And now that task was on Myreen's shoulders.

"And how am I supposed to do that?"

He straightened his back. This question he knew the answer to.

"We train you."

Myreen's brows furrowed. "Like what I'm already learning?"

"Yes, but more so. It's now imperative that you learn how to fight. Draven knows who you are, and he will stop at nothing to find you. What his desired purposes are with you, I don't know. But we must not let him find you. At least not until you are confident in your abilities to fight him."

She shifted uncomfortably, looking down solemnly. "I don't know how to fight. I freeze up every time."

He placed a hand on her shoulder.

"I will personally see to one-on-one defensive training with you, starting tomorrow. And in your next Defense class, you must spar. You can no longer afford to watch the others from the sidelines."

He hoped his offer to instruct her would help alleviate her fear and anxiety. He'd never offered such training to any other student, but Myreen was the most important person in the Dome. He'd make her the best she could possibly be.

"I hope I can become the shifter you believe me to be," she said.

"You will. I have no doubt about that."

"I do have another question," Myreen said.

"I have no more secrets to hold from you," he replied. "Ask away."

"How did you know to come looking for us?" Myreen asked.

He smiled. "You missed curfew, along with the others. I was notified that you four were missing. And I know you, Myreen. After what happened to Alessandra, I knew you wouldn't purposefully stay out past curfew. Which told me you were in trouble."

She nodded, and Oberon could see a gratefulness form in her eyes as Myreen half-smiled.

"Thankfully, the four of you were close to the subway," Oberon continued. "It made it that much easier for me and Ren to find you."

She glanced back at Kol, who was being carefully tended to by Maya.

"We're lucky you came," she said. "I don't know how we would've gotten Kol back here."

"Perhaps it wasn't all luck," he said with a wink. "I don't know how being a siren works, but it could be that I subconsciously heard your call."

He didn't know if that was true, but he liked thinking it was.

A trio of harpies entered the room and hastened to Maya's side.

"Come," he said to Myreen. "We should let them take care of Kol. And your friends are waiting for us in my classroom."

Oberon guided her out of the hospital wing, her pained eyes trained on Kol, even as his form was obscured by the healers.

The siren had a long road, but he'd stand by her side and guide her as much as he could. Draven would meet his end. And Oberon would finally have the peace he'd been seeking for twenty years.

Myreen

Myreen sat next to Kol's bed in the nurse's station a couple days later, holding his warm yet unresponsive hand in hers.

The harpies had gotten all the lead pellets out of his body, and in their place was square-inch gauze bandages over the slowly healing skin. His chest, which was bare and uncovered by the not-long-enough linen sheet, was scattered with them. Ms. Heather said that he was going to be alright. The lead in his system would make for slow healing, as lead was the one substance that weakened dragons most, but once it worked its way out, he would be okay.

She hated seeing him like this. Kol had always been an image of strength to her, seeming almost untouchable—on a number of levels. Now he was vulnerable, in pain. And it was all her fault.

Like a glutton, she replayed their kiss again and again. She could almost still feel the heat of his lips on hers. It figured that he would only finally open up to her when it looked like it was too late.

"You had better be alright, Kol," she whispered. "You can't just kiss me like that and then abandon me." Although, that would be a very Kol thing to do.

"Myreen?" Alessandra's voice sounded from the next bed. But it wasn't the feverish call of the last few days. It was a question. Was Alessandra awake?

Myreen turned her head in the mermaid's direction, and the girl looked at her through heavy eyelids. In a strange turn of events, Myreen's chest exploded with celebratory fireworks. She never thought she'd be so happy to see her schoolyard rival looking at her again, even if her eyes were darkened and bloodshot.

In her excitement, she rushed to Alessandra's side. "I'm here," she said.

Alessandra struggled to sit up, then grabbed Myreen's hand. "You have to listen to me. Don't go outside. Don't leave the Dome."

"It's okay, Alessandra," Myreen said in a soothing tone. "I already know the vampires are after me. They tried to grab me last night, but we got away."

"We?"

Myreen gestured to Kol in the next bed.

"Omigod, what happened?" Alessandra gasped.

"We were out after sunset and the vampires cornered us. We only got away because Juliet transformed and pretty much set them all on fire."

"Oh, so the fire-jinx is good for something."

Myreen frowned. Only Alessandra could still be nasty after waking up from a trauma-induced coma. "Never mind that. What happened to you?"

Alessandra cast her eyes down, and they were distant, unseeing. "My flight back from Thanksgiving break got delayed, so it was late at night by the time I was getting to the subway entrance. A group of guys came up to me, and one of them said, 'Hello, Myreen.' I didn't understand. Why did they think I was you? I'm so much hotter."

Myreen rolled her eyes at that statement, but didn't interrupt.

"But as they came closer, that same guy said, 'Wait, you're not Myreen. Is this some kind of trick?' I told him I didn't know what he was talking about. He got angry, and the three guys he'd brought with him attacked me. I didn't realize they were vampires until they were biting me, and by then it was too late to try to escape."

She stopped talking, and her face puckered up in remembered pain. A tear plopped as it landed on the sheet over her lap.

"It was a nightmare, Myreen," Alessandra continued in a small voice. "They didn't just drink from me, they… they…"

Although Alessandra's skin was smooth and unmarred now, Myreen remembered how many bandages had covered her body and knew that the vampires had beaten her up pretty badly.

"It's okay, you don't have to talk about it," Myreen said, laying a comforting hand on her shoulder. "It's over now. You're safe."

Alessandra's face flicked in her direction. "But you're not. They weren't looking for me, they were looking for you. If that's what they did to me, I can't even imagine what they would do to you if they got you. And you can't even use your mermaid abilities to defend to yourself."

The comment hadn't been meant to offend—surprisingly—but the confirmation of just how useless she was hurt.

"They left me for dead in the alley. But I knew I had to get back here, to warn you somehow. I crawled to the platform. And that's all I remember."

Myreen was lost for words, her brows twitching in uncertainty. She was truly touched by how much her supposed nemesis cared about her. And relieved that Alessandra didn't hate her for being the cause of her near-death experience. But then, Myreen hated herself enough for everyone.

"Why don't you get some rest?" Myreen said, patting Alessandra's hand. "I'll have the harpies bring you some food." Myreen made to stand up, but Alessandra grabbed her wrist.

"Wait," she said. "Please be careful. Don't let them get you."

Myreen smiled. "Everything is going to be fine. I promise."

Alessandra slowly released Myreen's wrist, and Myreen left the room to find a nurse, to let them know Alessandra had awaken.

But as she walked away, she worried she'd made a promise she couldn't keep.

***

Myreen was so nervous about her imminent spar in Defense class that her whole body seemed to buzz with electricity as she stepped onto the mat inside the gymnasium. The nervous energy both amped her up and made her fear she would shatter like a mirror at the slightest touch.

After the run-in with the vampires, Myreen was determined to learn how to handle herself in a fight, and not just for her own safety. Poor, wonderful Kol was laid up in the nurse's station at that very moment because of her uselessness. He almost died trying to protect her. In fact, they all may have died if it hadn't been for Juliet's explosive fire scaring the vampires away.

She could never allow a friend to suffer because of her again. Draven would keep coming for her. She had to make sure she was ready.

After visiting Kol and Alessandra in the nurse's station yesterday morning, Myreen had spent most of her Sunday training with Oberon. They had run more defensive maneuvers than she could recall, over and over again. It had been the longest, most intense physical exercise of her life. At the end of it, she felt limp—and still about as ineffective as jelly.

Now she had to spar with someone in front of the whole school. There wasn't a snowball's chance in hell that she was ready, but what choice did she have? She had to be strong, and to try her best. For Kol. For Nik and Juliet.

For everyone.

Everyone around her was looking at her, and she could tell that half of them were confused as to why such a fresh student had been called on to spar, and the other half—mer, mostly—were hoping to watch her get her butt kicked. She scanned over all their faces, wondering who Oberon was going to pair her with.

"Trish," Oberon called loudly. "Would you please join Myreen on the mat and demonstrate your skills to the class?"

That was the last name she wanted to hear.

Trish's perfect blond hair rose up from the sea of heads and she emerged onto the mat. "Gladly." Her eyes practically glowed as they locked and narrowed on Myreen.

Myreen flashed stunned, insulted eyes at Oberon. How could he pair her off with the one person who hated her most? And for her first real fight? What the heck was he thinking?

All he did in response was give her a single, almost imperceptible nod.

She exhaled her frustration and apprehension and adopted a defensive stance as Trish came close.

"I'm going to destroy you, little muckmaid," Trish hissed.

Then she spun around and kicked Myreen's legs out from under her. Fresh anger flooded Myreen as she landed gruffly on her back. She was mostly angry at herself for letting Trish get the jump on her like that, and she vowed that it wouldn't happen a second time.

Getting to her knees, Myreen dove at Trish, barreling into her abdomen and knocking her over like a cut-down tree. Once she had her on the mat, Myreen climbed on top of her, trying to get the upper hand.

Trish was just as swift on the ground as she was standing up, and she rolled so that she was on top. Myreen tried to slip out, but Trish had her trapped under her legs. Trish inched up to sit on Myreen's chest, then threw a punch right into her face.

The impact stupefied Myreen for a second. She had never been punched in the face before, and the pain to both her face and her ego was hard to ignore. When the second punch landed, all she could think to do was turtle up behind her arms.

In all the spars she'd watched in class, the fighters never went that hard at each other, and rarely threw punches, especially to the face. Myreen didn't know why she didn't expect Trish to fight as cut-throat as possible. Why did Oberon set this up? Didn't he know Trish would mutilate her? Shouldn't he be stopping this?

The punches kept coming, harder and faster. Myreen's forearms were screaming with pain as she hugged her own head. She struggled to focus, her mind rewinding over everything she'd learned, trying to remember anything she could use to get out of this. She couldn't do anything with her hands. If she moved her arms, Trish would have full access to her face, and Myreen was too afraid of the pain to risk it.

But her legs were completely free.

Using Trish's weight on her chest as leverage, she swung her legs upward with all her strength and wrapped them around Trish's torso, then pulled them down as hard as she could, slamming Trish backward into the mat.

Once Trish was on her back, Myreen wasted no time in getting to her feet.

Trish didn't stay down for long, and was standing up almost as soon as Myreen was.

"Nice move," Trish said. "But I don't need to even touch you to beat you." She pulled a vial out of her back pocket and opened it.

Before Myreen could ask what Trish was doing, water shot out of the vial and pelted Myreen's chest like a bullet.

"Ow! What the—?" Myreen looked down at the spot on her chest that stung sharply. Her shirt was dry. But she knew she had seen water come out of that vial, and she knew that's what had hit her. If that was so, where had the water gone?

Something flashed in the corner of her eye, and as she brought her head up to look, something cold and hard struck her cheek with a surprising amount of force. Her cheek felt wet after, and when she wiped her finger across it, the liquid was red. Whatever had hit her, cut her.

"I always make sure to have some water handy," Trish said with her hands on her hips. "Never know when I might need it. This is how a *real* mermaid fights."

The little water bullet zoomed around Myreen, striking her in different places again and again, stinging more and more each time it landed. The water was too small an amount to do any real damage, but it was still enough to piss Myreen off. Trish was just toying with her. *Well, no more!*

Myreen lunged at Trish again, but Trish dodged her this time, and when Myreen stumbled to the floor, the little water bullet splashed onto her face, getting into her eyes. Myreen wiped her eyes, but the water would not wipe away. Every time she pushed at it, it pooled over her eyelids again, blinding her. The strife was making Myreen's eyes tear up, which only gave Trish more ammunition.

Trish laughed darkly and came closer. Myreen was sure that she was going to mount her and finish her off. Myreen had had enough. In that moment, she hated Trish more than anything. She just wanted to hurt her.

She opened her eyes to try to see through the water. There was a long fluorescent light directly above her, darkening as Trish's head cast a shadow over her. Something clicked inside Myreen as she looked at the blurred light, consumed with the need to hurt Trish, to stop her from inflicting anymore damage.

In her rage, she could almost feel the glass tube break, and suddenly a burst of bright light slammed into Trish and sent her flying. The water spilled freely down Myreen's face just as the shattered glass of the light bulb above rained down on her. One stray shard nicked her arm, but otherwise she was unharmed by the falling light.

Myreen stood up, ready to rip Trish apart with her bare hands if she needed to. But when she saw Trish on the floor, staring up at her with terror in her eyes, she stopped. The silence of the room was suddenly very loud. Myreen looked around, realizing that Trish's horrified expression was mirrored on the face of every other spectator.

She saw the glass shards at her feet, then looked at the broken light on the ceiling. Did she do that?

She looked at Oberon for some answer as to what just happened, but his eyes held only questions as they stared back at her.

"What... What are you?" Trish said, breathless.

The accusation struck Myreen. It wasn't that a shifter had used light manipulation in a spar—Myreen had seen that one other time, when an older harpy boy had been called on to spar. No, it was the fact that a harpy power had been used by a *mermaid.*

Oberon cleared his throat, but his voice still came out dry and deep when he answered.

"She's a chimera."

Myreen

How could this be possible?

Only two days ago, she'd gone from being the most useless mermaid in school—and possibly the world—to being the siren that was prophesied to kill the most dangerous vampire alive. And now, she was a chimera?

She knew what a chimera was, if only from a brief lesson about it in Shifter Biology. A chimera was someone who was a mix of two or more shifter species, and such a thing was so rare that it was almost a myth. How could she be one of these creatures? As if being a siren wasn't rare enough!

Myreen hadn't stuck around Defense class after the accidental discovery. She needed time to process, and Oberon had respected that and let her leave before anyone else. She ran to Juliet's room, closed the door, and curled up on the bed, trying not to have a nervous breakdown.

It was just too much. What did this mean? She didn't even know how she had accessed what was supposed to be a harpy ability. She had just been so overwhelmed with hatred for Trish, and she knew there was no way she could fend her off with her own meager mermaid powers. Something inside her just took over.

Did this mean that her dad was a harpy?

That thought stopped her anxiety in its tracks, and suddenly hope sparked. Maybe this wasn't a bad thing. Maybe this could lead to clues as to who her father was. If he was still out there somewhere, she could find him and maybe have somewhat of a family again.

If he even wanted anything to do with her.

A gentle knock at the door startled her out of her ruminations.

"I'm not here," she called at the door with a tone of irritation that she hoped masked her fear.

"It's me," Kendall's voice said on the other side.

She rolled her eyes. Where was he when Trish kicked her out? Or after she got attacked by vampires? He had been MIA ever since the Alessandra incident, and now he wanted to talk? His timing couldn't be worse.

"Still not here," she hollered.

Kendall opened the door anyway and came in. She huffed and glared at him, wishing she'd locked the door.

"I know you probably don't want to talk about what just happened in Defense, but I have something hugely important to tell you. It's about your father."

All her walls went down. She was now very interested in whatever he had to say. She leaned forward on the bed, her tone much softer when she said, "Okay, what is it?"

"Not here," he said. "There's something I need to show you. I'll explain on the way. Come on." He waved toward the door, beckoning her to follow.

Her curiosity was on high alert, a burning need inside her chest. She swiftly followed Kendall out of the Mer wing and through the hallways.

"Alright, spill," she whispered urgently. "What do you know about my father?"

"You know that I'm a seer, right?" he asked instead. "We've talked about it before."

She shrugged and nodded brusquely, not seeing how this had anything to do with her dad.

"Well, ever since I was a boy, I've had horrible visions about the future," he went on as he led her through the Grand Hall at a brisk pace. "A battle between shifters and vampires. Our kind dying everywhere. I've tried and tried to focus my gift so that I can find a way to stop it from happening, but every time I have the vision, it's always the same. I'm starting to wonder if maybe the purpose of these visions *isn't* to prevent them, but maybe just to save myself... and those I care about."

Myreen listened to him with growing concern, not missing the fact that he was clearly leading her toward the exit of the Dome.

"Er, Kendall, I don't quite understand what we're talking about here," she said, slowing her pace.

"There's something else I've always seen in my visions," he continued. He slowed a little, not enough to walk beside her, but not going so fast as to lose her, either. "A beautiful girl with thick black hair. I never knew who she was or how she would impact my future, I only knew the feeling I got when I would see her. This girl was vastly important. When I first saw Alessandra a few years ago, I could have sworn she was the girl. She looked younger, of course, but visions aren't always clear. I couldn't know exactly when or at what age I would meet this girl. So I did everything I could to win her heart, waiting for the day that our purpose would become clear.

"But it never did. The more I got to know her... the less I liked the person she was. I kept thinking, 'Were my visions wrong? How could this girl ever be someone worth loving as much as I did in my visions?' And then one day, you came along, and I realized I had chosen the wrong girl. Don't you see, Myreen? You're the girl I've been waiting for."

He looked at her without slowing down and smiled that same charming, sweet smile at her. But she didn't feel the same warmth as before. She only felt a gripping sense that something was wrong.

That she needed to get away.

And they were coming very close to the door leading to the subway platform.

She stopped walking. "That's very sweet, Kendall," she said, trying to be as delicate as she could. "But, uh, didn't you say you had to tell me something about my dad?"

"Yes, I was getting to that." He stopped, too, and came to stand within inches of her, gently taking her hands in his. As much as she had appreciated being so close to him in the past, right now such proximity was alarmingly unnerving. "Your mother, her name was Zaia, wasn't it?"

Bells rang in her head. She had never told Kendall that detail before. In fact, she hadn't told anyone at school her mom's name.

"How did you know that?" Myreen couldn't keep the suspicion from seeping into her words.

"I knew it!" he practically shouted. "It all makes sense now."

She extracted her hands and took a slow step back, using her peripheral vision to take stock of her surroundings. "What does?" she asked, hoping to keep him distracted.

"You and I have been connected from the start. Before we were even born!"

He had a wild, excited look on his face, and Myreen was more than a little scared of him. He was talking crazy. He closed the distance between them and grabbed her upper arms. Myreen stiffened, her eyes

521

wide.

"Myreen, seventeen years ago, my mother befriended a fresh-out-of-water mermaid named Zaia. Soon after they met, Zaia told her she had fallen for a vampire who wanted to use her blood to create potential hybrids—shifters that could be turned into vampires! That vampire was Draven. He was attempting to fuse different shifter DNA together in order to come up with a shifter that was strong enough to be turned into a vampire. He told her that it was so our two races could one day live in peace and stop fighting. The great unification, or something. My mother warned her against him, but Zaia didn't listen. She agreed to help Draven with his experiments.

"One day, Zaia turned up pregnant. She said it was Draven's baby, and that it tested positive for multiple strands of shifter DNA. Zaia was suddenly horrified by all this, afraid of what Draven would do with her unborn child. Then she left, and my mother never saw her again. Draven has been searching for his lost child ever since.

"Don't you see, Myreen? *You're* the lost child! That's why he wants you."

Myreen flushed with panic from the top of her scalp to the tips of her toes. She didn't want to believe a word of what he'd said, but she knew in her heart it was true. That it had to be. It explained why her mom had been on the run all her life, always looking over her shoulder. Why they only left town during the day and why she was never allowed out after dark. Why her mom had never revealed that she and Myreen were shifters. And the no social-media thing—that must've been because her mom was afraid Draven would find her there.

Oh lord, her dad was a vampire.

And not just any vampire, but *the* most notorious, wicked, and feared vampire in shifter history.

Any fantasies she'd had of some heartwarming father-daughter reunion with an angelic harpy crashed and drowned.

There were so many frantic thoughts bouncing around in her head that she almost forgot Kendall was standing in front of her, still holding her arms. She came back to herself, and it occurred to her that the usual guards of this area were nowhere in sight. After the vampire attacks, that wasn't just unusual. There was something very wrong here.

She moistened her dry mouth, then said very slowly, "Kendall, what are we doing at the door to the platform?"

He let go of her and took a deep breath, running a hand through his hair, bracing for what he obviously expected to be an unpleasant reaction. "I've seen the future, Myreen. Shifters are going to be wiped out. Vampires are going to win, and our side loses. There's no way around it. But I know now why I've been seeing you for so long. You and I don't have to die. We can save ourselves."

"Wh— what?" she stammered, unable to believe what she was hearing.

"Draven wants you," he said, looking crazier and more desperate by the second. "He won't hurt you, not the daughter he's been looking for for the past two decades. If I bring you to him, you and I will be safe. He'll finally have you, and he'll reward me for delivering you. I'll be able to watch over you. We can be together, even as the world falls apart."

Her heart thumped in her chest like a trapped bird raging against its cage. She had to handle this situation delicately. She had no idea what Kendall was really capable of.

"You're talking about abandoning everyone here and selling them out to the vampires?" As she spoke, she backed toward the hallway as slowly and seamlessly as she could, waiting for the right time to bolt.

"Please, don't see it like that," he pleaded, his brows creasing in a way that made him look sweet again. "I've seen their end. Everyone here is already doomed. But I know that I can save you—save *us*. That's what my visions have been trying to tell me. You and I don't have join them in their fate."

"What if by doing this, you're causing your vision to come true?" she asked, drawing at one last straw to change his mind. "What if your visions are trying to warn you to take a different path?"

His jaw set and his brow smoothed. "That's exactly what I'm doing. Choosing a different path. One day, you'll understand."

As fast as she could, Myreen spun and sprinted for the hallway. But before she had gone five feet, Kendall's arms closed around her, lifting her off the ground.

"Hel—" she began to scream, but Kendall's hand closed firmly over her mouth, trapping all sound.

"I didn't want to have to do this, but you've given me no choice." He put her down next to the wall, then turned her back to it, keeping his hand firmly over her mouth. Pressing his body against hers to free up his other hand, he lifted something out of his pocket. In her peripheral vision, she could see a syringe with clear liquid coming toward her neck.

Her eyes widened, and she squealed, expelling all the air from her lungs in the hopes that any of it would escape between his fingers. She didn't know what was in that syringe, but she was terrified to find out. Despite her twisting and flailing, Kendall seemed to have her locked in an unbreakable wedge. When she felt the needle touch the skin of her neck, she closed her eyes, bracing for what was to come.

"Kendall? Myreen? What's going on here?" Delphine's silhouette appeared at the end of the short hallway.

The brief distraction was all Myreen needed. She put a foot on the wall and pushed forward with all the force she could muster, her skull crashing into Kendall's forehead and jarring them both. He stumbled back, and she crashed to the cold, metallic floor. She was so rocked by the impact that she was completely cut off from the world around her for a moment. She squeezed her head between her hands, waiting for the throbbing to stop.

Hands landed on her shoulders and she jerked away, ready to fight to the death, even if she was still dizzy. But when her vision focused, it was Delphine kneeling in front of her.

"Myreen, are you alright?" Delphine asked.

Slowly, the dizziness dissipated, and Myreen did what she thought was nodding. "Where's Kendall?" she asked, squinting one eye and rubbing her neck. There was a prick of pain where the needle had partially stuck, but she was grateful it hadn't gone any deeper.

"He's gone," Delphine said. "He ran to the platform and jumped onto the subway as it left. What happened? None of this makes any sense."

Myreen eased herself into a sitting position against the wall of the entryway. "He was trying to take me to Draven. When I refused, he grabbed me. I think he was going to drug me and take me by force."

"What?" Delphine gasped.

"Where are the guards?" Myreen asked, gesturing to the empty space around them.

"Well, Kendall told me that he foresaw an imminent attack on the other side of the Dome," Delphine explained, flustered and confused. "I gathered all our able-bodied personnel to the site, but there was no sign of danger. Even with my powers focused on this evening, I could sense no attack, which didn't make any sense. So I asked everyone to stay put while I searched for Kendall to ask for more details, but..."

Myreen shook her head. "He planned this."

"Why?" Delphine asked, her red hair somehow looking even more fiery. "Why would he do this? Why would he take you to Draven?"

"He said his mother knew my mother a long time ago, that my mother was Draven's lover, and apparently his willing test subject. Draven's not after me because he knows about the prophecy. He's after me because I'm his daughter."

Leif

Leif had been summoned to Draven's trophy room again, and he found himself stepping slowly down the staircase. He was glad to have some time away from Piper again, but meeting with the vampire leader wasn't something he was looking forward to.

He hadn't even seen Draven since they'd returned from Chicago. The attack had taken place two evenings prior, and they'd returned to Heritage Prep soon after their failed attempt at snatching the siren known as Myreen.

While the girl's siren moment had been something to behold, she'd been entirely lackluster the rest of the fight. In fact, if it hadn't been for her friends, Myreen would be in Draven's custody right now.

He remembered vividly the viciousness of the teenage shifters—how well-trained they were. Particularly the larger of the two dragons. And the phoenix had caught them all off guard.

Leif could still feel the relief he'd been hit with as the vampires were forced to retreat.

But guilt flooded him as well—if Oberon found out about the part he'd played in the attack…

Causing the car accident that blocked their way was his part in Draven's plan. He'd hijacked a car and drove it into oncoming traffic, causing a twelve-car pileup. The timing had been perfect: Myreen and her friends got stuck in the resulting traffic, and had been forced to attempt to walk the rest of the way.

Leif finally reached the Great Hall, and his boots noisily clacked against the polished stone floor.

The tall doors leading into the trophy room were wide open, like the mouth of a great beast waiting to consume him.

At last, he entered, and the doors behind him boomed shut like thunder.

"Welcome, my friend," Draven said in his typical cool voice. "Please, have a seat. We have much to discuss."

Leif walked toward Draven's desk, trying his best to avoid looking at the mounted shifter body parts plastered against the walls.

He hated these meetings. Draven was so casual all the time, Leif didn't know if he was about to be reprimanded or rewarded. Perhaps Draven just wanted a status update on Piper as an Initiate. Finally making it to one of the fine wooden chairs directly in front of Draven's desk, Leif slid into it, sitting up straight.

"I know you don't care for blood straight from the person, so I had a cocktail of sorts made up for us to share," Draven said, punching a button on his side of the desk. A hole opened on the left side, and up spun a glass pitcher holding an enticing crimson liquid, along with two empty glasses. "It's a mix of six different initiates, all different races. Freshly extracted."

"You try it first," Leif said, not trusting what this *cocktail* contained.

Draven smiled a toothy grin, then pointed a finger at Leif. "Smart boy."

Boy? Leif thought to himself. Draven's passive aggressive insult defined his arrogant elitism. Leif tried his best to hide his annoyance. *I'm far older than you.*

Grabbing one of the glasses, Draven poured the blood. Raising the glass to his nose, he inhaled deeply, like a professional wine taster sniffing in a competition. At last, he raised his glass and drained it.

"Exquisite," he said. "A good mix. Only the best for the elite, right?"

Leif didn't want to taste it. He wanted to defy elitism by knocking the glass pitcher to the ground, shattering it into a hundred pieces and spilling its contents. Draven was no better than any other vampire. In fact, he was probably the worst. The only division between vampires in Leif's eyes were the good and bad ones. And Leif had yet to meet any good vampires.

Not waiting for Leif to make a move, Draven poured Leif's glass and pushed it across the desk to him. Leif caught it with quick reflexes, a bit of the blood splashing out from the sudden stop. Raising the glass to his lips, he took a short sip.

He couldn't deny the burst of flavor that tickled at his taste buds, and he took his time swallowing. Grateful he hadn't been the one required to extract the blood, Leif pretended it was just another bag of blood.

"Delicious doesn't begin to describe it," Leif said, setting the glass down and looking back up at Draven.

The vampire leader continued to smile. "Indeed."

Leif raised it again and took another sip. As he brought his arm back down, he circled the glass. "Something tells me you didn't bring me down here just to share a drink."

Draven chuckled. "Intuitive as always, Leif. You see much that many others miss."

Leif saw past the complement and heard the caution of his words.

Draven gulped down another glass, then leaned forward. "You froze on Saturday evening. During the fight, you didn't get involved. I want to know why."

Leif had wondered if Draven had even noticed. He'd been so wrapped up in the capture of Myreen.

He shrugged nonchalantly. "You asked me to watch our backs, just in case the shifter military showed up. And that's precisely what I did."

Draven's upper lip raised as he nodded. "Yes, you settled for the bare minimum quite well. Which is quite unlike a vampire of your caliber."

Leif laughed. "You flatter me, Draven. You do realize how long it's been since I've been on an assigned mission, right?"

This time, Draven laughed. "Do you honestly expect me to believe that you've gotten rusty? You're an eternal being, Leif. You *can't* lose your touch. And I've seen what you're capable of."

Leif drank from his glass. "It's harder than you might think, after stepping away for as long as I have. Sure, my abilities might be as keen as they've always been, but the kind of mission we were on was more of a mental game than anything."

"Mental for you," Draven scoffed. "Extremely physical for the rest of us. Did you even notice that there were two dragon shifters involved, not to mention a phoenix?"

"They were kids, Draven," Leif replied. "Since when do we go around hunting kids?"

"They killed Theo and Amelia," Draven spat, slamming his cup down on his desk. "And so many others. And when did you decide we should go easy on younger shifters? Shifters are shifters, no matter their age."

Leif hated the whole situation. He hated that he was here in this fortress, surrounded by bloodlusting brutalists who couldn't just let life go on.

"Forgive me," he said, bowing his head and trying his best to sound sincere. "I won't let it happen again."

Draven wagged a finger at him. "You'd better not, because we have another mission. We're going after the girl again."

"What's so special about her?" Leif asked, knowing what Oberon thought of her. Now was his chance to get Draven's take.

Sitting back, another grin formed on the vampire leader's face. "The girl is my daughter."

Leif's eyes narrowed. "What?"

Draven's smile evaporated. "Did you not hear me? Myreen is my daughter. I've been searching for her for many, many years. Months ago I found her, but the shifters got to her first."

This was news Oberon did not have. Leif wondered for a moment what the gryphon would do if he discovered that Myreen was Draven's actual blood daughter. There was nobody in the world who hated Draven more than Oberon. And that kind of hatred could lead good people to do terrible things.

"You want a shifter to join the vampires?" Leif asked incredulously. "Even if she is your daughter, what makes you think she'd side with us?"

Draven bellowed a laugh that boomed around the room. "You of all people should know just how compelling I can make our side seem."

There is nothing compelling about our *side,* Leif thought. The torture he'd endured just to rejoin the vampires had been a terrible experience, full of memories mingled with falsities. Hallucinations. Was Draven really willing to do such a thing to his own daughter?

"Funny," Draven continued. "You've been living in Chicago for the past fifteen years, and that also happens to be where we found Myreen two nights ago."

He's already putting pieces together, Leif thought. He'd have to do a better job covering himself in the future. If Draven knew why he really came back…

"A frightening coincidence," he said. "Had I any idea we were in the same city limits, I would have told you."

Draven snorted. "I'm sure you would've. Fortunately, I've made a new *friend* from the Dome who has validated never hearing about or seeing you before."

"The Dome?" The nickname just spilled out of Leif's mouth, he was so shocked to hear that Draven knew about it. The location of the shifter school was a secret that no vampire knew about—besides himself.

Until now.

The vampire leader's eyes shifted to the corner of the room over Leif's right shoulder. Unable to resist following Draven's line-of-sight, Leif looked that way.

Standing sheepishly against the wall was a teenage boy with perfectly combed sandy brown hair and ocean-blue eyes.

"Leif Villers, meet Kendall Green," Draven said, winding his hand backwards like a fishing reel. "Come here Kendall and take a seat."

The young man walked toward the desk with his chest puffed out. Leif could sense the fear veiled by his strong stance.

"Kendall had enough good sense to seek us out," Draven said with excessive sweetness. "As you can probably guess, he's a mer, and is quite eager to divulge certain secrets to save his own scales."

"A traitor to his own kind?" Leif said, gazing at the mer with disgusted surprise.

"Oh, Leif, don't be so dramatic," Draven said. "The boy has been through a lot, and is a very gifted seer. You see, he has seen the outcome of the age-old war between shifters and vampires. He has seen the annihilation of his own kind. And like any survivor would, he has switched to the winning side." Draven smiled wickedly at Kendall.

"Haven't you, my boy?"

Kendall nodded quickly. "Yes, sir."

"Furthermore, his need for self-preservation has loosed his lips. We know that the school resides at the bottom of Lake Michigan." A holographic display popped up from Draven's desk, zeroing in on the structure that Leif had been helping to protect, though he'd never seen it. The vampire leader moved his hands away from each other on the holograph, zooming in on the structure. "Within, we have the layout, including entry points that are commonly used, as well as the secret ones. We know where the dormitories are, and we even know where Myreen sleeps." He pointed at one particular area where a red light blinked.

The blue lights creating the three-dimensional image reflected in the mad eyes of Draven. Leif had to alert Oberon about the leak of information, and about Kendall's betrayal.

"All this time, the shifters have been so close," he said, masking his true feelings.

The display blinked out as Draven swiped his hand from side to side. "Under your very nose, Leif. But do not fear for your own life. Kendall has told me that the school director would never have dealings with vampires. Oberon Rex has too much of a history with us."

With you, Leif thought. *You murdered his family in cold blood.* Instead, Leif said, "The last of the gryphons."

"His death is inevitable," Draven said. "Delayed, perhaps, but his time is running out. I'm assembling a team to make an attack. And as you're a daywalker, you will be crucial to the success of that team."

Leif felt his stomach sink. A direct assault on the school was the last thing he wanted to do. Instead, he bowed again. "I'm honored to be given a second chance."

Draven jabbed a finger at him. "And this time, you can't watch from the sidelines. You can't freeze. If you do, drowning in hallucinogenic water will seem like a mercy after what I put you through."

Leif nodded. "Understood."

"Now go," Draven said, sweeping his hand in the air like a broom. "There is more I wish to discuss with Kendall. But soon enough, you'll be back here with the team I assemble, and we'll finalize our plans to destroy the Dome, and every shifter inside."

"I look forward to it," Leif said, getting to his feet. He looked at Kendall and saw that the eel of a boy was physically shaking. Leif couldn't help but feel disgust for this betrayer. Resting a hand on the boy's muscular shoulder, Leif said, "Welcome to the winning side."

He moved to the massive doors, and one of them swung inward as he approached. Instead of heading to the staircase that would take him to his quarters, Leif took the stairs down a level to where the Initiates were located. Everything seemed to be a blur—his mind couldn't concentrate on anything but what he'd just learned.

Upon reaching the Initiates common room, he yelled, "Piper!"

The exclamation earned Leif the attention of the other humans in the room.

Glancing around, he couldn't see her anywhere.

Where is that girl?

"Sir," one of the human males in the room said. "I believe Piper went to bed for the night. But if you're needing to feed, I offer my neck to you in her absence."

Leif was barely able to hold back the things he wanted to say to the eager Initiate. Gritting his teeth, he said, "I need Piper. Now. Will you lead me to her quarters?"

The Initiate wilted, turning almost as pale as a vampire. "Of course. This way."

They walked into the north hallway, which was lined with small LED lights that barely illuminated the way. They came to a fork, and

Leif followed the human to the left. They continued until the hallway right-angled back to the north.

Three doors down and they came to a stop.

"This is it," the Initiate said, raising a fist to knock on the door.

With superhuman speed, Leif caught it. "I'll be the one to wake her. You go on back to the common room and… do whatever it was you were doing."

The Initiate hesitated a moment, which surprised Leif. They were always so overeager to obey.

Leif narrowed his eyes and released the young man's arm. "What's your name?"

"Adam," the Initiate replied.

"Well, Adam, do you have trouble hearing? Or do you really want to try the patience of an upset vampire?"

"S– sorry, sir," Adam stammered. "It's just that vampires usually don't go to their Initiates quarters. Vampires always summon their Initiates up to their quarters."

Leif ground his teeth and stared daggers at Adam. *Can't you take a hint?*

Seeing Leif's state, the Initiate turned around and sped away.

He sighed heavily. This place drove him so close to losing control. He longed to be back in his apartment, sitting on the Frosts' chair, sipping at a blood bag while holding Gemma's brooch.

Gemma. It felt like an age since he'd thought about her. Her grimoire was being used again after a century, and the selkie Kenzie had been successful with bringing plants back to life. Leif wished he'd had more time with her, but he didn't want to keep Draven waiting and wondering where he'd really gone. Leif had told him that he was going to scout out the subway area to see if there were better options than what had already been planned. Instead, he'd been able to meet Kenzie at his apartment for a minute or two.

She looks so much like Gemma.

He withdrew Gemma's brooch from his pocket and brought it up to his lips, closing his eyes and kissing it softly.

Hopefully not too much longer, my love.

Putting it back, he grabbed onto Piper's doorknob and pushed the door open. The hinges squealed like a shrieking gryphon, but to Leif's surprise, Piper didn't budge. She was laying on a bed mounted to the wall by two chains that angled away. There was a bunk above her, also held by chains, and two other empty beds on the opposite wall. They looked far from comfortable, but most Initiatives probably thought the need for sleep was a temporary thing, anyway. At least she was alone.

"Piper," he whispered as he drew nearer to her. Again, she didn't stir. Leif could hear her heavy breathing. He had no idea how long she'd been asleep, but it sounded deep.

Do not wake her. Find her phone. It was Gemma's voice, guiding him once more.

He looked about the room. Surely it would be close to a power outlet to charge overnight.

A nearby dresser was empty on top, and the last thing Leif wanted to do was paw through whatever belongings were in the drawers.

He heard a digital *ding* chime, and he turned to see Piper stir. Sitting next to her hand on her bed was a screen, lit up from a text message.

Stepping lightly over to Piper, he reached past her and grabbed the phone. He couldn't help but read what it said:

Phil: Miss you. Hope your day went well.

Piper had never talked about her relationships during their assignment together, and part of Leif ached to tell her to step away from the track she was on. If this Phil was her boyfriend... well, he knew firsthand what it was like to be turned by an old girlfriend.

He stashed her phone into his other pocket and walked as silently

535

from her room as possible, cringing as the door creaked shut behind him.

Sprinting down the hall, he zipped through the common room and up the stairs, stepping out into the Great Hall.

Leif slowed his pace here, not wanting to draw unwanted attention from any vampires. But luck was not with him. Beatrice happened to be sitting in one of the luxurious chairs off to the side.

"What's the hurry, Leif?" she asked. She wasn't in her typical black jeans and hoodie, but in a form-fitting sleeveless dress that ran down to just above her knees. She applied an extra coat of black lipstick to her lips and stood up. She was taller, due to the dark high heels she wore. Her white-blonde hair rolled down on her shoulders, a stark contrast to the rest of her outfit.

Leif stopped in his tracks. She looked beautiful, and he realized he hadn't thought that about her for a *very* long time. But just as soon as the thought came, he dashed it away, sticking a hand into his pocket and grasping Gemma's brooch again.

"I just need some fresh air," he said, moving for the door again. Quick as a flash, Beatrice ran in front of him. The high heels did nothing to slow her down.

"Mind if I join you?" she asked, smiling at him and reaching for his free hand.

"I'm actually going to watch the sunrise," he said, trying to move past her. She grabbed his arm as he went by, stopping his progression again.

"I can stay with you while it's dark," she offered. "You look like you've got a lot on your mind. I'd love to help you sort it out."

Leif looked into her icy blue eyes. "Not tonight."

Beatrice held on for another moment, as if hoping he'd change his mind. But Leif stood firm.

At last, she released him, the rejection showing in her

countenance.

Finally free, Leif ran out into the cold, wintry night, sprinting through the snow and whipping past trees. He didn't have anywhere specific he wanted to go. He just needed to get far enough away to make an important phone call.

He ran through the mountains for what seemed like hours, but pulling Piper's phone from his pocket, he saw that it had only been minutes.

Dropping to his knees in a foot of snow, Leif dialed a number he'd memorized years ago. One that he'd been told to use only in times of emergency. It was late at night, and he hoped Oberon would answer.

Raising the phone to his ear, he counted the rings.

One. Two. Three. Four. Five.

"Hello?"

It was the gryphon. He sounded wide awake.

"Oberon, this is Leif."

There was a brief pause on the other end. "High winds, Leif, where have you been?"

"Through too much. But that's not why I'm calling. Listen, trouble is coming your way."

"It already has," Oberon replied. "Four of our students were attacked a few nights ago."

"That's just the beginning," Leif said. "Listen, I don't have much time. One of your shifter students... he's betrayed the school. He's told Draven everything—the location of the Dome, information about Myreen."

"Who?" Oberon asked. "Which student?"

"His name is Kendall Green," Leif replied. "I don't know how long he's been working with Draven, but another attack is being organized. You're all in danger."

"We'll call in the military," Oberon said. "They can monitor our borders and protect us."

"That's a start," Leif replied.

"You've fulfilled my request, Leif," Oberon said. "I know going back to Draven was not an easy thing. If you need to escape, you should do so."

Leif shook his head, even though he knew Oberon couldn't see it. "I can't. Not yet. There are too many moving pieces right now, and I think the best way I can help you and the rest of the shifters is by staying here and keeping you apprised."

"If you can continue being our eyes and ears there in the heart of Draven's pursuits, that would be most helpful," Oberon replied.

"And that's what I will do, at least for now. But listen. There are a couple of other things you must know about Draven and his plans. When I first arrived back at his fortress, he told me that his intention is to find a way to make vampire-shifter hybrids."

"That's a lost cause," Oberon said. "Our genetic makeup is incompatible with that of vampires."

"He's figured it out," Leif replied. "I don't know the details, but he's recruited some insanely brilliant geneticists. They're on the verge of solving the puzzle."

Leif waited for a response from the gryphon, but all he heard was Oberon's breathing.

"Myreen," Oberon said softly.

"About her," Leif said. "She's Draven's daughter."

"Yes, that much we've discovered," Oberon replied. "From what Myreen recalls from talking with Kendall, her mother had joined with Draven in an attempt to bring peace between vampires and shifters. But Draven only used her to give birth to Myreen. We thought she was a mermaid, but she is in fact a chimera."

Leif gasped. "She's a hybrid shifter?"

"Yes," Oberon said. "And if what you're saying is true, he's

538

wanting to take things a step further with her."

A vampire chimera.

Leif's anxiety levels spiked. "Draven won't stop until he finds her. He'll tear down the Dome and kill anybody who gets in his way. And if he gets a hold of her, we're all doomed."

ABOUT THE SHIFTER ACADEMY AUTHORS

This series is the brain child of 5 best-selling and award-winning paranormal romance and urban fantasy authors. For the Siren Prophecy Series, each character was brought to life by a different author. For the remainder of the ongoing Shifter Academy series, a new book will release every six weeks by one or more the authors, as there are just too many stories to tell in this amazing shifter world.

Myreen was written by USA Today Bestselling Author Tricia Barr. Follow Tricia's work here: www.tricia-barr.com

Kenzie was written by Angel Leya. Follow Angel's work here: http://www.angeleya.com

Kol was written by Joanna Reeder. Follow Joanna's work here: http://www.joannareeder.com

Juliet was written by Alessandra Jay. Follow Alessandra's work here: http://www.joannareeder.com

Oberon & Leif were written by Jesse Booth. Follow Jesse's work here: http://www.joannareeder.com